The Redneck Run

Shay Lawless

The Redneck Run— Copyright © 2016 by Shay Lawless

ISBN-10: 1-940087-14-7
ISBN-13: 978-1-940087-14-6

21 Crows Dusk to Dawn Publishing, 21 Crows, LLC

Table of Contents

Chapter

Chapter –1

Friday Nights at the Crazy Kettle

I am sitting on a bar stool at the Crazy Kettle Bar in New Alliance, West Virginia. The stool is vinyl and ripped, and I can feel the tear against the skin of my thigh because I'm wearing a tight, black miniskirt. I am nursing my third drink and fiddling with my wedding band. It isn't in my hands. It is sitting on the damp napkin in front of me. 1980s rock from an old jukebox plays a muffled beat all around me. The lights are dimmed, and the air oozes with desperation, dust, and stale cigarette smoke.

A woman is dancing around one of the pool tables. She is in her mid-fifties, dressed in a skirt shorter than mine. A red tank top barely covers her size Double-D boobs and clashes with her home hair dye, red-orange with gray roots. She is barefoot, gyrates and wiggles, and holds her hands in the air. She does a little circle around one of the guys holding a pool stick, and she rubs her rear against him.

Her eyes are closed, and a smile flits across her pale lips when he takes a polite step away. He doesn't look like the rest of the guys here. He is chubby and has the kind of haircut that screams he got it done at an expensive salon in Charleston instead of his wife taking the electric razor to his head. He is dressed in designer jeans and a button-up shirt. He rolls his eyes and chuckles a little like he's embarrassed. He looks familiar. I wonder if I saw him at Holy Trinity Church when I went for Christmas Eve service. I'm sure he's thinking if he doesn't find anything better, he'll let the woman take him to her old beat-up car and give him a drunk blowjob.

To the unobservant eye, I look like I'm here to pick up a man for a few bucks to pay my rent. I'm wearing a black lace, spaghetti-string camisole top and high stiletto heels. The reason I know this is because seven men have sat down beside me in the last hour. Each has a story to tell. Every one of them is a lie because all of them tell me they aren't married. Every one of them is donning a wedding band. The last one is about forty and balding. He says he'd help me make my truck payment if I'd screw him in the men's bathroom stall five steps away.

I wish I had my ball cap. It is like a baby's pacifier to me. I wear it all the time, hide behind the bill. I think about that when I decline Drunk Number Seven. I'm not here to pick up a guy. I'm here to meet my husband. Ex-husband, that is, and probably a dead one at that. His name is Josh Devereauxs, and I bought him a beer tonight that stays full and warm next to my still-fizzy ginger ale. I suppose to the eight or ten locals eyeing me cautiously from their tables that I appear to be waiting for a ghost. I know they think it's creepy that I come here every Friday night, which is the same day of the week Josh disappeared and buy a dead man a beer.

I think I'm trying to make it up to him. If I could afford a psychiatrist, maybe she would tell me that it is the normal process of grief. Or perhaps she would tell me I've got the crazies like everybody else believes. I know my showing up here is an apology of sorts. I should have shown up the night Josh evaporated into the air like mist over a boiling pot. I should have picked him up at the closing time of 1:00 a.m. and driven him home. I did not. If I had, maybe he wouldn't be gone.

I've sat here from 10:00 p.m. to 1:00 a.m. and tried to make it up to him for the last three years, sipping on ginger ale and staring at the seat next to me that's empty most of the time, and sometimes it isn't because some drunk guy is trying to pick me up. Then I get up to leave. I turn to all the locals there and ask them if they are too drunk to drive. They all give me a cautious, sad gaze and shake their heads back and forth. They are always sober to me, even if they genuinely aren't. I know they think if they tell me they are drunk, I'll want to drag them to my truck like stray cats and take them home with me. Nobody wants to get in the truck with Crazy Brandy. They might go poof! like Josh into the air, too. They all shake their heads, and the bartender, whom I call Billy the Bartender, walks me out to my truck and tells me it wasn't my fault. Sometimes, people disappear. Tonight isn't any different.

"Baby girl, can you give me a ride home in a few?"

Did I mention the woman dancing around the pool tables is my mama? If I didn't, it is because she isn't much of a mama at all. The only time I see her is at the bar or when she wants to borrow money from me that she'll never pay back. She knows I'm here on Fridays.

"Yes, of course," I answer.

She's working hard on the chubby guy tonight. He looks more embarrassed than interested while she weaves belly-dancer-sexy around him. He's holding a pool stick and looking awkward while his buddies snicker under their breath at Mama and him.

"Hey, Bear, got yourself a girlfriend?"

Chubby boy's buddies make a few wisecracks while Mama leans in hard to balance. He reaches out a hand courteously to catch her elbow. I know he wishes he hadn't. He's way over six feet, young, and has a cute face with a perfectly slanted nose and lips that curve upward like he's hiding a smile or a kiss somewhere in there. Maybe he is. He's got a beard, so I can't see much more underneath.

He's Mama's type. She always likes the big boys with low self-esteem that would probably be hotter than hot if they weren't a hundred pounds overweight. She sees deeper than most, I suppose. At least, deeper than me. Or maybe she's looking in his back pocket for his wallet. He came up to the bar earlier and waved a hundred-dollar bill. Then again, I think sometimes her drunk eyes shrink them up a bit, minimizing their mass. Everybody's skinny after six o'clock at night through my mama's tipsy gaze.

"My friend's right. You're a sweet little thing," Up comes Drunk Number Eight fishing for a date. He's twenty-something and wearing a ball cap. I can see him sizing me up and down from the tip of my brown hair (Mama always says it is the color of chestnuts. I think my hair is more the color of fresh horse manure) to my toes sticking out of my stiletto heels. He reaches out, snags one of my curls at the middle of my back and tugs it. He's all red hair and freckles, rich boy cute with the same kind of cocky attitude my ex-husband used to have. However, where Josh was kind of a man's man, this guy is a little more girly man. He's not so much reeking of testosterone and looking like he's going to punch another guy out in the next ten minutes just for the hell of it.

"You've got the prettiest eyes," he says, leaning in a little too close. "What color are they? Pink? Gold? Damn, you're fresh. My friend over there—"

"The color of a Brandy Alexander," I interrupt him flatly. I hate my eyes. They are big and sad looking. And they are a vibrant tan-pink color, almost like burnt toast when I'm laid back. Pops tells me they get deep gold when I'm mad.

That's how I got my name, Brandy Alexander. However, I don't tell the drunk this little information about me. Mama told me the first thing she saw when I popped out of her was my big eyes, the color of her favorite drink. I suppose it could have been worse for me. She could have liked drowning herself in Tijuana Hookers.

Since I talk to him, Drunk Number Eight thinks he's got his little fish on the hook. He leans in to whisper in my ear. I think it's something about him and his buddy, and it might be a little racy, even based on what I've heard here. I can't tell. I know, though, that it is time for him to leave. The music is too loud. I look at the bartender. He is wiping off a beer glass with a white towel, and I can see him leaning in to hear what I am about to say. He has a funny little smirk on his face. Billy and I have a bet each week that I can get rid of any man in less than one minute. So far, I've won six times out of ten. I look at the clock on the wall and give Billy a little sideways glance. He looks at it too. I now have fifty-nine seconds—

"I've got five kids that are all under the age of six," I lie to Drunk Number Eight, "I'm looking for a deep relationship." He's not the usual redneck crowd. He is probably slumming this weekend, home from college, or traveling through and staying at the Sunrise Delight Motel next door. He is still leaning in, but I see a bit of light go out of his deep brown eyes. He's fiddling with the damp napkin under Josh's beer beside my ginger ale.

"I don't want a once-a-week relationship," I say, reaching for my ginger ale and taking a little sip. "I want somebody who is all-in, you know, who likes to watch sappy movies with me every night with a smile on his face, rubs my feet, and wants to be called Daddy by my kids. I don't like football or baseball, and I don't have cable. I go to church every Sunday, Wednesday, and Friday and expect any man I date to go with me and put twenty bucks in the plate."

Drunk Number Eight has the same pinched-lip expression all of us girls got when we walked past the men's restroom doors tonight. Something in there really stinks. It's almost like a possum died in there. "I don't sleep with anybody on the first four dates. After that, it's on a week-by-week basis, depending on how good you've treated me." He's still hanging on there, his finger twiddling with my hair. Maybe he's just flustered and is politely trying to back out. It doesn't matter. I'm close to beating my record of forty-five seconds. Crap.

I must go all-out. "By the way, I'm pregnant with number six. You in?" He's not. Imagine that. He nearly tears the back of the seat, slipping off the bar stool to get away.

Billy the Bartender saunters over. He's short and has a twinkle in his eyes all the time. He's digging out a bill from his wallet.

"Pregnant?" He shakes his head back and forth. "We'll have to adjust the rules a little in our bet, Brandy." He's got a hard twang as if he's from southern Alabama. "I say you have to keep it to three lies or four lies to keep it fair."

"Are you saying my life's that crappy I could scare them off telling the truth?"

He seems to ponder this a moment while he extends his hand with a crumpled dollar bill. "Maybe. I don't know. I'm just saying that you took it a little bit too far. I was even running for the hills after your *first* sentence."

"I didn't overdo it." I grab the dollar bill from his fingertips before he changes his mind. "I just don't have kids, and I'm not pregnant."

"Do you go to church?"

"No—I mean, I go at Christmas and Easter."

"Are you looking for a relationship?"

"Are you asking me this because you're asking me out?" I lean in like I'm flirting with him, wink. He settles against the wall behind him and holds out a hand. He's not too chubby, not too thin. He's right down the middle.

He folds his arms across his chest and gives me a wary gaze. "Not unless the first and last parts are a lie—that you're looking for a long-term relationship and you don't sleep with a guy on the first and only date. Because I'm all in for one-night stands."

"Maybe I'll just start with that next time." I decided the conversation was going too far. I get up and push my chair back. I can't tell if Billy is playing with me or if he is screaming that I'm the same old poor white trash he sees in here every day of the week that he sleeps with. He's elusive. I don't remember Josh ever saying much about him. Billy hides in the darkness of the bar. Maybe he murdered Josh because he didn't pay his bar tab, and Billy buried him out back. I ponder this very thought and then decide against it.

Josh was too poor to buy me new underwear. I know Billy the Bartender wouldn't give him a bar tab.

"Baby girl, are we leaving already?"

It is my mama. She knows I'm heading out. It is one-forty-five in the morning. I have left at this exact time on Friday nights for the last three years. One-forty-five was when Josh left the bar and headed for Fire Mountain View Trailer Park and Campground where we lived and where my mama still lives. I don't live there now. It is on my way home, though.

Of course, I tell her I can drive her to the trailer park in my old, beat-up red truck. But I won't go past the gates. She knows the drill. Before she gets out, she scoots her legs to the door, keels back toward me with her breath full of beer and her eyes swimming drunk, and asks me if I'm still working at Mister Smiley's Grocery and Beverly's Hometown Diner.

I try to breathe past her beer breath. The air is full of the scent of April in West Virginia when the trees are just easing into budding, and the grass is begging to turn from pale lime to dark jade. It sifts around her, and I can smell the sand-dirt soil, and catch a hint of spring while I tell Mama, yeah, I'm still working both jobs. Then she asked if I'd got a twenty that she could borrow.

"Yes, Mama," I tell her, digging a twenty dollar bill from my purse I have secreted between my hip and the driver's side door.

"Baby, you're my favorite. You're a hard worker," she tells me each time. "Don't tell your brothers and sisters I said that. They're already jealous you got a hamburger named after you."

I know I'm not her favorite. I'm just the one with the twenty dollars in my hand. And the hamburger with my name on it is just a regular old burger with a few spices I made up when I got bored waitressing one day. Beverly liked it so much that she used the recipe and named it after me. It's not like it is anything special. She's got five customers she likes that she named burgers after.

"You need to find yourself another man, baby. I don't think Josh is going to come back."

"I know, Mama. He's probably long dead and buried behind his mama's trailer. She probably got drunk and mad and took him out with a baseball bat."

"That's what they say."

"Promise me you won't buy pot with the money, alright?" I beg her. "Get some hotdogs and buns and some apple juice for Kaylee. There's enough there." However, I know she's already got it slated for a couple of joints. Feeding Kaylee, her youngest and four years old, comes secondary. It's hard to tell Mama no, even if she didn't raise me since I was four. She doesn't answer but hops out and signals me with a wave that I can go. Then she walks across the gravel lot toward a semi-circle of the first layer of seven trailers, around the crooked line of beat-up mailboxes.

As she passes, she bangs on the window of the second trailer. This is a signal. Little Pete lives there. He's twenty-six and has Downs Syndrome. He used to ride the bus, and two boys who sat in the back used to taunt him. Nobody ever stopped the boys because one of them was Judge Patterson's son. Judge Patterson was this big, angry-faced man. He was the kind of judge you didn't want to meet in the courtroom if he held a grudge against you. You might as well pack a suitcase and head yourself to the state pen.

But Little Pete would get to school and start yelling, *I don't like him. I don't like him. He's mean to me.* It would take an hour for the teachers to calm him down. One day, when I was a sophomore, I rode the bus home with him to find out who he didn't like. I suppose those bully boys weren't worried about the quiet, little scrawny girl sitting in the front seat. They didn't see the wild spark in my eyes while I watched the backseat through the rearview mirror.

When the two boys started teasing him, I strolled to the back of the bus and stood in front of them. I told them I'd be watching them. If they ever made fun of Little Pete again, I'd beat the shit right out of them. They laughed at me, so I dove right over the seat and started throwing punches and kicking like holy hell had broken loose. The funny thing was, they didn't want to hit a little girl three years younger and a hundred pounds lighter. They ended up with bloody noses, black eyes, and a different attitude toward Little Pete. I started following the bus home in the little truck I drove to school. I only had to do it for a few months because the judge moved on to politics, left his wife, and took his bully son with him.

I used to wait behind the bus until Little Pete got inside. He would wave to me from his window, and I knew he was safe inside.

Later, when we got older, and I visited Mama, he waved to me from his porch or the window. Every Friday, Mama bangs on his window and wakes him up. His light goes on, and I can see his smiling face and he waves at me. I wave back, and we make funny faces for five minutes. I do a thumbs-up, and he waits at the window, staring at me another ten minutes until I leave.

It is two-fourteen when I watch Mama wiggle-walk to the third trailer on the right that she shares with whatever new boyfriend is funding her habits this month. It is two-seventeen when I give Little Pete a thumbs up. I let my truck idle there by the rows of dented mailboxes for ten minutes. It was the same length of time Josh had waited to see if I was leaving for my job at Beverly's Hometown Diner on Main Street in town. I was supposed to come in and prepare the food for the next day. After that I waited on tables from six until ten. But the night that he disappeared, he saw my truck parked in the tiny gravel pull-off in front of the trailer.

I count down four trailers on the right and stop at the fifth. That's where my trailer used to be. It burned down three days after Josh disappeared. Mister Lawson, who ran the trailer park then, said the contractor who came in to fix our broken furnace must have done the wiring wrong. I knew better. We couldn't afford to pay the furnace company to fix it, so Josh tried to do it himself. I didn't tell Mister Lawson that. He wanted to sue the contractor, so he kept asking me who it was. I played like a stupid wife. I told him I didn't know because Josh hired him. And then, everybody was freaking out because Josh was gone, so nobody pushed the issue further.

Nevertheless, Josh saw my truck still parked in the street and left slowly as I do now. Missus Perry, who lives in the end trailer on the left, reported to the police she saw him leave when she went to her front porch to feed her cats. Then she said he went up the road, turned around in the third driveway on the right, and returned. He drove up and down the road three more times, then never returned.

I do the same. Then I drive the truck about sixty-five miles an hour until I come to a standstill on Township Road 482. I know he must have been mad that he couldn't go back to the house. He probably slammed his fists on the steering wheel, then finished his last can of beer. The beer can they found in the truck was empty, save for a couple of tepid dribbles in the bottom.

There's a little gravel pull-off about ten steps before the railroad tracks. I park at the pull-off for another twenty minutes, which was about the amount of time it took for Josh to screw Lisa Perkins in the seat of his truck. Here's where I'm not sure; I have to estimate how long it was they lay there. It was long enough for Lisa to pass out against the door, but that was the only part written on the report which became public information down at the police station. Josh usually didn't stick around with me unless he was too drunk to get up or the TV was on, and he didn't want to miss the end of a game. I guess it was about two minutes between the time he stopped grunting over the top of Lisa and before he pushed her away.

Tonight, I am trying out fourteen minutes. I open the door to my truck, snatch up my purse, and lean against the hood, waiting for the sound of the train's arrival. I stare at my phone, trying to balance the time it would take for a plastered, after-sex sleepy man to get out of his truck. Then I hear the grind of the train and see the lights slipping along the tracks.

I push away from the hood of my truck and saunter to the tracks. It is a slow pace. I am assuming Josh was dead drunk, so he wavered a bit here and there. I stop dead center in the middle of the tracks and wait for the train to come down on me. I wait, wait, wait. I can hear the engineer blasting the horn and see the light dousing me. I think I can feel the wind while I lean a little to look at my phone. Fifteen minutes and eight seconds.

BOOM! Something hits me, but it isn't the train. I see a shadow coming toward me out of the corner of my eye. It is a flash across the expanse of car lights, the passing of something fast eclipsing the car headlights stopped along the roadway in front of the railroad crossing sign. I am so focused on counting the minutes and seconds elapsing that I haven't seen the cars pull up along the roadway.

Somebody tackled me hard. I think there is a moment, we are both flying entirely off the ground. Then we hit the dewy dirt on the far side of the tracks hard, skidding and rolling in a flurry of feet, arms, and shoes. I am dazed for just a moment. I wonder if I have been wholly skinned alive from my right shoulder to my elbow. My flesh is stinging.

"What the hell?" I groan at the shadow next to me. I barely hear my voice screaming over the train wheels squealing on the tracks.

I can't see anything while I push myself up to my knees. I think there isn't a place on my body that hasn't gotten slammed and skinned against the sharp stones on either side of the tracks. "What is wrong with you?" I finally find my angry yowl. "Are you nuts? You could have killed us both!" I feel my shoulder for my purse and start to swing it at the shadow across from me.

Then I hear a deep voice screaming at me. "You're the freaking crazy one!" I blink in the blackness and make out the form of a man. I feel my purse impact with the silhouette, and it makes a wiggly bump into the air.

"What are you doing, asshole?" I step back, a bit dizzy from the tumble. "Jesus Christ, you could have killed us both!" I usually take one step to the right and miss the train entirely. The collision of my body with the man yelling at me caught me off-guard. "I'm not the crazy one." I take a step back. "You're the one who tackled me." I can see who it is. It's the chubby man that my mama was trying to pick up at the bar. He is wagging a finger at me.

"I tackled you so you wouldn't get hit by the train!" Then he stops, pushes both hands out, and steps back. His voice drops low, but I can hear it over the train's roar while the wind blows hair in my face. "Okay, I'm sorry. I'm sorry," he says in a consoling tone. "You know, I shouldn't yell at you. You're okay, alright? Having five kids and another on the way, I get it. You're what, twenty-five? You've got kids and no husband. My—my buddy, he told me about you. He tried to buy you a beer, remember? Lots of people have been there. You'll make it out alive. You don't need to do this. You can get help. You're going to be okay. You don't need to end it here." He is going to reach out and touch my arm to reassure me. I automatically repel the contact by taking a short step to one side.

"I wasn't trying to kill myself." I give him one of my eat-shit-and-die glares. I'm not sure he can see it in the dark. "I don't have five kids. I was trying to get your friend to leave me alone. I wasn't trying to kill myself. I was—" No one understands my intense and possibly obsessive desire to figure out exactly what happened that night Josh disappeared. It doesn't matter. While I was trying to think up something to say, the train finished passing in a whoosh of wind and a scream of wheels. We are standing there now, splashed in the light of a line of four cars stopped at the crossing.

"Damn, fat boy, you were fast." I hear someone say while they cross the tracks to get to us. "We thought we'd find a couple of mangled bodies here." They are stepping over the shiny rails, and behind them, a small crowd of people are hovering and staring at us through the car's high-beam lights. All the vehicles are stopped, and I can see doors open. It suddenly occurs to me that they all think I am trying to kill myself. Probably somebody called the cops.

"You are such an idiot!" I growl at the man who tackled me. I stomp off to my truck before the cops arrive and quickly head off into the night.

Chapter –2

Getting Fired from Mister Smiley's

If you look up the name Fire Mountain online, it comes up only under a listing of REAL GHOST TOWNS IN WEST VIRGINIA. Some of us are still very much alive here. The old Fire Mountain Coal Company that established the area as a mining community a hundred and fifty years ago is long gone. But most of the mining families stuck up on top of the mountain here because they couldn't afford to leave were able to procreate enough to keep it going.

It makes the eighty or so folks who've got trailers and old houses in the vicinity mad if you mention it. "Ghost town, my ass," Ellen Wells is saying to me. "It's like saying we're dead." It is closing time at Mister Smiley's Super Grocery Store in the town of New Alliance where we work. It is the only town in a twenty-mile radius and is sandwiched almost entirely in the center of the two most prominent mountains in the vicinity—Fire Mountain and Big Boar Mountain. Ellen's job is to restock the canned and packaged foods in Aisles One through Eight after the store shuts down at night. I clean.

I stand with my broom nodding. I've spent the last two hours listening to Ellen gripe and cleaning up the remnants of a collision of a cart and a hundred empty boxes of Real Meals for Real Men Weight Loss Meals on display in Aisle 12 that was described by Mister Smiley on his microphone: "Brandy. Cleanup in Aisle 12. Fat man knocked over the display of the Real Meals for Real Men Weight Loss Meals." Mister Smiley is tactless. I am happy it wasn't another kid throwing up in the fresh meat section.

Ellen juggles a plastic pack of egg noodles and stops long enough to wave it at me for emphasis. "Look at that sign, just look at it!" She points toward an open door and the poster of Noah Hartley that Mister Smiley stuck up on the wall in the employee breakroom last week. I peer to my left and take in the poster. It says: GET YOUR GHOST TOWN ON—FOURTH ANNUAL FIRE MOUNTAIN REDNECK RUN. And it has a picture of a man running splashed across the front. He is almost invisible, and mist comes off his back and head like he's a ghost.

"Who gives them the right to just write us off like that?" She grouches with an indignant head wag. "It's a bunch of rich folks from Charleston and Huntington wanting to make money off us poor folks. That's who it is." She pokes me in the chest with the egg noodles and leans in so I can smell the cigarettes on her breath. "They think they can just come out here, make fun of us, and take over; that's what it is."

I nod politely and grab the bill of my ball cap that isn't there. Mister Smiley won't let me wear a hat here. It makes me antsy, and I peer toward the line of two cash registers by the store's front window. I am worried that the four girls who run the checkout can hear Ellen complaining. There is a certain pecking order here. We're all like a bunch of my pop's chickens he keeps in the yard. The bigger ones get all the little bits of feed he tosses out. They eat and eat until they can't take anymore, and even then, they are still poking the ground with their beaks so the others can't get any. These are the four girls who work at the register—they are like a team. Two girls run the register and check folks out, two bags. They come from the subdivisions in New Alliance, and their families have a lot of money. The Check Out Girls get twelve dollars an hour, vacation days, and leave work at a timely hour. Mister Smiley always comes out to walk them to their cars in the evening.

The little hens in the back are the ones like Ellen and me who come in after the store closes to stock the shelves and clean the floors. All we get is minimum wage and the crappy night shifts. Mister Smiley is long gone when I get off my shift at one in the morning. Missus Smiley turns on the security cameras to ensure we don't take any free groceries home. The only thing that walks to my truck with me is an old stray tomcat that shares my midnight lunch.

"I'm doing the run," I tell Ellen behind my palm. "I'm probably the only one in it raised redneck." It's true. I have been preparing for it for almost two years. As soon as I get home from work, I sleep for four hours, then get up and run twenty-one miles. I get done in about three and a half hours.

"What made you decide to do that? You'll never win," she says. She pokes a finger at the man running on the sign. "They got professionals running it. They use these amateur runs for practice.

I seen it last year and read about it online. These guys come in and run the race and win by a long shot. They use the races to get corporate sponsors and rack up money to pay for them to go to the big races. You ain't going to win. You ain't, so don't try. You'll just get hurt."

She is probably right. I won't win. I've spent most of my life, though, with people telling me I wouldn't amount to anything. They said I'd have a baby at fourteen like my mama did. I'd never finish high school. I'd never do anything more than work at Smiley's. That's why I want to do it. And because I have Pops. He's one of Mama's old boyfriends. He's taken care of me since I was four, and Mama left me at his house one weekend and didn't return. He tells me the only thing holding me back is my big ears. He says the sky is the limit if I hide them behind my hair.

"Look at my ears, Ellen," I say, pushing my hair up on my head. "Pops says big ears are the only thing holding me back from doing anything I want. Are they big or what?"

"No, they are tiny." Ellen eyes me with a tip of her head.

"Yep, so nothing is holding me back."

She doesn't know what I'm talking about. But I get what Pops means. He's all old camo pants, worn-out ball caps, and Confederate flags flying on his front porch. He talks with a thick accent when his friends are around, and he always has a raggedy, beat-up truck sitting on the front lawn he's working on. But he's really smart. And he's the closest thing I've got to a daddy. Most of the time, I listen to what he says.

Then I hear the soft voices of the cashier girls coming our way, heading toward the breakroom to clock out. I hurry, push the broom across the floor, and eye them cautiously as they walk by. Janie Mills and Carrie Edwards were in my high school classes. The twins, Michelle and Meghan Reynolds, were a year below me. I still can't tell the twins apart, but everyone stares at them like they are gingerbread cookies on Christmas Day while they twitter and giggle, cuddling close and keeping some big secret from the rest of the world. They are all beautiful, moving past me in slow motion and ripping off their cash register aprons with SMILEYS written on the front. They have long, smooth hair, perfect complexions, and rich mommies and daddies waiting at home for them.

One of them leans into another and whispers something leaving them all laughing and looking back at me. "Did you rob the Goodwill again this week?" Meghan Reynolds asks me. They look at me and burst into laughter. I look down at my jean shorts and tank top.

"I ran here tonight," I shrug it off. But I suddenly felt vulnerable like she opened the bathroom door while I was peeing, and everybody got a good look at me sitting there.

I choose my words carefully. I have learned to watch my grammar and bypass the *I ain'ts* and *he don'ts* so people don't taunt me. "I'm working out for the Redneck Run." Then, too eagerly, like I need to impress her, I add, "I'm going to call myself the Fire Mountain Shadow. That will be on the back of the T-shirts I get."

"Oh, my God," Michelle draws that one out latches on to Meghan's arm and rolls into another fit of laughter. My face burns a self-conscious red.

I try not to listen. Still, I can't help but chew on the cruel words for the next half hour and long after everybody's gone but the night shift. Regardless, there are five people working tonight. They are all tired and grumpy. It is between paydays and the bottom of the ridge flooded out with a good downpour last night, leaving some of them with soggy floors in their houses.

I go up to the registers, turn on some music on my phone, and start dancing down the conveyor belt and doing some cartwheels to cheer them up. They still don't do anything more than roll their eyes, so I start singing to the music through the cashier's microphone. Ellen thinks this is funny, and even if I'm not wacky enough, her laugh is contagious. You can hear it echoing off the walls and mingling with the others.

It is right about the time I am on the second verse and second cartwheel when I am reminded who the chubby guy is who Mama tried to pick up at the Crazy Kettle and who tackled me on the railroad tracks. He goes to Holy Trinity Church in New Alliance. Sometimes, he helps Preacher Murphy pick up almost-expiring food for the church pantry and hand it out to people who need it. Mister Smiley always lets them in on Wednesday after closing to pick up the food. It is Thursday, and they are just as surprised to see me dancing and singing on the conveyor belt as I am seeing them coming down the aisle at me on the wrong day.

I don't think the song is spicy, but obviously Mister Smiley does. He nearly jerks me off the belt. I must make an awkward jump to the linoleum floor and catch the side of Preacher Murphy's arm to keep from falling. Preacher Murphy is tall and old-guy handsome. He's like the weatherman on the local nightly news my aunt watches with a funny little smile hiding on her lips even if he's telling us that we'll get ten inches of snow. He's got short, gray hair and wears a big, toothy smile on his face. "Is this what goes on in here when I'm gone?" Mister Smiley is keeping his voice down because the preacher is here. It is grating, as if he is whisper-yelling. He grips my skinny arm, and is one step away from shaking me like a kid.

"No, not usually," I mumble. "I was—I was just trying to cheer everybody up. It rained hard last night, and Jimmy Moody's house flooded. He can't find his cat, and his couch is soggy."

"Who is Jimmy Moody?" Mister Smiley is staring at me with a furrowed brow. He has a round head shaped like a basketball and hardly any hair on top except a little crown of fine black fuzz. However, he has thick eyebrows that look like wooly worm caterpillars creeping across his forehead.

"He's the one that unloads the truck at night," I answer. Surely, Mister Smiley signs the paychecks, so he knows Jimmy's worked here for over four years. Still, his round cheeks turn irritated red, and he looks at the preacher and shrugs.

"It's hard to keep track of all of them, especially the needy ones the state sends me." Mister Smiley's head snaps back to me. "But this one, I remember this one's name. It's a booze—Bloody Mary or something."

"Yeah, Mary," I lie to him right in front of the preacher. I cautiously look up—no lightning bolt to strike me dead.

"Well, Mary, I didn't see your little red truck in the lot. I thought you weren't working tonight."

"I didn't drive. I ran here," I tell Mister Smiley, hoping he is impressed with the fact that I did a twelve-mile run. I'm hoping Mister Smiley will sponsor me for the Redneck Run.

"You—ran all the way from Fire Mountain?"

"Uh-huh. I was running low on gas. And I wanted to practice for the Redneck Run."

I look over Mister Smiley's shoulder and bounce my eyes past Preacher Murphy's stern but patient gaze. I think he is trying to read the situation. I'm not sure. Maybe my family's reputation precedes me. Everybody in New Alliance always tosses all of us Devereauxs, MacCabes, and McAllisters into the same pot like we're all a part of a good old-fashioned Irish vegetable soup. My mama is a MacCabe, my Pops is a McAllister, and Josh's family are the Devereauxs. Even though we're as different as carrots and potatoes, we're supposed to mix well. Not so. We don't get along at all. It's more like eating pickles and pumpkin pie together. Yuck.

It doesn't help that I don't go to Holy Trinity except for major events like the Christmas Eve service, so the preacher doesn't know me personally. After Josh disappeared, I went to Fire Mountain Community Church, thinking that maybe if I prayed hard enough, we would find him. It didn't work, and after a while, I got tired of putting money into the offering plate and not getting results. I figured if I was going to pay for a show, I'd go to the movies in town.

I can't read the preacher, so I work my way back to the man who nearly killed me on the tracks. He thinks Mister Smiley getting mad at me is funny. I can tell because he is hiding a smirk behind his hand that he is rubbing along his cheeks. However, he can't hide the laughter in his eyes. They are chocolate brown eyes that crinkle up at the corners. I decided to call him Bear, as his friends call him. He is enormous and looks like a big grizzly bear with a scruffy chin beard. I note this before my gaze sets on Mister Smiley again because I hear the word *fired*.

"You're firing me?" I asked him.

"I have no choice," Mister Smiley is wagging his thumb toward the back door. "If I didn't, what kind of message am I giving the other workers, Mary? Is it okay to play around instead of working? No. I'm not paying you to dance and carry on, maybe break my conveyor belt."

"It won't happen again," I plead, holding my arms out in front of me with hands clasped, begging. "I swear to God." Oh, I wish I hadn't said that. The preacher's eyes widened, looking upward as if waiting for a bolt of lightning to come through the dusty ceiling and strike me. My own eyes follow warily. No lightning. I look back to the preacher. "I mean, I swear to—*me*."

It was all I could think of to correct myself, and then I reckon the preacher probably thought I was comparing myself to God, which was perhaps just as bad. But the worst was yet to come, "I suppose I just swear," I say, then try to shake that off, "I don't swear that much." I swallow hard and turn away from the preacher. "Oh, never mind. Mister Smiley, I've got a million things to pay for this month. I've got my tuition and my mom's trailer rent due. I have to pay for my little sister's babysitter. I can't lose my job. I *swear* it won't happen again."

"You know, her singing was unique," the preacher interrupts. "We could use another soprano in our choir." He turns to Mister Smiley. "How about if she comes to church on Sunday and sings soprano in the choir, you keep her on." He reaches up, latches onto Mister Smiley's shoulder, and gently shakes it. "She likes to cheer folks up. Maybe Brandy can cheer up the everyone from the first row—"

"And all the way to the Baptist Church in Beckley, two hours away," adds Bear. They all think this is funny and laugh. I see Ellen peering around the corner of Aisle Three, a can of peas in her hand. She is stifling a giggle in her palm. I scratch my chin, narrow my gaze at Bear, and give him the stink-eye. He shrugs, turns his eyes to the floor, and his cheeks turn a bright pink.

"You won't let this happen again, Mary?" Mister Smiley isn't happy about the proposition. Still, he reaches over and snatches up the broom against the cash register. He sticks it up between us until I take it in my hand.

"No, sir," I say. I know I'm gritting my teeth anxiously. I turn toward the preacher. "But you are kidding about the choir thing, right?" I ask. "Because I'm not great about getting out of bed on Sunday morning until ten or eleven. It's my sleep-in day. It will eat up the gas in my truck. I've got just the right amount of money—"

"I'll have someone pick you up." He holds up a finger. "And another thing, no more saying the Lord's name in vain, no more swearing to God. No more—swearing."

"Yeah, okay." Great. I puff out my cheeks and snatch the broom from Mister Smiley's hands. About twenty minutes later, when he is about to leave, I catch him just as his hand is on the latch to the door.

"Mister Smiley," I mutter. I am nervous, rubbing my own hands together. "I know the timing probably isn't right, but I was wondering if you thought about what I asked you the other day. You know, could your store sponsor me for the Redneck Run?"

"I'm still thinking about it."

I realize Pops used to always tell me the exact same thing when I would ask him for a new pair of jeans and a pretty shirt from the mall shops just as all the winter bills were coming in. It gave me hope because it wasn't a downright no, but in the back of my mind, I probably knew the outfits weren't coming anytime soon, or at least until his tax return came in sometime in March.

However, I know Mister Smiley can afford the thirteen hundred dollars. I don't know if he really wants to sponsor me. Still, he won't reject me in front of the preacher and Bear. I'm hoping he'll believe in me.

"Okay," I concede. "But you'll think about it, right?"

He grunts. "Uh-huh."

"One more thing." I watched him slide out the door, and I step forward. "It's still alright if I buy the dented cans of food at a discount for a couple of folks I know, right?"

"No stealing. And you can buy only the ones dented at the discount price," Mister Smiley growls, pointing to the cameras at the corner of the room. "Any funny business, and I'll call the cops."

Chapter −3

Getting Shot at by Crazy Willie and getting Kicked out of church

I'm staring down a double-barrel shotgun. I'm not quite ready to terror-pee my pants. Nevertheless, if the sweat dribbling down my forehead right now is any indication of my fear, I think I might. There are six drops of sweat and counting settling on my eyelids. It's Crazy Willie standing with his legs splayed state highway patrol style in front of me. He's about six foot ten inches tall and has a wild, rabid dog look to his eyes. His hair is sticking up on his head, and he's wearing blue coveralls and a light gray sweatshirt with black streaks.

"Woman, you are encroaching on my property. I'm going to kill you. I got the right." He's right about one thing. I'm trespassing. I'm not sure he's as clued in on the laws as he thinks. Regardless, it is just him and me in the middle of a few hundred acres. If he murdered me and buried me three feet under in a black plastic garbage bag anywhere around here and took the secret of his killing to the grave with him, nobody would ever know.

He doesn't care that I'm giving him the kind of puppy eyes that always work on my pops when I've done something wrong. I'm just standing here nervously twisting my fingers together and, like I already said, almost peeing my pants. It is seven in the morning and Sunday, and I promised Mister Smiley and Preacher Murphy that I would be at the church. But my day has been crappy from the start, and so I'm expecting the worst.

You see, they never found Josh's body. I find it hard to close the book on him because I still wonder if he isn't out there somewhere. Some folks say he's buried on Crazy Willie's property. Rumor has always been that Willie's got illegal moonshine stills and marijuana patches running up and down the mountainside. He's been known to wander around town after dark near my old trailer park. Folks said maybe Josh was trying to steal the piping on Willie's stills to turn in for recycling money. Or maybe he harvested a patch of pot.

Regardless, some believe Crazy Willie shot Josh and buried him somewhere on his property.

I wouldn't be on Crazy Willie's land at all and facing a rifle if there wasn't a question about who killed Josh or if he was dead. For one thing, I can't go straight down. The straight path takes me through Fire Mountain View Trailer Park and Campground. I can't go into the trailer park without his sister, Crystal, chasing me down to beat me up. His mama says I was the one who murdered him, and she told the cops I shot him and buried him on Pops' property. She started telling everybody about all the girls he'd screwed while we were married. I got really mad. Pops helped me file for a divorce.

The other reason I cut through the property is because, in my mind, I'm still married. I feel like a ghost walking around in a haze most of the time with unfinished business. Maybe Josh hit his head and doesn't know who he is. Maybe he's homeless and sitting with a grocery cart underneath an overpass in Charleston. Maybe his body is moldering underneath one of his girlfriend's trailers that he ticked off. Maybe, maybe, maybe. I've got a thousand of them that roll through my mind at about two in the morning because I can't sleep thinking about them. The ghost of Josh haunts me. That's why I started running. It helped rid my head of all those maybes.

It can't just be any run. It has to be something challenging to keep my mind busy, something scary to keep me from thinking. I start by running along the highway and dodging the coal trucks on the night shift. Then I take off down Fire Mountain along an old gravel road. I trip and skid all over and have to jump downed trees in the moon's light. About halfway down, I cut through Crazy Willie's property right in front of his house and past his TRESPASSERS WILL BE SHOT and BEWARE OF DOG signs. He thinks it is okay if his dogs always chase my cousin and me on the ATVs. It is not, however, okay if we cut through *his* land.

I climb under Crazy Willie's seven-foot-high fence. If he's still awake, he's watching for me. Then, he lets loose his three Hellhound-Rottweilers and his two or three beagles and mixed-mutt hounds. If I'm lucky, it is just the dogs chasing me for a half mile through the woods, baying, barking, and carrying on. Then I climb under an old chain-link fence, and they stop once I'm on the other side.

If I'm not, Crazy Willie's got his shotgun, and he shoots it a couple of times at the trees and over my head, screaming cusswords and things he'll do to me if he ever catches me. He never does, so I cut through the gravel pit and get yelled at by the truck drivers. Then, I tear down to just about the bottom of the mountain and stop just short of a small ridge. That's where I come to a standstill and stare down at New Alliance. It looks so pretty with twinkling lights.

I usually stare at it for a few minutes, drink it in, and pretend it's mine. Then I head to the very bottom of the hill to where the highway comes in. I'm careful there now. People fly down that road. A month and a half ago, some man in a big, new truck nearly pancaked me because he was talking on his phone. I made a flying leap to his hood and called him a stupid, pretty boy, dumbass. He stared at me with wide eyes when I came down the other side. He probably peed his pants and thought that he hit a deer. Now, I'm running in the gravel to avoid stupid dumbasses, and I shortcut it to Township Road 436, which is a straight run back up Fire Mountain and home. Or, in today's case, a quick right to Holy Trinity Church so I can sing in the choir and keep my job at Smiley's.

Today, I still haven't made it. Like I said, it has been a bad day. My truck battery is dead, and Pops has already left for his Sunday morning visits to the flea market. I don't have a choice but to make a run for it. Now Crazy Willie has his double-barrel shotgun six inches from my sweating forehead. One of his beagles keeps nipping at me, and I have to keep jumping from right to left.

"I'm sorry—um, Mister Reads." That's his real name, Bill Reads. What else can I say? I am looking around wildly, trying to find a way to duck out of this situation. "How—how about I won't do it again?"

"You won't because I'm gonna kill you!"

And damn, if he doesn't push his index finger on the rifle just at the exact moment, I dodge to the right. I yelp. Afterward, I hear a crash and a boom, and my legs move faster than my body can keep up. I bob in and out of the trees and take giant leaping steps. I swear, at one ridge, I am flying through the air for nearly the count of ten.

I can hear Crazy Willie. He is shooting and hollering. Today, his dogs crawl under the fence and chase me straight down Main Street. I don't stop my wayward flight until I am slip-sliding to a halt in the parking lot of Holy Trinity. The crazy dogs are nipping at my heels.

I shove my arms on the glass double back doors, slide inside, and pull it close just as one Rottweiler hits the glass. Smack! He smashes it hard, his muzzle slapping slobbery, cream-colored drool while another tries to paw its way through the glass.

"Holy crap," I mutter, take my hand off the door gingerly to make sure they can't get inside. I step back. "Frigging hellhounds can't come in here." I taunt them with my hands on my ears and blow them a raspberry with my lips while I wiggle my butt.

It isn't until I turn that I realize the door opens to the choir room. Preacher Murphy is standing there with a hymnal pressed to his chest as if he is preparing to say a prayer. The entire choir is standing with folded hands, gazing at me with their heads tucked to their chests, as if meditating.

"Hey, Preacher Murphy, I'm here." I greet him while trying to pull twigs from my hair. I get a peek of the church through the doors and a long hallway beyond. It is big and pretty, with natural wooden pews, an altar, and a red carpet. It is stuffed full of people all dressed up in their Sunday best. I got a pair of running shorts and a T-shirt with smudges of shotgun powder. "I'm here. I'm sorry. I got chased by Crazy Willie's hellhounds. Well, that's what he calls them when he sees me coming. He says: 'I see you, little she-devil. I'm letting loose the hellhounds!'" I let my words trail away. Preacher Murphy has a strange purse to his lips. "I guess you didn't need all that information. Still, I suppose that's why folks think he's crazy. I'm a mess. Where do you want me to go?" He opens his mouth to say something. His lips move, but nothing is coming out. He stops and gets a funny tip to his head before he scratches it with his fingers. "My truck wouldn't start. I had to run here," I offer up. "I didn't want to be late. Old Bill Reads caught me taking the shortcut through his place and shot at me. You know, Crazy Willie. He got me a bit." I poke a finger at my shirt, then realize both my knees are skinned and bleeding a bit. "Oh, and I fell at the gravel pits. The dogs usually stop before I hit the road. They didn't. I didn't see a truck coming. I thought they were closed on Sunday. Guess not. I can go to the bathroom and clean up."

I can hear the organ playing near the front of the church and see Preacher Murphy snap his attention to the heads turning toward us. He smiles and tugs my shoulder, pointing to the back of the room.

"We can cover you in a choir robe," he says, herding me toward the rear of the room, where I can see more of the bright blue choir robes hanging on a rack. "Are you alright? Do you need Band-Aids?"

"I'm fine," I say. "I just don't know the songs that well."

"All you have to do is mouth the words. We'll give you a hymnal." In other words, he is begging me to *not* sing.

It should have been that easy. I follow the white-haired lady in front of me out to the choir chairs right in front. She keeps turning and nodding to me to let me know I'm doing alright. Twice, she stops to lay a hand on my arm and herd me in the right place. We're all in robes, whooshing out with hymnals in our hands, twenty-two figures marching to the beat of the opening song.

They stick me in the back with a handful of gray-haired sopranos with way too much cherry-red lipstick and pink-cheeked blush. I can't help but note that the Cash Register Girls, Michelle and Meghan Reynolds, are two rows in front of me. The twins are like two sticks of cherry candy to all the men sitting in the pews with wives who started wearing stretchy pajama pants around the house two weeks after getting married. They look like two angels with their perfect, pale complexions and bleach-blonde hair straightened to a soft river stopping just short of their shoulders. I suppose I can't blame those poor guys for ogling those angels. Their voices are sweet and melodic, two crystal glasses. I try not to whisper-sing loud enough that my hoarse voice cracks and breaks one of them.

I can't help but notice everybody is staring at me curiously now. I'm the Devereauxs-McAllister-MacCabe girl from on top of the mountain wearing dirty running shorts and a muddy T-shirt hidden under robes who suddenly shows up to sing among the blessed ornamented in pretty white dresses, brush-on makeup, and high heels below. I realize while I'm up there, everybody in the audience is staring at me in the same way they did in elementary school, thinking the girl with the drugged-out mama and the worn down, thrift shop, hand-me-down clothes shouldn't be anywhere near their kids. Maybe they think I've got head lice, or I might perhaps have the same weed-smoking, beer-drinking disease my mama has, and I'll give it to their kids. Then I wonder if Mama isn't just going to, right out of the blue, show up drunk and make a fuss because she heard I'm singing in the choir. She's done it before.

I feel dizzy and lightheaded thinking about everything they think of me. I can feel their eyes burning a hole through my choir robe, seeing the real me underneath. I remember what used to happen to me when I tried to sing in the choir at school. I would— *oh, crap*, faint. And the next thing I know, I'm blinking up at Preacher Murphy while he's huffing and carrying me to an old leather couch in the choir room.

"Get her a pack of ice from the kitchen!" he belts. "And some Band-Aids," he says as an afterthought. I watch while three old ladies stare down at me with concerned faces. One pats my hand until it feels raw.

I start to sit up. "Preacher Murphy, I don't need any ice. I just forgot I'm afraid of standing up in front of people."

"Honey, you hit your head pretty hard," one lady says. She points a wrinkly finger at my noggin. "If not for Beauregard, you would probably be singing with the angels upstairs."

"The choir director caught you after you hit the first stand and before you hit the floor, you know."

I wheel my eyes around, following three sets of old lady eyes to a man standing awkwardly by the door.

"Beauregard," I whisper. Ug, no, Bear. I lean out and groan at him. "Oh, please stop trying to save my life."

Yes, it is the chubby guy. I missed him somehow in the choir. He thinks this is funny and gives me a little smile. I see him nearly jump into action. One of the twins is handing him a box of Band-Aids and a plastic baggie full of ice cubes. She rolls her eyes at Bear. The gesture is aimed at me.

"Reverend Murphy said to give this to you," she says while her matching sister peers through the door at me like Mister Smiley stares at the toilet bowl in the men's bathroom when it is overflowing. "He's going to start the sermon. He said that you could patch her up while I do my solo." She's not looking at Bear, snapping her eyes back and forth. I know she is lying. My little sister does the same thing when she comes over to Pops to visit, and I ask her if she got into my stuff in my room. I know she did because there's stuff all over my floor. Kaylee can't look me straight in the eye and tell me she she didn't trespass without wavering.

Bear is looking at me like he would rather walk into the bathroom while his grandma is in there naked than put a Band-Aid on my knobby knee. "Just give it to me," I say, wiggling my fingers while I sit there. "I can do it myself."

Bear lets his shoulders fall and takes the ice pack and Band-Aids she is stuffing into his hands. I see him cringe a little next to her like shy boys do, his head dipping low with a little smile tweaking his lips.

"I can do it," he shrugs. "Unless you bite. You don't bite, do you?"

"Why—why would I bite?" I ask him, unsure. Was he calling me a dog?

"I don't know," he stammers. "I mean, no. I was making small talk. You looked like you were in a dogfight earlier. You didn't look beat up; you were just being chased. We all saw you running down the road. And now, you look like you'll faint again because I am talking too much." He hunkers down on one knee while I look over his shoulder at the twins staring at me like I'm a sideshow freak. Bear follows my gaze for just a split second, then hands me the icepack to put on my head.

"You ladies can go on out. I'll be there in a second. I'll be there for your solo, Meghan."

The one he calls Meghan looks relieved. "Thanks; I don't know if I can do it without you." She still lingers there, looking at us and then toward the sanctuary where I can hear Preacher Murphy droning on about something.

"How do you tell them apart?" I ask Bear while he unwraps a Band-Aid. I tug up my choir robe to expose my skinned knees. He cringes. "Those two remind me of the matching set of coffee mugs my pops got us to drink coffee out of last winter. They both were identical. I couldn't tell them apart until I dropped one and it got a ding." I thought about it momentarily while he patched up my knee and rubbed the sticky end so it stuck to my skin. "Maybe one of those two will fall, hit her head, get a dent in her temple so I can tell them apart."

Bear looks up and ponders this for a moment with his hand on his chin. "Well, if you look at it that way. It's easy." He leans a little to the right on his knee. I see a twinkle in his chocolate-brown eyes.

It reminds me of how Pops always looks at my mama, even though he tells me he would never come within a ten-foot radius of her again. "Meghan's the one on the right. She's the one with the dent." He leans in a little and works up a sly smile he hides behind his hand. "Just at the bottom of her collarbone, right where it dips down by her shirt, she's got a teeny-weeny little scar from having chicken pox when she was five."

I snap my head to him, knowing my mouth is slightly agape, and my eyes narrow knowingly. "Holy crap, you noticed that." I smile, a twist of my lips telling him I know why he noticed her dent.

"Shhh, now, she'll hear you." He pushes a finger to his lips. "And yeah, of course," he says. "Anyone with a canny eye, as my mother would call it, would see that."

"Naw, Bear," I laugh softly. "Any man with a huge crush on a woman would notice that. Are you a couple?"

When I say Bear, he looks at me with a tipped head. "It's Beau." He turns around and seems to note the two women have left, "Beauregard Rodriguez, actually." Suddenly, he drops his happy face. I wonder if I said too much or if he doesn't have to be nice to me anymore because nobody is watching him. He seems to shake away the happiness and suddenly goes downright mean. "And no, we're not a couple."

"Why don't you ask her out?"

"Why don't I ask her out?" he repeats with a cranky twist of his lips. "Well, for one, I'm fat. Did you miss that?"

"No, I didn't," I say honestly. "You're chubby. Why don't you lose weight?"

I think my words must have been like a knife slashing through his ribcage, letting the anger seep out into the air from wherever he kept it in there. His eyes narrow, and his face turns beet red. "You wouldn't get it, would you?" he asks me, pushing himself to his feet with one hand on his knee. "I know it must be nice never to work at being skinny. But maybe if you'd eat a little more and smoke and drink a little less, you wouldn't black out in the middle of the church service. I suppose, though, you can't change that when you're surrounded in—that redneck crap."

"Surrounded in what?" I ask him.

"Bars and trailers."

I want to ball up my fist and lay him flat then. That's what my mama would do. I try hard not to be like her, especially in church. I know folks who act like him. They smile at you on a busy street, but when you go down a back alley, they whisper mean things.

"You're going there, aren't you?" I say, not believing I'm suddenly in fight mode. "In the way rich people say things without using insensitive words, you're calling me trailer trash."

"You said it. And it wasn't as rude as you calling me fat. At least I didn't describe you as skanky, which is what you look like right now and something you can't hide under a choir robe. Who wears shorts and a dirty T-shirt to church on Sunday? Who bolts into a church and cusses. It is disrespectful to God and everyone here. Did you not notice everyone in suits and dresses and think, maybe I should go home and change into something less skanky?"

I stand up, shove off the choir robe, and let it fall to the couch. "You called yourself fat. You asked me if I had noticed it. I did. I may come from a trailer park, but I'm not trailer trash. I may be a redneck, but I've got more class in my little finger than you've got in that big old pudgy body of yours." I stop and wag a finger at him. "You are nothing but a rude, chubby man hiding behind a bible and pretending to be a Christian when you are nothing but meaner than the devil," I spit back.

"You need to leave. You disrespect this church by saying that."

"Is everything alright?" I hear another voice coming from the hallway. Bear turns and tugs a little at the collar of his choir robe. I can see a brown-haired woman standing there, looking back and forth between us. She is probably our age and is wearing a black church dress.

"It is fine, Lilly," he says. I figure this is probably another one of the girls he likes.

I lean in any way, look up skyscraper high past his beard and to his eyes. "You know what?" I ask. "I don't like this church so much. You are all mean. You can kick me out if you want." I turn to Bear. "You know, all you folks talk about is putting money in the plate and patting each other on the back when you do something *you* think is good. It doesn't work like that." I reach out and poke Bear's tummy with my index finger. "You know, it doesn't come from down here."

I can see his face turning a bright red. I reach up and knock his temple with my knuckles. I can barely reach him on my tippy toes. "It comes from up here—all that stuff. Not just deciding not to eat but also being mean and calling other people names right out of the blue. It is called restraint and taking control. Neither of which you have."

I push past Bear, stomp to the front door, and leave. I run like hell is chasing after me like I always do when I wish things were different, wish I was different.

Chapter –4
Sucking it up

I live at Pops' house about three-quarters of the way up Fire Mountain. It is about a quarter mile down on Locust Ridge Road, an old gravel road that the township only plows in the winter if we get twelve inches of snow or more. Most people call it Fire Mountain Road. Fire Mountain Road used to keep going all the way to the top of the mountain. Now, it stops at Locust Grove and ends with weeds and gravel.

There's a big wooden sign where it comes off Fire Mountain Road that says: McAllister Sawmill and Tree Cutting Service. That's Pops' mill, and he does really well in the summer. In the late spring, like now, we're both cutting it close on the income we've lived off of for the winter, so we're doling every last cent out to pay for gas in our vehicles and food on the table.

It doesn't stop Pops from feeding everybody around if they're eking out the last few pennies they've dug out of the cushions of their couch, too. That's what he's doing when I return from church on Sunday afternoon. He's got his entire family and some folks I don't even know lounging around his house and pouring out to the yard.

I meet him coming in the front door. He's not too tall and not too thin and looks in good shape for a man who never lifts a finger to exercise. I suppose all the tree-cutting and lumbering he does, makes a good workout for him. He's got sky blue eyes and red-orange hair he keeps cut short and almost always covered by a raggedy, old ball cap. He's also got lots of freckles like me.

"Brandy, can you cook us up that turkey I got thawing on the stove?" he asks me, tugging on his ball cap. It is his scraggly gray hat I got him for his birthday three years ago. I know he's wearing it to suck up to me. He wants me to cook an entire three-course meal for more people than I saw at the Sunday service a few hours ago. "And maybe some corn, potatoes, and things you wrap in bacon?"

"Which *things*?" I ask him flatly. "You know it hurts my feelings when you call the creations that I got an A in on my finals *things*."

He gives me a crooked smile. He thinks my dream of becoming a chef is silly, a pipe dream. He feels that instead of wasting my money on college tuition to learn my profession, I should wander into a kitchen and read the recipes from a cookbook. "*Things* are what the D students made, and there were plenty of them. However, Pops, if you mean those bacon-wrapped drumsticks with marsala sauce and skewered apples with mango chutney boiled eggs wrapped in breaded bacon, I will make them. But only if you call Mister Smiley and see if I can get my job back."

"What'd you do this time, sweetheart?" he asks. "You didn't burn the place down, did you?"

"No," I mumble-groan so it sounds like *no-wa*. I wiggle my finger for him to follow me toward the kitchen. "He caught me doing a cartwheel on his stupid conveyor belt when he brought Preacher Murphy from Holy Trinity to the store to pick up food for the poor box at church. Then, the preacher made me join the choir at Holy Trinity to keep my job. I got to the church today, and when I looked out over the crowd—"

"What the heck were you thinking about joining the choir?" Pops gives a hearty laugh, and everybody sitting on his old brown couches and watching TV, with an odd mix of recliners in the living room, looks up at us. "Crap, girl, you get dizzy at a four-way stop if there is a car at each sign."

"Yeah, right?" My back is to him. I toss my hands into the air. "I guess I just got caught up in the moment."

"That hardly seems a rational explanation that Mister Smiley called a little bit ago and told me to tell you to apologize to the choir director for cussing him up one side and down the other."

That's when I pivot on my feet and gaze hard at Pops. "What are you talking about?" I ask. "Mister Smiley called? I didn't start the argument. That idiot choir director did. He called me everything straight down to poor white trash and said I was skinny because I went to the bars and smoked. Do you know how insulting that is to someone who works out and runs as much as I do?"

"That don't sound like something a choir director would say, Brandy. And churchy folks don't lie—*much*." Pops looks grave now while I turn to walk into the kitchen. "And I know you've got a smart mouth on you."

I stop and glare at him hard. "Fine. Side with the rich people. If you had a kitchen door anymore, I would slam it shut right in your face. Oh, what the hell. I'm going to do it anyway." I move my hand out, pretending I'm slamming an invisible door shut between us. Pops starts to say something, and I put up my hand. "The door is closed. I can't hear you."

I should have let him finish what he is saying. If I had, I would have known that Preacher Murphy had called not long after Mister Smiley left the message with Pops. The preacher was going to make a stop out at Pops' to talk to me. Needless to say, I didn't listen. I didn't know. So just as everybody starts converging on my meal three hours and forty-five minutes later and I am checking on two pumpkin pies in the oven, I see the broom Pop keeps between the stove and the wall start to fall. As I catch it, I see Pop's shadow behind me, hearing him clear his throat.

"Oh, now that the food is done, you're coming to apologize," I growl and turn. I am tired and a little grumpy from cooking. Pops hurt my feelings when he didn't side with me. I think it is him. It is not. Instead, when I shove my hands on my hips and give a little waggle, I'm staring between Preacher Murphy and Bear. "Oh."

"Yes, I am." It is Bear looking pale staring at me. "I mean, I didn't come just because the food was done." Then his face turns crimson red. Probably because he thinks I made the remark because he's chubby. It is funny because everybody in the living room who can see them through the open kitchen entranceway is watching him. Considering that he did the same to me this morning with the twins, I should feel like I've just recouped some of my pride. I'm a little indignant; it is not fair that I must make sorries to him.

I realize he is standing there, eyes darting around scared-rabbit like he wants to bolt. Everybody is suddenly quiet, barring a bit of lip-smacking around the turkey, trying to hear what is going on in the kitchen between me, the preacher from Holy Trinity, and a snobbish man in a Sunday suit. It's undoubtedly better than what they are watching on satellite television.

"I ain't sure if this is what Mister Smiley meant as an apology." Pops is snickering while he rounds the corner smiling. He probably thinks he needs to officiate like a referee at one of the boxing matches he likes to watch. He thinks I have Mama's cheeky temper.

"A sassy sorry from you," Pops goes on. "and this poor man running to the hills because you're going to ride that broom off in hot pursuit, isn't what I would call appropriate."

I look at the broom in my hand and give Pops the stink eye. "I'm not a witch. It wasn't my fault."

"Pride goeth before destruction, and a haughty spirit before a fall. Isn't that what it says in the bible, preacher?" Pops nods his head toward Preacher Murphy.

"Proverbs 16:18," the preacher replies with a healthy nod to Pops. Pops looks smug as if he made that statement himself, and it is God patting him on the back for all his cleverness.

"Okay, fine." I feel my lip twitch, and I know Pops can see it, and I know he knows what this means. I don't particularly appreciate being put against the wall. I'm not particularly eager to get ganged up on. I'll take a punch, but whoever beats the crap out of me better not turn their back for a second. I will get my revenge.

I look Bear in the eye, but he isn't looking at me. "I apologize for calling you Bear instead of Beau. I thought it was your name. I am sorry that you think you are better than us trailer trash and rednecks like the ones you see all around you here." I wave a hand around the room, and I see Bear's eyes getting antsy while my Uncle Pete, sitting on the couch in the living room, rises up. He takes offense at being called a redneck by anyone other than a bigger redneck than him. Pops puts out his hand and stops Uncle Pete, who is eyeing Bear like he's a mean old tomcat and me like I'm a little hurt mouse with big, sad eyes.

"What'd he do to her?" Uncle Pete's got my back even if Pops doesn't.

"He called me skanky," I tell Uncle Pete.

"No, he didn't do nothing." Pops holds up a hand and shakes his head back and forth. "Brandy, stop. That's enough."

"How does the word skanky come up in a conversation during church?" My cousin, Kenny, yells out from the other room. I can see him in there trying to stifle a laugh between bites of food. He has red hair, a state highway patrol buzz cut, and tattoos up and down his skinny right arm. He's only a month and two weeks older than me and the closest thing I've got to a smart-alecky brother.

"I don't know. But it did twice," I answer.

"Yes sir, I did," Bear interrupts quickly, turning his attention to Pops and then me. He would love to slip through a crack in the floor and slither away in the darkness of our crawlspace underneath. "She's right. It was me. I didn't come here to get *her* to apologize. I came to tell her *I* was sorry." He looks me right in the eye for just a split second. And for just that split second, a sparkle there reminds me of the shine Josh would get in his eyes when he was flirting with a pretty girl. "I'm sorry. I'm not usually like this."

"You should probably get used to it. Brandy Hard Candy tends to bring out the worst in all of us." It is Kenny who says this. I drag my eyes away from Bear's, and they stop at my cousin's hard stare. I see Kenny give me a funny squint of his eyes. He is coming back in to dig his fork into the turkey for thirds. He puffs out his cheeks and does his weird duck call. I don't know why he is as skinny as the broomstick in my hand. He hasn't stopped eating since the day he was born. He is odd. He's got this thing he does where he always puffs out his cheeks and makes a sound like a duck. He also makes up names for me to suit his mood or whatever awkward situation I've gotten myself into. Today, I am Brandy Hard Candy. "Screw off, Kenny," I tell him, tossing the broom in his direction. He catches it easily and throws it back at me. "What is wrong with all of you today?" I ask while I resist the blow and watch the broom slap on the ground. "Nobody's got my back today but Uncle Pete?"

"The other dude's got God on his side," Kenny points at the preacher, who is eyeing the turkey with a rather lustful look in his gray eyes. "Who do you got?" He looks around. "By your broom there, we can all assume Satan? Who wants to be on that side?"

"It is done. Apologies accepted, right Brandy? Bygones," Pops interjects, stepping forward so I can't see Kenny like he can cut some cord between us and stop me from diving across the expanse and killing him. He doesn't wait for me to answer. He looks all happy and slaps a hand on the table. "You two hungry? Let's eat."

"Your dad said you were in here."

I am in my papasan chair in my bedroom, trying to hide in the dim light of my lamp a half hour later. On the floor, I've got a furry deer hide Pops shot a few years ago, with a pink rug tossed on top.

I've had enough insults today. I've got my music on, and I'm reading one of my books from class. I see the shadow at the doorway. I quickly pull out my earplugs and drop my book onto my lap. My room isn't too small, but Bear's shadow extends all the way across the pink throw rug, over the cozy quilts and pillows on my queen bed, and to the far wall where I still have posters on the wall from high school. He has a massive plate of food and shoves a fork into the turkey I made.

"He's not my dad."

"Don't be mad at him for my sake."

I want him to go away. "No, I'm not saying that because I'm mad. He's really not my dad. He takes care of me."

"Isn't that what dads do?" he says and then gets a look of realization. "I'm sorry again. He's your boyfriend. Reverend Murphy told me you weren't married even though he called you Missus Devereauxs. I just figured— I'm just really good at saying the wrong things today."

"Are you sick? He's like a hundred. He's not my boyfriend," I say flatly and start to put my earplugs back on. "He took me in when I was four and raised me." I sigh. "Okay, yeah, he's my dad, I guess. Is that all you wanted?"

"No. I want you to understand that I won't yell at you again. I really have never called anybody a skank in my life. My sister was there. She was the one who told everybody you were angry at me. She's never seen me get mad. But they put me on some—" Bear stops, throws back his head, and puffs out his cheeks. "I'm fat, and I know it. My dad died this year. He was always fat and depressed. Everybody thinks I'm going to follow in his footsteps. My mom had the doctor give me some pills to help, and they make me—mad all the time." Bear comes into the room. I see he's not letting this go.

"So stop taking the pills," I offer, hoping he'll leave.

"And just get fatter? I know you probably think I'm weird for discussing this with you."

"I do," I say. Then I feel bad. He looks like a spanked four-year-old. "It's true what I said. It starts up here in the head." I tap my forehead. "Why don't you try exercising?" I look at the plate he is holding in his hand. "Have you ever portioned your food?"

"I'm not an idiot," Bear tells me. "I don't mean that in the wrong way, but I've tried everything. I'm in the desperate phase."

I laugh out loud and sit up a bit. His face gets red, and I put out a hand.

"Bear—I mean, Beau, I'm not laughing at you." I scrub my hand over my face. For some stupid reason, I'm always picking up stray kittens and thinking I should help folks. "Do you think you're the only one who believes they are sitting on the brink of insanity because they can't control everything around them? I mean, you're talking to a woman who sits in a bar every Friday night waiting for her probably dead ex-husband to show up. Then I go through every detail of the last night before he vanished, step by step, just to prove to myself he's not dead and I didn't kill him because I did something wrong."

"I'm sorry. I get that. I miss my dad."

"I buy Josh a beer, dude. It just sits there and gets warm." I laugh when I say it. It really sounds funny now that I think about it. Bear chuckles half-heartedly too.

"Did you cook all this?"

"Yeah."

"It's delicious."

I hold up my book and poke a finger at it. "I went to a culinary arts school for three years. Now I'm two semesters away from a degree in restaurant management." I sigh. "I can help you if you want. I can show you how to exercise and portion your foods."

"Naw," he says.

"I suppose if you'd lose a little bit of weight, it might get you enough confidence to ask cute little Meghan out on a date. Just saying."

He shrugs and looks away. "Maybe I'll think about it."

"I work out every morning at six. Just show up if you change your mind."

Chapter –5
Josh's Secret Lockbox

Bear never shows up at my front door at six in the morning. On Friday night, however, he's at the Crazy Kettle. I wouldn't have noticed, except when my mama comes in surrounded by a wisp of thick cigarette smoke, I see her looking toward the yellow lamps hanging from the ceiling over the pool tables at the back of the bar. I'm in a sore mood. For the twelfth time at the grocery, I asked Mister Smiley if he could please sponsor me for the Redneck Run. He mumbled, "I'll think about it." I follow Mama's gaze and see Bear with his friend. They are both holding pool sticks and talking to some girls. He doesn't look up. I roll my eyes. "Mama, leave him alone," I tell her. She isn't interested in what I say.

"Huh?" she mumbles and I see her eyes are bloodshot.

"Leave him alone," I tell her. "He's churchy. He's the choir director at Holy Trinity, and not looking for what you've got to give."

"You can be mean, you know that?" She looks at Josh's seat and hesitates as if she wants to sit there. She doesn't. Instead, she goes around and sits down on the stool to my left. "I'm still cute. I got a long line of good-looking men still knocking on this door." Mama raises up her hands and waves them in front of her chest. I can tell she used to be pretty when I look at her face. It isn't time that's taken away her beauty. It is drugs and drinking and too many mean men. Her cheeks are sallow, and her eyes have wrinkly bags. She usually doesn't sit near me, so I wonder what she wants. She has something tucked into the crook of her arm, which she brings out and sets in front of her. It is one of those cheap gray-metal lockboxes. "What do you want, Mama?" I ask her.

"I found this in your old room." She leans back and pokes it over to me with her bent knuckles. "It was in your closet."

"So?" I look at the box, then at Mama. It is sad that she still calls the little room in the back of her trailer with dusty pink curtains and musty carpet, *my room*. I only lived in it a year before they started taking me away from her. "I haven't lived at your place since I was two. I don't think it is mine."

"I think it is."

I sigh and tug it over, flipping open the top. There's a little basketball the size of a fist and some old notes crumpled into squares. I see some tiny knick-knacks and marbles rolling around the bottom. On top are six or seven plain white envelopes with names on them.

I feel my stomach wiggle and feel a spark of curiosity creep along my spine. My finger pokes at the envelopes. They are all open, torn across the top with jagged edges. "This was in my old closet?"

"At the top where it is hard to reach," she says. "I found it looking for the Christmas ornaments last year."

"Last year," I repeat. "This is Josh's stuff, Mama. What's it doing at your house?"

"He came over one night, He asked to store some stuff in your room." Mama looks nervous. She taps her fingers on the wooden bar counter. "It was about three months before he disappeared."

"Why didn't you give it to me sooner?"

"Baby girl, he came and got everything else after a few weeks."

"What else?" I ask. "What was he storing at your place?"

"Brandy, I don't know," she says. "Boxes, I reckon. Back then, you was married to him. I just figured you knew about it. Figured it was your stuff too. He filled up the room. It took him three trips in his truck."

I reach in and take out an envelope. It says: ASHLEY on the front in lead pencil. Next to it is a phone number scrawled in Josh's handwriting. I feel strange, thinking maybe there are eyes on us. But I open it nonetheless, peer inside. There is a copper-colored key like the kind that Pops uses on his garage door lock. Then there's also a driver's license. It has Josh's face on it. In the dim light, it looks like the name on the permit is Johnathon Mills. A fake ID? Why would Josh need a fake driver's license? He was over twenty-one.

I don't want to look in the next envelope that says: KATY-DID. Like the idiot I am, I peer inside. There's a key and a driver's license with Josh smiling on the front. He's William Hill Junior in this one. "Why didn't you give this to me when you found it, Mama?" I jerk my gaze to Mama. "And don't tell me you didn't want to see me hurt. You haven't cared about me since the day I was born."

"Why do you say that?" She snake hisses. "Why do you always toss that in my face?"

"I don't know," I grumble sarcastically. "Maybe because you left me alone in my playpen for days at a time with nothing more than a half-eaten box of cereal, a bottle filled with soda pop, and the TV turned on to cartoons? You think I don't remember that?"

"You survived."

I stare at her, then let out a deep breath. "Did Josh tell you anything about what he kept at your house or why he had this box?"

"Baby, the boxes were all taped with silver duct tape, and after he took everything else, I didn't know he had left anything."

"Was there money in these envelopes?" I wiggled the envelope at her face. "Mama, tell me you didn't take money out of them."

She stares at me with her lip twitching. "It wasn't like Josh said he left it for you. He's dead, sweetie. He's not needing nothing where he is now."

"You think?" I ask her. "Because there are —" I stop and count the envelopes quickly, one by one, with a flip of my fingers. The last one is just an open envelope with a name on it. Crystal D. Oh, no. That is Josh's sister. "There are seven clues in here that would, in theory, say otherwise." One more for his sister makes eight. Why would he have one for Crystal?

"You're talking Latin to me." Mama digs a cigarette from her purse and holds it to her lips. She takes out a silver and turquoise lighter and starts to flick it with her finger.

"You can't smoke in here," I tell her, taking away her cigarette and slapping it down on the counter. "I am telling you that each license has Josh's picture, a different name, and probably address."

"Maybe they're just old fake IDs he used to get into the bars when you two were in high school."

"Yeah, I don't think so. How much money was in each envelope?" I growl at her. I close the box and rub my forehead with my fingers. I don't know whether to laugh hysterically or burst into tears. Maybe both.

"A couple hundred," she tells me.

"And you used it all."

"I figured he wasn't coming back."

Mama wiggles her fingers at Billy the Bartender, and asks for a beer. While she digs out a few dollars from her purse, I see him looking back and forth between us. After he leaves, I lean into Mama. She is shoving her cigarette in her mouth and getting up to go smoke outside. I feel woozy, half wishing I could throw up. "Promise me you won't tell anybody this, swear you won't."

"Why would I do that?"

"Just don't."

"Are you okay?" I must have sat there staring at the wine glasses hanging along the wall for five minutes before Bear's voice behind me forced me to blink. He is standing right behind my stool.

"Yeah," I say, closing my eyes and rubbing a finger on my forehead. "Just dandy."

"Alright." He leans into Josh's stool. I think he is going to sit down. However, I'm sure he knows enough of my story by now to think that I might believe he is sitting in a ghost's lap. "I was just a little worried. The creepy homeless lady can be intense. I wasn't sure if she was pestering you for money."

"She's not homeless. She lives in a trailer at Fire Mountain View Trailer Park." I turn to take Bear in, my eyes narrowing to tiny slits. "Her name is Ruby MacCabe. The reason I know this is because I pay the creepy homeless woman's rent. She is my mother."

"Oh, for the love of God." Bear pushes a hand to his face. "I am so sorry. I really struck out this time with you, didn't I?"

"I wouldn't call it striking out," I tell him. "I'm not planning on any man even making it to first base with me right now. If you are looking for somebody to screw in the back of your truck, it isn't me."

"Oh, no, I didn't mean that. I meant as a—friend or something."

"As a friend, you struck out when you didn't show up at my front doorstep at six in the morning for the last five days to work out."

Bear leans into the stool and looks at it. He is wearing cologne. It smells good. Then he slips into the seat. "I thought you were just offering to help me to be nice."

"I was," I say, glancing up, and catching Billy gaze hard at me. "I meant it." Billy gives me a wink and looks up at the clock. He thinks Bear is trying to pick me up. I know Bear isn't going anywhere soon.

I dig my hand into my purse and pull out a dollar bill. I carefully slide it across the counter toward Billy. "Here, take it. I lose." Billy tips his head a bit to the right, questioning. Then his lips twist into a knowing smile. He walks over and picks up the dollar. "It's not what you think. He's a friend, Billy," I gruff. "Shut up."

Bear watches carefully but doesn't ask any questions. I have a horrible lump in my throat. I'm still trying to wrap my mind around the envelopes in the box. I really want Bear to leave. *I* want to leave. I feel like my head is simply going to explode into a million pieces.

"I'm sorry about what I said about your mom—"

"Hey!" I hear the shout from across the room. It splits Bear's words right in half. He snaps his head to the door. I do the same. It is a woman's voice. It is deep, though. I'd recognize it anywhere. It's Josh's mama, two of his sisters, and one cousin. One of the sisters is Crystal. All of them are standing there holding bats and my eyes roll to Billy, wide and surprised.

"Oh, what the hell," I hiss. "Can this get any worse?"

Crystal Devereauxs and Josh were a lot alike. She was older than him by one year. It isn't their looks that are the same. She's got bright red hair and stone-cold blue eyes like her brother. She's nothing like me. She's a good foot taller, mean as hell, and has more attitude in her little finger than I have in my whole body. Crystal is always mad about everything, and it doesn't take a stifled sneeze to make her go off, throwing punches every which way. When Josh and I were married, I spent more time avoiding family get-togethers she attended for the simple reason that she would hunt me down, find places we were alone, and shove me hard against the closest wall. "Oops, sorry," she would say. "Little b—itch." And she would hold out the B long and hard and hiss out the last part. I stay out of her way. I think I'm going to be shoved into a corner tonight because her mama's eyes are on me. I'm terrified. The one thing Crystal and I have in common is our hot-tempered mamas. Her own mama, Lizzy, is rough on her. She's big and ruddy-complexioned and carries herself like a man. Her hair is the color of carrots because she buys cheap boxes of generic hair color. It sticks out from beneath the dirty ball caps she always wears. Lizzy carries a baseball bat everywhere she goes. She's got one now. The local police chief, Big Don, has arrested her for fighting in every bar in town.

She drives home drunk every weekend. She's been in jail for carrying concealed weapons into Beverly's Diner and flashing them around. When I look back on it, I wonder how I stuck with Josh at all. His family is the craziest, most criminal bunch of rowdy asses this side of the county. Oh, yeah, as I recall to answer my last question, he was dang hot and a bad boy. Who doesn't have a side that longs a little for that?

But, ninety percent of the time, Josh's family and I avoid each other. On Friday nights, I meet my dead ex at the Crazy Kettle. On Saturday nights, the Devereauxs are at the Crazy Kettle, starting fights, drinking hard, and getting into trouble. Lizzy's told me a million times she's going to beat me until I admit I killed her son. Then she'll kill me. She's got this idea that I buried him underneath my trailer and tried to conceal the body by burning it down. That's why I avoid Saturday nights here. It still leaves ten percent of the time that we accidentally run into each other. It's a small town we have to work with, and there are only so many gas stations to pump gas, diners to eat in, and bars to get a beer.

I'm at that ten percent right now. I see everything stop in the bar, people looking at me and then looking at the women facing me off. Only the music blares in the corner. "I heard tell you still been comin' down here celebratin' my son's dyin'," Lizzy growls between the gap in her front teeth. "I heard tell you been sayin' it was me kilt my son and buried him out back my house."

My eyes roll to my mama. I curse her under my breath. She is the only one I've ever kidded with about that. I'm just sitting there, knowing I've got to scoot out of my seat. "I don't want to fight, Lizzy." I let my feet hit the floor and tug my dress down to the midway thigh. "I don't know where Josh is. He could still be alive for all we know."

"Why'd you send cops to my house the other day? That ain't cool."

"They brought me a picture of a hand and wanted to know if it might be Josh's. I can't do it anymore. Lizzy, I can't. Tag. You're it. You start talking to the cops from now on. You knew him just as well as I did." I breathe in, breathe out. There's no nice way to say it. They keep calling and coming by with bones they found here or a shirt they found there. John Does, they call the pieces they find.

Maybe I might recognize something. I never do, and it makes me go into a funk for three days after they stop by. I've got no clues.

"I'm sick of your mouth. We ain't playin' a game of tag with you." That's Crystal talking now. She tosses down her arm and wiggles the bat in her fingers. "Let's tear it up, Mama."

"Brandy." It is just one word that Billy says. I turn. For just a millisecond, my eyes catch Bear's face. He's as pale as a ghost. But Billy is tossing a bat at me, which I catch in my hands. He nods his head and wiggles a finger in the air. He's got four bouncers that hang around the bar. They slip out of their seats and stand up. They don't have a weapon, but these big boys don't need one. Anybody can see that while they cross their beefy arms over their chests. They could crack Lizzy in half with a slug from their thumbs.

"It's four against six, ladies," Billy says. "What do you say we call this a night. Otherwise, I'll have my boys get started while I call Big Don." Actually, it would be four against five. I would trip over the bat trying to get to them. Regardless, that catches their attention. Big Don. He's the local police with jurisdiction over Fire Mountain and New Alliance. Nobody wants to deal with him and his lack of Southern charm. He'll just as soon crack a head open than ask any locals if they have a side to a story. Most folks around here think he's nothing less than Satan himself. Lizzy is probably so mad because I sent that fallen angel from hell knocking on her door.

Lizzy narrows her eyes. The room is so tense and stifling —it is thicker than my Mamaw's can of pig lard, which she kept in the refrigerator and had to cut with a knife.

"Come on, Mama, we'll catch up to her later." Crystal shoves her mama with her shoulder. "When she's alone without her gorillas."

I watch them fade away into the oozy darkness at the back of the bar. I see one of those gorillas following them out. I know he's waiting in the parking lot until they are gone.

"Hey, are you alright?" Billy reaches over the counter with his baseball bat and gently nudges me. I hand him my bat, and he starts to shove it away. "You can keep that if you want. You might need it."

"Who—who was—that?" Bear interrupts while I'm shaking my head back and forth. He was still pale around the lips, almost like somebody had drained him while I stood up. His eyes are still locked to the door.

"Lizzy and Crystal Devereauxs," I tell him, puffing out my cheeks. They are numb, and I poke one side with my finger. "Josh's mom and sister. It's okay. They won't bother you. It is me they want to murder. Any excuse will do." He's such a pampered pup. I don't really want to hear it. It just makes me feel like a bigger freak than I already feel. "Listen, will you excuse me?" It just happens like that. I feel the lump burn its way up my throat. I hate crying and don't do it in front of anyone. I snatch up the box, hug it, and weave to the door. I push it open with my back and feel the cool April air from outside before I'm consumed by the pungent reek of cigarettes from the smokers outside the door.

My little beat-up red truck is halfway through the parking lot, and I get in and slam the door shut behind me. I barely even lay the damn lockbox down on the seat beside me before I count to five, start punching the steering wheel, cuffing the air, and screech-hollering cusswords at my ex-husband. I am in mid-son-of-a-bitching when I hear the knuckle knock on my driver's side window. I can do nothing more in my misery and humiliation than lay my head in one hand and roll down my window with the other.

"Yes, Bear, what do you want?"

He is so tall that he must lean over to face me in the driver's seat. I realize I should have nicknamed him Sasquatch, not Bear. I am trying to pull off that I came out to the truck to use my phone to call somebody. It is loud inside, and sitting here is a good excuse. I don't want anybody to know I'm having some crazies.

"I'm an idiot, okay?" he says. "I shouldn't have sat down in the seat. I shouldn't have said anything about your mother." He keeps looking up over the truck hood like he's expecting Lizzy and Crystal to return. They won't. I'm sure they are ten miles down the road smoking weed and popping open cans of cheap beers.

"Okay, this is a church thing, isn't it?" My stomach is in knots. I want to go home. My fingers play with the phone like I'm texting somebody. "Is Preacher Murphy paying you to stalk me and get me to join Holy Trinity? Because it isn't happening. I'm not some lost soul you've got to save. I've got issues, yes. Who hasn't? Go away."

"You were freaking out. I don't want to leave you," he says. "And not because I'm a church fanatic. But because I feel bad for hurting your feelings. Are you drunk?"

"You didn't hurt my feelings. I wasn't freaking out. I came out to call somebody. And no, I am drinking Shirley Temples—ginger ale."

"Okay, what was this?" Bear has the audacity to raise his arms in the air like an exaggerated version of me thumping around in my truck a minute ago. He pushes his voice a pitch or two and echoes a much-embellished version of me screaming and cursing.

I should have been really irritated. There is a second that I want to stretch my arm out the window and punch him. I am on the verge of a mental breakdown, I think, so it would have been excusable. He stops, and he has this funny little grin on his face like a six-year-old kid who just got caught putting a cricket down his sister's shirt.

"You were freaking out, Brandy." He shrugs his shoulders. "I'm just saying. It is not the crazy my sister used to get when I left the toilet seat up in the middle of the night, and she came later, sat down, and fell in, but it comes a close second. A real close second."

I stare at him. The mental image is funny. Pops has done this to me occasionally. I feel the giggles bubbling up in my belly, and I finally shake my head and laugh out loud. "Bear, really," I say. "It wasn't you who hurt my feelings. It was my mama."

"I get it. My mom is—" Bear is resting his arms on the window. He winces, then looks resigned. "My mother is a controlling, scheming, conniving witch sometimes. Maybe she doesn't get drunk and dance around the bar, but she's got her issues. Control issues." He leans in while I smudge away the tears from my eyes with my fingers. "Oh, man, does she have issues. Why the heck do you think I came back to this God-forsaken town, huh? She coerced me into it. I didn't want to come back. You see, I'm in the same boat as you. You can say something crappy about my mom. We'll be even."

"I don't know your mom." I look at Bear. He seems a bit stunned. I'm not sure why.

"Well, it doesn't matter." He scrubs a hand over his face. "We're friends, right? You're not mad at me?"

"Bear—I mean, Beau," I realize I have been calling him the wrong nickname again.

"You can call me Bear," he says. "My family does. My father used to call me Bear-Regard. Then it got shortened to Bear." I don't need his life story. I want to be alone.

"I'm not so good with relationships," I tell him. "I'm not looking for anybody to sleep with, to date. I'm not even looking for friends. You understand, right? It's another consequence of having a mama who dumped me and a husband that vanished into thin air. I don't want to lead you on, make you believe I'm not a flight risk. I am. I've been known to bolt at a 'Hey, let's go get some coffee.' I don't like to let anybody any closer than—" I hold out my hand at arm's length between us. It stops at his belly. I gently nudge it. He takes a step back. "Here," I say. "I'll be honest upfront. If you take two more steps back, I'm less likely to run over your toes when I leave."

Bear stares at me for a second like it is starting to sink in. "Oh," he says. "Yeah, okay, I get it."

"Hey, Brandy, are you okay?" He's about a stone's throw away, but Billy is standing in the parking lot, looking back and forth between me and Bear. I can't believe he left the bar unattended. "He's not bothering you, right?"

Bear puts up his hands. "I was just checking on her."

"I'm fine," I yell through my window. Billy nods and waves then turns to leave. I can see he is hesitating, kind of taking slow steps, waiting for Bear to leave. He does, starts to go, and turns slowly.

"I told you I get it. I'm leaving. You don't have to call your friends in to drag me away like some creep."

I didn't say anything or realize I was still holding my phone. I just sat back and wished I wasn't myself anymore, hoping I didn't have the urge to drive to the train tracks and figure out why even Josh didn't want to stick around.

Chapter –6
Bear

Obviously, Bear doesn't get it. It is half past five in the morning, and I'm sitting in my room. I've got the lockbox on my lap, and I'm sorting through the contents again. I'm sure it isn't the healthiest thing for me to do. Nevertheless, I'm trying to wrap my mind around the envelopes and the meaning behind them.

I heard a throaty engine of a truck pull in about a half hour ago. I think one of Pops' lumber yard guys is stopping in to pick up a building key. They always forget them and wake us up in the morning to pick up a duplicate. I didn't bother to get up. I know Pops is sitting on the front porch with Kaylee plopped on his lap and a cup of black coffee in his old white porcelain mug. Mama was too drunk to watch her last night, so I brought her home with me.

When I came back from my morning run, Pops and Kaylee were sitting on the porch. She was wrapped in a little blanket even though it wasn't cold. Kaylee is brown-haired, skinny, and freckled, just like me. She is lucky, though, and has sky-blue eyes. Kaylee was chewing on toast with honey, dribbling all over Pops' shirt. She was looking self-assured and a bit overstated in her raggedy, pinkish pajamas propped like a princess on a parade float on Pops' lap. It doesn't seem so long ago that I had the VIP seat there.

"You tell me when you're ready for me to fight for this little one," Pops told me. "I'll do it all over again even if she is as ornery as you."

"Not now, Pops," I told him. I know he wants to take her in, adopt her like he did with me. But it isn't Pops who will end up watching her all day. It is me. It is another cheap shot at keeping me from finishing college. I don't want to think about it. I don't have time to watch a kid all day long. I've got my whole life ahead of me. He gave me these doleful eyes. I just walked away and settled into my room to study. I hear a knock on my bedroom door. That's what Pops always does, knocks if my door is almost closed. I don't answer unless I *don't* want Pops to come in because I'm getting dressed or something. I wait for him to come barreling in after the allotted amount of time he usually waits for my answer. He doesn't, so I lean forward on my chair.

"Just come in, what's up?" I say, slanting at an awkward angle and latching on to the door to open it. I am wobbling there like I'm walking a tightrope, the height of wavering in one direction or the other before I lose my balance. The door opens wide, skidding over my deerskin and the little pink carpet in front of my bed. Then it catches and stops.

I am poised for the fall long before I stop midair and feel the chair beneath me slip to the left. I keel forward and collapse on the floor with everything in my box flying into the air in a horrible-sounding crash and bang.

I no sooner look up from the top of my head while I'm lying there flat on my back and see Bear taking up the expanse between door and door frame. He's got this expression on his face, eyes slightly closed and lips pursed tightly. It is an *oh-shit* look if I've ever seen one. And I've seen many. In fact, I am surprised to see it again on Bear because I saw the exact same expression on his face not more than four hours ago. I did not expect to ever see him again after the last time I saw him.

It was at the Crazy Kettle. I had waited until Bear disappeared into the front doors after I yelled at him before I turned off my truck. I wasn't really leaving. It wasn't quite my scheduled time. Besides, I had to drive my mama home, or I figured she would pick the drunkest man she could find and stay with him the night, maybe end up dead in a ditch off the highway.

I waited in my truck for her to come outside for another smoke. The later it gets, the antsier I get sitting in my truck. Finally, at 12:30, I sigh and get out of my vehicle, knowing Mama has been sneaking a smoke in the bathroom. I work my way back into the bar. I look around in the oozy black, but she's nowhere in sight.

"You're evil. You are a real wicked witch, you know that, right?"

I heard those words and turn to see Bear's buddy, who tried to pick me up last weekend. He's wearing the same ball cap over his red-blonde hair and has that rich boy, pretty boy swagger about him. He puts his hand on my shoulder. I step to the right and turn.

"Excuse me?" I say, scrubbing off his fingers. He lets his hand fall and stands in front of me. I don't think anybody else hears his words. It is a full bar tonight, but the jukebox is playing loud. There are a few tables next to us where people are eating pizza.

"You heard what I said," he almost has to yell over the jukebox. "Beau comes up, tries to be nice, tries to talk to you, and you treat him like a piece of crap you accidentally got on the bottom of your shoe. Women like you—"

He doesn't get to finish what he is saying when he is cut short by my mama barreling into him from behind with both her fists flying. "—don't talk to my baby girl like that—" is all I hear before the man is shoved straight into me, his chest hitting my head.

I take two steps backward until I bang my rear off one of the pool tables. This leaves me keeling to the left, which would have been fine if Bear's friend wasn't getting pelted by my mama's fists now. He is trip-marching forward with this wild-scared look in his eyes, something akin to a cat that's got its tail caught in a fan. His hands come out right toward my chest and in realizing he is three inches from grabbing my boobs, he jerks them away and is simply free-falling flat straight at me.

I yelped just as my rear hit the floor. It was hard, but I didn't have time to assess the pain. Bear's friend is flattening me in one breath with his one-hundred and sixty pounds of solid man. Adding Mama to the top of the pile, still beating his back with her fists, I nearly couldn't move or breathe. Mama yowled when Billy grabbed her arms and tossed her to the side.

"Get her out of here!" he yelled just as Bear's friend's weight was lifted off me by Bear himself. I will only say that they dragged Mama out kicking and screaming and sent me packing with her. It was a bit unfair on my part, but I guessed Billy knew I was driving her home anyway. Right before I walked out the Crazy Kettle doors, I turned for just a split second. I caught Bear's face and gave him the meanest stink eye I could manage. That's when he gave me the expression I am getting now while he wavers above me in the hallway. It is something short of the sad-eyed, hurt expression Pops' old beagle dog, Boo, gave him last December when he lifted his leg to pee on the Christmas tree, got yowled at, and thrown outside.

"We've got to quit meeting like this," I say to the puppy-eyed gaze. I can't be mad at him any more than I could have made Boo stay out in the snow for more than five minutes. Still, I'm lying there looking like one of those chalk mark-ups they make at a crime scene on cop shows where the dead body was found.

It was a corny remark, but Bear started laughing like it was the funniest joke he'd ever heard. I mean, he is wiping away tears from his eyes. I stretch out my arm, and he leans over, snatches it up in his huge paw, and drags me to a sitting position.

"Yeah," Bear says. "I saw you do that same trick last night, except you fell backward instead of forward."

"Glad I could mix it up a bit for you." I glared at him. "Make it a little more exciting the second time around."

"Third," he says. "Don't forget the time you fainted at church and fell off the stands."

"Thanks for reminding me of that." I sigh, and look around the floor. The envelopes are scattered all around, and a couple of the driver's licenses barely cling to the envelope that had housed them. I quickly snatch up and push the cards back in before I yank the lockbox upright and lay them within. Bear squats across from me and starts reaching for one of the envelopes, but my hands in the air stop him. "I'll get it."

"I don't mind," he says. He picks up one of the licenses anyway and kind of waves it in the air between us. "What's with all the driver's licenses? You're either underage and like to hit the bars, or you're a serial killer." His words are nonchalant while he reaches out and hands it to me so I can shove it in the proper envelope. "Is there something you need to tell me like: *Bear, don't turn your back to me because I've got a knife in my pocket*?"

I think he is funny, and I laugh a little. "They aren't mine." I tug one out of the envelope and hold it up for him to see. Josh's face is smiling at him from the card. "Does this look like me?"

"Not unless you're a dude on the weekends." Bear pushes it up so he can get a good look at it. "And I know you're not because Gabe said that, although you're a heartless witch, and that is a direct quote from his lips, not mine; you were also soft and cushy when he landed on you last night." Bear lounges on this thought for a moment. "Gabe's my buddy."

"The one that called me evil."

"That's him," Bear pokes a finger at the license. "I have to assume you're a serial killer. I suppose I should have suspected that after the bar incident last night."

"It was your buddy who attacked me," I reminded him. "He actually called me a wicked witch. I've been called a lot of things, but I've never been called wicked." Then I stop to think it out and push a forefinger on my chin. "Oh, no, wait a minute. We had a pastry chef come into one of my classes first semester. He had some cinnamon biscuits he kept calling The Best Little Wicked Hillbilly Biscuits. He keeps looking at me the whole time that he's showing us how to make them. I finally got mad and pointed it out, telling him it had to be racist or something to keep drawing attention to the fact I came from the mountains and all. And do you know what he said? He says: *I wasn't looking at you because you're a hillbilly. I was looking at you because you're just plain wicked cute.*"

Bear stares at me with a funny, cockeyed grin. It reminds me of Josh, and I know it isn't normal to keep seeing my husband's ghost in every man I meet. I suppose it is probably some step in the grief process. "That's funny. Did he ask you out?" He plops the license into the envelope, leans over it, and picks up a marble from the box.

"No, he was just saying it to cover his ass."

"Oh." Bear seems to analyze my answer, then he rolls the marble between his hands. "When I said *bar incident*, I wasn't talking about the fight with Gabe." Bear's face turns red. "I meant the thing with the money. Do you always pay the bartender a buck to keep all your murders under wraps? Or did he win the bet that the guy you liked the least was going to sit down next to you that time?"

"Well, Billy and I actually have a bet to see how quickly I can get rid of the creeps who come and sit next to me," I divulge to him. I point to my stack of books on the little pink shelf by my bed. "He has paid for my books through my wins for the last two years. I thought you might be good company, so I just gave him the dollar." He nods. I say: "Hey, Bear, tell me the truth, is Preacher Murphy sending you on a mission to save my soul? Is that why you're here?"

"Kind of," he tells me. "Does that bother you? I won't preach to you or make you read the Bible."

"What good is that going to do?" I stuff all the envelopes into the lockbox, close it tight, and shove it beneath my bed. Then I push myself to my feet. Bear rises too.

"I'm really hoping you're a witch like Gabe said. Maybe you can work some magic on me and make me skinny."

"It isn't magic, Bear." I reach up on my tippy-toes and touch his head. "Remember what I said? It's up here. It's grabbing life by the balls and taking control." I wave a hand at Bear, then snatch up my shoes on my desk. "Let's walk today and see where we're at. Then we can work out in my pops' garage. Every time Pops goes to a flea market, he brings me back some new pieces of workout equipment. Most of them are brand new. Folks go out and spend a thousand dollars on stuff to get their bodies in shape, then they turn around and decide it just isn't worth it."

I had just put on a fresh layer of glue between the soles and uppers of my tennis shoes. I wiggled my finger between them to make sure they were sticking. Pops always laughs at me and tells me I train so much that I've run the soles right off my feet. Maybe so, but mostly it is because I can't afford another pair, and my tennis shoes are just the right kind of comfortable now.

Twenty minutes later, we're strolling down an old logging road. Bear is quiet so I chatter on about the birds and the trees and working at Mister Smiley's. Then we trek down a hillside, and I bump him hard with my hip. "So, I really need to know something, Bear," I ask. "I know she is beautiful, and her voice is like an angel singing. But lots of girls have that. What does a girl like Meghan possess that makes a guy so flipping crazy to please her he'd risk sitting next to Crazy Brandy at a bar and asking her to work him into shape?"

"I— I don't know." He doesn't look at me and settles his eyes on the ground in front of us. "She's got something other girls don't. But I don't think walking is going to help me lose weight," Bear gripes. "I'm just being honest. I've done it before, and it doesn't work."

"Well, we aren't just walking. We are hiking. We are going to do this for a week, and then you're going to start running," I retort. "I'm also going to show you how to portion your foods."

"I've done that. It doesn't work."

"It didn't work because you just didn't care. Look for the prize at the end of the line, Bear," I tell him. "If nothing else, just pretend you're looking down a long tunnel and Meghan's standing there at the end." I push out my hand and stop him, making him turn to look down at me. "Listen, let me tell you something. On the outside, other than being a little unhealthy, you're just fine, you get that?

You're an attractive guy." I have latched on to his arm, and his eyes roam down to where we are touching, so I release my hand and step back. "Every step down the tunnel, you are getting skinnier. Every step down that tunnel, you are taking control of your life. Making good decisions about your health, that's grabbing life by the balls. I'm willing to believe in you. I believe you can do this." I drop my voice to a whisper. "My big question is this: are you willing to believe in me to help you do it?"

"Brandy, I—"

"Oh, for God's sake, all you have to do is show up every morning," I tell him. "It ain't that hard." Ain't. I try not to use that word. It has been so shoved into my vocabulary growing up that I found it difficult to leave behind for so many years. Now, occasionally, it comes out when I am getting mad. "I mean, it *isn't* that hard," I correct myself. "I'll help you out, and you get a free chef-made breakfast every day." I waggle a hand for us to start again and take a step forward.

Bear pushes out a hand between us and forces me to stop. "Let me rest a minute," he utters. He is still almost out of breath. "Why are you doing this, Brandy? Why do you give a crap about me? I don't even know you."

I don't tell him the whole truth. I haven't even wrapped my mind around it. I have a huge crush on him. He's big and cute, like a teddy bear, and I feel safe around him. I don't say that. I get crushes on men all the time. Then I get to know them. They say something stupid or screw something up or screw every girl I know, and I wonder what the hell I saw in them. I figure, how can this guy screw it up any worse than he has up to this point? "I dunno. I'm weird like that," I tell him. "I want to help everybody. Pops tells me I want to be different from my mama so badly that I try to be the opposite of her. So I marry an idiot who has seven different aliases. Then I sit around and wait for him to come back to me after he disappears."

"Ah, the licenses in the envelopes." Bear nods his head and looks a little relieved.

"Promise me you will keep this a secret. Nobody needs to know this. It just might open up a whole new box of worms with those people with baseball bats at the bar," I tell him. "That was why I was doing this in my truck last night—" I wave my arms wildly in the air.

"My mama had the box and plopped it in my lap. It was like a slap in the face. I've been standing in front of trains for the last three years trying to figure out why my husband hated me so bad he committed suicide, and now, I'm thinking— I don't know what I'm thinking." I do know what I am thinking. I am wondering what I was so bad at doing that he had to get what he needed from seven other women.

"I won't tell a soul," Bear promises.

"But you'll tell me what you talked about with my Pops for a half hour before you knocked me over in my room?"

"Yeah, sure. All he said was that you wear armor around your heart, and you ought to let it down once in a while, let folks in." Bear waves a hand. "I've caught my breath. We can keep going—but he also said that he'd shoot me with his rifle if I hurt you." I sniff a laugh and start the march again. That's Pops.

Forty minutes later, I'm using my fist for size to show Bear how to portion his food. Then I go into my room and pick up one of my college-rule composition books. I open it up, make sure there's no writing in it, and then I take it into the kitchen to Bear. "Here, this is your clean slate." I hand him the book. "Don't count whatever you've done in the past. Just start from this point on. Forget all the times you messed up the diet or gave up or didn't follow up. You're not going to fail this time. You're going to succeed."

"You sound like one of those motivational speakers they have on Sunday morning T.V."

"If you're going to make fun of me—"

"I'm not."

"Okay, then, write down what you eat every day and how much you exercise. Don't lie. Write down your weight."

"Please don't make me write down my weight."

"I've got to know if it is working. Your buddy called me a witch, but I'm not magic. The broom in the kitchen was just a prop. It doesn't really help me fly." I try to kid with him. He's all serious and has this doe-caught-in-the-headlights gaze at me. "Listen, I've got to figure out foods for you to eat and a fitness plan. I guarantee you'll want to know when the weight starts going off. However, in the meantime, I don't want to kill you."

"I don't want *you* to know."

"I'll let you see my tits every time you stand on the scales," I toss out like we're negotiating a contract. I think he almost faints when I say that. Bear's mouth is working, nothing is coming out. His cheeks are burning red.

"I'm just kidding," I say. I hold up both my fists like I'm going to duke it out with him and give him a gentle chuck on the arm. "Pops would kill me if I did that." I pause and nibble on my lip. "No, he'd kill you."

Chapter –7

Old Bobby Reese

Pops told me that the Fire Mountain Redneck Run was started by Hensley Peters, who used to own the Crazy Kettle. He said back in the day, when Hensley put on the event the first weekend of September, folks from around the state came to watch the locals compete. Hensley had competitions like a mud bog ATV marathon, sledding down McAllister Hill in old bathtubs, and target shooting at big paper mâché mosquitos the fifth graders at Fire Mountain Elementary made for their art fair projects.

Things have changed since the local tourism agency came about five years ago. Hand-in-hand with the big new country club on Big Boar Mountain, the next mountain over, and settled above New Alliance, they took possession of the Redneck Run. Then, to add insult to injury, the country club and the tourism agency kind of shook the redneck out of all the events. They made it upscale—something I call *fancified* so the mollycoddled rich people at the bottom of the mountain could participate or be included in making a profit from it.

Nowadays, four competitions comprise the National Fire Mountain Redneck Run. An ATV race along Fire Mountain Creek at the bottom of our mountain replaced the mud bog marathon. And there is swimming because, at the clubhouse, there are three Olympic-sized pools. Third, there is a running competition as the country club has the largest inside running track in a five-state region—

"And lastly," I am telling Bear. "There is archery—shooting at fifteen paper targets of wildlife along a trail at varied distances. Did I mention that the resort at Big Boar has three professional-size ranges for their patrons to practice?"

Bear contemplates what I am saying. We are standing out back behind Pops' garage. Pops has a bunch of hay bales with targets still on them leftover from hunting season. He uses them to sight his bows to get his shots right on the mark. I went to Grant Rehabilitation and Nursing Center just off the main highway between New Alliance and Fire Mountain to sneak out Bobby Reese.

I've been doing it for nearly six weeks. I have yet to get caught. I know he doesn't look like he can lift a bow, much less pull it back. He's seventy-four and gangly with wrinkled, chocolate-brown skin. He is also the best bow hunter anybody here has ever known.

Pops said that in 1978 when we had a blizzard, nobody could get down the mountain to get any food. Bobby Reese got out his bow, and two days later, everybody who was hungry had a fresh deer or turkey sitting on their porch, skinned, and ready to pop in the fire.

"Why don't you get a membership so you can practice at the country club?" Bear asks.

I look at Bear, thinking that he's kidding at first. Pops is standing next to me and clears his throat, bangs me in the arm like I might say something heedless. Be nice, his eyes say when I look up to see Pops shaking his head back and forth gently. It is subtle, something I would only notice, and isn't so anybody can see. Still, I don't even know what to say. Maybe I should tell Bear nobody from Fire Mountain has ever been invited there. We would be like a buck deer accidentally strolling into a meeting of the National Rifle Association. I'm not so sure it would make it out alive. Or maybe I should say that even if I dug out every last dime I had in the old, aluminum coffee can I've got hidden on the bookshelf in the living room that holds my tuition money, the money Billy the Bartender loses to me every Friday, and every cent I don't spend on groceries, it would only pay for a half hour on the archery range. I know he wouldn't understand, though. While I mull it over, it is silent.

"Dude, she can't afford it. Nobody can afford that place." That's Billy the Bartender telling Bear those words. He stopped by to check on me and ensure I got Mama home on Friday night.

"Yeah, if she could, she'd know how to swim," Kenny says beside me. "And she can't. She sinks like a Bud Light can full of quarters."

"How are you going to swim for the event?" Billy asks.

"I'm gonna get a fishing pole, tie her on like a worm, and pull her from the other side. She's a sinker." Kenny laughs. He isn't kidding. It is like I get into the water, and suddenly, I'm three hundred pounds and sink like a bag of bricks. "I had to pull her out twice last time."

"I've gotten better." I hadn't. I still sink.

Billy starts chit-chatting with Pops about a good place to fish along the creek. Now he's got a beer in one hand and is stifling his laughter at me while I miss the target with the bow by at least five feet. "Oh." Bear just kind of looks at the ground, then shrugs at me. I think he might have lost more than a few pounds in the last three weeks since he's been showing up at Pop's place to work out with me. I can see it in his cheeks and in his waist. I can also see the muscles on his arms where fat used to be. He won't say if he's lost anything; he shrugs when I ask him. He won't step on the old weighing scales I have in the garage even when I tease him by tugging up my shirt and exposing a little bit of skin from waistline to tummy button and doing a wiggly dance for him.

Right now, Bobby is standing around with nine of his friends that he refused to leave back at the nursing home. I had to break them out, too—climb in his window, slip through his room, and unlock the back door to liberate them. Then, they had to duck down in the back of my truck until we got past the New Alliance Police Station. They whooped it up all the way up the gravel road to the top of the mountain. I think one of them was smoking weed and trying to cover it up with a cigar.

Bobby's friends are all shapes and sizes but have two things in common. They're all old and wilder than a bunch of escapees from the West Virginia Correctional Facility. One with big teeth keeps grabbing my butt and making a whistling sound. Another tried to take off on Pops' ATV and nearly rammed it into a tree. A third snuck into the garage, past my exercise equipment, and to the rundown refrigerator where Pops keeps a couple of six-packs of beer. He has one six-pack in his hand at this very moment, and he's dancing around the rest of them. Now that I think about it, I bet those nurses know I sneak them out. I'm babysitting this rowdy crew. It is probably the only time they get a break from their rebelliousness.

Alas, Bear looks like he's going to bolt. I don't want him to leave. I know he comes here because Preacher Murphy asked him to make sure I don't lose my soul somewhere between the church parking lot and my back door between Sunday afternoon and the following Saturday night. But I feel something spectacular when he comes around, something I haven't felt since Josh and I first went out.

Bear makes my tummy get this tickle when he's nearby and even, sometimes, if I think he is coming the following day.

Regardless, it doesn't last long because he never stays more than a few hours while we walk, then work out in the garage. He doesn't talk much; he smiles at me and asks me general questions like what the weather will be or if I got a good grade on the test I was studying for two nights before. We go inside, and I make Pops and Bear breakfast. Just out of the blue, he will suddenly say: "Thanks, Brandy. Are we doing this tomorrow?" Then he gets up and walks out. I keep getting the weird vibe he'll be toting a bible beneath his arm the next time and reading verses while he's trudging along the elliptical. He hasn't yet.

However, today, I got a treat. Bear forgot his wallet and came back to get it at noon. I think he wishes he hadn't, though. Everybody is staring at him like he's a turtle that showed up on a snowy winter day. I nudge him with my knuckle and turn to Bobby Reese. "Well, I don't need the country club. I've got Papaw Bobby here." I turn and pat the short-sleeved shirt to my left. It is a lime green button-up fastened somewhere near his belt and belongs to Bobby Reese. "He knows everything there is about shooting a bow. He's trying to teach me."

"How's that working out for you?" Billy the Bartender laughs while he takes a swig of his drink and points to my fifteen arrows lying around the ground. "I watched Bill Pierce in the archery world championship last year. He's the celebrity shooting the archery on the team that's coming this year and bringing in the bucks with him. Damn, it was just bing, bing, bing! Brandy can't even get bing."

"I got to admit, darlin', that you just might be in trouble if they are going to be shooting bows in this event," Pops is standing with a beer in his hand, and his arms crossed over his chest. "You couldn't hit a buck deer three feet away last hunting season."

"Because that buck gave me *that* look, Pops," I try to defend myself. I furrow my brow, work up my eyes, and imitate a puppy-eyed gaze. "It just tore my heart out. It was like he could see into my soul. A paper target can't give me that look."

"He didn't give you any *look*, baby girl," Pops mutters. "You were just playing princess diva again. Because you were not anywhere near where you could have made a meal or two out of that old buck.

If I remember correctly, by the time I marched over to the deer blind to see if you died or something, the damn deer was looking through the slits at you. And you were rocking to the beat of some song on your phone and texting some little girl from your school."

Everybody laughs at his joke at my expense. I laugh softly, too, but it hurts my feelings. I know the celebrity team the visitors' bureau is flying in are all off-season professionals. I'm not an idiot. They are the ones that bring in the crowds. I've read the newspapers. I've seen it in the magazines. I can do it even if I don't scream it out loud to anyone. I really think I can beat them if I practice hard. Then I can show everybody that this poor, white trash, redneck girl from a trailer park can amount to something.

"Screw off," I tell Billy instead of how I really feel. Because I know they'll laugh like everybody else does. He has a deep voice, and his chest vibrates against my side.

"You tell him, little girl," Bobby Reese backs me up and hugs me around my shoulders. "It just takes time."

"She's been at this six weeks," the man who keeps grabbing my butt says. "How much time are we looking at?"

"I've been doing this for seventy years," Bobby says, reaching over and grabbing up a bow. "I've got bad eyes and shaky hands. Seventy years and sometimes I miss." He pokes an arrow in it three times, and three times, he hits the mark right in the dead center.

"You didn't miss." I scrub my hand through my hair and give him glum eyes.

"And it took me seventy years to get to this, sweetie."

"The Redneck Run is in less than four and a half months." Billy gulps down the last beer in his bottle and tosses it over at the fire ring. I've decided he might be cute, but he's also annoying outside the small talk at the bar. Everything he says is almost like the slap-happy remarks you hear on a sitcom. I see the girls give him moon eyes. He doesn't return the gaze often. He tells me he can get the pick of the litter working at the country club as the afternoon bartender. Why waste it on poor, drunk girls at the Crazy Kettle?

"I'm teasing you." He reaches out and tugs on a tendril of my hair like it is an apology. "I've just been watching those four beautiful girls from New Alliance everybody's been talking about.

They are so friggin' hot," he doles the words out like he's making love to them one at a time. "They've been at the club preparing for the competition daily. They are perfect and might give that professional dream team from Washington State something to worry about. You should come up and see them."

"I read in one of the big Huntington newspapers that they're *hometown girls with hometown hearts*," one of the guys adds. "Ain't never seen them up close. Man, Brandy, maybe you can run Bobby and us up there to see them one of these times. I bet it is one hell of a show."

I look at him, insulted. "I am not going to run you up there and watch you drop your jaws like a bunch of horny old fools so you can cheer on my competitors."

"Competitors? Come on, Brandy, give it up. Do you even have a sponsor?" Billy the Bartender asks. He looks around, waiting for everyone to join in. They all stand there looking awkwardly at each other. "They really are just like they say in the newspaper," Billy goes on like I'm a two-year-old he has to scold into using the big potty instead of wearing a pull-up diaper. "These girls aren't just goodlooking. They've got skills to match. Come up and take a look at them. You'll see what I mean, see the difference. They aren't just a bunch of dumb hillbillies. Security will let you through with an hourly pass, won't they?" He looks up at Bear and Pops like they have the answer. Both shrug. "Well, I've seen them. They let people park at the overflow parking lot and watch as long as they stay outside the gates."

I try to shrug Billy off. His words poke in my mind like one of Mama's boyfriends' wet Willy forefinger used to stick in my ear and make me so irritated I would scream. Billy keeps coming up and bumping my arm while I'm trying to shoot, then smirking. He tells me he can teach me better by coming up behind me and putting his arms around me to show me the proper way to shoot. I finally make an excuse to return Bobby and his friends to the nursing home. It isn't just that the nurses are probably noticing the men are not back from their speed walk through the park in town. Today is Thursday, and Millie Piper, who lives in a little house on the ridge next to ours, needs a ride to the cemetery so she can talk to her dead husband, Ivan, for eight minutes before I turn around and take her home.

Eight minutes is the time it takes for her to sing *Amazing Grace* and say the Lord's Prayer before her grand finale of pouring a cup of tepid coffee with six teaspoons of sugar mixed in over the ground.

I know I've only got four hours until dark, and I think one of my taillights is out. I don't want to take the chance of getting pulled over because there is also one thing I want to do after I drive Millie home. In my glovebox, I've got the envelope that says HANNAH on the front. I looked in the old phonebook Pops keeps in the kitchen drawer and did a search online. I found Tyler and Hannah Heaton an hour and forty minutes away in Fairview.

It is killing me to figure out this great secret of who these people are and why my ex-husband has fake driver's licenses. I've got time to myself without working at Mister Smiley's tonight. I'm taking a short road trip, following the trail to 1055 Robin Lane, where the couple is supposed to reside. I've got ten dollars in my pocket for gas. I've got an extra hundred dollars in my glovebox that I took out of my tuition money coffee can just in case I break down.

My fingers impatiently tap on the steering wheel while Bobby and his buddies scramble into the back of the truck. The scent of freshly mowed grass wafts past. The sound of crickets and frogs creep up from the woods. It mingles with the grind of my engine, and I can't help but wish spring wouldn't end. I think about Bear. The cooler weather will eventually shove him away along with the cicadas and warm, sweet breeze. That is just the way it is. I peer at the rearview mirror to make sure the men are all sitting in the bed and not being adventurous by balancing on the sides. I catch a whiff of aftershave, peer to my right, and Bear is standing at the window.

"Hey, I'm taking off. Did you remember your wallet this time?" I ask him, scratching my knee and feeling a little mosquito bite bump. You would think there wouldn't be any mosquitos this far from the creek, but even here, we get them. Ah, something I hated about spring, those little beasts.

"I did." He pats his rear pocket and looks to his left. I follow his gaze to where Pops and Billy are jawing again. "You want some company taking your buddies back?" Ug. No, not really. I snatch up my ball cap from the dashboard, push my hair back, and wish I had a tie to pull it up and away from my neck. Instead, I shove what I can into the ball cap and slap it on my head.

Bear is watching all this, not saying a thing. Something in his eyes tells me he doesn't understand. I don't care. Josh bought me the ball cap when he and his buddies went to a Reds game in Cincinnati. After the trailer burned down, all I had of Josh was the ball cap because it was sitting on the dash of my truck.

"Well, Bear," I say. "For one thing, I have to sneak the old guys back into the nursing home. I'm not sure if you're up for that. I mean, you could sit in the truck by the back door, but if I get caught, I'm not sure if they'll call the cops or not. Even if I get out without going to jail there, I've got to take Millie Piper to the cemetery. And last, but not least, I am heading out for a few hours to do some personal stuff. I won't be back until late."

"Okay," he says. I think he is going to leave while I slip my arm on the steering wheel to turn the truck around in my pops' gravel drive. Then Bear pats the window with his hand just as I push my foot on the accelerator. "I'm off until tomorrow morning. I can ride along. I mean, if you want me to go."

At that moment, I had never asked Bear where he worked. I don't know much about him except polite conversation we have while we walk or jog. Right then, Pops walks past my truck and pats the hood as he goes. "They are all loaded." He nods toward the back. "Put your shield down, baby. Take the ammo back out of the gun."

"Huh?" I twist my head questioning Pops. "I don't understand what you're saying."

"If I got to tell you, it don't matter."

"I think he's saying you should take me with you," Bear offers. He has that same silly, lop-sided grin Josh used to get.

"No, I don't think he's saying that at all." Now Pops is grabbing at his head like he is taking off a hat that isn't there, and then he pretends to toss that invisible hat to the ground. Bear doesn't see this. I roll my eyes. I'm not taking off my hat. I really don't *need a man* like Pops is implying.

"Get in. But you've got to promise you'll keep this secret, right?" I hear Bobby banging on the top of my truck. "No telling anybody where we're going."

"It is a deal," Bear says, getting into the truck. "I can keep secrets."

Chapter −8
Hannah

Bear is along for the ride. That includes jumping the hill on Roller Coaster Road three times so the guys in the back of the truck can have a bit of a thrill before taking their meds at the nursing home and going to bed. He waits in the vehicle while I climb through Bobby's window and unlatch the security entry. He even hops out and holds the door for them while I make small talk with the nurse at the front desk so they can slip in undetected.

He takes to Millie right off and even escorts her by the arm to Ivan's grave. Then he waits with his elbows on the hood of my truck and ushers her back when she's done. She smiles at him and pats his hand, something she's never done to me.

"What is your job, Bear?" I asked him twenty minutes before Fairview. We were listening to music, enjoying the wind coming in the open windows. I turn the radio down with a twist of my fingers.

"Oh, I just do stuff up at the country club. Security and stuff."

"That's why Billy looked at you when he asked about people coming to watch," I say. "That's a cool job. You carry a gun?"

"No," he laughs. "I don't. Should I?"

"Yeah, that would be sexy," I say. "So that's where you see Meghan most of the time?"

"Every day."

"You know, if I was you. I'd talk to your boss and see if you guys can carry guns on the morning shift. Tell him there might be a rough crowd at the Redneck Run, and having one on your hip might help keep the crowds from getting too rowdy. I can tell you right now that Meghan will see that gun and think it is hot."

"You think? It's that easy?" he asks, chuckling. Before I can answer, he turns to me and pokes me in the shoulder. "I just wanted to tell you I lost eight pounds in the last two weeks. That makes twelve total."

"No, shit!" I say it and almost want to pull off the road to celebrate. Instead, I let go of the steering wheel for a minute and do a car dance, waggling my arms in front of me and then into the air.

"Stop that!" Bear's eyes are fist-size in terror. I think he is going to reach out and grab the steering wheel. "What are you doing?"

"Celebration dance," I say, my hands back on the steering wheel. He looks relieved. I felt like a proud mama right then. "Eight pounds is a lot. I was sure I saw it, but I didn't want to say anything. You're eating well, aren't you? You're not starving yourself?"

"No, I'm portioning everything just like you said. I mean, most of the time," Bear confesses, nibbling on his lip. "It's hard when I go out to restaurants. I want the big steak. I got to order the girly-girl steak."

"I told you restaurants do that on purpose to belittle your manhood, didn't I?" I divulge. "They call the bigger, more expensive stuff the Bob or the Ed and the petite sirloins the w and the Ednas, so you're too proud to ask for them."

"I know. I ask for the Marys and the Ednas now," he tells me, that silly lop-sided grin slipping up on his lips. He's got angel lips that turn up at the corners. I didn't see them as well when he was chubbier. I see them now. "My mother just doesn't understand. Gabe and my sister make fun of me, call me a girl."

"Show me your muscle, Bear." I reach out from the steering wheel and nudge his arm. He pulls up his T-shirt sleeve and flexes his arm. Yes, he's got muscle where a thick layer of fat used to be. Damn, it makes me a little warm where warm shouldn't be right now. "Next time your mama and your sister lay into you, you just pull up your sleeve, give them a little flex. Tell them you don't have to be girly-girl to order meals with feminine names on them. Because you're not."

"I will," he says, then his smile drops to a wince. "It's tough waking up in the middle of the night and hearing my stomach growl. That's my low point, the point I got to work on. I thought of that halfway through a cheesecake in the kitchen at midnight last night."

"Cheesecake is a good excuse to fall off the wagon, Bear. I think, however, the image of my mama dancing around the pool tables at the Crazy Kettle is what keeps me up at night. Talk about nightmares. I've been known to get up at two in the morning because I've heard a knock at the door. I dream all the time Josh is still alive and standing at Pops' door. Now you know my weaknesses."

"You are so forgiving," Bear says.

"And you are hard on yourself. Twelve pounds is a lot to lose. So, has it given you enough confidence to ask Meghan out yet?"

He doesn't answer. I don't pursue it. I realize I've come to the town of Fairview when the little white and brick houses start coming closer and closer together. The little hill rolling into the main street suddenly opens up to tiny homes, one after another, and then an old school building. I must have missed the road. It is supposed to be outside town. I assumed it was in a subdivision. I turn around and backtrack a few miles, turn around again, and this time creep along until I see a street to my right like I saw on a map online. I pull off the road and get out the folded-up map I've got sitting between us.

"You know, I have GPS in my truck," Bear says. "We could have used that. It's a lot easier than these maps."

"Now's not the time to tell me that." I look up at him, furrow my brow, then set my gaze on the road to the right. I'm not sure I want to go down this road. I'm not sure I'm ready yet. Maybe that's why I didn't grab the little GPS that Pops keeps in his truck. I'm terrible at reading maps. Perhaps I really didn't want to find it.

"So where are we going?" Bear asks, leaning in and peering at my finger rolling toward Robin Lane. The town is almost non-existent except for the dot on the map. The road I see to my right that corresponds to the road on the map is barely paved, a grayed asphalt street creeping up into the hillside.

I look up at him, trying to take in those brown eyes staring at me. Trust. It's a little tricky for me. It's funny. I've had more people in my life I can rely on than those who have hurt me. But the ones that skinned my heart by dragging me through their own problems seem to override the good of others. I feel like I know it is going to happen; I'm just waiting out the seconds to get hurt again. Pops says I put up a shield —oh, that's what he was talking about earlier. Of course, he didn't know I was heading where I am going now.

"Pinky promise me you won't tell anybody this." I hold out my right hand with the tiniest finger extended and wiggling. Bear doesn't hesitate. He brings up his hand, latches on to my pinky finger, and shakes it hard up and down. "I promise." I reach into the glove box and tug out the envelope. Then I pull out the driver's license inside. "It's from that box I had the other day in my room.

My mama brought it to me at the bar a few weeks ago. She said she found it in the closet in my old room. The picture is my ex-husband. His name is—" I pause, try not to doubt myself in telling Bear my secret. "His name was Josh Devereauxs. But on here, he is—"

"Tyler Heaton," Bear finishes before me. He takes the card and holds it up. "I take it we're heading to —" He squints his eyes to read the address. "1055 Robin Lane."

"Uh-huh."

"You sure you want to do this?" Bear asks me. He scoots around in the faux leather seat. I know it has to be uncomfortable for him. It is old and stiff. "Do you want to hunt down this ghost? What if he is alive and sitting on the front porch with some woman? I don't know you that well. But I'm thinking that if you have been spending the last three years of your life sitting on a bar stool on Friday nights waiting for your husband to return, then you stand in front of a train to prove to yourself he's not dead, I don't know if you're prepared."

"It is worse not knowing, Bear." I push the map down between us, ready myself to go up the hill. "Everybody's got their demons. Mine is sitting here, never knowing why Josh just vanished. I mean, is he dead? Is he alive, or did he get bored with me? Was I too stupid or not pretty enough or—" Bad in bed? I don't say that; instead, I wave the thought away with my hand.

"Brandy, you are beautiful." Bear reaches out and gives my head a playful shove with his hand. "I guarantee it wouldn't be that." I know he's just saying that to wipe the sad expression off my face. I blush, grab my hat bill, and tug it self-consciously. God, I feel like a bumbling idiot around him sometimes.

I force a smile, lean over, and shove him back. "I think you've got a crush on me."

"Oh, you wish," he answers. "Smart college girls with attitude and a sweet little redneck swagger just aren't my type." He does this little waggle back and forth like he's imitating me.

I shake my head, give him a faked suspicious gaze, and chuckle. "Oh, you're going there again calling me a redneck."

"I said it in a positive context. And I didn't use skanky with it in the same sentence." He stops, loses his grin, and gives me a sober gaze. "You were never skanky, alright?"

"I know." I roll my eyes, and poke at the map. "I'm going. You're either with me or not." Why do I still look at him and think he really means it? I don't know, so I start down the road, my tires grinding over gravel. Bear's not done. I am sure he is on some crusade for Preacher Murphy. I'm okay with that. I don't really have a choice. If Mister Smiley fires me, my tuition check's going to bounce.

"Yeah, okay, I get it. Everybody's got demons. You're right. However, not all of us chase them down, Brandy." He shrugs. "Regardless, I'm in. I'm going. You know that."

"That's the difference between you and me. When the bull comes at me, I grab him by the horns. You run."

"What makes you think that?" he asks.

"Have you even bothered to ask Meghan out yet?" Ha! Did he really think he was so perfect?

"Have you bothered to take that stupid hat off your head every time you get scared or mad?" he spats at me with a mean twist of his head. I turn to glance at him, but his eyes aren't angry, just concerned like Pops gets when I come home too late.

"What?"

"Take off the hat and keep it off, and I'll ask her out on a date."

"You are just plain mean. It's not stupid." I snapped my attention back to the road, wishing I hadn't brought Bear. "Josh gave it to me, jerk. It's about the only thing I've got left of him."

"Yeah, that's what makes it stupid," he tells me. "Brandy, it isn't the way it looks so much. It's the way you treat it like it's your husband. You recognize that. You grab at it like you're grabbing a guy's hand, using it to have your back. It's his replacement."

"You're not my therapist, Bear," I tell him. My eyes are following the three house numbers I see on mailboxes along the road. 1053, 1054.

"No, I'm not." Bear scrubs his forehead. "I'm just trying to help."

"Then use your eyes and see if the next box has 1055 on it." As I climb up the hill, there is a long expanse before I see a clear spot ahead and a rickety mailbox sitting sideways in some tall grass. I slow, not really wanting to stop. My heart is making a thump, thump, thump in my chest. I feel a little dizzy as my truck grinds to a halt at the end of the gravel drive.

"There's a house across the street that says 1056," Bear mumbles. I'm hardly listening while I shove the brake on and slip out the door. Yeah, there was a house there. It doesn't have a number because there is nothing left but a charred shell of beams keeling inward. I rest my hands on the truck's hood and stare at it. The house looks like the burned carcass of a fish lying in the aftermath of a bonfire. A gentle wind picks up, and the waft of overcooked wood tickles my nostrils.

Bear gets out and slams his door behind him. I watch him walk over to the house and stop at the three rickety burned steps still left behind. "It looks like it's been a while since it burned, Brandy." He stretches out a leg and uses his foot to push on a bit of wood that was once the front door. "It's the house you were looking for." He reaches down, slips his hand beneath a little cedar sign, and holds it up for me to see: The Heatons. 1055 Robin Lane. Welcome.

"So now what?" he asks, dropping it to the ground and turning toward me.

A dog barks behind me. I turn to see a little beagle tied to a doghouse on the property's front lawn across the street. A white and green trailer is plopped there, and a woman about Pops' age is standing on the porch. "You here from the insurance company to take more pictures?" she hollers across the short expanse. Her southern accent is thick, and she's wearing a tan knee-length dress with pink and blue flowers on it. A skinny black cat weaves in and out of her legs. "Jenny said you'd be out sometime this week. I told her it's been three years. You really should let these poor folks get what's due them."

"No, ma'am," I reach into the truck and pull out the envelope with the license on it. "I'm not with the insurance company." Then I turn at the exact moment I see Bear shaking his head, looking up to the sky like he can't believe I'm doing this. "I'm just looking for someone. Could you tell me if this is the guy who lived here?"

I jog across the road while she walks toward me. We meet by her mailbox, and I see her squinting into the picture of Josh. "Yeah, that's Ty." She pokes the picture with her finger. "Red-brown hair like the burly man across the street." She points a finger at Bear. "He had sneaky eyes. He was really skinny, like he was sick. He was the daddy. He was hardly ever there. Hannah didn't seem to care.

She liked keeping house for him. She loved him, loved those kids. He drove this big truck and would bring it up the hill, park it almost in the middle of the road so Gil at the post office couldn't get through to get the mail up the hill. I'd hear that truck, and Hannah would, too. She'd come running out, jumping right at him so he'd catch her in the air."

She stops and shakes her head. Maybe she sees me wince. I know I'm feeling something strange quiver in my chest. I imagine Josh giving her a piggyback ride to the house like he used to do with me. Seeing him doing it with somebody else hurts and aches like a leg cramp in my belly.

"I knew that little girl since I taught her in Sunday school at the Fairview Baptist Church," the lady goes on. "I was watching the kids the night this place went up. It was Christmas Eve. They were supposed to be wrapping up the presents. I was reading the babies a book and boom! Next thing I know, half their house is on my front lawn."

I hear the crunch of Bear's feet tramping across the road. I stand there, trying to decide if I can ask the question I need to ask. My mind is whirling with the thought Josh lived there. Three years ago. With another woman. He was a daddy. I see him driving his big old semi-truck up here, parking it in front of the house. He'd climb down just like he did outside the trailer park while I ran up the road to meet him. I remember his silly grin and his hand coming up to push away his hair hanging in his face. I remember —

I shook off the thought, realizing all she said was in the past tense. "Where is he now?"

"Fairview Cemetery. They buried them both there side by side. Well, what was left of them." She stops, and I feel Bear's hand on my shoulder.

"You alright, sweetheart?" she asks. I know what they mean by the blood draining from my face now. I feel the oozy sensation of something falling from the top of the head to the neck. I must be pale. I feel dizzy.

"He—died, did he?" I am staring at the license, not really comprehending I am looking at anything at all.

"Yeah, burnt to a crisp. Don't know if there was enough left of them to put in a casket, but they did."

Chapter –9
Letting it Soak in

"I'm driving."

"No, you're not driving."

"Well, you aren't driving, that's for damn sure," Bear is slipping his fingers into mine, stealing the keys away. "Not right now."

"I'm going to the cemetery."

"No, you're not. Just—just let it go. He's not your husband anymore, right? Pops said you got a divorce after he didn't come back. He was with another woman, Brandy. You need to stop doing this to yourself."

"You can't stop me!" I scream at him. "How much do you know me?" I ask him. Then, I pinch my forefinger and thumb nearly together. "This much. That's all. You have no right to decide what is good or bad for me. If I do not go today, I will go tomorrow. If you don't like it, you can walk home."

Bear comes to a halt in front of me, so I have no choice but to stop at my truck door. "Look at me," he says, touching my shoulder until I glare at him. "I will take you to Fairview Cemetery if you let me drive, alright? Please, Brandy. You look as pale as a ghost."

I suppose Bear is probably wondering how the hell he got involved with all this while we drive to the cemetery. He's mentally pushing a gun to his head thinking it is the only way out. At the same time, he watches me stare at the headstone with their names etched into a pretty marble stone: Hannah and Ty – Together in Eternity.

When Preacher Murphy passed around the names of folks who are lost souls in the neighborhood, and mine fell on Bear, he probably thought he could drop off a batch of chocolate chip cookies and walk off into the sunset. Nope, he is one hour and forty-five minutes away from home and staring at a girl with the crazies, staring at the grave of her husband who is, strangely, twice dead.

"Do you want to find a police station and tell them what is happening?" Bear asks. I turn and shake my head.

"No. Why? They already think he's dead. Besides, I don't trust cops."

"Brandy, I really think they need to know what he's done."

"What?" I spit at him. "So that they can come knocking at my door more than they do now? You don't understand what I went through when he came up missing, do you? I was the wife. He was screwing around with every girl in town." I puff out my lips. I knew this was a mistake bringing Bear along with me. "Listen, I got hammered with questions, cops knocking on my door night and day. They figured I caught Josh screwing around, killed him, and hid the body at Pops. They brought police teams out to walk his property and check for a grave. I had no clue he was—he was doing anything at all. The night he disappeared was the first time I found out he was screwing every girl in town. Little Pete told me Josh brought 'another Brandy home' on Friday nights. I stayed home that night and parked my car around the side of the trailer to see if he was really bringing Lisa Perkins to the trailer. Josh must have seen it. I made the mistake of telling some homicide detective from Charleston this. He took it and ran with it, pointing the finger at me. I can't—I can't do it again. Bear, there's no way I'm telling anybody this. And if you have any compassion in your body, you'll never mention this to anyone."

"I told you I wouldn't."

Everything's a blur while we drive back to Fire Mountain. I know an hour passes while Bear drives and keeps turning the radio stations nervously. He reaches up on my dashboard, grabs up my hat, and tosses it to me. I know he is trying to be nice, but I throw it out the window. He turns around, gets out of the truck, and picks it up off the grass.

"Are you going to do this thing?" He tries to joke with me, waving his arms like I did in the truck the night Mama gave me the box.

"Ha ha," I say without luster. I stare out the window as we pass a little car on the side of the road. Three little girls are sitting beside it, squatting in the shade away from the setting sun. About three minutes later, a guy is walking up the road with a gas can in his hand. Bear scratches his head and looks at me. "Do we stop?" he asks. "It could be miles to the next gas station."

I nod, and he works his way around. It's just a remote four-laner. The guy's probably twenty-four or twenty-five. He tells us his name is Travis Larkins and looks exhausted. He tells Bear the reason why.

His wife, Tiffany, just had a baby last night and they are bringing her home from the hospital. It is his fourth little girl. He didn't have enough money to get both gas and diapers. He had to make a choice between the two, so he opted to keep his baby's butt dry.

Bear drops me off with the wife and kids while he runs up to the next exit or two until they can find a gas station open. The mama is sitting on the passenger side seat with her door open and feet hanging out. It is hot. The little girls looked scared, hunkered down next to her. I take them out to a little field by the car, and we catch lightning bugs in the dewy grass and the layer of fog coming up from a creek nearby. They giggle and dance while we put lightning bugs on each other. Then Bear returns with Travis, and we wait until he gets his car going. All the little girls cheer. They don't care if Daddy has to make a decision between gas and diapers. They've got each other. And now, they've got a hundred bucks of my tuition money I had in the truck for an emergency that I slipped into Tiffany's hand. She kept shoving it back. I wouldn't let her.

Bear and I drive off in silence. It's getting late, the sun is setting. "How much did you give them?" he asks me. I knew he probably saw me slip the money into Tiffany's hand. "Oh, come on. I saw you."

"A hundred bucks."

"I bought three bags of diapers at the gas station. I gave Travis sixty. It was all the cash I had in my wallet." Bear smiles. It is good to see him smile. He doesn't do it too much. "That ought to get them a couple meals. I told him to call down to the security office at the resort, and I'd talk to somebody about getting him a job. He got laid off from a contracting job a few months ago."

I scoot up in the seat. "I didn't know they were hiring up there. One of the guys I work with at Smiley's applied, and they told him that he had to have a college degree to work as a busboy. Maybe you shouldn't have done that, Bear," I say. "Get his hopes up, I mean."

"He'll probably get a job there. I can put a good word in for him."

"Really? I doubt he has a high school degree, Bear. He got laid off from a roofing job." I look at Bear and know he doesn't understand. He probably comes from the subdivisions in town, and his daddy built him a tree house in the backyard next to the expensive store-bought metal swing set.

"They must have changed their standards since I applied last year," I tell him. "Because the witch who owns the place told me right to my face: 'We like to hire a higher caliber of workers here at our resort and country club. We don't usually hire locals. We only go for the cream of the crop.'" Actually, she had looked me up and down and rolled her eyes. Amelia Vega. I think that's her name. I saw a posting at the college that they were hiring kitchen workers. I thought a job at a resort would be good to add to my resume when I was finished. I sat down in her big, expensive office at the far end of a long, hardwood conference table. In front of me, I had a green folder they had prepared for all their applicants. It contained an application I had filled out and detailed information on their resort.

On top, I laid my résumé and little folder, which I saved to keep tabs on the places I applied for jobs. In mine were newspaper clippings and articles I cut out to get a good vibe of what each offered. I noted Big Boar Mountain Resort and Country Club got terrible one-star reviews on their menu. While I was waiting for Missus Vega to look up, I saw a bit of the poor restaurant review sticking out of a magazine in my folder, along with an article that talked about a long line of Missus Vega's business ventures that failed. I had pushed them in quickly so that nobody saw both.

On either side of me, she had four employees sitting in to listen to the interview. Eight people were staring at me. Ten people staring at me is my limit for feeling uneasy and thinking I will faint. At that number, I would have just gotten up and left, which would have been better in the long run.

I didn't leave. Missus Vega primped her short, brown hair with one finger and looked down the long expanse of the table at me over her designer glasses. She didn't ask me anything about myself, who I was, or what I had to offer. Missus Vega didn't care about my insides. She just took one look at my outsides and didn't like what she saw. She asked me why I even bothered to apply to the country club. *Jeans and a button-up blouse? Who wears that to an interview? Do they not teach you the basic skills of applying for a job at your high school? With that look, you'll never get a job here, much less waitressing at one of your local diners down in whatever little hick town from whence you come.*

I remember hearing chiding laughter on either side of the table.

My cheeks turned hot. It made me so mad I felt my tummy rumble. I stood up and snatched up my folder, ready to bolt. I started to turn, then stopped cold. I felt Missus Vega just wasn't making fun of *me*. She was making fun of *everybody* who hailed from a million little hick towns all over the place.

I looked Amelia Vega straight in the eyes and told her I didn't come to get a job waitressing. I came to apply for a job assisting the chef. She didn't let me finish. She dared to sniff a haughty laugh: "Oh, my God, don't waste my time. Get out of here."

"So you know what I told her?" I am telling Bear the story, sitting back in the seat, watching him drive. "I said this: *I think it is my time wasted, not yours. Maybe this will be a lesson to you someday when you're sitting in a cardboard box instead of your big house on the next hill. Because from whence I come is Fire Mountain. And perhaps your clientele don't come here to savor the local fare, but they expect good food. And that diner just outside New Alliance has a full parking lot every weekend for customers who have tasted the crud you offer here. They hop in their cars and take off as fast as they can down that mountainside to Beverly's Hometown Diner. Let me tell you something. It isn't just manners you lack. It is the ability to open your eyes and see that you should probably take a little advice from the hicks that surround you. Because your food reviews are a steady one star along with your competence and character*. I plopped the magazine down on the table and flipped her the middle finger right there."

"You probably could have stopped before flipping her off." Bear didn't speak during my entire tirade. He looks stiff driving, though. Big guys like him don't understand what getting a pie in the face is like whenever you turn around. Everybody's friendly to the big guy because they're afraid of him.

"Bear, she compared me to day-old white bread."

"What?"

"Yeah, when she was escorting me out the door with security on either side, Missus Vega said that people are like white bread. Some come out of the oven with a good start. They are fresh and perfect and ready for the shelf. They are the ones who succeed, who folks go right to and pick out to take home. Then there's the rest of the bread, ones like me. It comes out a little burned or undercooked.

Nobody wants it because it didn't bake right, and you can't hide that it got burned or broken. You can't change the way it looks. It is poor quality. Especially if the cook who makes it is a drunk or in prison. It's the kind that ends up in the bin at the back of the store. The bread isn't good for much more than the food pantry at the back of the church or the garbage. Poor white trash."

"Surely you are improvising." Bear was shaking his head. "She didn't say all that."

"Yes, she did. But that isn't the point. The point is that she just looked at the outside of me. She didn't even bother to look inside."

"Well, maybe if you wore something a little more appropriate, she would have taken the time to check out the insides."

I see Bear looking over at me, looking me up and down. I'm all T-shirt, old tennis shoes, and jean shorts. My hair is shoved into the hat I am wearing again. He's wearing khaki shorts and a button-up over a clean T-shirt. His haircut is fresh and stylish. Maybe he's right. But who has the money for all that?

I don't say that, though. Because I've got a lot of hillbilly inside me that thinks I should be who I am and be proud of it. I can't afford new dresses every week and pay for my college. Still, I sigh. He really doesn't understand, and it isn't his fault. "Bear," I say softly. "I can't afford new clothes. If I could buy a dress every day, I would. I can't. And I couldn't afford it for the interview. That's why I needed the job to earn money and buy clothes and food."

"You shouldn't listen to people, Brandy," he says. "Especially me. I'm sorry, that was a stupid thing to say. Don't let it bother you."

"It really doesn't bother me, Mister Beauregard Rodriguez, to be exact," I say. I use his real name just like he did when he was Band-Aiding my leg at church, "unless it is the middle of the night. You probably know what I'm talking about. Maybe your demons call to you to get up and eat. Mine sit on the end of my bed and tell me I'm just what everybody says. *Nothing.* I lay there in the dark for hours, thinking about it over and over all the shitty things people have said to me. Now I've got to add your stupid little remarks to the pile every time we see each other. Do you get it? You hurt my feelings. I don't think you care if you hurt my feelings. It is like you say something insulting, but it is okay if you backtrack and tell me I shouldn't listen to you. That's—mean. You need to work hard on that, Bear.

You need to learn to quit being mean to your friends just because you know they like you and aren't going to leave you. It hurts." I slap my chest above my heart. "Pull over, I'm driving."

He does what I say. He tells me not to be mad at him, but I am. The last twenty minutes of the drive are quiet, awkward, and excruciating. When we got back to the house, I get out of the truck and tell him goodbye.

He stands there for a minute, wondering if he should go or follow. Then, like he does each time, he says, "Thanks, Brandy. Are we doing this tomorrow?"

"Not tomorrow." I know I am just tired, just being cranky because the image of Josh and a faceless girl named Hannah lying side by side for eternity is swimming in my mind.

"Does that mean just not tomorrow or not ever again?"

"I don't know, Bear, you hurt me." I'm hardly three steps away when I get a text from Bear. It has three phone numbers on it and a little sad-faced emoji. It says, *When you wake up with those demons, call me. I'll be at any of these and sit up with you until they go away.*

It is sadly hilarious. Right now, he is one of the demons that make me feel small because of what he said. I turn and throw my hands in the air. "Yeah, because you're so good at it." That is all I say. I walk up the steps onto the porch and slam the door hard behind me.

Chapter −10
Demons

My phone is going off. I'm sound asleep. My hand is patting at the table next to my bed. It is 3:30 in the morning.

"Hey, it's Bear."

"Are you dead?"

"Huh?"

"It is 3:30 in the morning, Bear. This better be an emergency like you are dying and need CPR because you woke me up."

"No, I just can't sleep. It's those little demons again."

Again. This happens at least twice a week. He can't sleep. Now, I can't.

"What is it tonight, Bear?" I sit up in bed and yawn.

"Cheesecake. With cherries and this pink-red sauce on top."

"Where did you get it?"

"It was in the refrigerator."

"Well, go put it back."

I hear a grand sigh, a rustling, the opening of a refrigerator door, and then footsteps.

"Okay, now *really* put it back."

"Holy hell, how did you know I didn't put it away?"

"I'm not telling, just go put it away. Go to bed. Maybe this will help." I yawn loudly on the phone. "That lady who lived across from the Heatons, she called you *burly*. You are not chubby or fat anymore. You are officially one step farther away from being fat, and what people call burly. Put your phone up to your ear, and I'll sing you to sleep. Once you hear my voice, you'll be so sick to your tummy that you'll never want to eat again."

Chapter –11
Bear's Treasure Box

We have a meeting at Mister Smiley's Super Grocery Store on the first Monday of each month. There are about thirty people who work at the store. We all have to show up and sit around the break room. Missus Smiley usually brings in homemade donuts and apple juice. She is a frumpy woman with long gray hair that she keeps in a bun on top of her head. She always tells everybody that they are so sweet.

Today is different. Mister Smiley brings everybody outside to the front of the store. He has a huge cake on a fold-up table that is placed adjacent to the big sign with Mister Smiley's Super Grocery Store on it. There are a bunch of reporters. I think for a minute that it must be Missus Smiley's birthday or maybe the store's anniversary. Everybody is standing there waiting in anticipation of something BIG. I see the Cash Register Girls, Michelle and Meghan, standing up front, holding hands, giggling, and dancing on their feet like they are waiting for the last letter and number to be called in a game of Bingo and they are sure to win. Janie Mills is trying to look cool next to them. She's the dark-haired one of the bunch. Carrie Edwards is talking smugly to Mister Smiley and fixing her hair in a mirror. They are behaving more like movie stars preparing for their names to be announced at the Hollywood Hall of Fame than subdivision girls who work at cash registers in a dumpy grocery store in the middle of nowhere, getting ready to eat cake

"What's going on?" I asked Kim Wells, who works in the office. She shushes me with her finger and tells me to keep watching. It's a big surprise. Mister Smiley pulls out a wireless microphone and clears his throat in it. "Testing. Testing," he says, and everybody gets quiet except for a couple coming out of the store with a shopping cart of groceries. They stop and look at everybody like they are surprised. Everybody laughs, and the cameras start rolling.

"As you all know, in less than four and a half months, the National Fire Mountain Redneck Run will be coming to our little village in the Mountain State—"

That's when I see it coming. I suppose I knew all along Mister Smiley was never going to sponsor me. I reckon he was my only hope, so I just banked everything on his store. If my mama was here, she would laugh, telling me how unrealistic I could be. *Baby girl, why the hell are you always building castles in Spain, huh? Get down from your high horse. You ain't better than nobody else 'round here.*

"—so today, we are announcing that Mister Smiley's Super Grocery Store in the beautiful town of New Alliance, West Virginia is sponsoring four of our little ladies who have grown up in the shadows of Fire Mountain and who have worked at the store for over a year. And that is Jane Anne Mills, Carrie Lynn Edwards, and the cutest little twins this side of West Virginia, Meghan, and Michelle Reynolds—the team we are calling: Fire Mountain Shadows."

I felt like a fist gutted me. *Fire Mountain Shadows.* Not only did they steal my name, but they also stole my sponsor. The crowd bursts into applause, and the local reporters converge on them as if they were superstars. I feel sick to my stomach and wish Josh was here to defend me. I think he would have fought his way through the crowd of well-wishers, grabbed the microphone from Mister Smiley's hand, and hit him over the head with it. If he was here.

But he isn't. I stand there clapping with everybody else, listening while each of the girls gets up on a makeshift podium of mobile home steps shoved up against the curbing. She tells us how utterly surprised and thankful she is.

I opt out of getting a square section of the cake. It isn't that I don't want to take a bite out of one of the girls whose picture is right on the front. I feel queasy and want to leave. Of course, I can't. Mister Smiley waves me over after he talks to the reporters. He points to a big splash of punch someone spilled near the grocery store's front. "Clean that up, would you, Margarita?" he grouses at me, poking his fat forefinger on the ground.

"Margarita?"

His face screws up like he's either pooping or thinking really hard. "You know, I can never remember your name. I know it's something alcoholic, isn't it?" He scratches his balding head and wrinkles his nose like a rabbit.

"It's Shirley Temple," I lie to him. "Shirley isn't that hard to remember, is it?"

"Oh." he bobs his head up and down. "Well, Shirley, clean up the punch on the ground before they get it on camera." As he walks away, he scratches his head, mumbling, "I don't remember signing any paycheck with Shirley on it. Damn, I've got to pay more attention." He's high on all the fanfare. People are clapping him on the shoulder. Heck, they even let a dozen doves fly out of a cage. I sop up the punch on my hands and knees and stick around to help clean up the tables and trash on the ground.

"So, you are giving up, Dandy Brandy?"

My cousin, Kenny, thinks he is being funny when he pokes me in the shoulder with his skinny forefinger. I know why he's asking me this. Pops is always telling everybody everything about us. It makes me mad in instances like this. It is insufferable to know the whole world knows you failed. He probably told them I was crying about it. I wasn't.

"Just because I don't have a sponsor doesn't mean crap," I tell him while he puffs out his cheeks, makes that weird duck call. One day, somebody is going to shoot him during waterfowl season, and I'm going to laugh.

Pops is taking a bunch of guys out on the river in his pontoon boat. It holds six people. He's got eight here. They are all staring at me with the kind of smiles people give when somebody is trying to tell a joke, but they are completely screwing it up. "I wasn't counting on Mister Smiley sponsoring me. It was just a thought. I've got a whole list of people who might do it."

"Like who?" That's Billy the Bartender sitting in the kitchen with a couple of my uncles. Suddenly, he is becoming a fixture at this house, buddying up with Pops. I'm not sure if I like it or not. He stares at me all the time and follows me with his eyes like he's waiting for his prey to break from the herd so he can hunt me down. Every time I head to my room, I see him following and I make a veer to the bathroom.

"Like nobody I would ever tell because you might steal them from me," I yell back into the other room. "And God knows nobody wants to see you run in the event. You sprint like a prissy, little girl."

I feign running across the room with my arms flapping and waving.

"Babe, you going out with us?" Pops is coming through the living room with a bunch of fishing poles in his fists, and I almost run into him. "I got your pole all ready."

"No, I've got stuff to do."

"Stuff," he asks. "Like what?"

"Like stuff that is none of your business." I shouldn't have done it. But I told him about the lockbox and fake driver's licenses last night. He told me to take it all, throw it in the dumpster behind Smiley's, and forget about it. Nothing good is going to come out of that box, he said.

Pops stops and eyes me carefully. "You need to respect me, Brandy. I put a roof over your head."

"Not much of one," I tease him. "It leaks."

I can't say I've ever seen him get angry with me. Not the kind of right-in-my-face fuming mad. One time, when I was seven, he caught me climbing on the roof and screamed at me. He's never laid a finger on me, though. However, right then and right in front of everybody, he throws the fishing poles against the wall. They bang and clatter, and everybody stops talking while he stomps across the room, grabs me by the shirt collar, gives it a little shake, and leans in hard. "Then if you don't like it, get the hell out of here," he growls like a grizzly. "I'll hold the door open for you." I know my eyes are wide. I stand there staring at him. "I threw your mother out. I'll do the same with you if you disrespect me or if you bring drugs into my home." He leans forward, pulls me one step, and points to the ashtray on the table. "You know better than this." It is a joint, nearly smoked to the end and smashed to the bottom of the tray. It isn't mine. I don't know whose it is. I think it is Kenny's, and I don't want to tell on him. "Do you understand?"

I'm too stubborn to answer. It makes me mad that he thinks I did it. He growls: "Get out." He knows I don't smoke weed. Still, when I look back and forth in his eyes, I don't think he believes me. I wriggle free of his fingers, don't look at anybody's face while I walk to my room, grab up the lockbox, and stick it into my book backpack. When I gave him a wide berth and headed out the door, he had already picked up the poles and laid them on the kitchen table.

"Hey." It's Bear's voice, and I don't want to deal with anybody. I didn't even know he was in the house.

"Yeah," I say, plopping my backpack across the expanse of the driver's seat to the passenger, looking at him, who is staring at me through the passenger side window.

"Okay," he says. "You haven't been making the best decisions over the last week."

"Like what? Don't tell me you think that joint was mine too."

"I'm talking about Billy."

"Okay, it was a lot less than you are probably going to make of it," I say. But please be more specific, so I know we're on the same page."

"Okay, when I walked into your room last night, you were on the bed with Billy. He had his hands up your shirt, feeling you out."

"Oh, stop! Please be less specific!" I groan. "I didn't mean to go into detail about that moment. I meant over the week. And you're not my boyfriend. What is it to you?"

"I'm your friend, and I think you're better than letting Billy climb on top of you and—"

"Stop!" I have my hands in the air in front of me, and I'm in mid-wince. "Bear, I am not discussing this with you!"

Okay, it is true. Billy the Bartender and I had a moment. It was a bad moment, a bad decision. But sometimes, a girl has her needs, and if the time is right, it is right. It was just one of those moments. With respect to Billy, it was the wrong person. He is attractive and well-built, and he just happened to walk in when I was all nice and cozy on the bed watching T.V. However, he's shallow, and the thought that he's slept with a thousand girls doesn't appeal to me. Still, he stood at the door talking, then worked his way across the room. Then he was on the side of the bed talking sweet and soft to me, leaning over and kissing me. He's an okay kisser. He was the only kisser for the moment, so it worked for me. The next thing I know, he's kissing my neck, shoving his hand up my tank top, and grappling underneath my bra.

I would have stopped him. Unfortunately, Bear came barreling through the door before I either got to the point of stopping it or made a wrong decision and didn't.

"The point is, Bear, it is my decision if I choose to fool around with Billy in my bedroom or on the front porch or the rooftop, for that matter. I just needed a little something something. Let's leave it at that."

"That's classy."

"What? Are you a virgin?" I ask him. "You've never fooled around just to—fool around?"

"No, I am not a virgin. But I don't go flopping around my bed with every girl that walks in the door just when I need a little *something something*, isn't that what you call it?" Bear looks at me with a snarky smile. "I suppose that's the difference between you and me."

"Are you calling me poor white trash or a slut?" I turn my head and tip my chin. "Are we going there again? Right now? Are you going to shove a couple skankies into a sentence and this time, with negative context?"

"I'm not touching that with a ten-foot pole." Still, he opens the passenger side door, pushes my backpack, and hops inside. I know he notices it makes a rattling sound, and now, he knows the lockbox is hidden in the pack. "Okay, no, I'm not calling you any names. I know he's been following you for weeks, staring at you like you're a piece of meat. That's just crude. I'm trying to use the right words to avoid insulting you. Please don't bait me with stuff."

But I'm more concerned because he's settling in the truck. "Really?" I ask him. "Did I invite you along?"

"No, but I'm coming."

I don't say anything for a few minutes; I just drive. Bear doesn't, either. Finally, I reach over, flip open the backpack, and pull out the lockbox. I open the lid and pull out an envelope. I set it down in my lap.

"Hey, butt wipe." I turn my attention to Bear and make him look over. He's mad, irritated.

"What?"

"I'm not like that. I'm not my mama."

"I know." He situates himself and looks down at his hands. I can tell when he's nervous. Bear starts rubbing his hands together, twiddling his thumbs, patting his legs. "Then why'd you do it?"

"I miss it. I miss being close to somebody." I'm not really comfortable sharing my feelings. The guys that hang out with Pops make fun of me when I do it.

"Find somebody you like then. Some nice guy."

The truth is, I don't really want to find a nice guy. I thought I'd done that the first time. Josh was a bit wild, but I can tell you nobody would have expected he had a string of wives. I'm still wondering if this isn't all just a bad dream. Maybe somebody used his picture, and that is it.

"Right," I say. "They are all over the place, oozing out the bar's walls, sitting beside me at church."

"I can tell you he isn't in that envelope you've got in your lap." Bear reaches out and snatches it up. He looks at the writing on the front. "Ashley." He breathes in and lets his eyes roam over to mine. "I guess we are going to visit Ashley." He reaches into the envelope, pulls out the driver's license, and squints against the sunny windshield to see the name.

"Johnathon Mills on Hill Road in Brink Hollow," I tell him before he reads it aloud.

"What's your plan this time?" he asks. "What can this possibly do for you. You know your husband is dead. Are you going to approach Ashley if she is there and ask her if she knew him? There's a phone number on the envelope. Why don't you call it?"

"I can't just call, and I don't know. Bear, I'm freaking out about this. And I'm already having a crappy day."

"Okay, I get it."

It is five o'clock when we pull into Brink Hollow. It is just off the highway, on the corner of two old backroads. It's the closest thing I've seen to a ghost town. There are two rundown buildings in town pushed up against the hillside. The paint has long been rubbed off of them, and there aren't any windows in them. Nobody's lived in the tumbledown structures for a long time. "Let's explore," I say, pulling off the road and turning off the truck. Bear looks skeptical.

"You're going to get us arrested."

"By who?" I ask. "There isn't a police station for miles. Don't be such a baby. If the cops come, tell them I told you I would beat you up if you didn't go in."

"Ha ha," he says flatly. "Why am I getting a bad feeling about this?"

"Because you've been locked up in a convent for the last ten years." I jab him in the shoulder and push myself out the door. "Come on, Sister Beauregard, let's walk on the wild side." I do a little twisty dance, revolve around a couple times, and wiggle my finger at him. "Do I look like a stripper?" I ask him, blowing him a kiss from my palm.

I got a smile out of him. "You look like my sister when she stepped on a ground hornet nest when she was eleven or twelve."

I stop and make a funny face by crossing my eyes and sticking out my tongue. "Fine. I was going to take off my clothes. Now, I'm not."

"No, you weren't."

"You don't know that." I have to go around the truck's hood and grab him by a flap of his shirt sticking out. Okay, I notice something right as I reach for his shirt. His belly isn't as chubby as it was. I don't say anything. I don't act like I notice. But I do. It almost feels like the bad things from the morning are being erased away just by this simple fact. *I* helped him do it. I continue, dragging him onto the tall grass before the buildings.

One building has a crooked sign that says RINK HOLLO GROCER. I peer inside. I see a worn wooden floor with flaps of old linoleum sticking up. Along the front, part of a counter is still intact. There isn't much more but a few broken stools and rotting shelves.

"Oh, please don't go inside," Bear tells me. It is too late. I am already pushing open the door with shoulder and hip and stealing inside. I strut to the counter and slip behind it. When Bear walks in, I pretend I am running a cash register. "Welcome to Brink Hollow Grocery. What can I help you find, sir."

"Okay, I'll take six rolls of toilet paper and a side of beef," Bear tells me. "And I would like to order a new brain for the girl who drove me here. I think she lost it when she decided to come into this dump."

"I can do that." I turn around and pull down make-believe supplies for him, setting them on the counter. That will be a million bucks."

"Ow, that's a bit steep. Leave out the girl's brain. It wasn't much of one before we got here anyway." Bear thinks he is funny and laughs. "I'll just stuff her head with toilet paper instead. Nobody will even notice."

"Oh, you are funny, Mister Rodriguez," I point a finger at him over the counter. "In fact—" I never got to finish my sale. The sound that I would describe as a single pop of a tiny balloon just beneath my feet was followed by the ripping, tearing crunch as the counter keeled toward me. It wasn't until that moment that I realized the boards beneath my feet had decayed to mush between the wall and my shoes. The weight of the old wood counter, with me leaning my bony elbows hard against it to ring up the imaginary cash register, had pushed it over the edge of its ability to hold.

"Oh, Bear," I whimper just as the floor beneath me gives way. I remember seeing his eyes get as big as fists disappearing as I fell straight down.

I don't know how he grabs one shoulder of my shirt in the fingers of his right hand, but he does. The initial shock as the tank top slips up and catches around my neck takes my breath away. I gag just in time to feel his left hand latch onto my wrist as I involuntarily snap it upwards blindly.

"God almighty," Bear grunts. There I dangle, wiggling like a moth desperately trying to come out of its tank-top caterpillar cocoon. The sideways counter is leaning over the edge above me with Bear's weight. I hear it grinding. It is completely broken on my end, terribly close to coming loose on the other.

"Hey, don't look down."

Why do people say that? I hadn't thought of it until he told me not to do it. I'm not particularly afraid of heights. I climbed trees to the tippy top from the time I was four. I probably would have climbed straight up his arm like a rabid monkey had he not said those words. Instead, I look down.

"Holy shit," I gasp. It isn't that it is far from the tip of my toe to the floor. I would gauge the height from where I was dangling to the floor at not more than twelve feet. No problem. In most circumstances, I could have Bear release my hand, and I would drop and land on my feet. There is one problem. Three massive shards of thick window glass are directly beneath where my toes are dangling, wedged between an old stairway and a rusted, busted freezer.

"Please don't curse."

"You're kidding me," I hiss.

"And you looked—down, didn't—you?" Bear is grunting with my weight. I can't feel my hand. His death grip on my wrist has left it a numbed, tingling fist. I know he is probably desperately trying to figure out if his weight will send us both into the glass if he tries to adjust his stance and pull me up.

"I did." I think I am going to hyperventilate. A dribble of hot sweat slips down my forehead. I smell old books and dust and believe that this is how I will die. "And that makes it twice I didn't listen to you. I should have listened to you the first time. I swear if you pull me out, I will listen to you next time. And I—I won't cuss. Let's do this. I'll count to three. If you think you can pull me out, do it. If you can't, just let me go. Don't tell me which one you're going to do." I close my eyes and take a deep breath. "One—" I stop. Did he hear me?

"Why are you so quiet?" I ask.

"I am praying."

"Oh, okay, two—" That little dribble of sweat on my forehead trickles down to my right eye. It burns. "Can you say a little prayer for me while you're at it?"

"Brandy, you are who I'm praying for."

"Oh, yeah, the glass." I take my last breath. "And—"

"Oh, for the love of God! Just say it. Three!" Bear yells those words. I swear my arm is ripping off, my flesh is being skinned from the bones of each one of my ribs when he snaps upward. I feel myself lifting up and nearly over the counter like a seesaw. Bear is squatting, leaning back, and dragging me the rest of the way across the old boards of the counter. When he pulls me all the way over, the entire counter and a good piece of the floor flip over and make a sickening screech as the wood is ripping away.

My upper half partially lies across Bear while I wrangle my shirt back in place. I know Bear had to get an eyeful of my breasts. My legs were dangling where I was making my grocery sale. I half-crawl and half-roll to a safe distance from the gaping hole in the floor. Then I lay there a big pile of shivering scared.

Bear is pushing himself to a kneeling position. I think he is going to yell at me. He is looking me up and down without expression. Then, right out of the blue, he gets a funny twist to his lips. I know I'm dead meat. Kenny got the same look last hunting season when I almost rammed his ATV with mine going down a hill. Bear doesn't get mad, though. "You know," he says, matter-of-factly, "If I could describe your face when I said three, it would be the same one my mom's little poodle gets when he poops."

"Oh," I mutter. "I thought you were going to divulge that in a moment of weakness, you didn't pray I'd not fall on the glass, but you'd get to see my tits before I died." He bursts into the most hysterical fit of deep laughter I have ever heard. I mean, he is almost rolling on the floor while he starts to relate to the traumatic event that just occurred as if it were a classic cartoon. I am lying there on my back, staring up at him, and he can't stop laughing. It is so hard, and tears are running down his face. "You did, didn't you?" I glare at him, pushing to sit and crossing my arms. "Incredible. Just incredible. I'm getting ready to die, and your brain is in the gutter."

"No, really, I didn't," he says, wiping tears from his eyes. He holds me at bay with his hands. Then, just as quickly as his wild laughter begins, it ends. "Oh," he says in a single huff. I think I am bleeding or something, so I get up on my knees, pat my arms and legs, and rise. His eyes aren't on mine, though. Instead, he is staring hard to my left.

"Look," he says. "Check it out." My eyes follow. But while I stand still, Bear gets up and eases himself over to the small section where the counter had once been. Only a lighter section of wood remains where the nails popped out off the floor. I watch as he kneels down to the long section of the base of the counter that did not collapse into the basement. "Bejesus, come here." It is the first time he has called me anything besides Brandy. I'm unsure if he adjusted my name, made it smaller, or concocted a nickname for me. I do what he says, scramble, and approach him. I lean a bit with my hand over his shoulder, peering down toward his knee. He is staring hard into the shadows, and I see him picking up something in his hands.

"What is it?" I feel like I have to whisper. I don't know why. He is just kneeling there on one leg so hypnotized. I feel like if I speak too loudly or move too fast, the air around us will shatter.

He holds something square and wooden up in his palm and pushes away a layer of dust on the lid with his fingers. It is a tiny metal trunk not much bigger than his palm. Bear is silent while he kneels there. He doesn't shift, doesn't move. Then it is like he is holding onto the air in the room with the one breath he is gasping from his chest. His left hand comes up, and he uses two fingers to unclasp the little copper-colored hook that holds the lid to the base. He opens the lid wide. We both peer inside with bated breath.

"I can't believe this." Bear breathes out. It is nothing more than a single marble, a beautiful brown and gold tiger eye rolling around within the raggedy, red torn velvet inside. Back and forth, it rolls. I think time is lost to the man beneath my hand because I feel him huff a raggedy breath against my knee.

"Bear, are you alright?" My words are a hoarse whisper, and they seem to shave back the dust filtering in the air. He acts like he has found a million dollars in gold, but it is just one marble.

"I—I don't know."

Something crashes from the floor on the far side of the room. I snatch his shirt and nod toward the door. "Outside. Let's get out of here."

Chapter −12

Ashley

The moment I set foot on the wood of the front porch, I knew it was a mistake. To my left, there are three black garbage bags. The smell alone is enough to discourage me. It doesn't, however, repel the opossum growling and munching the skeletal remains of a chicken carcass. He turns and looks at me, skitters off into a jagged hole in the plywood board tacked to the porch railing.

The open bag is the first one of the three that is stinking the most. One side had been peeled away by a cat, dog, or raccoon, and its contents spilled on the shabby wood. There are a few poopy diapers with coffee grounds scattered on top and something that looks like a peach moldering between. I am stifling a gag when I knock at the door of the old brick house. We are about two miles from where the town center of Brink Hollow once stood. It has shifted south and adapted itself to the modern world. I am standing on the porch of one of a long line of old company houses, still standing from a coal mining business long gone. We are on the outskirts of the new town and up a hillside. In the distance, I can see the top of a courthouse and several town buildings.

"Wow," Bear is huffing. "That was the biggest rat I've ever seen!"

"It's just an opossum. He won't bother you unless you stick your hand down there and grab the chicken away from him." I turn. Bear is staring at the black hole where the opossum disappeared. His right foot has yet to scale the top step. "I cannot believe you've never seen an opossum, Bear."

"An opossum," is all he says. "I'll just stay here."

"Yeah, big boy," I shake my head, teasing him with a scathing roll of my eyes. "Good to know you've got my back."

"I had your back, Brandy, when your butt was dangling Indiana-Jones-style over those two spears of glass ready to impale you."

"I suppose I have to wait for you to hand out another coupon before you save my butt again? I'm going to start calling you Possum instead of Bear. Because that's what possums do. They faint and froth at the mouth when something scares them."

"Funny, haha. I am not frothing at the mouth." Still, he doesn't move. I bring my knuckled hand back up to bang on the door, and it opens about six inches.

"I don't have the payment for the T.V. this week, so you might as well take it." The girl inside is holding back a little boy with her hand. He's probably two or so and only wearing a saggy diaper. He's pushing hard with his head to the back of her knees and wants to get around her legs. He wants to hit me with the little plastic orange and green hammer in his dirty, chubby fist. His nose is snotty, and there's a brownish streak down his chest. I'm hoping he doesn't get past his mama's right leg.

The girl has frizzy red hair and freckles. I can also tell she's got attitude. Her lip keeps twitching on the right side. "I'm not with the T.V. place," I say. "I'm Brandy, and I just wanted to ask you a quick question."

"I don't have any money to give you. Are you an idiot?" She turns around and screams at the little boy while she drags him back so he falls with a thud on his rear on the floor. He yowls in frustration. I know she is getting ready to close the door. She is pushing it with her hip, forcing it across the grimy brown shag carpet. I smell cigarettes wafting through the crack. "I got three babies to feed, and I can't even pay rent this month."

"No, no—" I have the envelope in my hand. I see the door closing, closing, closing. I wiggle out the driver's license and hold it out for her to see. "Do you know him?"

I hear the scuffle of Bear's foot on the step behind me while he adjusts his position. The girl's eyes go from the license to Bear and then back to me in the tiny crack she allows between us. "Who are you? What do you want?" she hisses. "Because if you know where that shit is, I want his address." She opens the door just a little, shoves her hand out, and snatches onto my hand holding the card. I see her narrowing her gaze, focusing on the contents. "I'm the first one in line tearing Johnny's balls straight off his body."

"Johnny," I say. It is quiet. She releases my hand, and the little boy squeezes between the door and her skinny leg. I see him barreling toward the steps. The red-haired girl points a finger at the diaper and screams at Bear to catch the boy before he gets to the road. "Jared Michael!"

Bear's eyes are more terrified than when he saw the opossum while he stretches out his hands, and he hesitates. I know he is trying to find a place that is halfway germ-free between the poopy diapers and a dirt-smudged head to grab him. Bear does snatch him up. It is funny. He is holding him straight out in front of him, and the little kid kicks, squeals, and tosses his fists into the air. I can't help but think of Kenny. My cousin decided to raise a pig for the fair one year, so my Uncle Craig bought Kenny a little piglet. It was all hellfire and squirmy, and Kenny never worked with it all spring like he was supposed to. The pig was just plain wild when it got big. I snuck out into the barn and covered him from head to toe with lard on the day Kenny had to take him to the fair. He slipped right through Kenny's legs, got loose, and it took half the town to chase him down. Uncle Craig finally caught him, and he had to hold him with his back to his belly and his front feet in the air, just like Bear is holding Jared Michael now. I'm not sure, but I think he would have been more comfortable wrestling that opossum in the garbage.

"See, this is exactly what that crappy piece of shit man left me," she tells me while she pushes her way past me. She extends her arms and snatches Jared Michael from Bear's grasp. I can almost see the relief flood over Bear's paling cheeks. "I got three kids, but I can't pay the rent. He took my car and the one damn credit card I had and racked up a thousand dollars' worth of God-knows-what." She backs up around me, pushes her butt against the door to open it wide. Then she shoves Jared Michael in and closes it behind her. "What did he do this time, rob a bank?"

I look at Bear. He gives an eye roll upward like he's saying, I told you we shouldn't have come here. I think you are crazy, and I have collected enough evidence to have you committed. "Um, I don't think so," I stutter. I look back.

Bear is absolutely no support. He is scratching the back of his neck with his hand, shaking his head back and forth like he knows what I'm going to say, and he can't believe I'm doing it. "You're Ashley, right?" She nods.

"Josh, I mean Johnny, I think he got killed in a fire."

I'm trying to read her eyes. They are staring hard at me. Jared Michael is hitting the door with his hammer. I'm rolling my hand through my hair, nervously pushing it away from my sweaty face.

The trash is wafting to my nostrils, and I'm hoping I don't throw up on her pink flip-flops. "Three years ago. I just found his grave. I—I was married to him too."

"Three years ago," Ashley replies, her eyes working downward, her head shaking slightly from right to left. It is more a tremor than a denial. "Let me see that picture again." I hold it up, and she squints again into Josh's face. "Sweetie, this is Johnny and he ain't dead. You got the wrong guy. He was sitting on my couch six months ago with his feet propped up on my table, drinking a beer, and screaming for me to keep the kids quiet so he could watch some stupid science fiction porn movie. Three years ago, we were making babies on that same couch."

"He was alive six months ago," I repeat, letting the words echo through my mind.

"Yeah, Johnny. You know, nothing would surprise me with him. Listen, you look like I just gutted you with my fist. Maybe you've got the wrong guy, huh?" She pushes back her hair with her hand just like I do and smiles. "My Johnny, he's got a scar on his left butt cheek, can't miss it. He's got this crazy laugh like this—" She throws her head back and lets a roar-like laugh trickle down. "He's got this stupid orange bird thing with wings spreading out on his arm."

"A phoenix," I say.

"I dunno." She lifts her shoulders and throws out her arms like she's preparing to take flight. "It's like a bird with a dragon face. But he drives a white truck. I met him at the diner outside town, Annie's Burgers and Dogs. I waited tables there until I had the kids. *His* kids. He wasn't wearing a wedding band—"

"Crud," I spit it out with a stomp of my foot. I don't know why I turned around and looked at Bear for support. I think he's probably still eyeing the hole in the plywood.

"Maybe not," she says. "It looks like he pulled a fast one on you."

"He married you too?" I ask.

"At the little white Hope Prevails Church in town. Reverend Myers performed the ceremony. It was four years this June. I'm sure he'll be back. He takes off sometimes and doesn't come home for a few months. I can tell him you stopped in. That would freak him out." Ashley giggles. I feel like I'm going to faint.

I'm just staring at Bear, listening to her words zooming past my head like little hornets stopping long enough to sting me as they pass.

"Well, thank you." That's Bear who says it, waves at me. "C'mon, Bejesus." I realize he is digging in his wallet. I'm pushing past him, shoving down his hand. "Not now."

"But she needs money."

"Bear!" I know she is looking earnestly at Bear. I can't see her, but I feel her eyes on my back. He's got a wad of cash in his wallet bigger than the tire on my truck. "Not now. Don't."

"You're not okay, are you?"

No, I'm not okay. But I've been not okay for so long. I'm starting to let it fall off me and onto the floor like a pair of underpants that are too big. Later, we are sitting at the diner outside town at a booth and sipping coffee. I'm tapping my fingers on the table, staring at the white porcelain cup. Bear's still clinging to the little treasure box. He's got it sitting right in front of him, and he keeps opening and closing the little latch and then peering inside.

"I'm obviously not taking this as well as Ashley. It's like matter of fact with her, no big deal. Inside, I am going to explode. I was married to Josh or whatever his name is now for three years."

"The three-year glitch," Bear mumbles to the box. "It used to be the seven-year itch. They say people get sick of each other around the three-year mark now."

"Really?" I spat at him. "Are you my marriage counselor now? *I* didn't have a problem with *him*."

He shrugs. "You're going to stop this now, right?" he asks. I swear I saw his hand come out like he was going to pat mine. He stops and crumples the napkin under my water with his forefinger and thumb instead.

"I'm going to have to stop sometime." I take a ringlet of my hair and wrap it around my finger. It's a bad habit, but one I can't break. I read online that it will increase my chances of split ends. "One of the licenses is from Ohio. I've never been out of West Virginia."

"You've never been out of the state. This state?"

"Don't look at me like I'm strange. I've never had reason to go. Everything I want is right here."

"I would think somebody who laughs while she's hanging over a shard of glass wouldn't want to be cooped up in one state."

"I wasn't laughing."

"Yeah, you were." He sighs. "Bejesus, you—"

"Why do you keep calling me that?"

"Bejesus?" He does that little shrug with his shoulders that goes lazy from left to right. "I don't know. You scare the bejesus out of me."

"Seriously?" I say flatly.

"You need more refills?" the waitress slips by in skinny jeggings and a tight T-shirt. She has enormous boobs. I know because Bear keeps getting this funny little smirk on his face when she leans over to fill his coffee. He's up to five cups.

"I'll take a piece of pie," Bear says. Then he stops and looks at me before his eyes turn to the waitress. "Change that pie to a salad."

She's cute with a button nose and big blue eyes. She keeps smiling at Bear and forgetting to give me refills. It's okay. She'll be back in five minutes to flirt with him again. "I'll take a piece of apple pie," I tell her. I turn to Bear to let him know his eyes are trying desperately not to lounge on her boobs again. I smile slyly. "I haven't had as many cups of coffee as you."

He waits until she leaves and leans in. "Listen, that's not my fault. She keeps refilling it."

"Then don't slug it down like it's the last cup of cold water on earth. She won't come back."

"Come on, Brandy, she puts those babies inches from my face."

"Those *babies*," I say with a funny twist to my words. "You're as bad as Kenny. I swear, sometimes you guys think I'm a dude." Bear shrugs. "Listen, I'm just saying," I go on. "And I'm not making thirty restroom stops on the way back so you can get your porn on in this old diner." I smile and hold my hands out.

I know he doesn't get it. Bear is as pretty as the piece of pie the waitress gives me. When we walk in anywhere, women crane their necks to see around me to get a sweet sip of him. Bear isn't so big anymore. He's more muscular than chub. He doesn't see it, I suppose. He's not used to women's heads turning when he walks in the door.

Bear ignores me, tugs out his phone, and starts tapping it. "I'm not being rude," he tells me. "I'm doing what you said. I am writing down everything I eat on my phone notes. Later, I transfer it to paper. I can't lug around that 'clean slate' theme book. People stare at me."

He makes me smile. I realize it isn't just the thought he's using my idea and sticking with it. He doesn't know that I've got twenty-five of those damn theme books partially started, never finished. I realize he hasn't wholly irked me with an insult since he got into the truck. He's trying hard to be friendly and polite.

"Yeah, I can see the difference. You look different every time I see you. I have to adjust each time." I shove the hair from my face. "Don't forget to add your workout in the little grocery store, dragging me out of the depths of hell."

Suddenly, he puts down the phone and pokes his finger at the treasure box. "My dad used to get me one of these every time he went on vacation." Bear shifts in his seat. I don't understand why he doesn't tell me much about himself. I don't ask him, though, considering I do my best not to tell anyone about my mama. "He actually even kept sending them even when I outgrew them every year until, well, you know last year when he—"

"Died," I say softly for him.

"Yeah. He'd put some little treasure inside. When I got a little older, he put in money. One time, he bought a real gold doubloon from a shipwreck."

"Do you believe in ghosts?" I ask him. I'm serious. I mean, what are the odds a kid left a treasure box under the counter in the grocery store?

"I don't know," he says, looking up at me. "I'd like to right now. I'm just not sure what a marble would mean. Every time he sent something, the contents had some meaning between us."

"Maybe he's giving you back some of the marbles you lost— haha," I clown around, but my voice is even-toned. "You know, you lost your marbles?" Bear is learning how to make stink-eye. He does it at me, holding a scalding glare until he laughs. I tell him that he makes me feel better. We leave, and, surprise, Bear has to go to the restroom before we even get to the door.

I'm standing there rocking back and forth on my heels. The waitress walks up, holding a fifty-dollar bill and flapping it in the air. "Your boyfriend left this on the table."

"I think he meant to leave it," I tell her. I don't tell her why. I think she knows. Seven cups of coffee and a fifty-dollar tip probably cost him less than the X-rated movie he'd have to rent to get the same thrill he had looking down her shirt. "And he's not my boyfriend."

"Really."

When Bear and I get to my truck, I toss him the piece of paper the waitress gave me. It is one of the little tear-off guest check sheets she carried in her pocket. It has her phone number on it and two little scraggly hearts.

"What's this?"

"Her name is Lilly. The waitress, that is," I tell him. "She said to call her. She gets off at six."

"You're a better wingman than Gabe." Bear is grinning while he stares at the paper.

"Gabe is the guy that sat down next to me and called me fresh and then called me wicked because he said I wasn't nice to you." I wait for Bear to nod at my question.

"I wasn't trying to pick you up at the bar. He was until he thought you had a crap load of kids and wanted more than a one-night stand—"

"Then why'd *you* keep looking at me?" I'm teasing him. I don't think he even saw me that night. He was too busy avoiding Mama's lap dances on his chest.

"I dunno. If I was, it wasn't because I wanted to pick you up. You're not my type. I like the skinny blondes with something to show when they pour my coffee. I suppose you were the only fresh meat there under thirty. Better to look at you than the dirty bathroom door."

Chapter –13
Martha Hershberger

"Well, you sure can pick 'em."

That's Martha Hershberger talking. We are walking through the campus at Fairview State Community College. The college isn't huge. I can walk to all my classes within ten minutes. There are twenty-one buildings, all within a few blocks. Martha and I have many of the same classes together, so we walk from one to the next, lugging our backpacks against the rain, snow, or unbearable sunshine. Today, it is a misty sprinkle under gray-black clouds.

Martha grew up in Owl Hollow, only a few miles from Fire Mountain. Her dad is Born Again Christian, and her mama is Amish. However, I don't think she is either. She dyes her hair pitch black and adds purple highlights at the bottom. She wears pink contacts in her fist-size eyes. She puts on the same Amish baby blue dress and leather shoes daily and plops a little white bonnet on her head. She is only five feet tall and skinny, and Martha even has to look up at little me with the wind blowing my words away.

"My family allows me to experiment until I join the church," she told me once. "I've got to be honest. I'm torn. I don't want to hurt anybody's feelings. I'm probably going to be Born Again Amish forever." Martha told me her mama and daddy have a sizeable organic mushroom farm in Owl Hollow. She is the oldest, so her daddy sent her to college to learn how to manage the property.

She told me that she had gotten baptized twenty-six times because she kept running away to some boyfriend's house in Ohio. She said she would walk until she got to a creek or stream, then swim across bare-naked with her clothes held out of the water. She even did this along the Ohio River. This is another one of the reasons we walk together. She is trying to teach me to swim for the Redneck Run. I told her what Bear had said about me in the restaurant for chit-chat. "Uh huh, right?" I declare. "I'm not crazy then?"

"No." She walks with stomping steps like she is moving through tall grass. "You should pray for him."

"I should," I agree. "But Bear attends church every Sunday, Tuesday, and Thursday because he directs the choir. He has lots of people praying for him already."

"Maybe it isn't working because they aren't praying for him to be a better person. Maybe they don't know him like you do, and they toss out random prayers. You know," she says. "They probably just ask that he doesn't get sick or his crops grow well. He needs you to pray to make him a better person."

But Martha makes me believe that Bear has not shown his churchy friends his mean side, so they don't know to say prayers to make him nicer. I nod but find it difficult to believe God would listen to me over everybody attending church. Besides, I'm just holiday devout. I'm just not a praying kind of person and so I have changed the subject to talking about classes. We have this job fair today. I don't want to go. Beverly's Diner called and needed a waitress, but I had to turn it down. Attending the fair is part of our grade. We must plop down our resumes and talk to different places about the jobs they offer. Most aren't hiring. They are just there to support the college or to boost their clout with local tourism. I don't have a lot of faith in them. The big ones, like the Boar Mountain Resort, don't even bother to come.

It doesn't matter anyway. I'm not in the running for any of these jobs. I've got another school semester to go before I can get my degree. Besides, the primary instructor doesn't even know I exist, and I've been here for three years. I think I'm like one of those faded yellow buttercups on old wallpaper nearly hidden behind the couch, blending into the background. I know I'm nothing special, not too pretty, not exceptionally bright. My grades are Bs. I barely scrape by in chemistry and math. Nobody would notice if I sat on a bench with my clothes off for three days. I'm constantly reminded of that whenever I go into his classes. My professor will point something out to one girl, then turn and suggest something to another. He singles everyone out, one at a time, ensuring they each get a sprinkling of attention. I don't even warrant getting yelled at when I'm the only one with my phone out texting instead of listening to him. Everybody else, he gives them holy hell. His name is Dean Popovich. Everyone calls him Professor D. He's the one I've talked to about a couple of people I have designed meal plans for.

Pops went gluten-free last year, and my cousin Kenny's daddy has diabetes. My aunt, Jenny, is vegetarian and refused to eat anything at the table until last Thanksgiving when I made her fake turkey and fake gravy. I also asked him about Bear and how to plan some meals for him. I didn't tell him who it was. I only told him it was a friend. He didn't suggest much; he just gave me the names of some books that might help. Then, when I saw Bear losing weight, I told him what I'd done. He just nodded his head. Then he gave me a funny look and turned to talk to someone else. I was embarrassed and thought maybe I'd repeated something stupid. I didn't think much of it until the job fair.

Before the fair, a couple of restaurants came into one of my culinary classes, and the owners gave a speech. They are business owners and could be better at giving speeches, so they are boring. This is how much my instructor doesn't care what I'm doing. He plops down next to me, and even while I poke on my phone and scoot around my seat, he doesn't criticize me. It doesn't matter. I am more worried about getting my tuition payment in next week. I still need to add two hundred dollars to the bundle of money in the old coffee can on Pops' bookshelf to pay for next semester. I should be working at Beverly's right now and skipping the class. Nobody would know I'm missing. Well, not entirely, because I would know I wasn't there—I can't skip.

"I thought of you when I heard about this place."

I am in mid-text on my phone to Pops, asking him if he's still mad at me. He hasn't talked to me in the three days since he found the weed in the ashtray. I think my instructor is talking to someone else, but I look up at him, nonetheless. He is looking at me, pointing a knuckle toward the lecture podium. I follow with my eyes, letting them fall on the carpeted stage below.

Most of the restaurant owners coming in are wearing suits and ties. The one sitting on a bar stool in the front of the room isn't. He's got long hair, and it looks a bit uncombed. He is wearing a T-shirt, jeans, and a beanie. He talks about this little resort at Salt Springs, where his parents started as a bed and breakfast forty years ago. Now he's the owner, making it bigger and better. What caught my ear was that his restaurant catered to customers with special eating needs who want to have a vacation and still maintain their diet.

"You— thought about me?" It sounded stupid when I said it. The instructor just nodded.

"You are one of my students, aren't you?" he whispers with a funny smile.

"Yes. I didn't think you even saw me sitting here."

"Of course I have. Why would I not?"

"No, I figured it was because I was on the tuition payment plan. I didn't matter."

"I don't know who pays and who doesn't. The administration doesn't give us that information." He is dipping his head down, trying to whisper low beneath his breath. "I know you pulled me out of the ditch last winter in your little truck when we had that ice storm. Everybody else just went flying on by. On your term paper, you wrote a damn good essay on diabetic meal planning with recipes because you had an aunt or uncle that had it. Every time I turn around, you're picking up somebody's pencil when they dropped it or making them smile when they had a bad day. Just listen. And—" he holds out his voice. "You're the one that didn't show up the day we did the speeches and food tasting."

"I—was sick."

"It is more than half your grade. You're not going to pass without it."

I don't say anything more; I just put down my phone and listen. Later, I take an old sleeping bag outside behind Pops' house, lay it down, and stare up at the stars. Pops was still mad at me when I got home two hours earlier. I can't stand when he doesn't talk to me. It is almost worse than if he raised a fist to me. When I entered the house, he made an excuse to go to his barn. He has a bunch of friends and some of his cousins over, and they all stare at me with indignant gazes, talking low like someone died.

It is my punishment because they think I will turn out like Mama now. One joint in an ashtray, and I'm the one dancing drunk at the bars. I'm so mad at Kenny. It had to be him who left it there. Uncle Craig is always saying: *that boy just ain't right*. Maybe he's right. I laid into him in the kitchen in a yelling-whisper. I knew he'd deny it. He didn't want the angry glares at him. I hear a rustling in the tall grass just outside the area cleared for the lawn. It isn't Pops' dog.

He's tied to the shed and baying at the wind on the other side of the house. Sometimes, Kenny comes out and tries to scare me while I've got my earplugs in and I'm staring at the stars. I narrow my gaze in the black and try to pick out any shadows that move.

There is something by an old oak tree. I can barely make it out at first. I sit up and twist my head to ensure my eyes aren't playing tricks on me. Then, with a shuddering startle, I can see an entire body blending into the tree bark. It is a grown man with legs slightly splayed. His hair is wild. I can see it darker than the ooze behind him.

"Crazy Willie," I whisper his name. Strangely, although my heart is pumping hard, I'm not terrified enough to scream. I think maybe he has come to murder me for cutting through his property again. I've seen him in town at night when I'm home, but I've never known him to come to Pops' property. Never. But that's expected. He doesn't like folks. He's the closest thing to a hermit anybody's ever known.

I swallow hard. I'm terrified to move from my sitting position. I finally muster the courage to lick my lips and clear my throat. "Crazy Willie?" I ask the air. I don't hear his hellhounds. Maybe he's come to drag me off into the woods, tie me up in his bed, and make me his wife.

He moves. It is slight at first. "Don't scream," his gruff voice growls. I don't think I could even if I wanted to yell. I imagine him putting his old dirty hand over my mouth and then grunting over top of me. Then, the next thing I knew, he was hovering over top of me, his body shadowing the light from the round moon, so I was utterly consumed by his black.

"I need some things from town," he grumbles. There is no hand reaching for my mouth. I nod my head slowly up and down. "You can drop them off on your way past my cabin."

"Okay."

He thrusts something into my hand. I take it, and it is a crumpled piece of a used mailing envelope and three one-dollar bills. Even in the dark, I can see the envelope has scribbled writing on it. It looks like something a six-year-old would print. "That's what I need."

I don't tell him that three dollars is not enough to pay for all these groceries. It is just all that he's got. I say: "I'll get them for you."

He stares at me for a minute, ogling him. My heart is still racing even when he is consumed by the thick layer of wood as quickly as he came. I'm too nervous now to put on my music. I am left listening to the sound of laughter coming from the house and staring at the envelope before I fold it carefully and push it into the back pocket of my jeans with his money.

"Hey, Brandy."

I think I shoot six feet into the air. I know I gasp a high-pitched gulp of misty air when I hear Bear's voice behind me.

"Cripes, Bear, you nearly scared the crap out of me. Literally."

I am shaking. I don't know what I am thinking. Maybe I believe Crazy Willie is coming in for the kill. I am sitting with my arms behind me. I scoot a little to see Bear outlined against the porch light. Another silhouette is beside him, smaller and wavering.

"I'm sorry. Gabe and I were bored. We thought we'd stop by."

Well, this is something new. I share my gaze with the two shadows behind me. "It's pretty boring here. I'm just sitting here watching the stars. I've taken boredom to a whole new level."

"That's not quite the sense expressed in the living room right now." Bear walks up and sits down next to me. He lounges back with his arms around his knees. He smells like the moonshine I saw someone passing around in a little Ball Mason Jar earlier. I heard Kenny telling Pops that he and his daddy made some in their garage last week. Pops took a sip and said it tasted like gasoline. "Talk is there's a storm brewing." He waves Gabe over, and I scoot across the sleeping bag so they can sit on it instead of on the dewy ground.

"I promise I won't wrestle you to the ground like my mama," I tell Gabe. "Unless you call me a wicked witch again."

"Ha ha," Gabe answers. "I'm sorry. I was a bit drunk that night."

I'm not sure if Bear would have cared right then or not if his butt got damp from the wet. He is wavering. If I didn't know better, I would say he is almost dead drunk.

"The atmosphere is a bit tense. World War III is being played out between three warring countries." Gabe doesn't have the usual awkward stance of a preppy fish accustomed to a swanky tank in the city being flopped to one of the cheap glass jars you get at the fair when winning a gold fish. He must have been sipping the 'shine too.

Bear's friend lays back, puts his arms behind his head, and relaxes. He's designer red-haired, skinny, and city boy pretty like Bear. Maybe I'm the one who should feel awkward in my country girl tank top and old jean shorts. It wouldn't matter. The two men beside me are probably seeing three of me.

"It did take the attention off two city boys crashing their redneck party, though, I would presume," I sigh. "Oh, God, I wish they would let this rest."

"Then don't smoke weed." Gabe makes it sound easy.

"I've never smoked weed," I groan. "It was my idiot cousin who smoked a joint in the house when nobody was at home. I got blamed for it. And I can't tell my Pops about it because if I do, Kenny will get the crap beat out of him by his daddy. Now I'm the weed-smoking mirror of my mama. Pops won't talk to me because I'm stubborn, willful, and turning out like her."

"Ah, family drama," Bear says. He starts to lean back like there's something to rest his back. Then he laughs and catches himself.

"You've had your fair share." Gabe laughs at Bear while he wavers to the left. "You wanted to taste moonshine for the first time. Now you did. Whoa, right?"

"Yeah, I'm sure Brandy doesn't want to hear more." Bear reaches into his pocket, pulls something out, and thrusts it toward me in his fingers. "Here, I got you something." I don't move for a second, and his hand wavers there. "Please take it."

I reach out and try to read his face. I can't in the moonlight. There is a dark side and a light side caught in the shadows of the sky. "Is this for heartlessly comparing me to the bathroom door?" Gabe laughs out loud. He obviously knows what I'm talking about. It is an envelope, and I open it up and peer inside. There's some cash or credit card inside. "What is this?" I take it out and hold it in front of me.

"It's a thousand bucks. Go buy something." Bear sounds smug, like it is a bandage that will cure the wound he stabbed into my flesh at the diner.

"This is a Band-Aid to heal the sword you stuck in my gut?"

"A thousand-dollar one," Gabe snickers. "I'd take it. He likes giving money away. Especially when he's drunk."

Gabe's words are mean, just offhand about it, like a thousand dollars isn't anything more than a two-dollar beer he just handed me. "I don't want it," I tell him. "Do you not realize you insulted me by assuming money will buy self-respect? Why don't you tell me you're sorry. It's free." I push the card back toward Bear. He shrugs and takes it. I should know better than to try to reason with a drunk. They either get sad, slap-happy, or downright mean when I'm sitting there in the Crazy Kettle sober and sipping my ginger ale, and they come up to flirt with me.

"Suit yourself."

I wait for him to apologize. It seems the simplest solution. Bear says nothing and tucks the card back into his wallet.

"So, are you going to tell me you are sorry?"

"That would imply I was wrong."

"You *were* wrong. You were mean and impolite. Just because you have money doesn't mean you can be shitty to people."

"It kind of does," Bear answers. "It got me laid the other night by Lilly, who works at that diner. Everybody loves you when you've got money, Brandy. It's fun to watch them begging with their hand out." Bear is drunker than I thought. "You should have seen what she would do just because I took her to a nice restaurant and bought her bracelet."

"Is that what you're expecting from me?" I spit out hotly. Mama's temper inside me flares. If Pops was sitting here with us, he would tell me to walk away before I say something I'm sorry about later. But Pops isn't here.

"You just had your hand out, didn't you."

Holy shit. I'm listening to Bear, thinking I'm not hearing what is coming from his mouth. Maybe it is a good idea that he doesn't talk much about himself when we hang out. Now, my little refuge beneath the stars and away from the inside of the house is becoming a prison.

He reaches out. I think he is trying to poke me in the side. I push my hands up and lean back. He misses the mark. I push myself to my feet and slap my hands together to get the little bits of grass from my fingers.

"You are drunk and saying things I know you're going to regret tomorrow. I'm going to ask you politely just once to leave," I growl between my teeth. Bear doesn't say anything; he looks over at Gabe. I think he is rolling his eyes. "If you don't, I am going to go inside and get my Pops' double barrel shotgun, and I'm going to start shooting at you. I might miss. I might not. You would be an easy target right now because I don't even think you can hardly crawl. I will tell you this. You have no right to disrespect me. You have no right to treat me like a whore who will accept payment for being verbally screwed. And if you ever, ever imply I am anything short of a vestal virgin as far as you are concerned, I will grab you by the balls, swing you around until you scream like a two-year-old girl, and turn you into a eunuch."

"Ouch." That's Gabe. "She said that in big kid words." He seems to be listening. He gets up and nods toward the front of the house where they are parked. "Come on. I think she's made her point."

Bear doesn't say anything. I want to cry. I've been hanging out with him for almost five months, thinking he's something short of a chubby superhero. Now I find out he's nothing but the wealthy villain in every grocery store comic book.

"Pops, those two boys are too drunk to drive." I am leaning against the door frame in the kitchen. Pops is sitting at the table playing poker. He stops long enough to glare at me. Everybody is looking from him to me, eager anticipation in their eyes, waiting for the fireworks to explode. I don't think he is going to talk. He does, but his lip makes a subtle twitch.

"You want me to try and stop two grown boys from leaving that I never invited in the first place? They are your friends. You take them home." He stares at me hard.

"Alright." I nod my head. I don't want to go back out there and swallow my pride. However, I don't want them to wrap their truck around a tree on the way down the slippery gravel road, either. I turn, thinking that maybe by the time I get to the front door, I'll hear the rumble of the truck already leaving. If they die, it will be off my shoulders.

"Baby, you know you are only as good as the company you keep," Pops says. He tells me this like it will solve all of life's problems.

"They came here. I didn't bring them in," I tell him. Then I realize what he is implying. He thinks I was probably partying with them the night he found the weed. It just isn't worth another fight. "Yeah, okay. I'll take care of it."

I'm almost to the front door when Pops, Kenny, and Uncle Craig push past me. "Stay here." Pops points to the front porch. They smell like cigars. Kenny's still giving me the stink eye every time I see him. It occurs to me that maybe it wasn't Kenny at all smoking the dope. Perhaps it was Gabe and Bear. Maybe they entered Pops' house and slipped the key out from under the mat at the front door. I'm almost sure of it when Kenny glares at me again and shoves me with his shoulder. I can't imagine why he's mad at me because I never told Pops it might be him.

I stand on the porch and hear talking in the drive. I wait there an eternity. Almost an hour and a half later, Pops comes barreling up the drive in his truck. Kenny and my uncle get out first. They putter around a minute by the truck. It is because they know Pops is going to yell at me.

"Did you get them home okay?" I ask him when he's mainly across the lawn. My voice is hoarse and scratchy. I see Kenny coming up behind him. He's got the ha-ha-Brandy's-gonna-get-hell look on his half-smirking lips.

"They had somebody meet us at the bottom of the mountain at that Holy Trinity Church you go to next to the New Alliance Quick Stop." Kenny says, looking at Pops, who looks hard as coffin nails at me.

"It was Preacher Murphy that met us." Pops has stopped at the bottom of the steps. I am leaning against the rail.

"Preacher Murphy?"

"Did you know that red-haired boy is one of his sons, Brandy?" Pops comes up the steps, two at a time. He pauses right next to me. It's the closest thing to saying he's ashamed of me, the look he gives me with his jaws working hard. "You're going to give us a bad name, girl. What were you thinking bringing those boys up here, letting them get drunk, disappearing off in the woods with them."

"Pops, they were here before I knew they were drinking. I was out looking at the stars. Besides, they are grown men. I can't make decisions for them."

"Yeah, that's what I'm worried about."

I realize what he is implying. Again, what Mama has done never fails to haunt me. "I don't do that."

"Uh huh," That's his uh-huh that tells me he thinks I'm lying. "You're playing with fire, and it ain't the happy fire that lights a birthday candle. It's the scary kind that burns down a house, baby girl. I told those two they weren't welcome here anymore."

I stand there feeling slighted, wishing I could tell him everything I do is to make him proud, even if I will never admit it, and he will never understand it. College. The Redneck Run. Making sure Mama makes it safely home from the bar on Friday nights. I know he took me in, so I didn't rot in that trailer park with a drunk mama.

"Maybe you should take some time off that college stuff you do. It's not working. Quit throwing money away at something that's no good. Maybe, Brandy, you should focus on finding some nice man and settle down like a normal girl."

"Normal girls go to college, Pops." Maybe not in his book because I know he doesn't get it because nobody in his family ever went to college and hardly got through high school. I think he believes I go and smoke pot there and sleep with all the guys. "You have to go to college to get a good job nowadays."

"Like cleaning the bathroom stalls at Beverly's," Kenny snorts. Pops narrows his eyes at the remark.

"I just think it would be for the better," he says. "You can stay here. We'll talk to your mama about us taking Kaylee in until she gets better."

I stand there, feeling the wooden porch rail on my fingers. It is old and has little slivers sticking up that scratch my palm. I don't know how to answer Pops. I don't want to throw it all away. "I'm not Mama," I whisper. "I want to be better than her. Pops, I want to finish college."

"You want to be better than your own mama," Pops chews on the words. "Well, then, do something for everybody else, not just you."

Chapter –14
A little short on friends

I have two bags. One is a large brown paper bag filled with four rolls of toilet paper, two packs of menthol cigarettes, honey ham lunch meat, a loaf of bread, mustard, and a small plastic jar of pickles. I whistle and toss the items at Crazy Willie's front porch from his clothesline out front because as soon as he sees me running along his muddy driveway, he still sends his hellhounds chasing me.

It wouldn't bother me much if I didn't stay up all night making him beef jerky snacks with fresh apples and oranges. He looks tired, and he's undoubtedly moody. I don't think he's getting enough fruit. This is the second smaller bag. The dogs tear into that one like they haven't eaten in years, ripping at each other's throats and rolling around in the muck. Willie clips another grocery list and three dollars onto the clothesline four days later. When I bring the bags, I fill a third with leftovers from last night's dinner and let it fly at the dogs. I reached the bottom of Fire Mountain, under the chain-link fence near the Quick Stop gas station, and then to the other side of the highway without getting my rear nipped once.

I stopped at the Quick Stop and bought a popsicle in the freezer section. I set it down on the wooden counter and forked out the one dollar and fifty-five cents to pay for it. Standing at the register, Buddy Webber looks at me and shakes his head. "It's all paid for."

"But you didn't take my money," I reply while he shoves my money back at me.

"A guy came in and gave me fifty bucks if I told you that he said he was sorry. He said anything you want is paid for."

"Was it a tall guy six and a half feet high, short red-brown hair with whiskers on his chin?" It's tough because now I can't even describe him as chubby. "Oh, he's kind of built like he works out."

"Yeah, Brandy."

"Well," I say, tugging my last dollar from my pocket. I slap it on the counter with the popsicle money. Then I push them both back toward Buddy. "Here's a dollar for you. Tell him I said to screw off. I don't want his money or his apology."

I'm a bit cocky and irritated when I push open the doors and step outside into the misty early morning air. I take my usual route back up the mountain along the highway toward Fire Mountain Road. I walk it for a while so I can lick the popsicle. I'm only three steps off the highway and on our road when I see a flyer on an old tree. I think it is a missing dog poster, so I ease my way to the other side of the road and peek at it.

It is white copy paper clipped onto the tree with an electric staple gun. *I'm SoRRY*. That's what it says. It is Bear's writing. I know it is because I noticed when he fills out his books, he makes the Os smaller than the other letters. I glance up the road while the popsicle melts cherry red along my fingers, down my arm, and almost to my elbow. There are thirty more, one on about every other tree. I try to ignore them going up the incline. I must keep on the road because little rocks and ridged cliffs are everywhere on either side. I stop just short of the gravel turn where High Ridge Road intersects. Something is shiny in the gravel.

I squint in the milky morning air, lean down, and poke at one of the shiny things. It is a little green gemstone, the kind they sell at the gift shops in town for a buck or two a piece, along with little velvet bags to hold them. I take a step back and let my eyes skim across. At the same time, I catch a glimpse of our neighbor's truck barreling around the turn. It's Junior McPherson. He passes me every day while heading for his job at the sewer plant. Today, he careens sideways to miss me like we haven't met at this exact point every day of the year for the last two years. He does his usual horn honk and points a finger at me. I shift to the right to get out of the way, but not before I make out what is written in green gemstones on the road. Of course, I'M SORRY.

The sorries are everywhere Bear knows I go and all the way until Pops' property begins and ends. When I take Millie Piper to visit her husband's grave on Thursday, Bear puts a little Post-it note beside Ivan's grave. When I pass the Holy Trinity Church parking lot, there are three SORRY, SORRY, and SORRY on the church sign board. When I pick up Bobby Reese at Grant's Rehabilitation and Nursing Center, Bobby's laughing because he's got a felt SORRY sewn on a hat. Bear even has one posted on the Fairview State Community College website. I can't imagine what he paid for that.

There are only two places I know that aren't covered. One is the last pew at Holy Trinity, where I had been sitting each Sunday morning since Preacher Murphy gave in and told me I didn't have to worry about singing in the choir because of the fainting incident. I don't go there anymore. I can't imagine what the preacher thinks of me after picking up his son, dead drunk on moonshine, after coming to Pops' house.

The second is my chair next to Josh's ghost on Friday night because I'm sitting here tonight, and I don't see anything remotely reminding me of Bear. I'm also torn. I wonder if Josh is alive and sitting out there somewhere laughing at me. I'm almost inclined to move over to his chair like I am saying that I never sat around with his ghost next to me in the first place, wishing he was here instead. I don't. Instead, I scowl and don't look at Billy. I keep thinking about laying in the bed with his hand up my shirt. He has been flirting with a dark-headed girl who comes up and starts giggling when he smiles at her. She slaps a hand on her lips and then runs back to her chair with her covey of friends. Bear is right. Billy is a jerk.

Holy Hell. I want to go home and stuff myself between the sheets with a bottle of bad wine and a good book. I can't. Mama is here tonight, and I've got to take her home. "Mama, let me take you home." I catch her when she walks past me to go to the bathroom. There are only ten of us, and I'm ready to go. To hell with three years of sitting in this bar on Friday nights.

"Ten more minutes." She is reeling drunk, staggering, and bumping her hip against the barstool. She grabs my arm to stabilize herself. "I'm buying rounds, baby girl. Do you want a drink?"

"How are you buying rounds?" I ask her. Her face is three inches from my own. Her breath reeks of beer and cigarettes. "Where'd you get money? Because yesterday, I took a hundred and thirty dollars of my paycheck down to the rental office to pay your trailer rent."

"I just ran into some cash."

"You just ran into some cash?" I pull back a little. A guy passes and stares at us. "You need to pay your rent if you have cash. If you've got it, I can't afford to pay my tuition and your rent. I can't even buy a pair of new shoes." I point my finger at the worn sandals on my feet. "I'm gluing the doggone soles back on my tennis shoes every morning."

"Then, baby girl, go barefoot like me!" She slips off her shoes and does a little dance, leaving her shoes scattered across the floor. I can only release my hand from her arm and scrub my fingers across my face. She twists and spins like a macabre ballet dancer to the bathroom. I watch her until she disappears behind the slamming door. Last week, she lost her little silver lighter from high school. Said she left it sitting at one of the tables. She got back, and it was gone. I don't wonder why.

"She can't be any worse than my mom," I hear a voice behind me. It has a southern tone; I recognize it as Bear's friend, Gabe. He walks up behind my chair and places his hand on Josh's bar stool as I turn. "Oh, you think you've got the monopoly on crazy parents?" He laughs. "Oh, no. My mom's the one that stands up front in the choir right by the microphone." He opens his eyes wide. They look like colossal baby blue marbles. "She can't sing a note to keep herself alive. I mean, she sounds like a dying cat squalling. Everything's all screeches and yowls. But because she's the minister's wife, everybody pretends like she's been brought down straight from heaven with an angel's voice. Last week, she forgot the words for Amazing Grace and ad-libbed them in front of the congregation. I think she even added some words from the National Anthem and an old Aerosmith song by the time she was done. I thought Beau would fall off that little stand they put up for him to direct. He didn't know what to do, and I'm sitting in the front row, tears coming out of my eyes, falling down laughing."

"Please, go away." I'm torn between running after Mama into the bathroom, getting up, and leaving her here. "Please don't come around me. My pops is hot about you guys getting drunk and then having to meet your dad. Somebody will see you talking to me, and they will tell him." Gabe isn't coming close; he's wavering between the chair and me. I glance up at Billy. He is eyeing the clock. I shake my head. I've got no clue how to get rid of Gabe. He knows me enough, and I can't lie my way out of getting him to leave.

"I'm not sitting down if that's what you're worried about." He sticks his hands in his pockets. I realize he is in a suit and pleated Sunday pants. His tie is long gone, and his button-up shirt is unbuttoned at the top. He seems to take note that I notice his clothes. Gabe rocks on his feet and looks down at his pants.

"We had a church dinner this evening."

"Does your daddy know you're here tonight?" I waggle my finger in the air above us. "At a bar."

"I hope not. He wasn't really thrilled to drag us home the other night." He looks over my shoulder. I don't follow because I assume Billy is not far away. "I was supposed to get here an hour earlier and before you got here to put this on your chair." Gabe holds up another envelope into the air. "I think my mom knew I was up to something. I lost my job in Cincinnati and needed a place to land for a while. She's been all up in my face. It is suffocating." I glance up at Billy. He appears fascinated at what he can see but not hear. "Regardless, take this. Bear wants you to have it."

"Oh, no," I push my hands before me. "Just go away. Please don't stand in a bar with everybody looking and hand me an envelope. Good God." That's all I need, Big Don coming up here and arresting me for prostitution. "Period. Tell Bear to leave me alone. I don't want anything to do with him or you. My Pops wants me to quit school because of you two going home drunk. He says you're a bad influence, and I should focus on —" I stop. I don't know why I'm telling Gabe this. "I don't like Bear, and I don't like you. Just leave."

"Only if you open this and look inside."

I breathe in, breathe out. I roll my eyes around and take in a couple faces around the bar, lapping up what they see but cannot hear, like kittens licking the bottom of a bowl of warm milk. I warily snatch the envelope from Gabe's fingers and give him one last glower. "If I open this, you will leave me alone?"

"If you want me to, I will." He stops. Maybe he realized that the massive sum of money inside the envelope would not change my mind. He looks up at the ceiling and bites on his lip. "Brandy, I don't particularly like you either." Gabe laughs softly and leans into me. "You can be backward and caustic. For God's sake, it is downright weird that you sit here at the bar waiting for some dude who will never appear. I think you like sitting there turning guys down repeatedly. Then, you don't have to put up with them being human and making mistakes. But for some damn reason, Bear's taken a shine to both of us. And you have—I wish I didn't have to say this— you've changed him. And it isn't because he's handing you money. So now, I'm seeing you in a whole new light."

"Hey, sweet thing, I'm buying tonight. What can I get for ya'? Mama swoops past again and gives Gabe a wink. I realize I've got the envelope in my hand.

"No, thank you, ma'am." Gabe shakes his head.

"Mama, go away." I wave a hand, then look at Gabe. I feel like I am opening Pandora's Box and letting all the evils spill out into my world. Still, I open the flap and peer inside.

"There's nothing in here."

Gabe shrugs. "He said you'd get it."

"I—I don't."

"What is it?"

"Nothing."

Gabe leans over. I turned the envelope so he could see inside. Nothing. He runs his hand through his hair. "You did get mad because he was giving you money to be his friend."

"Has he ever done that to you?"

"Yeah, all the time. I'm like you. I ignore it." Gabe looks toward the door again. "Listen, I've got to get home before my mom realizes I'm here tonight. I know. I'm way too old to worry about how she sees me. Do you want me to tell Beau anything?"

"I'm not sure. My pops doesn't think it is a good idea you two come around. I don't think it is a good idea."

"Yeah, well, that makes three of us whose parents don't want us hanging around," he says. "But sometimes, everybody else just doesn't get it. I understand. Okay, I'll let Beau know."

He starts to leave. I reach out and snatch Gabe's sleeve. "Was it you two who smoked the weed at my pops?"

"Weed? No way. I have a beer once in a while, but that's it. I've got a million people from Dad's congregation spying on everything I do. So, no way." Gabe shakes his head back and forth. "I thought you said your cousin did it."

"I don't think so," I say. He looks like he's telling the truth. Nothing in his eyes tells me he might be trying to hide a lie. Then again, I married Josh. He looked me straight in the eyes two nights before he vanished and told me he'd never let me go. Aw, crap. Here it comes, the flood of memories pouring into my mind that would be better off forgotten.

I remember. I remember Josh standing there above me while I still lay in the bed with the old torn sheet tucked up to my chin. He was there, all skinny and sexy, putting back on his ripped jeans. Josh didn't have his shirt on, and he dipped his head to his right to get the hair out of his eyes. He just stopped when he'd pulled his pants up to his waist, zipper still undone, showing his belly. Sexy. He was so damn sexy. He bent down then and kissed me tenderly on the forehead, one hand on my cheek. God, baby, how do you do those things you do? There ain't nobody else I'd be with but you. Nobody.

"Nobody," I say the word out loud and realize it is too late. Gabe furrows his brow.

"So that's *no*?" He is looking down at my fingers, still clinging to his sleeve. He doesn't look mad, just confused. I release it and take a step back. "You're sure?"

"Tell Beau I don't usually give second chances, but I'm short on friends right now. I'll text him. We can be a threesome." As soon as I say it, my hand slaps over my mouth. My face is hot and red with embarrassment. "I didn't mean it that way."

But Gabe thinks this is hilarious and leans over to belt out a loud laugh. He points a finger at me and starts to leave. "I'll tell Bear that. He'll think it's sexy."

"If you do, Gabe Murphy," I tell his back. "We will have words."

I'm driving up the main highway about twenty minutes before the turnoff to Fire Mountain Road. I see a banged-up truck sideways in the ditch along the brim, facing where I am heading. I know the truck. It is big and orange and belongs to Lizzy Devereauxs. Against my better judgment, I pulled up beside it to see if there was anyone inside. I can see a shadow near the rear. I know it is Crystal Devereauxs even before I back up beside her and roll down the window. I call out: "You need help?"

"I got to get my truck out of the ditch before Big Don comes." She looks at me with no expression. "I don't want to go to jail. My plates and license are expired. I got beer on my breath, and Mama left a big old joint in the ashtray. The truck smells like a 1970s rock concert, and some old lady is driving past. She looked too scared to get out. I know she called the cops. I saw her using the phone."

"You got a rope or something I can tow you out?" I ask her.

She nods. "I got a battery charger we can wrap around your bumper and mine." We wrap the charger around our bumpers, and I drag her truck out of the ditch. There's no thank you. Nothing. She unwraps the cord, tosses it in the back of her truck, and takes off in a spray of dirt. I realize I better take off before Big Don thinks it was me in the ditch.

Chapter –15
Then the lights go out

It is two in the morning. I know this because I can barely see a black plastic clock radio on the floor six inches from my face. The clock is sideways. It is blasting and blinking out red numbers: **2:00. 2:00. 2.00**. It is in battery mode because the connected cord just got ripped out of the electric socket when I tripped on it in the dark, coming through the bathroom door.

The batteries must be old because I can see the numbers fading away. I'm begging the staticky country music that turned on when it fell doesn't turn off. This terrifies me. He will hear me trying to use my fingernails to peel up a board where I've pulled the dingy linoleum from the floor beneath the small bathroom vanity sink in the trailer. He will hear me breathing, hear Kaylee sobbing quietly underneath my elbow. Then we die. I don't want to die. "You've got to do this, you hear me?" I am whispering to Kaylee. "You can do it. I'm making a little hole in the floor for you." She stares at me.

"Kaylee, Kaylee, Kaylee," a man's voice calls from the other room. He's in the hallway of Mama's trailer. "Tell John John where you're at." I kneel on the mildewed carpet, listening to his stocking feet pad down the hallway. My bottom lip is bleeding. It tastes salty and warm and makes me want to gag. I swipe it away with my knuckle.

I know there is a hole here. When I was three, a pipe broke underneath the trailer connected to the sink. Mama used a hammer to break three boards out and wrap some duct tape around the crack in the PVC pipe. Then, after her fix, she just laid a couple of busted boards she found out in the trash on top and half-ass hammered them on top. Sometimes, the feral cats in the trailer park would hide under our trailer when it was cold. I could hear them meowing, and I'd go and peer down through the cracks with a flashlight to see them. "Kaylee, come on, baby," the man coos. "I'll give you candy."

His voice makes me shiver. It is high-pitched for a man. "Don't answer him," I tell her. "He doesn't have candy."

"I know," Kaylee whisper-sobs.

"Come on, Brandy, I won't hurt you." His voice cracks when he tries to sound gentle and sweet. I should get up, but I've got nothing left in me to do so. My nose is bleeding, and my left eye is already swelling shut. He's kicked me, hit me, thrown me. I smell mildewed carpet and think that this will be the last smell on earth I will have before he kills me. *Kills us.* But he's going to have to kill me before he gets to my little sister.

"Oh, did I hear something?" John John's voice slips down the hallway. I know he knows where we are. His fingernails are scratching and grating squeamishly slow and bit by bit along the wood paneling, getting closer and closer. He is just toying with me. He bangs the wood hard with his fist. I jump and wince.

"Oh, Brandy, where are you?" his voice says singsong. I wonder where Mama is. She is long gone.

Pop! I feel one board come loose. Kaylee sniffs hard. She is still wearing a silver plastic tiara with tiny little fake diamonds on her head that Pops got her at the New Alliance Dollar Store. I don't know how Kaylee managed to keep it on when John John kicked her with his stockinged foot. I believe my little sister pushed her hands up to shield that stupid little tiara instead of protecting her face because her nose was bleeding too. I suppose she's like me. She loves Pops and wants to please him, and it's like a little piece of him keeping her company while she's scared. Kaylee keeps reaching up to ensure it is there in the same way I snatch at my ballcap.

"Hush now, baby," I whisper. "You've got to be quiet." It doesn't sound like me. "I'm going to pull up these boards, and you'll crawl out. It is dark. But you can see where Mama's porch is, and you *must* crawl toward it. You hear me?"

"Yes," she murmurs. "I don't want to."

"You *have to*. Then you run to Little Pete's house. You'll see him looking out the window. He'll see you, alright?" My words are shaky. But I know Little Pete is waiting for me to leave. He will be standing next to his window, looking out. He watched me go in. He won't leave until I start my truck, give him a thumbs up, and pull off. I know that his brain is a little slow to get started, but he remembers when I lived here. He remembers me banging on his window and giving him the thumbs-up every time I went to work at three in the morning.

It was our thing. The night me and Josh's trailer caught on fire, he was waiting there for me. When he saw the flames in the window and realized I hadn't left, he told his mama and saved my life. Little Pete takes great pride in that and continues our tradition when I come to my mama's and drop her off on Friday nights. I'm begging in my mind, tonight won't be different. "Oh, looky here." John John's feminine voice matches his long, greasy hair and too-long chin. "I've found a door open."

It is the only door left in Mama's trailer that is still intact. John John is Mama's boyfriend, and he has used my body to knock down two others straight from the hinges. I think he might have broken one of my ribs. My shoulder hurts, my head hurts, and my tummy is nearly scraped raw because he dragged me across the top of one bedroom door to bring me back out.

"Time to go," I tell Kaylee. "I love you. I'm going to push you through."

"Then I run." I hear the bottom of the trailer door slide across the carpet. I'm only an arm's length away once it opens.

"Then you run."

My night didn't start off this bad. No, not at all. I dropped Mama off at midnight. Leaving early was different for me. I felt like I was trying on a new pair of tennis shoes, leaving earlier than my usual one-forty-five. They felt a little tight, not worn in. Different. I'd rather wear my old ones because they are more comfortable. I'm used to them. I don't have to worry about blisters on my ankles and toes again. I'm unsure but ready to climb out of my old shoes. I've worn them for three years. Three long years. I suppose I am still going through the motions just by being there.

Nevertheless, I drove to the railroad tracks. I don't wait for the train. I sat there long enough to stare at the tracks and think everybody was probably laughing at me. They've probably been doing it for three years. I don't know why it didn't bother me before. Now it does.

"Aw, crap." I squinted into the little bit of my headlights, hitting the metal post of the railroad crossing sign. I'm sure it is illegal, but Bear taped a torn cardboard to the post. It is crooked from the breeze. I turned my head sideways to mirror it. *Sorry*, it says.

When I got home, I dragged my books out and sat in the living room with Pops. I curled up on the couch. He sat in his old green recliner and watched the end of some 1980s sitcom. It was just us and the sound of the T.V. At least he didn't get up and go to the other room tonight. "You're home early for a Friday night." He didn't look away from the television but reached out with his little white remote and changed the station. There was a baseball game on.

"I am. I got paid." I touched the tip of index and middle finger to my thumb, rubbing them together. "I got cash to pay a few more bucks on my tuition. Mama was at the bar. I was afraid she'd talk me out of drinks and spend it all."

"She didn't, did she?" Pops looked up. He was wearing his glasses. They are bifocal lenses, so he looked at me from the top of the rims.

"No, she said she had a bunch of cash."

"Does she got herself a new man?"

"I don't know." I shrugged. Pops stared at me hard. "Mama was buying drinks for everybody."

"The dogs were barking tonight. I think we've got coyotes coming up the hill."

"It might be Crazy Willie," I told him. "I've been getting groceries for him."

"Cripes, girl." Pops moaned while he shifted in his seat. He snatched up the beer bottle stuffed in the little beverage organizer I got for him last Christmas. Then he took a drink. "Crazy Willie? You know he was in the state pen for killing somebody. You can't save every stray cat you come across."

"It is a bartering deal. He's got the best trails for practicing for the Redneck Run," I told him. "He lets me run them if I buy him lunch meat and stuff."

I think he is going to ask me if it is really worth it. Pops doesn't. He said: "I guess that don't hurt nobody."

"It *doesn't* hurt anybody," I corrected him. It is our usual banter that's been missing for the last week.

"You're still not too big to spank," he countered, and I breathed a sigh of relief. "You're done hanging with those two boys from town, right?" That's Pops. He gets right to the point.

"I wasn't with them tonight if that's what you mean," I said. "The preacher's son was there. But we didn't hang out or anything. We just crossed paths because my chair is by the restrooms."

"It's just I've been noticing more than a few boys up here sniffing around. I'm just concerned they are here for the wrong reasons."

"Pops! Please!" I hate it when he does this; it embarrasses me, even if it is just him and me. "I swear to you they are nothing more than friends. They're nice boys."

"Yes, but maybe you think that, but they don't understand it—" I started to push my hands up, rebuffing his words. "No, sweetie, hear me out. They aren't from here, didn't grow up in the mountains," Pops said. "I'm just saying: stick with your own kind, sweetie."

"Who, Kenny?" I asked him. "Because he's all I got now, and all he thinks about is hunting. And there isn't a damn good-looking boy in a fifty-mile radius."

"What happened to Lindsey that you used to hang out with?"

"Lindsey Wells from fifth grade?"

"She was a nice girl."

"In fifth grade, yes. In eighth grade, Lindsey got pregnant." The conversation wasn't getting any better. "I'm getting some chips. Do you want something?" I said, pushing myself up from the couch. I don't know how else to change the subject. Pops declined, and I pushed myself off the couch and went to the kitchen. I saw something shiny, just barely peeking out from beneath the sofa.

I bent down and nudged it with a crooked finger to get it to a position where I could snatch it up. You would think this seemingly trivial act would not change my life forever. Had I not caught the glint, I would have gone on, and there probably wouldn't have been a crucial fork in my road of life until I needed to pay my tuition.

Of course, on the other hand, you could say that my mama dropping the lighter on the floor while she sat on Pops' couch two weeks ago was the turning point. Either way, it doesn't matter. Mama's silver lighter with the turquoise horse was there. As I slowly picked it up and held it aloft, I let my eyes work to the ashtray only an arms-length away.

"Pops, when was Mama here?"

"She wasn't."

"You're lying to me." I held the lighter aloft for him to see. "Here's her lighter." I don't know what was worse, catching Pops in a lie or delving through the few reasons she would have been there.

"Oh, well, maybe she was," he told me casually, just like that, then turns his attention to the TV.

"You don't know?" I demanded. "You're not making sense. You either know she was here, or she wasn't."

"She stopped by the other day. She needed some cash."

"And she, perhaps, smoked a joint?"

"Oh, no, she knows better." Pops nervously shifted in his chair. He leaned back. "Oh, well, baby, I'm sorry. She probably smoked it after I left. It didn't occur to me she'd do that here."

"You left her in your house by herself?"

"Sure, why not?" Pops told me. "There's nothing here she'd want or take. I only had twenty bucks to give her."

The lighter. The weed. The wad of cash that Mama had in her purse. I felt the blood drain from my face like the rush of water flushing down the toilet. My eyes worked upward, shelf by shelf until I came to the old coffee can I hid on the second shelf from the top. There is an old dusty plate, pictures, and six or seven books. There are three vintage cans: an old oil tin, a white and pink cookie canister full of my grandmother's cookie cutters, and my coffee can. When I rose up and walked to the shelf, I knew the money was gone.

"What's the matter, Brandy?" Pops asked. I knew he knew, but I pushed the little footstool by his chair and clambered to the shelf. I have a couple stages I undergo when I suffer a traumatic experience. One is disbelief, two is freaking out, and three is anger. I stood in disbelief and reached up, feeling my fingers on the coffee can. Then, I pulled it down and tugged off the top.

Pops stood. He held out his hand to help me down. I pushed it away, slid down, and sat on the stool, staring into the can. I was starting to freak out. I felt it. It was like I was smothering. "I'm going to kill her. She took every dime of my tuition money that was due. There was almost eighteen hundred dollars in here, Pops!" I stood up and, in the freaking, out stage. "Holy shit! How am I going to pay for this! I've been saving this up for four months! I've been working every shift I can work to get this!"

"We'll figure something out."

"*We'll* figure something out?" I screamed at Pops. "*We* didn't practically suffocate cleaning up vomit at Smiley's to get in an extra ten minutes of overtime. *We* didn't work the fifty hours the last two weeks at Beverly's, so there was enough to cover my mama's rent, too. *We* didn't put off buying a new pair of shoes for three years until the soles were worn off so I could finish school. No, *I did*. *You*, Pops, don't want me to finish school. You let her in that door, and I know why. You fell for her stupid flirting shit and slept with her. Then you had the guts to blame me for smoking a joint in your house! Oh, God." It slipped through my lips like the ghostly sound of wind through the tops of the pine trees on Crazy Willie's side of the hill. He stared at me. "I'm going to kill her." Then comes the anger.

"Listen, sweetheart, it isn't the end of the world. Maybe it is all for the better. You can do what we talked about now, stick around here. I'm not too bad to hang out with, huh?" Pops was really laid back while I shoved on my shoes, grabbed my keys, and headed to the door.

"You're kidding, right?" I swear, I was so angry that the hair on my arms was standing on end. "Did you give the money to Mama, so I'd stick around? Is this what this is all about?"

His hand came out and tried to catch my arm. "You know I wouldn't do that."

"I'm not so sure. You slept with Mama, didn't you? Did you pay her with my tuition money? Because she isn't worth the rent money that I give her every month or the fifty dollars I fork out for Kaylee's food. She definitely isn't a two-thousand-dollar whore!"

"Stop talking about your mama like that!" He shouted at me. I could see his eyes turning bloodshot red. His cheek trembled. "Do not push me, Brandy. I will not justify anything I do with your mama to you. It is none of your business."

"It is *my* business when she steals my money when she is with you!"

"Oh, you're not thinking with your head, Brandy. Don't lose your temper. You said you didn't want to be like your mama. If you go out that door all hot-headed and ready for a fight, you're being just like your mother."

I lingered at the door, standing at the fork in my road. It isn't exact, but an hour later, while I feel like I am taking my last dying breath, I remember what I said to Pops: "That's not how she left the other day, was it?" I felt my hands shake and heard the keys trembling as they dangled from my fob. "Why did you even bother to take me in, Pops? Why was it? Was it so you could get Mama to come here even when she had a boyfriend? Was it so you could have a link to screw her?" I groaned and grabbed my head. "Mama doesn't have to visit anymore because I'm grown up. I suppose that's why you want to take in Kaylee, right? So that you have another reason for Mama to come here?"

I've said some nasty things to Pops before. He's never lifted a hand at me. I saw his hand rise and his lip twitch this time, and I expected the slap. He stopped not a quarter inch from my left cheek. Then, Pops glared at me. "Get out."

And my final words to him ring in my mind right now while I'm pulling up the last piece of wood from the floor and careening backward as it lets loose: I told Pops, "You know, sometimes I wish she never had me. Nobody gives a rat's ass of what I want. Nobody. Sometimes, I wish I was just dead." Because I know I am going to die while I stuff Kaylee out through the hole and down into the cat poop and pieces of pink insulation and tiny broken rat bones beneath. And probably a flashlight or two I lost looking for the cats when I was three.

"Crawl, baby, crawl!" I am whisper-screaming before John John uses his shoulder and knocks open the door. I should have never stomped into Mama's house, screaming at her. At the same time, she knelt there at her dirty little sofa table with eighteen hundred dollars of my money in baggies full of white powder sitting out in front of her and her boyfriend. But I did. There was Kaylee, sucking her thumb, watching late-night adult cartoons right behind them. I kicked over the table, spilling it all out on the floor. And John John, he grabbed me by the waist, tossed me like a floppy teddy bear into the T.V. and into the doors—

His foot hits me in the chin now, sending me keeling backward. I've got enough in me to slam the vanity closed with my foot before he starts pelting me with his fists.

I can only fend off his blows with the back of my arms. I hear myself kind of beg-sobbing that I want to live. Please, let me live. I swear to God, I won't do anything. I won't call the cops. I won't tell anyone. They can keep my money. Then I'm just kicking and baby-hitting with fists that aren't doing any damage. Then it is just me mumbling sobs. Did I hear Pops' voice? Crap, he was mad enough at me when I left. I can't imagine what he'll do to me now. I think I did. Then the lights go out.

Chapter –16
The Visit

It is stifling hot in Pops' house. He goes to New Alliance and buys a window air conditioner with money he doesn't need to spend. "You saved my life, Pops. You don't need to do anything else," I mewl while he and Kenny are trying to figure out how to fit it into a window that's too small and slightly askew. Uncle Craig and Aunt Jenny ran down to New Alliance to get more screws and some two-by-fours to make a frame. I'm lying on the couch because Pops won't let me get up. Two days in the hospital, and Pops says they shouldn't have sent me home so soon. But I didn't have insurance, so they booted me out with a load of forms to apply for medical financing through their loan department and a couple of seventy-dollar ice packs I could get at the dollar store for fifty cents each.

Kaylee is sitting on his recliner, staring at me and eating a cold hotdog. She looks like her usual smug self. Glad I could save her life. She hit me with the toilet plunger this morning to wake me up and ask me if she could watch cartoons. But we did my little celebration dance, gyrating across the living room, marching and waggling our arms in the air that we are okay. Now we are three hours later. Pops is cussing and putting in the air conditioner. Kaylee is turning up the T.V. volume with the big toe of her right foot on the remote in the beverage organizer on Pops' recliner.

"Little Pete saved you." Pops corrects me, grunting with the weight of holding up the air conditioner while Kenny uses a chain saw to cut out a more significant gap in the window. He is right. When Little Pete didn't see me come out, he opened his bedroom window facing Mama's house. He wears glasses and can't see well, but his ears are better than anybody I know.

He heard me screaming and then heard Kaylee crying under the trailer. He was afraid to crawl under the trailer but coaxed Kaylee out. He broke down the front door to get to me. Pops was a close second—he sat up at the house for twenty-five minutes pacing until he figured he would have to tear me off Mama. Pops took off down the mountain twelve minutes after Little Pete, hugging John John around the waist and dragging him down the hallway.

I heard Pops' voice coming up through the hole in the floor underneath the vanity in the bathroom. I hardly remember the rest except Little Pete, who came to visit me to make sure I was alright. He kept telling me: "I don't like him. I don't like him. He's mean to me. He be mean to Crazy Brandy. She's not crazy. She's just Brandy." Just like he used to in high school when those two boys would tease him on the bus.

My grades came out today from Fairview State. I got straight A's except for one class where I was supposed to do a brief speech as a final project. I couldn't do it. I just knew I'd faint dead away up there on the podium. I got an I for incomplete. I don't tell Pops. I close my little laptop computer and smile to myself. I quit. I'm done. At least I went out with A's—well, almost. I know the college will hold my transcripts and grades until I pay. It isn't happening anytime soon. It doesn't matter. At least I got to get a little taste of the dream.

"Did you hear me?" Pops asks. I didn't. I scooch up on the couch and feel every bone in my body ache. I am sweating bullets in here.

"No."

"The preacher just pulled up in his car." He is trying to get the air conditioner situated and ready to add the frame when my aunt and uncle return. I don't know what to say.

"Why are you telling me?" I ask him. "If a soul needs saving, it is yours or Kenny's. Neither of you have been to church in ten years." I, however, said a bunch of prayers three nights ago when John John was punching me from head to toe. "When Mama's boyfriend tossed me through the second door, I prayed he'd either kill me or send me to heaven." I also said a few prayers for Bear because I thought in that moment of complete catastrophe, he might be listening more.

"And you are here, Brandy Pandy, right?" Kenny grunts his reply and makes a smothered duck call. Pops is making him balance the air-conditioner while he answers the door. "That means you're no angel, then." I suppose he's right. However, word has already gotten out about my fight with John John. It has spread like wildfire up one side of the mountain and down the other. I imagine the whispers are far tougher on me than Mama and John John. They are both in jail for drug charges and assault. Everybody at the trailer park is mad at me for turning them in.

Pops didn't say it, but I can see it in how he looks at me. *We take care of our own problems. We don't need the cops involved. We don't need outsiders knocking on our doors.* They say it is my fault, and I should have never gone to Mama's trailer the other night. Others whisper that maybe it was me who got rid of Josh, murdered him, and burned the trailer down to hide the body.

Of course, they ran a piece on the local T.V. station. They called it a domestic dispute and a drug bust. Now, folks in town have devised their own set of rumors. I suppose Preacher Murphy, standing at the door with a box of canned food he collects for the Holy Trinity church pantry, saw the twenty-second story. He's probably come to exorcise me. If the box of food for the needy isn't a crushing blow in itself, I hear him asking Pops if Bear and Gabe can come in and visit. They are waiting on the porch.

Pops turns his head around and eyes me. I can't read his expression. It is as blank as it gets. "You tell me, baby girl."

I'm not surprised he says this. I know he doesn't trust those two men. I think a tiny part of him worries if he doesn't do what the preacher says, he'll go to hell. Instead, he'll let me make the decision, take the chance.

"Pops, I don't feel good. Tell them to come back in a few weeks."

There are muffled murmurs. Pops is rubbing his chin with his hand, a sign he feels he is in a precarious position, wobbling somewhere between heaven and hell. He looks at the door and looks back at me. Kenny's face is getting redder by the minute, trying to hold up the air conditioner by himself. Pops obviously thinks my soul is in danger because he gives me one last look, then waves the men inside. "You can come in, but you must give me a minute. We're in the middle of something." Pops lingers between us a minute before the preacher tells him that he didn't want to impose, and to finish what he was doing.

"Do you need help?" Preacher Murphy asks.

"No, sir."

Preacher Murphy drops the food box on the table stand by the front door. I see Pops trying to keep his cool. His jaws are working up and down while he blinks at it. He is insulted. I'm surprised he isn't getting angry and saying something about not taking the food pantry box—we don't take handouts.

Pops doesn't have time to object. The preacher tries to stop me from sitting in my bed on the couch. He is dressed in black suit pants, a button-up white shirt, and a tie. He is also donning a suit coat. I know he is roasting in here. He keeps swiping a cotton kerchief across his forehead and saying: "It's going to be a hot one today." It only seems to spur Pops on, making him want to get the air conditioner settled into the window more quickly. He's still waiting for my Aunt Jenny and Uncle Craig to return with more wood. Every now and again, when something breaks in the house, Pops yells out that we're standing on the threshold of hell. If one more thing needs fixing, we might as well fall right in. I'm a little worried he's starting to believe it with the preacher looking so hot.

His two cohorts are not as fancy. They are both wearing cargo shorts and T-shirts. Thank goodness, none of them are toting around a Bible in the cleft of an arm. Kenny looks nervous enough being this close to the church. Bring in a Bible, and I think he might believe I called them in to smite him for pulling back on the couch this morning and rocking it back and forth, teasing me that he was going to tip me over. I wave the preacher away and feel the jarring ache in my ribs while I sit up. The doctor said my little ribs aren't broken, just bruised. Bruised? They feel like they got ripped out of my flesh and pushed back inside. The only thing broken is my left wrist, which isn't so bad. It just seems weird to lay there while they are staring at me, taking in my puffy black and green eye and my busted lip. The rest of the bruises are mostly hidden under my shirt and sheet over my legs.

"I'm fine. I need to get up," I muster. It is awkward. I look at Bear.

"How are you feeling?" He reaches out and gives me a little shove on my shoulder.

"Wonderful," I return. I look at Gabe, and he smiles like an idiot at me. I have a good feeling he got dragged here, not on his own accord. The preacher sits down at the end of Pops' table. Bear and Gabe drop on the couch like they've lived there all their life.

"So, how are you really feeling?" Preacher Murphy keeps looking over his shoulder at Pops as if he feels he should help.

"Sore," I tell him the truth.

"You look like you got beaten with a Louisville Slugger," Bear offers. "Better now than when we saw you at the hospital."

"You were at the hospital?" I don't remember much of the hospital; it was just a bunch of nurses gabbing at the nursing station so raucously that I could not sleep. Then, when I finally felt my eyes start to close, they would stomp in, turn on my bright ceiling light and holler, "HOW IS BRANDY?" at me, to make sure I wasn't dead.

"Yeah, you left your phone," Bear says. "Your Pops found it and called me to see if I knew where you were. In the middle of the call, your mom called him and said there was some guy at her house, and he was going to kill you. I got to the trailer park when the ambulance was pulling out. I stayed until that little dude that dragged you out started screaming for me to leave. You said it would be a good idea."

"Little Pete told you to leave?" I feel uncomfortable.

"Yeah, it's alright. He was freaking out. I think he thought we were with John John. Your family was all there."

"Dammit, Kenny, hold it still!" Pops interrupts our conversation. Then his head slowly turns to the preacher. "Sorry, preacher."

"I am holding it still," Kenny replies, his teeth gnashing together. I can see the preacher eyeing his arm tattoos guardedly. "You keep dropping it on my fingers." There is nearly inaudible bickering between the two. Pops hammers something in the wall, Kenny curses aloud, stops, and both look back at us. They bump shoulders like two seasoned warriors getting ready for an epic battle. Kenny steps back and holds his hands in the air. Preacher Murphy's eyes are wide. Bear and Gabe are looking at each other. They believe there will be a knockdown, drag-out fight between the two.

"Should I do—something?" Preacher asks.

"Oh, it's okay." I push a hand on Preacher Murphy's arm. "It's how they work together, how they ride. Kind of like Cain and Abel. It'll be alright."

"Cain killed Abel in the bible," Preacher tells me.

"Oh, well, maybe not them." I shrug. "Let me translate. Pops is saying: 'Son of my brother, I know you are handsome and young. However, your strength is not of your father yet. Be strong." I pause and point to Kenny. "Kenny is saying: 'Dear Uncle, I am of little strength. But I am trying to make you proud with every muscle in my weak body. But please, kind sir, do not hammer my fingers again. It hurts really bad.'"

"Son of a bitch!" Kenny yowls the curse, steps back, and the air conditioner starts to fall. It is Pops who catches it. The two come to a complete halt. Both are staring at us like two little boys who just got caught tying firecrackers to the family cat's tail.

"That was really, *son of a bitch*," I say. "I can't translate that any better," I tell them.

Gabe thinks this is funny. He bursts out into laughter, doubling over. It really wasn't that funny. But Bear is laughing, too. I think it is more to break up the feeling of dry ice in the air between us.

"Pops, you got anything out in the kitchen I can cook?"

"You're supposed to be resting. If you wait a few, I will make us all some potpies or something."

"*Frozen potpies*," I hiss and shake my head. "I am not feeding the preacher from Holy Trinity Church potpies from the frozen food aisle at Mister Smiley's. At least, not if you want us to get to heaven."

Chapter −17
Box of food from the pantry

There's always something to cook in Pops's kitchen, so I dig out some deer steaks and put them in a mini-smoker on the back porch. Pops is always going to yard sales and bringing me back expensive cooking appliances he finds really cheap. People buy them but never use them. They spend too much time going out to eat.

"Hey, you mind telling me the whole story of what happened?" Bear slips into the kitchen. I turn and shrug.

"No. I don't want to talk about it."

"Okay." He nods. "Let's try this. I've never asked you why you decided to be a chef," Bear says to me. I'm frying some potatoes because I know Bear likes them. I know he knows. That's why I'm making them because he dips his fingers in the pan and pulls a hot one out. He juggles it back and forth until it cools and pops it in his mouth.

I look at him. He must know everything about me, down to the underwear I wear, because he's seen it in my bedroom laundry basket when he visits. "I'll tell you, but you won't understand." I add some of my spices to the potatoes, then hold one up for him to taste. "When I was really little, my mama used to leave me with a box of cereal and be gone all day and most of the night. I was always hungry." I'm waiting for the pity expression. He doesn't give me one. He nods while I hand him the spoon and tell him to stir while I dig some veggies out of the refrigerator. "When I moved in with Pops, his kitchen was stocked and looked like nothing I had ever seen." I turn around with a bag in my hand and point to a wooden kitchen chair. "I would sit on that chair and stare at the open cabinets for hours."

Bear nods. I hear my aunt and uncle coming in the front door. I stop long enough to hear Kaylee jabbering up a storm. "Pops just ate frozen food before I came. He had an old freezer in the garage, and he'd reach in, take out a box, and stuff it in the microwave. He didn't think that would be good for me. He went to Smiley's and bought a cookbook, and we learned how to cook together."

"My mom didn't cook. We ate out all the time." Bear kind of tips his head right to left. "Could you tell?"

"Maybe a couple months ago, not so much now." I reach out and pat his belly with my fingers. "Pretty darn flat."

"Bejesus, I'm so sorry," Bear just spits out. He looks sincere, starts to stick his hand out, and stops. "I don't blame you for hating me, for saying that stuff at the hospital. I just wanted to say that."

"I said stuff to you?" I ask. I'm embarrassed and disconcerted at the thought that I talked to someone and said things I might regret. "I don't remember. I was on painkillers. What did I say?"

"Just stuff." I think he will leave it at that, but he doesn't. "You were right. I do treat people like crap. I do try to buy people's affection. You were right that I do it because it is easier to hand somebody a fifty dollar bill and get a smile instead of working a little to figure out what people like above the almighty dollar." He is stirring hard, mashing the potatoes. I reach out, grab his hand and the spatula, and slow it down.

"You don't need to slaughter the potatoes, Bear, before eating."

"And I miss this." He holds up one hand like he is encompassing what we are doing. "I like it that you show me how to cook things."

I stand there and listen to him. I miss him, too. But my reasons are different and not so innocent. I remember last month Bear and I standing in almost the same position. We were making pancakes. They weren't the usual kind, but special ones without a ton of sugar, butter, and eggs that I had spent an entire day testing and retesting from a recipe I had conjured up one day for a class. Because there's a little diner along the highway in New Alliance that has all-you-can-eat pancakes and sausage on Sunday morning. Bear said he had been passing this little restaurant every Sunday, and the scent of sausage, bacon, and pancakes filled the air around the diner and seeped into the windows of his truck. It was killing him, the craving for them. It was all he thought about. He was tired of toast and grapefruit. He was sick of mushy oatmeal from a box.

He was going to break. It was to the point that he had driven past the diner twice last Sunday before church and even pulled into the lot. I got a text from Bear: *I'm breaking. I'm going down. Talk me out of it. I'm sitting in the parking lot of Dana's Home-style Restaurant. Non-butter popcorn is not going to help. Help.*

By that evening, we were spooning batter into a hardly oiled pan, elbow to elbow, and he was standing over me like I was some goddess. I swear, even his eyes were fevered, staring at me while the small, delicious pancakes sizzled beneath our noses. I can still remember the scent of his shirt, slightly sweaty with a hint of real maple syrup. Man smell. Hungry man scent. God, what a turn-on.

I fathom that he's become my man candy, my cooking whore. If I keep coming up with tasty, low-calorie recipes, he'll come running back, begging for more. He'll be standing there close enough I can feel the heat from his body, looking up long enough to appear as if I'm just trying to read his eyes to see if he is hungry, but knowing damn well I wish he was hungry for more than those damn pancakes and maybe he'll forget about Meghan and bend me over the kitchen table and—

"—sometime next week or something?" Bear drones on.

"Huh?" *Oh, crap.* I had not heard a word Bear was saying. I bob my head and realize the vegetables in my hands are dribbling juice to my elbow. "I mean, of course, whatever."

"I'll go tell him then."

"Okay." I wondered what I had agreed to. I go outside, return with the smoked meat, and lay it on a plate. Gabe comes back in by himself and leans with his butt against the table.

"What time?"

"What time—for what?" I ask him. Then I think he is talking about the food. "We're eating like right now. It's done."

"No, Bear said he talked to you about going out to a restaurant next week. It would be you and me, and him and Meghan."

"Bear said that?" I must look like an idiot when I pull my chin up and turn my entire attention to Gabe. My eyes are looking up to the ceiling.

"He said he just talked to you about it," Gabe says. "It isn't a big deal. I thought—he asked you." Gabe's face is red. He's stammering, and I feel horrible because he looks like a doe that just got shot. "I mean, we don't have to be a couple or anything. He just thought it'd be fun. I don't know any girls here. He said he never knew what to say to Meghan, and it might be easier if he wasn't alone. I'm tired of being a third wheel. I'm talking too much, aren't I?"

"Wow," I say. "You are." I laugh, and it hurts my ribs.

"You're laughing at me. Great."

"No—" I lie, telling him I'm not laughing at him. He's really nice-looking. I know he has to be doing this for Bear because, other than the incident at the bar, he's never looked at me the way a man looks at a woman. I could have sworn Kenny told me once that Gabe wasn't into girls. "You said you didn't like me."

"You're not as bad as I thought."

"It was the threesome thing that was the game changer," I tease, "wasn't it?" I felt he was going through the motions like he likes someone else who doesn't give him the time of day. I reach out and poke him with the baster on the deer meat. "Okay, yeah, you are talking fast. But you want to go out with—this?" I ask him, standing back and holding out my arms. "People will think you beat me."

"I don't care. Toss some makeup over it. My sisters do it with their zits. It's just going out to eat and maybe playing putt-putt golf."

Then my face gets serious. I nibble on my lip. "Gabe, I haven't been on a date in a long time. I don't have a nice dress. I'll probably say stupid stuff that will haunt you for life."

"You are funny. Just wear what you've got on now and tell people you got in a car wreck."

I look down at my pajamas. "What about your mama and daddy?" I ask him. "Won't their heads explode if you go out with me?" I bring my hand up and make fake fireworks with my fingers.

"I think they will be so happy I am dating a real live girl; they'll rent us a limousine and buy you a corsage like we're going out for prom even if you wear a pair of flannel pants and a t-shirt with—" He reaches out, tugs the bottom of my t-shirt. "—camo and big-time wrestlers on it."

"As opposed to a dead girl you've got hidden in your closet?" I look down. It occurs to me that my entire wardrobe is a bit on the rough side compared to the girls I've seen him hang around with on Sunday mornings. I suppose it is what happens when you're surrounded by nothing but men in camo pants and the high-visibility bright yellow safety shirts Pops' lumber workers wear. Gabe stops short and snaps his eyes at me. I'm not sure he realizes I'm kidding until I smile. He laughs a little. "I was just kidding, too."

He was. Still, I'm sure he is backtracking now, recognizing the fact my entire closet is filled with t-shirts and jeans.

"Then okay. I can deal with that."

I have a curious feeling in my belly after our conversation. I haven't accepted a date since Josh disappeared. I'm not ready to take the step. I'm just not. I know I need to walk that walk sooner or later. I take a deep breath and tell Gabe yes, like I am accepting a wedding proposal. Mixed feelings or not, I snatch up some plates and go to the doorway to tell everybody that the food is ready to eat. I stop short. Bear is lingering near Pops, his hands in his pockets.

"You know she's not going to win this. There's no way in hell she can." It is Bear. I know he has no clue that I have slipped into the living room threshold because Gabe is right beside me, and he's got a look on his face like a ghost just jumped out at him. Bear's back is to me. He is standing up with his arms crossed. I can't believe they are having this conversation. What did I miss? "You need to stop her before she gets hurt," Bear tells Pops. "She can't shoot the bow, hardly doggy paddle long enough to save her life. Maybe she can drive an ATV better than she can drive a car. But she went left of center six times the other day, driving those old men back to the nursing home. I thought we were going to die jumping hills."

Kenny laughs a little like it is a joke. He is stifled by Pops' stern glare. "But she can run," I hear Pops sniff. "I'm not worried about her getting hurt. She's been down that path a thousand times. Hurt, she'll get over. She was discarded like trash on my front porch by her own mother, told she'd never make it past sixth grade without being on drugs and pregnant with three kids. She's been dumped by her husband, told by her college she's nothing but a hick and every guy that shows up at my front porch sticks around long enough to find out she's not sleeping with him." Pops gives a harsh glare at Bear. "She'll just find another project to work on to cover it up, make up for whatever wicked thing she thinks she's done to deserve another heartache. She'll pick up another stray cat to bring home to feed and find an old lady to stand with at the cemetery while she grieves her dead husband. My little girl pays for her mama's rent and groceries, so she can't afford her tuition or the gas to get her to work. It's knowing her own friend doesn't have enough guts to believe in her that I'm worried about."

"It isn't just losing, Lee," Bear gripes. "People are going to make a laughingstock of her. She doesn't have the right stuff."

"Well, I'm not quite sure how most folks get this *right stuff* you're talking about," Pops says. He is standing before the window, leaning a little to the right to scrutinize his work.

My aunt is turning the T.V. channel for Kaylee. She is a big-bosomed woman who always wears these prim flowered dresses that come to her knees. She could walk straight out of a 1950s movie. She's wearing one now with a pair of pink pumps. She is trying to pretend she is not listening to Pops. She is. She is a little hard of hearing in her left ear, and she tips her head while she gets Kaylee situated with a blanket on the floor. I can see through the opening that my uncle is out on the front porch, sawing away at the two-by-fours to make a frame. It is loud. They have yet to notice I am here.

"But it doesn't have to come from an expensive racetrack at a country club or brand new ATVs donated by some retail store in California." He pauses and turns his attention to Bear. "Brandy's been to hell and back a couple of times. The other night was just a silly drop in the bucket, a coke-crazed idiot trying to beat her dead with a baseball bat because he was insulted that she was mad he kicked a little baby girl. He beat her with his hands, a kitchen chair, then when she was wedged between the back of the couch to get away, he grabbed a lamp and tried to shock her with it." He pauses and rubs the grizzled gray on his chin. "You know she tore the bathroom floor out with her bare fingers so she could stuff that baby girl out through the trailer floor before she got killed?"

Bear stares at Pops with no expression. I feel humiliated, woozy. I know I'm rubbing my arms like I can hide the bruises there from resisting John John's blows. I wished I could fall through the floor then. I really didn't want my suffering blasted out to anybody. I see Gabe looking at me. I didn't want anybody to know the details. He has the same expression in his eyes as I saw on my city-born kindergarten teacher the first time she saw head lice crawling all over Bobby Henderson's little head.

"Pops, please stop." My voice is nearly a whisper. I'm not sure he hears it over my uncle's footsteps on the porch and the bang of boards that he lays just outside the window.

Pops turns his attention to me. I don't think he knew I'd come in. He doesn't look surprised; he's just angry and concerned. "No, baby girl. You shouldn't be embarrassed by what you did just because your mama didn't lift a finger to help you. I'm not an idiot. I know why you won't talk about it. You think she thinks that dumbass boyfriend of hers meant more to her than you. And maybe he did. She might be your mama because she gave birth to you, but inside your head, she isn't anything like you. You are mine, and I didn't have a damn thing to do with making you before you were born. I did after, though. And that's me inside your head."

"Pops, please stop."

"No." Pops turns to me. "You mean more to me than anything in the world." Then, he turns his attention to Bear, raises a finger, and points at his chest. "So—boy, before you pass judgment on any of us up here on the mountain. You'll have to understand there's more to what's inside somebody than blood, guts, and things you can see with your eyes. Before you put down my little girl, act like she's some idiot that's going to turn out like her mother, think again. Maybe she knows something from the stuff I taught her and something from her experiences that might give her the *right stuff*."

Translation: Pops loves me. I realize then that I am never going to fit in with folks like Bear, Preacher Murphy, and Gabe. They don't know me. They don't understand. I gently lay the plates on the table before the couch. I don't bother to look at Bear. I can see his eyes working down my arms and stopping at those chipped and broken fingernails nearly gone from popping the boards off the bathroom floor at Mama's. Now he knows the story. "It's time to eat." My voice is cool. I fake a smile. Pops waves a hand to my uncle on the porch.

Bear doesn't know when to stop. "Brandy, listen to me. You can't do all of those events by yourself. That's what I'm trying to tell your Pops. They came out with the regulations last week, and I read them over. They won't let just *one* person do them all. It has to be a team."

"I don't care." I feel deflated inside. I'm all redneck and don't give a crap on the outside. You know why? I believe that Beauregard Rodriguez, standing in front of me in his cargo shorts and pretty button-up shirt, had that rule made just so I don't compete with the pretty little girl he'd do anything to date. Anything. "I won't race then." I shrug. "Eat up."

It was a strange meal with Preacher Murphy trying to keep up a conversation. The problem was that he only seemed to know stuff about church. Pops makes a meager attempt to keep the house from being completely quiet except for Kaylee's cartoons. He only appears to understand hunting and logging. It is just about as dull as knowing the church picnic is coming up next week. I poke at my food. Gabe's scratching at his neck like he's got a nervous itch. Bear is trying to eat because he knows I'll be even more insulted if he doesn't.

When they leave, I walk over and grab the box of food Preacher Murphy set on the end table. I can see my aunt, Kenny, and Pops looking at me. Kaylee is bouncing around on the floor. She even ganders a peek in my direction. "Please do not insult us by bringing a box of food from the poor pantry. We are not needy," I tell Preacher Murphy, who is rising from the couch. "Next time, bring a bag of potato chips or potato salad from the store. It is kind of how things are done up here." Nobody says anything. Pops nods at the preacher and Gabe and Bear as they quietly walk out the door.

I knew Bear would come back later. He left his phone sitting on the table. I'm lying on the couch with my feet propped on Kenny's knees while we watch T.V. Bear comes in, and Kenny gets up and offers him his seat. I don't say anything; I raise my legs and sit up. Bear lounges on the couch, watching T.V. He says nothing. Every now and then, he laughs at some stupid joke on the T.V.

For an hour, we sit there in silence. I'm really mad at him, so I keep giving him a stink eye. He ignores me until I push myself far enough to ram him once with my heel.

"Ow, Brandy." Bear finally turns to me. "What the heck?"

"I don't understand why you can't just be my friend and have my back," I declare bluntly.

"Are you still mad at me because of the race?" Bear turns to me and grabs my foot before I kick him again. "I'm trying to protect you."

"Stop trying to protect me. I'm not a frail child. I'm not your prissy girlfriend."

"Fine. I know that. I just didn't want you to be alone."

"I had Kenny until you came along."

"I should have known that too. But I don't think you're okay, do you get it? I don't think you are frail, but you're not—okay." Bear's eyes are easing to the door. "You want me to leave?"

"No." He's right. I know it. My tummy is all knotted up, and I keep seeing John John's face flashing in my head. I try to dose off, and he's there in my head, taunting me. I tell Bear that, and he nods.

"John John's in jail now, so you're safe," he says. "We know he'll be there for a while."

"He's in my head." I poke a finger at my forehead. "I can't even watch T.V. He keeps climbing in. When you told Pops I was too backward to compete, I felt like you were jumping in with him."

"Um," Bear seems to think this out, then he nods his head up and down. "Here." He stands up, approaches my side of the couch, and makes me scoot over. Then he sits down and tugs me over. I'm shoved up next to him with his arm around my shoulder and my back against his chest. I think it should feel awkward. It doesn't. It's like getting smooshed between Pops and Kenny when I sit between them in the truck—comfortable and safe. "Okay, so I didn't have many friends before I moved back. Not a surprise to you, I suppose." Bear reaches over to the table and picks up his phone. "I could say it was because I worked twenty-four hours daily, but you'd know better. I'm just —not a good person to be around. People tend to figure that out quickly."

I twist my neck so I can see his face. "I like being around you most of the time. Gabe likes being around you."

"No, you don't. I can't believe you let me back in your house tonight. You're nice. Everybody says that. And Gabe, he's used to me. We were friends in school before I left. I'm working on it, though." He turns on his phone, scrolls to his pictures, and starts flipping through them until he stops. "I don't want to go back to where I was, but I'm scared I might. I got these if I have to go back."

He starts flipping through the pictures, and there's lots of me being silly and some of Gabe fishing and swimming at the resort pool. There's Pops and almost everybody in my family. There's one of Kaylee on Kenny's shoulders and Bobby Reese and his buddies locking arms for a posed picture. I vaguely remember Bear tugging out his camera and taking the photos.

Then he turns to another of me, giving him a stink eye, but this time I'm flipping off the camera. I remember doing that when he wouldn't stop pestering me in the kitchen one morning.

"Get rid of that one," I tell him.

"No, because that's the one I always turn to when I am starting to do something that is—mean."

We lay there looking at pictures, then watch T.V. until way into the night. I fall to sleep to the beat of Bear's heart on my back. I remember the exact moment I did. His fingers are tangled in mine because we were fighting over turning the channel on the remote, and I grabbed his fingers to stop him. They stay that way in a sudden silence. I don't know what Bear is thinking, maybe nothing at all. I feel my heart pounding and hope he doesn't feel it and understands how he is making me think. I lay there against him, and our fingers are clasped long after his snores ring steady in my ears. I lounge there, feeling the moment and wishing it would never end.

Sometime during the night, Kaylee creeps in and lays down on my belly. When I woke up, she was still sleeping soundly. Bear stays until I wake up at seven, and he excuses himself because he has a meeting in less than an hour. Pops doesn't say a thing when he passes by in his pajamas. He just shakes his head and grumbles his usual grouchy words before his first cup of coffee: "Are you making breakfast or what?"

Chapter –18
Lies and Truths

The road to Boar Mountain Resort is long and winding. It is new asphalt, so even the worn tires on my old truck hardly make a sound when rolling over it. This stretch of Bear Mountain Resort Road meanders through a thick pine and maple forest. To the city-born eye, it would appear an old, deep forest. To those who have grown up around the woods in the mountains, it is nothing more than a replanted clear-cut leftover from mining in the 1920s and 1930s. It is clean and sterile, with hundred-year-old trails made wide from the lumber trucks that crossed the mountains of trees years ago.

Near the top is a gatehouse shaped like a little white gazebo surrounding the parking lot. Twenty-four-hour security guards check each visitor who comes into the lot. A sightseer can get an hourly pass to look around the building grounds. A vast wooden overlook with a clear view of New Alliance is below.

Although no chain link fences surround the grounds, you can't enter the parking lot unless you pass through two big iron gates on either side of the pavilion. I am stopped at the gates by a clean-cut guard. He looks more like a buff bouncer at the Crazy Kettle than security at a country club. Except, of course, he is wearing a brown and green uniform. His name tag says Evan B. He is smiling at the cars in front of me with big yellow passes dangling from the rearview mirrors. He waves them past. When he gets to me, I see his hands come out in front of him, palms up, as if he were going to stop a truckload of drunk and rowdy teenagers. One look at my raggedy truck, and I see him pull on his invisible armor. He suddenly becomes stoic and expressionless when he hustles out and asks me for my membership pass. He peers into the back seat and eyes Kaylee, playing with my cell phone in her car seat.

"Well, Evan," I tell him bluntly. "I don't have one."

He gives me a funny look like how the heck do you know my name? Then I see him tip his chin and look at his identification tag. "Oh. I can give you a one-hour pass if you are here to watch the Fire Mountain Shadows. However, you must remain in the parking area." He holds a little pad, clearly marked with 1– HOUR PASS.

"I just have to tell you that if T.V. or news reporters come, you must stand out of the way. You can't get autographs from any of the girls. Children aren't allowed on the grounds unless attended by an adult at all times." The Fire Mountain Shadows. I still feel gutted by that blow. I worked hard at coming up with that name.

"Really," I laugh. "They work as check-out girls at a grocery store. Why would someone want a check-out girl's autograph?" He doesn't laugh with me. I think about just leaving. I don't want to be here when the Cash Register Girls flit past me in all their pomp and glory and my stolen name. I've still got bruises on my bruises. That, I note, is obvious to the security guard, who keeps focusing on the green-blue shading of my left eye that even makeup and sunglasses can't hide.

"Yes, ma'am," he says. "Are you aware of the famed National Redneck Run? Boar Mountain Resort sponsors the national team. They also have a deal with the Smiley chain of grocery stores, allowing their team to work out here. The girls are the poster children for the event. There is a huge couple million-dollar commercial deal for the sponsor whose team wins. We've gotten it every year so far, and the longer, the better. This whole event is getting big like the Olympics. They are like movies stars."

"Well, I doubt that," I utter. I'm trying not to chuckle. Six or seven cars are lining up behind me. I see the guard getting antsy and wanting to take care of the paying customers. "No big deal, I don't really need a pass. I just wanted to see if Bear—" I pause, correct myself. "I mean, Beau was working this morning," I tell him. "It looks like you're getting busy. I can call him or something."

"Beau—Vega?" The security guard asks.

Okay, I'm staring at him. It takes a moment for the realization to seep in. It crawls slowly, creeping past my mind like Pops' old tomcat tries to slink past everybody's legs at the front door in January to get into the warm living room. I think my mouth drops for a split second. I know I must look like an idiot staring at him.

"Oh, I suppose," is all I can muster. "Beau—Rodriguez?"

"I think Rodriguez is his middle name."

"Who has a middle name like that?" I say aloud. Beau Vega. Amelia Vega. BEAR IS AMELIA VEGA'S SON.

I should have known. Who has thousand-dollar money cards to toss at people they've pissed off? Why didn't I know? Because the idiot called himself Beau Rodriguez. What the hell?

"Let me give him a call. Why don't you pull around the building, then over to the side—over there," the security guard points to where the little drive goes around the pavilion and shoots cars out the other side to the exit. "Please don't get me in trouble, alright? I can't just let —anybody in."

Anybody with a crappy car, jeans, and t-shirt, and a little kid with a snotty nose, I think. I don't say anything, though. I comply. I saw the guard take my license plate number as I pulled around and put my truck into the lot. I can see I am facing the direction they all wish folks like me would take—back down the mountain road and to whatever hick town from where I hail. Ten minutes pass before I see a shadow at my window. The security guard is beaming like a first-time daddy holding a newborn baby. I look at the tag hanging from his pocket.

"Hey, you're Brandy Devereauxs, right?" he asks. I nod, looking up from my phone in my lap. "I'm so sorry. I didn't know you were a friend of Mister Vega. My apologies."

Funny thing. I didn't either until ten minutes ago. I don't say this. I wave to him with my hand. I think I want to leave. Yes, I think I'll leave. Kaylee is getting fidgety in the back, and the little crackers I hand her will make her thirsty soon. I'm not the best mama material. I forgot her sippy cup. I can't, though. "You know, you're somewhat of a legend here." The guard is now leaning up to the window. His breath smells like peppermint gum. He reaches in and touches me with his knuckle. Suddenly I'm good enough to be his best friend, regardless of the crappy truck and clothes. "Everybody still talks about how you gave Amelia Vega a verbal spanking." He almost whispers at me. "Nobody ever sticks up to her and comes out alive. They said she ended up getting security to throw you out. I wasn't here that day. I had strep throat. Wish I was here. They said she went into the back room and literally sobbed for an hour." He draws out the literally and gives me a thumbs up.

"I —I wouldn't go that far." I am still letting the idea that Bear is Amelia Vega's relative sink in. Between Josh and my mama, I'm learning to roll with the changes.

"Is it true you told her she was going to end up in a cardboard box?" Evan has his hand on the top of my door and keeps peering behind him. "They said you said she'd end up in a cardboard box in some city park. But not a big city like Charleston. She wasn't good enough for that. It'd be some crappy place like Carrolton —"

"Yeah, I guess I did."

"How the heck did you get in good with Beau Vega after tearing his mom a new asshole?"

His mom. *Crap. Crap. Crap.* "I dunno." My fingers are twiddling on my key chain. "Maybe he's using me to get back at her for something, huh?" I swing it back and forth, thinking of a quick excuse to tear out of there. He believes this is funny and laughs.

"You know, she copies your hamburgers from Beverly's now. She paid some big California chef to figure out the recipe. It isn't the Brandy Alexander up here. It is the Amelia Sirloin Petite Burger. She paid a mint to that chef."

"And she could have just asked me for the recipe," I bantered back. "I would have given it to her for free." Suddenly, Evan leans back and pats the window. He looks up and waves behind my truck. In my rearview, I can see a man in a suit coming down the stairway. Even now, I hardly recognize him compared to four months ago. His steps down the stairs are light and not the thick gait of men who have to balance because they can keel sideways from being heavy. He looks ten pounds lighter than the last time I saw him. His suit is form-fitting. But it isn't the weight he has lost. It isn't his stature. There's something in the way that he carries his shoulders, something in his straight posture that shows he just might be hitting that point, the one of self-assurance he simply didn't have four months ago. The one that comes from his mind and not his body.

Bear thanks the security guard with a quick wave and some small talk before he comes over. I tell Kaylee I'll just be a second. I slide out and meet him at the front of the truck. He takes off his suitcoat and holds it in the crook of his arm. We both lean against the hood.

"Well, surprise, surprise," he says, looking over at me. "I would have never expected Brandy Devereauxs to show up at the witch's castle. Should I check in the back of the truck for a bucket of water in case she flies outside—"

"At what point in our relationship were you going to tell me Amelia Vega was your mother?" I interrupted him. I'm not giving him the benefit of an expression. The July heat is beating down on me. I'm really mad at him. "It isn't something you leave out of a friendship. It is as simple as this: *Hey, your mortal enemy is my mom.* Just saying."

"Would it have made a difference?"

"Yes."

"Then my decision was warranted," Bear says, giving me a sideways shrug. "I just can't believe you didn't figure it out."

"What would have been my clues, Beau *Rodrigues*?" I asked him. "I've never been invited to your house, and you don't open up much. I had nothing to work with, no clues."

"Would it make any difference if I told you I was adopted? She's not my real mom?"

"No."

"It's true. She was married to my dad, and she adopted me when I was little. I heard the words relationship and friends a couple sentences ago. We're still friends?" He asks. I roll my eyes.

"Beau, I'm still dating my maybe-dead husband on Friday nights. The other day, I almost drove to the prison where my mom's incarcerated to sit out there. What do you think?" I put up a finger to stop his words. He pauses with a smug smile, lifting his lips. "No, don't say it. I'm crazy, that's what you'd think."

He ignores that whole idea. Kaylee is calling my name in the back seat. Bear shifts enough he can see her while I hold up a finger and tell her I'll be just a second.

"Do you want to get her out? Let her play a minute?"

"I think I saw a sign that said this is a child-free zone," I tell him. He furrows his brow like he thinks I really mean it.

"I'm just kidding." It is sterile here. No kids. No playgrounds. "There's a cliff edge right over there." I point ahead of us.

"I can hold her."

"No, I'm only going to be a minute. I'll never get her back in."

"How are you?" he asks right out of the blue. "You look much better than last I saw you."

"And here we go again, talking about me." It doesn't matter, though. I don't even know why I bother to ask him. "I'm sick of one-sided conversations with you. You realize you manipulate the conversation with me each time, right?"

"What's wrong with that?" he shrugs.

"A lot." I grunt. "I don't even know you. I don't know what your job is. I don't know why you flew under my radar for ten years. I don't know why you hid who you were and why you still do. You're just this blank-piece-of-paper guy who used to come and work out with me every day for almost five months. I didn't even know your real last name. I thought it was Rodriguez."

"It's Vega. Rodriguez is my middle name." He still can't look me in the eyes. He seems bored and detached. My heart suddenly feels sad. I'm trying to figure out what made my heart thump-thump-thump around him. It isn't doing it so much now. It's more like the sound the hospital monitors make when somebody is flatlining.

"I know that now because the security guard told me. You're obviously better friends with him, Mister Vega." I roll my eyes.

"What do you want to know about me?" Bear shoves his hands in his pockets. He stares at the ground, but I can see him glancing at his watch before he does.

"Oh, it isn't a big deal." I know he's watching for Meghan. I can see him glancing up again and again toward the far side of the building. "How long have you been living here?"

"Just since right about the time we met."

"Why'd you come back if you aren't happy here?"

"What makes you think I'm not happy?" he asks, staring across the woods. He shrugs. "I'm happy. My dad died. Mom needs help running the place."

"Did you do this where you were?"

"Why do you want to know all this?" he asks me.

I don't know and I tell him that. "Small talk, I suppose. You started growing on me—" Then I add: "Like poison ivy on a tree. Oh, regardless. My instructor called me yesterday and gave me another chance to pass his class. I'm failing if I don't. I was supposed to give a speech. I skipped it. He said if I come in and do one for one of his first-year orientation classes, he'll give me another chance."

Bear starts to chuckle, then tips his head to the side. "You are kidding me. You think you can do it?"

"No." I am honest. "I'm going to throw up in the parking lot and buck like a wild pony. But I need the grade to apply for a job as an assistant chef."

"I thought you were waiting until you finished school to apply for the full-time jobs."

"That was the plan." I scrub my hand through my hair. Bear watches me do this, then furrows his brow. "Somebody's got to take care of Kaylee. And there's the hospital bills and attorney fees. I've got to pay the trailer park for the two doors John busted with my head. My mama stealing my tuition money was a ball-buster. I'm dead broke again. I've got to pay back the loans before I go back next semester. I kept going down to the administration office and making excuses as to why I forgot the money. I've dragged it out until the end of this semester and after finals. I think they are on to me. I'll have to put it off. The speech is my final straw, breaking the camel's back. You know how that will end if I don't have somebody to catch me when I fall."

"You're quitting?" He reaches into his back pocket and pulls out his wallet. "Let me pay you for everything you've done for me, Brandy. I can help." He whips out a credit card and extends it toward me. "Don't quit school. I won't let you quit school."

"Haven't we been through this once before?" I can't believe he's doing this again. "I don't take credit cards, Beau." I hold out my hands, fending off his hand waving at me. "And I'm not quitting. I'm just moving on. Everybody's right. Your mom, my mom— I could go on with a long list of everyone I know. I won't. Because even God seems to think I'd be better suited waitressing at Beverly's and stocking shelves at Mister Smiley's. He sent Preacher Murphy to offer me a job cleaning the church on Mondays. You said it yourself. *I don't have the right stuff.*"

"I didn't say you didn't have the right stuff—" He just halts and stands there like I splashed a bowl of freezing water on him. "I guess I did." His eyes latch on mine. That damn thump, thump comes in.

"Hey, who's in there?" Bear asks. He reaches out and taps on the top of my head. "What'd you do with Brandy? Because she wouldn't listen to somebody's crap, much less mine."

"Stop it, Beau," I say, pushing his hands away with both of mine. I know he notices I'm using his real name. I can see how he keeps glancing over when I say it.

"Quitting just doesn't sound like you," he tells me. "What happened to the girl who runs down the hillside laughing like an idiot with hounds on her ass and gunshots over her head."

"Excuse me?" I twist my head up so my eyes meet his. "You were the first one in line to knock my dreams—" I stop. It isn't worth the fight. I say: "Naw, I'm sorry, it wasn't you. The girl got reality knocked into her. I think it was looking down that hole in Mama's trailer and realizing I couldn't fit through it with Kaylee. I started to pray for God to save me and realized I was asking way too much for God to figure out something I couldn't figure out myself."

"What do you mean by that?"

"I don't know. I just prayed for something else." I shrug it off. I push myself up from the hood of the truck. "Listen, I'm not here for a pep talk. I'm here to have you test something for me. It's for my job interview."

"Will you finish the part about praying, please?" Bear leans in, brow furrowed. "Finish what you were saying. It's important to me."

"No, just listen. The snacks are gluten-free and fat-free and, hopefully, don't taste like a piece of cardboard." I force a smile and shove away a hand he is holding out to snatch my arm. "I'm calling them Midnight Stash. I'm applying to a resort that focuses on health. It's the kind of thing they can put out at night for clients to snack on."

"Okay." He draws the word out. He's still giving me a stern gaze.

"You inspired me." I walk around my truck and reach into the passenger seat. I pull a brown paper grocery sack from Mister Smiley's and hand it to Bear.

"Enjoy. Be brutally honest," I tell him. "I've got a stone's throw chance of even making it past the first interview, but I need the job. I need out of here. It pays a little better than minimum wage and is far enough from Fire Mountain that folks don't know me."

"You're leaving?"

"Cross your fingers for me." I hold up my hand, forefinger and middle finger crossed. "All I had was Pops, and he has Kaylee now.

I got a restraining order on Mama and her newest boyfriend. I want to go somewhere nobody knows my mama or my past. Where it is too far to drive to a bar and obsess about a husband who obviously didn't think I was special anyway."

"Oh, like a place where you can take off your armor long enough to clean it and put it back on again before anybody really gets to know you? A place where nobody knows you're a quitter." Bear is biting on his lip, twiddling his thumbs, patting his leg. It is a sure sign something is bothering him. He holds out his credit card again. "Pay for whatever you want with it. New clothes. A car. Brandy, buy yourself a house with it, I don't care. Please stay around. Don't leave because I brought you down."

"A house," I laugh out loud. Then I realize he isn't kidding. My smile drops. "You didn't bring me down. I did it myself. I should have never thought I was good enough for anything more than being trailer trash." I shake my head and push his hand away. "I don't want your money."

"Then what do you want?"

"What I prayed for when John John busted through the last door, and I shoved Kaylee under the trailer. I want you to feel something with your heart, you know? Find a way to put yourself in somebody else's shoes for long enough to figure out who you are inside and up here." I point to his head. "I was afraid nobody else would pray that for you because they didn't know you like I do. Or maybe they didn't care as much as I do. I don't know. I just wanted to do it before I died." I snap up my keychain in my fingers and swing it in a circle. I snatch the key from the air, walk to my door, and latch on to the handle with my fingers. "Just try the snacks. Let me know what you think."

It is right then when I hear the whistles and cheers. I look up and see the cars parked in the lot waiting for the Cash Register Girls to come gliding past in their three-hundred dollar running suits and two-hundred-dollar practice running shoes. And there they come, their long blonde hair blowing in the wind, their hands waving beauty queen style at their admirers.

"Since when did they get celebrity status?" I sniff, watching them soar past, cameras flashing at their every step.

"Makes you just want to bring them down, doesn't Brandy?"

Bear leans in toward me and pushes off the truck. He walks around and jabs me in the ribs right in the sensitive spot. It burns. "Or maybe this?" He throws his hands like I did in my car at the bar that night. "You know how I know this? You look like the little prissy girl playing prim and proper in the sandbox with her toys all laid out in a perfect little row and who just got sand tossed in her face."

"That's what I'm talking about. Stop being mean, Beau," I retort. Then I look up and catch his eyes just as he locks on to my own. "No, it doesn't. I wish them well." He looks away, so I jab him in return. "Did you ever ask Meghan out on a date?"

"Megs?" he says her name like he just popped a candy honey drop in his mouth for the first time, and it is the best thing he's ever tasted. "Yeah, we've been out twice this week. She asked me both times. We met in one of the gyms at the club. I started going there late after everybody left to work out when I couldn't visit your Pops' place. She hunted me down. At least that's what Michelle says."

"Cool."

"That's all you're going to say?" He sniffs, pushing himself from the truck. Yes. That is all I am going to say because I feel a giant ball in my throat begging to get out.

"What do you want me to say?"

"I don't know. I worked hard to get where she'd go out with me."

"Bear, she would have gone out with you four months ago, dumbass," I tell him. "Come on, I saw how she looked at you the day I fainted and fell off the back of the choir stands."

"I guess I just didn't notice."

"No, because you were too busy worrying about everybody else's thoughts."

"Maybe. I guess. Kind of like you, now," he says. I climb into my truck and close the door. He is standing over it. "You're not the only one who doesn't want to turn out like her mom. I was in management if you really want to know. I hate working here. I hate it. I hate the suit, working with my mother, and sitting around and making decisions that could make or break this entire complex. You are the only damn thing that makes it bearable—that made it bearable. Were you serious when you said you prayed—?"

"Hey, Beau!" Right when he says that I see Meghan running up.

She breaks from her little pack and wheels around my truck while I get it started. She acts like she must use Bear's arm to come to a stop, standing there giggling and clinging to him.

"Hey, I know you, don't I?" she says. Her voice reminds me of bubbles popping in the air. Meghan puffs out her cheeks, crosses her eyes, and blows some air at her bangs. "Yes, I do," she answers, pointing a finger at me. She bounces up and down like Kaylee when Pops gives her an ice cream cone. "You are one of the janitors at Mister Smiley's. I remember you mopping up a little boy's puke the other day. Remember? He puked in the toilet paper aisle. I don't know how you stand doing that. It's so gross. Oh! And you're the one whose husband is missing. I remember that too—did they ever find his body? Ew, my daddy is a police officer, and he told me he had to come to your door and tell you they found bones in a field, but then it turned out to be a dead deer. He said it was horrible watching your face—"

"If you don't get her out of here," I growl. "I'm going to punch her in the face."

Bear knew I wasn't kidding. He snaps Meghan back a couple steps. I hear him consoling her until I start my engine. I hit the gas a couple of times so a black cloud of exhaust fumes bursts out and consumes the two, and then watched with a sight smile as the sound of the engine backfiring makes them jump as I pull away.

Chapter –19
More Demons

It is 2:45 in the morning. I know this because my cell phone's bell is going off as an alert for a phone call.

"You better be dead, Bear. Or I will kill you. Did anybody ever tell you it is rude to wake people up in the middle of the —" I cut the last off with a yawn.

"Holy Hell, your snacks are phenomenal. I ate the whole entire bag. I can't stop. I want more. More."

"I see you found the chocolate with the coffee beans in them," I tell him. "Those had a special note on them to save until you had a craving in the morning. They have caffeine. Lots of caffeine."

"You're kidding, right?"

"You're buzzing, right?"

"Will you sit up and talk to me until it wears off?"

"Where is your girlfriend? Can't she talk you down from a caffeine ledge?"

"Please. She's such a prude. She won't even kiss me goodnight."

I sigh and push myself up in bed. "Since I'm awake, lay back and push the phone to your ear. I'll sing you a lullaby."

"Oh, that's okay." He laughs. I don't. "I'm just kidding, Bejesus. Sing me a song."

"No, Bear, you sing me one tonight."

He does. His voice is deep, soft, and close to the sound angels make when they sing above the clouds. I don't sleep because I can't. It makes my tummy jumpy when he sings to me, even from a mountain away. I realize Bear's my caffeine. I'm addicted. And I smile to myself, hoping he doesn't force me off a ledge one day.

Chapter –20

Beverly's

I can't even stand to sit in the front rows of the church. It isn't that I feel I'm right within scrutinizing view of Preacher Murphy. I really don't fear that he might pick me out of the crowd and use something stupid I'd done recently to stress a point and parallel whatever bible verse he is ranting about in front of his congregation. I fear having to turn and look back at everyone looking at me. Boom! The lights will be out.

I tell Bear this while I'm washing off the counter where he has settled in at Beverly's Hometown Diner. He lifts his cup of coffee into the air so I can clean beneath it. He says I should've started at the back row of the church each Sunday and worked my way up one row a week. "But I suppose we don't have time for that if you're doing your speech in three days." Then he finishes with my personal sore spot: "Tell me something. When you were working on being in the Redneck Run, did you not think for one moment there might be crowds along the route to watch?"

He's so confident now. No, I would call it cocky. "I guess like everything else," I say flatly. I'm still wearing a soft bandage around my left wrist. I start to lean my hand on the counter. I remember it still aches when I do this, so I lean back a little. "I just didn't think it out."

Bear had pulled into Beverly's when I was just about to end my shift at 10:00 in the morning. I'm tired. I want to take off this itchy 1940s gangster-style dress Beverly makes me wear to wait tables, go home, and sleep. I think it must be a child's size. It is so tight that I can hardly breathe.

However, Bear sits down, orders a cup of coffee at the front counter, and won't stop talking to me. He tells me I fell asleep last night in mid-song. He could tell because I started snoring. I think he is lying, though. He thinks sitting down and chitchatting while I'm on Beverly's clock is okay. I have washed this section of the counter six times since he sat down, appearing to be doing my job while she eyes me carefully once in a while.

"Hey, this reminds me of something. There was this cute little blonde at the diner we went to. Do you remember her? Lilly, that was her name. You think you can lean over more and —"

"Go to hell, will you? You are twisted, Vega," I growl at him. He notes I use his real last name with a quick snap of his eyes upward. "Don't even go there with me."

"Brandy! Did you swear at that gentleman?" It is Beverly. She is wearing the same dress as me, but it fits her better around the chest. She has chestnut brown hair in a short bob and super high heels. She likes to live the part and dons a veil while sitting with her legs crossed on one of the cherry-red vintage bar stools reading a book. She keeps peering over the top at Bear, giving him a sexy look.

"No, ma'am," I say, glowering at Bear while I've got my back to her. Just as I turn to acknowledge her, he flirts a smile at her. She sinks her chops into it and breathes in deeply.

"Please go away," I turn back and whisper to him. "I've got ten more minutes," I tell him while a little lady with white hair waves a hand in the air and points to her coffee cup. "I've made it through three days without more than an hour's sleep. If I don't cuss some idiot out in the next eight minutes, I'm home free. I just have to finish my shift with a smile on my face, or Beverly is going to fire me." I pause and turn to the impatient old lady. "I'll be right there," I go over, grab the coffee pot, and work around the tables, doling it out. Bear is behind me, chattering away like we're at my Pops' house, not the diner.

"I want to take you somewhere today. It's a surprise."

"I've got plans," I lie. "I'm taking off for France."

"Really?" He actually believes me.

"No, butthead, I've got to work at Mister Smiley's in five and a half hours." I narrow my eyes. "Guess why. No, don't. I'm covering your girlfriend's shift. I've moved up to cash register girl for two and a half months, so the pretty girl can strut her stuff all day for the cameras at your country club."

"Wow, you're grumpy. When will you be done?"

"Well, if Mister Smiley can hide it from the West Virginia Labor Department, I go home again for an hour and come back to run the cleaning crew for the third day in a row until two in the morning.

I do my run, and I will start back all over again tomorrow at four." I stop, get right up in his face, and glare at him because I am tired-angry. "Then, little buddy, I'm flying to Hawaii with a guy I met last night in the parking lot."

"You're going out—with somebody?" he asks, cutting me off from one table. "Really? You won't go out with my best friend, but you'll fly away to Hawaii with a dude you met in the parking lot?"

I look at Bear. He is serious as heck. Do people really do this in his world? I can't even get to Charleston with the gas I bought for my truck by digging out the change in the seats. I take a quick look toward the front of the diner. Beverly keeps looking up from her book, eyeing me.

"I thought I was your best friend," I tell him, giving him the sad eyes I give Pops when I need to borrow five bucks.

Bear's head does a quick cock to the right. "Bejesus, I can't tell if you're playing with me."

"Dude, I'm messing with your head. I told you I haven't even been out of this state. Do you really think I could fly to another country with a stranger?"

"Hawaii isn't another country. It is part of the U.S."

"You do realize you will get me fired, right?" I tell him, pushing him to the left and out of the way with a gentle hand pat. "And it isn't just because I'm going to crawl across this table and wring your neck because you annoy me." I lean enough to pour the coffee with the white-haired lady at the table and sigh deeply. "No." I turn to look at Bear. "I'm not going out with someone; if I was, it isn't your business. I don't have time to date. I don't have time to go to the bathroom. I'm going home and sleeping. I can't afford to stop." I pause, pour the white-haired lady her coffee, and turn my head to Bear. "Why aren't you at work? Surely you run the show up on the mountain, right?"

"No, they just make it look like I do."

I know better. Since he came through the doors, he has received about a hundred texts and calls. He gives me a funny smile and shrugs. "They probably don't even know I'm gone. Therefore, I am here. I am going to take you somewhere." He tips his head and points his finger downward. "Hey, you're going to spill—"

"Brandy!" Beverly's scream forces me to turn my head to her, pointing frantically at the coffee pot I'm pouring past the top of the little porcelain coffee cup. It forms a hot river down the table, and I make a bumbling attempt to swipe it up with the dirty napkins the lady piled on her plate.

"It's a good thing you can cook. You're a lousy waitress." Bear is just standing there telling me. "No wonder my mom didn't hire you." He doesn't bother to grab a towel. He is just watching me bumbling around, scrambling to keep my job. I don't think it even occurs to him to help out.

"Can you not pick up a towel and help me?" I ask him. I snatch a clean napkin from the vacant table behind me and thrust it into his hand. He stands there, stares at it, then nods his head up and down. "Bear, you don't know how badly I need these jobs. I can't frigging buy toilet paper, and I'm almost out. Do you get it? And I'm not a bad waitress; you are just following me around like an idiot, and I can't do my job!"

"I will get this." Beverly swoops in, pushing me away with her hand and apologizing to the white-haired lady and then to Bear. I snatch the towel from Bear's fingers, but Beverly turns to me and shakes her head. "Maybe you should take a couple days off, Brandy. Just go home. I'll call you if we need help next week."

"You are too good to be working at that place anyway." Bear is trying to console me while I walk out to my truck. He is six inches from my left ankle on every step. "Maybe this will give you time to finish your classes."

"You can't do this. Bear, I know this is difficult for you to understand, but some of us don't have a mommy with her hand stretched out full of money." I'm ready to cry. "I can't finish my classes because I can't pay my tuition. It isn't just being unable to stand up in front of a class full of people and make my speech. A hundred things are currently stopping me, including the man who puts a roof over my head. Can you please leave me alone?"

"Go for a ride with me. I can call Don Smiley," Bear tells me, "I'll talk to him about letting you off today. How's that? It's not a problem. He'll do it. If you want, I'll tell Beverly that she better expect you in tomorrow to work, or I won't visit there anymore."

I'm wiggling my key fob, listening to my keys jingling on the end while I walk. It is hot already. I can feel the heat permeate the hair on the back of my neck. I come to a standstill and pivot to face Bear. I push my hand out to stop him from barreling into me. "Listen, Bear, I like you. I really do. But we are from two different worlds. I know it. You know it. You've never said it out loud, but you've shown it every time you see me. That is why you've never invited me to your house or asked me to have dinner with your family. We go into a diner, and you're looking around, seeing how people view how I dress and talk. Until last week, I didn't even know your last name. You didn't even talk to me when I went to your church. I don't get you. It isn't okay where I come from to bother me at work just because your family owns the country club. It isn't fair for Beverly to think your family will do something to her if she doesn't hire me back."

"Come on, Bejesus, I don't know what you're talking about. What could my family possibly do to her diner?" Bear rolls his eyes and shakes his head back and forth.

"Put her out of business." I point to the vacant building next door. "That used to be Pickett's Grocery. They weren't big, but they'd been in business here for sixty years. That is until Don Smiley started rubbing elbows with your people up at the resort on the mountain. I went to school with Zach Pickett. He said your mom went to the tourism association there, and suddenly, they wouldn't advertise with Pickett's anymore; they advertise with Smiley's. Everything they tried to buy started costing twice as much. Then, one day, they couldn't afford it anymore."

"That's not my mom's fault."

"Yeah, in my book, it is," I tell him. "That's what I mean when I say we don't see eye to eye, Bear. I'm sorry, but I'm just not like you. If I did the same to your mom's country club, you'd be all up in my face about it." I shrug. "But it isn't just that little store. Three gift shops went out of business because your mom put up a huge gift shop along the road leading to the resort. The riding stables outside town couldn't compete, the restaurants along the highway shut down when you put the buffet in."

"We are not responsible for folks going out of business. It is bad marketing or bad management on their part. They can compete.

For every business that can't keep up the pace with the economy, three benefit from having our resort here."

I really thought Preacher Murphy sent Bear to help me out. As I'm listening to him now, I'm not sure the preacher knew him well enough to figure out he was not such a good person inside. "But Bear, yes, you are," I tell him softly. The sound of a car coming down the road behind us nearly cuts off my words. "We are all in this life together, messy or not, like me and Pops. We fight all the time. We can't always see eye to eye, but at the end of the day, I'm not trying to hit him in the shins with a baseball bat, so he goes to bed hurting." I reach out and poke Bear in the arm. I watch his eyes follow my finger. "This town isn't any different. Your place can grow and prosper and still support the rest of these little places. In the long run, people come to see them to get a feel for the little town at the bottom of the mountain where the big resort is. It's all about the environment and the character of the region. And it is real live people you are hurting when you put them out of business."

"Where did you come up with all this?"

"You think I'm stupid because I'm from here? I'm not. I went to college, I took classes that had to do with the stuff I know." I bite my lip from saying more. "Why don't you just tell Preacher Murphy your job is done with me. I think I've done more for you than you've ever done for me. Have him send some other bible-toting do-gooder. Somebody more like me, someone from *my* world."

"You're right. We are from two different worlds. I guess I'm the survival of the fittest type. You live, or you die." He is quiet for a minute, stands there while I start to lean against my truck, and realize it is too hot already on its surface to let my butt rest against it. "But honestly, I've never really known anybody hurt by what my mom's done. It would help if you looked up to her. She raised two kids nearly by herself and built a huge business. She's rich. I don't see it, Bejesus."

"You don't see it," I say softly and nod. It didn't surprise me. Maybe I should have pointed them out along the way. "Well, you have met many people your family has hurt on their charge up the mountain." I sigh. "You see, Boar Mountain wasn't always called that name. It wasn't called that until your mama built her place there. Together, our two mountains were The Fire Mountains.

When the Civil War tore through our state, the mountain we lived on mostly had the McAllisters. And they were southern sympathizers. Boar Mountain had mostly folks whose boys fought for the north. It was the MacCabes, Pipers, and the Picketts and the Dinsmores. Now, everybody fought back and forth, mostly yelling and carrying on. But stuff started to get split down the middle, like the churches and the stores. Then, one day, there was a fire. It went up one side of what Fire Mountain is now and then started up what Boar Mountain is. It could have been bad because there were Yankees and Rebels. In all likelihood, they should have been happy to watch each other's homes burn. But they weren't. Both of them worked together to stop the fires. In the process, though, the old church got burnt down. But the preacher came up and said that they should build a place in the middle where the church once stood where everybody, no matter what they believed, would be the same. And that the two mountains on either side be as one."

"I don't think it is anything more than a story."

"Really. Because of the town in the center, they named New Alliance. Millie Piper's husband, Ivan, was his great-grandpa, and he was the preacher at that church. And it was Ivan who worked at Pickett's. When he lost his job, he didn't have insurance and couldn't afford to go to the hospital when he got sick. Billy Finch and Ellen Dinsmore, for which you pick up the food pantry stuff at Smiley's, had a two-hundred-year-old cabin on the creek at the bottom of your property. The town bought them out for ten thousand dollars, said it flooded down there too much, and they couldn't live there anymore.

"Okay, I get it."

"No, I don't think you do. Billy and Ellen Dinsmore are the ones at the apartments that used to be a hotel out on the highway. My cousin, Kenny, and his dad, his grandad, and his great-grandad lumbered off the Finch's property and owned the lumber yard up there. They're part McAllister, part Dinsmore. My Uncle Craig lost the business when your mom came in. He was probably one of thirty back then whose work went to hell. She contracted out to big businesses for everything that had to do with the resort and country club and said a bunch of hick locals didn't know what they were doing. You want me to name more?"

"Not really."

"Oh, sorry, not done," I snap. "Because Bobby Reese, who shoots the targets, used to feed half the community from the deer he hunted in the fall off Boar Mountain. He fed Grandma Pearl and the Heeter family, who now live off the state because they can't get a job because there are no jobs except for the country club. Do you get where I'm going? Your mama doesn't like hunting and says it is murdering animals. More than a few bellies go hungry now."

He shoves his hands in his pockets and rocks back and forth on his feet. I imagine he'd have that same line, the one where he said: *To say I'm sorry would imply I was wrong.* I cut him off before he says it. I didn't want to hear it again.

"A thousand sorries written on cardboard and torn pieces of paper all over town won't bring back what the Fire Mountains used to be, Bear," I say softly. "And not ones that aren't sent from the soul but just from the head. Although they are heartfelt, you are right; you and your mama don't ever think you are wrong because you don't have any understanding or empathy for those people you are hurting. We are just a bunch of stupid locals, hillbillies or rednecks. I took your shallow sorries because I felt sorry for you and figured, well, that's all I thought you could give."

"You felt sorry for me? I can't imagine that."

"Yeah, sucks being on the other end of the stick, doesn't it, Bear," I say, leaning forward and pushing my hand on his chest. "See, when I first met you, I thought what you were missing was up there in your head—self-control, confidence, the ability to have a character and be proud of it. I was wrong. It isn't. It is right here. You've got no heart, no soul."

He shoves my hand off. I think he is going to walk away. He doesn't. "Okay, you've had your say. Now let me tell you how I see you. I think that's fair."

"Go for it, Vega, you don't scare me."

"You are a hick, a hillbilly, a redneck, or whatever you want to call yourself to show how tough you want to be on whatever day it is. You do realize people roll their eyes when you hang it out like a banner, don't you?" He pauses and looks at me. I don't give him the benefit of an expression. Just fold my arms across my chest. "On the outside, you wear your flannels, tank tops, and old blue jeans.

It is like you are waving a flag to rebel against society that doesn't care about you. You refuse to change. It might make it look like you're surrendering everything you believe in. Your mama is a crud. She uses you for a ride or money, and you let her. She sticks up for her boyfriend in court and tries to make you look like it is your fault he nearly killed you. It's just sad. Your husband was a jerk; he went out on you and left you. I'm sure he told you a time or two that you were trailer trash or you couldn't do better than him. You run around chasing him all over the place, thinking you can latch on to some old memory that probably never existed in the first place. It was all in your head. You're stuck here in this shithole town, and you've got nothing, and nobody but your Pops. But there's something you have that most people don't. And whatever it is, you use it to start digging your way out. But you get so far and start thinking that maybe everybody else is right. You're never going to amount to anything. You're not good enough to reach the top of the hill. You stop. Instead of figuring out what got you stuck in the first place, you—stop."

He's not telling me anything I don't know. However, it still hurts to hear it from somebody else's lips.

"You want me to stop."

"I'm a girl. I can take it."

"You bank everything on a stupid competition you'll never win. It isn't that you're not tough enough or tried hard enough, Brandy. Because God knows, I think you would win if there was a contest of who had the biggest heart, the one who won't stop until she drops dead. You surely didn't give up on me; I had given up on myself. Now I'm wearing T-shirts again." He kind of forces a smile. I'm not feeling it. "Big marketing companies like The Texas Advertising Team and Rainn Promotions have worked with the tourism offices all over the United States to bring in the best athletes, so there is no way anybody else can win. They can't. Period. I've sat in on the meetings. Because there is a lot of money involved and politics involved. Even some big churches have tossed in a million bucks to get their name on a ballot. It isn't just the commercial at the end of the rainbow folks are vying for. Every one of these athletes is marketable." *And some ugly little girl from Fire Mountain is not.* "Whoa, stop." I push my hand between us and shake my head.

"You can stand here all day long and tell me everything that is wrong with me. I know they exist, and if you're doing it to try and hurt me because I said you didn't have a soul, it has already been done over and over again. There isn't a night that goes by that I don't wake up in the middle of it and stare at the ceiling and wonder what it'd be like if I had a real mama and daddy around if I didn't cuss if I would have been a better wife for Josh. A hundred ifs. I can think of a thousand things I should have done or could have done but didn't. Those old ghosts will haunt me forever, I suppose. But about the Redneck Run, that's where you're wrong. It wasn't the race up the mountain. It was getting there. It was everybody coming together just like they used to back when there were two Fire Mountains and not one Fire Mountain and a castle with an evil witch and her sinister, dark son at the top of another." I stop and take a breath. "I suppose I was hoping if one of us just got to be in the Redneck Run and maybe placed less than a millionth, we'd have something to hope for. All those people you met, that's all they need, Bear. Not your money. Not your pity. And certainly, not somebody that tells them that it is great they have heart, but not the ability to succeed. That's all they need. That's all I needed."

But it was too late now. I pull up my phone and look at the time. "Okay, I think we've torn enough wounds into each other for today, Bear. I got to go and stitch myself up before my next shift. Thanks for the advice. Thanks for summing up my life and putting it in a piece of toilet paper so I can flush it down the toilet."

Chapter –21
Riding ATVs with Kenny

On Saturday, Kenny and I drive a couple of Pops' ATVs to the very tip-top of Fire Mountain, which faces Boar Mountain. You can see the resort and a few huge log cabins. One is, no doubt, Amelia Vegas' home. We turn off the engines, sit back, and share swigs of bottled water. You can see forever from up at the top of this mountain, or at least until the clouds or the last misty fog gobbles up the next set of mountains beyond. I can't help but wonder what Bear's doing over there at this very moment. He's probably sitting at some swanky desk the size of Pops' living room and signing contracts for something. It is nearly silent up here except for our conversation—hunting, Kenny's job at Trimble's Hardware Store, and hunting again.

"I can't wait until hunting season," Kenny remarks and sighs.

"No wonder you don't have a girlfriend." I take a big swallow of the water and plug the top with the lid. "All you talk about, Kenny, is hunting."

"Okay, how's this?" He turns to me. He got his hair cut last Friday, which is way short on top. He's not used to it and keeps patting his head like he's wondering where it went. Kenny is smiling, and his eyes sparkle when talking to someone. "I think you should still do the Redneck Run, Sandy Brandy."

"I appreciate your support, even if it is a bit belated, like all those birthday cards you gave me two weeks too late." I smile. He knows I'm kidding.

"I'm serious. You're looking at me like you are waiting for a punch line, Brand New." The nicknames from Kenny are never-ending.

"I am." I see him get this little smile on his lips. "I can't do it. I don't have a sponsor. I don't have a team. Bear said that the teams have sponsors donating millions of dollars. It is all a political thing, a way to market their businesses. I can't even get Beverly's to donate the thirteen-hundred-dollar entrance fee. She says it is demeaning to call people in our town rednecks and refuses to get involved."

"Well, Beverly is weird. And Bear, he don't know shit, Brandy," Kenny stretches his arm out, wiggles his fingers for the water. "Do you know how many folks in town were talking about how they thought you had a chance?"

"Like who? The only chance I had was to make a fool of myself. That's what Bear thinks," I reply.

"Everybody who came into the hardware store, that's who. And everybody at Fire Mountain Community Church."

"That's not a lot of whos, Kenny, compared to what the Fire Mountain Shadows have following them."

"I'd do it with you," he tells me then. "I'd be a part of the Redneck Run. I would."

"You would." I think he is getting ready to burst into laughter for a moment. He doesn't. My cousin loses the smirky smile he's trying to hide and gets serious. "You think I'm kidding. I'm not."

I am thinking about Kenny's words four hours later while I'm ringing out Rita Henderson's groceries by running them over the scanner on the checkout counter, one by one until each makes a tinging sound to show it rang up correctly. Toilet paper. *Ting.* Carrots. *Ting.* Butter. *Ting.* Premiere Women's Maxi Pads. Getterman's Sausage. *Ting.*

"The Women's Maxi Pads didn't scan." That's Mister Smiley standing behind me, arms crossed and rolling his head back and forth impatiently. "Shirley, did you hear me?"

I forgot I told him my name was Shirley. I'm not quick enough to snatch them up while they continue their roll down the counter, so he shoves himself around me while the rest of the groceries back up on the counter. "Good God, Shirley, are you deaf?" Much to Rita's embarrassment, he takes the plastic bag of pads and starts swooping them over the scanner wildly again and again.

Next, he holds them up and grabs the microphone like he will announce to the world that he needs the price of Premiere Women's Maxi Pads for Rita Henderson in Checkout Aisle Two. But before he does, he turns to me and mumbles: "This is what we get when we must hire half-ass, backward employees from the county poor box. They can't label the groceries properly and are too stupid to run the register. I cannot wait until *my girls* are back from their training."

I feel my lip twitch. I see his hand reaching for the microphone and the panicked expression on Rita's face. I try to hold my temper at bay. I can't. Pops is right. I'm like Mama when it comes to having a problem with anger management. However, unlike Mama, I don't always need to scream. I say how I feel in a calm, cool, and irritated manner. Such I do while my hand gently pushes the microphone away from Mister Smiley's pink, puffy lips. He doesn't even get to clear his throat while I stand there and shake my head. "No, by the way, I'm not deaf," I say flatly to him. "I can hear every word you say. But my name is not Shirley. It is Brandy. And Brandy can hear every word you say about her butt when she leans over to clean the mop bucket in the back room. Yes, you could probably bounce a quarter off it. But you're not going to do it unless you want my fist in your face and your own butt on the floor. And no, you're never going to get sugar-sugar like that from me, as you call it."

I lean in and focus my eyes on him. "I'm not deaf. I hear you talking to the guy who brings in the frozen pies and saying he better not let Missus Smiley see them. She gains twenty pounds in her ass just looking at the lemon meringue ones, and she's got a freezer full of them at home. You laugh. I hear it. It isn't funny. Do you know how much liquor she sneaks out of the refrigerator section to deal with your nagging mouth? I do. A lot. I hear you mimicking your customers' accents and drawing them out slowly so we all sound like idiots. You've make fun of Little Pete's lisp when he comes in to buy Super Super Bubble Gum. I heard you saying cusswords that I did not even know were real words when Preacher Murphy was late picking up the pantry food. And you can't tell us enough how bad it is you must hire us locals, us hillbillies, us redneck trailer trash. I hear you. But if you look around, that's also who buys your stuff."

I am staring at Mister Smiley, who is frozen to the spot where he stopped only inches from my face. His face is deep cherry red, and he's shaking somewhat. "And just because I am local and you make me clean the toilets does not make me an idiot," I tell him. "Just because I missed one thing on the scanner doesn't push my IQ down to ten." I had my say, but I could have gone on longer. Everything in the store had come to a complete halt. Everybody just got off work about a half hour ago, and it is a busy time of day, with folks stopping in on their way home.

I catch Ellen Wells coming to a standstill at the end of the register line in her white Mr. Smiley's apron, cutting a line across her neck with one forefinger and then shoving it up to her lips like she is telling me to cut it and shut it. I peer to the right, look down Aisle 5, and a young woman with a baby in a cart has stopped to look up front. And Missus Smiley is back by the deli, swiping her hands on the front of her apron and stomping down Aisle 5 towards the front.

"Oh, shit," I say. And that, too, was blasted over the microphone for everyone to hear inside and out to the speakers in the parking lot.

"Get out." Mister Smiley lifts his hand into the air, pointer finger aimed toward the front doors. He uses the other hand to flick off the microphone at the register, and he leans into me and grits his teeth hard. "I don't care if Mister Vega specifically asked for you to deliver supplies to the resort this afternoon. I don't care. I don't get enough sweeteners in my coffee from the church or that resort to take in dumbass hillbilly rednecks like yourself. So be it if I don't go to heaven because I fired you. I'll go to hell. Get out. You are fired."

"I've hit my lowest point."

"Well, good, that means you've got nowhere to go but up." Pops is trying to cheer me up a couple of hours later. "You know, there's nothing to stop you but those big ears of yours." He makes me a huge bowl of chocolate ice cream, and it is a mixing bowl, so it is an entire container. Then he dribbles half a bottle of chocolate syrup on top and tosses in some cherries.

"Enjoy that." Kenny is sitting next to me on the couch. "McAllister and Devereaux's clans will have to drive an hour away for groceries now. Thanks, Branding Iron. That means no ice cream because it will melt in our trucks." I've got the blanket over me. It is freezing in here. Yes, we finally got the air conditioner into its frame. However, Pops bought it at one of his beloved flea markets, and it doesn't know when to stop. It must be thirty below zero in his living room right now. Kaylee has a big mixing spoon and is helping me eat the ice cream. She thinks it is the most fun thing she has ever done. It probably is. I remember coming to Pops' house, feeling safe and loved for the first time.

But Pops says there is one good thing about today. He said Mama called from jail, and if I talked to her and dropped the charges, she might sign the adoption papers for Kaylee over to Pops. I suppose that's a good thing for Pops. Not so much for me. I'm walking around looking over my shoulder for John John all the time, worried they'll let him out again, terrified he's going to hunt me down.

Thus, I'm still sitting on rock bottom when there's a knock on the front door. We all know it is a stranger or a cop when somebody knocks because family and friends usually walk right in. Suddenly, it is quiet in the room. Pops is talking to one of his workers on his cell phone and stops dead still. Kenny's head snaps up toward the front of the house. Strangers or cops. I never noticed how funny we look when an outsider comes to visit. It is like we are a little family of wary bunnies chewing away on the grass, watching for hunters, and with the sound of footsteps, we all shut up and look wide-eyed at where the steps are coming from.

"It's Bear," Kenny says loudly. "You know how I know? He's so damn tall. I can see the top of his head at the upper window on the door. Who agrees? We can all pretend we're not here. Maybe he'll go away."

Kenny was kidding. He didn't know about Bear and me fighting in Beverly's parking lot a few days ago. Honestly, I wish I could hide from him right now. I want to sit here and gorge my newest failure away with ice cream. It's not that easy because Pops doesn't know an enemy. He hops up like Bear's got a bag of his favorite candy at the door and opens it wide, inviting him in.

"My wounds are still healing," I tell him, pretending I'm pulling a fake knife from my chest. "You hurt me. Go away." I drop it to the ground with a shaking hand, then fall back dramatically, almost losing my bowl of ice cream. Kaylee thinks this is funny and shoves herself next to me, laughing.

"That's not fair. You had the bigger sword."

"I actually had the *better* sword," I tell him. "I just needed a shield to block your blows. You hurt my feelings." His words hurt me, but I suppose if I got Mama's temper, I also have my pops' ability to forgive after a few days.

"Do you want me to leave?" He jabs a finger at the door.

"Because I can." He's not looking at anybody else. I know he thinks I told everybody about our fight. In that light, I am surprised he has the guts to even come in the door without fear of getting shot. "But I hear you're not working at Smiley's this afternoon, so I came to see if you wanted to ride somewhere."

"How'd you hear that?"

"From what I gather, the entire town heard it broadcast over the loudspeaker."

I know I'm staring at him. You see, I had this love/hate thing going with Bear from the very start. I liked his looks even when he was chubby. I like how he's gone from shy to having the same kind of cocky swagger Josh used to have and the way he has a hard time looking me straight in the eyes but forces himself to do it. The way he tugs at those little chin hairs and then rolls his hands to get his hair out of his eyes nearly makes me speechless. It's a nervous habit for him. It drives me wild inside. I forget just for the moment I hate that he's got a girlfriend and he's too embarrassed to be seen with me. But he is right. Who wouldn't be mortified to say they were my friend? I'd try to stand in front of me, hiding the raggedy clothes.

I also realize I look beautiful to him, too, right now, with my crappy ripped-up jean shorts, a tank top, and my bare feet. Add in the mixing bowl full of ice cream and dribbles of chocolate running down my arm from Kaylee smacking her spoon against my shoulder; I am sure I am a wonderful sight to behold.

"Brandy!" They all say it at once, smacking me out of my daydream.

"Huh." Oh, no. My mouth is probably wide open, too.

"No wonder you got fired today." Pops shakes his head back and forth. "You're loopy."

"Well, not barring the fact she dragged out all of Mister Smiley's dirty laundry in front of everyone," Kenny adds.

"God! Leave me alone!" I'm embarrassed because they are all snickering at me, so I shove the ice cream toward Kaylee and stand up. I stomp across the room, snatch my keys off the little table in front of the couch, slide on my cowboy boots, and make my way to the door.

"Listen, I had nothing to do with you getting fired this time." Bear is following me out to my truck. Pops' yard and driveway are covered in trees. It is not very cool beneath them but shaded. Sun dapples the dirt ground at my feet. Summer. I love summer, the green grass and trees, and the sound of cicadas humming.

"It isn't like you are big on apologizing anyway."

"I shouldn't have said what I did the other day, I'll admit it," Bear says. "But what you were saying, it was freaking me out." He reaches out and tickles his fingers along my arm to get me to stop. I come to a standstill and look down at my elbow, where he is gently laying his hand. "I took a hike on Boar Mountain with an old plat map I got at the county offices, went out, and found all those places you were talking about—the old lumberyard, the cabins, and a couple old houses they tore down. I even found a mailbox with the name of Reese on it. I saw the foundations, the old asphalt roads."

"Did you think I was lying?" I asked softly. "I don't understand what you're getting at."

"No, Brandy, I didn't think you were lying. I just wanted to see it for myself, feel it for myself, like you said. It was surreal. It was like an old ghost town. I put the faces with the names and the houses and—I think you've introduced me to everyone on that mountain."

"I probably have, barring a few who have died. Many of them were at Pops' house when you were here. I suppose it is a ghost town now." I shift somewhat so his hand falls away. "At least that's what they call it on the posters for the Redneck Run. They say Boar Mountain and Fire Mountain are ghost towns."

"The only thing I didn't find any sign of on the old map or off the trail was the church."

"You go to the church. It is Holy Trinity."

Bear lets this sink in. "Oh. But I got the feeling from your story that it became common ground between everybody. It's kind of—"

"—the church for the rich people in New Alliance now? Yes, but it wasn't always like that," I finish for him. "Yeah, another product of the resort high on the hill. We've got the little Fire Mountain Community Church. It's an old metal pole barn, and our preachers don't have a degree in anything. It is just a few folks that talk about God and read from the bible and tell me I'm going to hell."

"I wish it wasn't like this," Bear says. "I wish—" He chews on whatever thought is working up in his mind. Bear's quiet, reserved. "I wish I could give it all back to your family, the Reese family, and Ivan Piper's wife. I wish I could rebuild all those cabins and stick those families back like before they had to move out. I wish I'd never met any of you. Then I would not have to feel this incredibly bad." He shoves a fist to his chest and pounds it. "Because it is killing me. I wish I'd never let Gabe talk me into going to that bar, so I saw you sitting alone. Because I could have gone my entire life over there—" he lifts his hand, pointing toward the direction of Boar Mountain. "—without any worries about the things that I do and how it affects everybody else. I could be like my mom and just skate through life. And now, dammit, I can't."

I'm not sure what to do or what to tell Bear. Welcome to being human! I can't do that. It is a strange and wonderful wound he has now, one that a Band-Aid won't protect. My eyes wander then, down the driveway. The bit of light trickling through the trees makes it hard to see the truck sitting there. It is one of the big trucks, not quite a semi, but the ones they keep at Holy Trinity for their food drives. IT IS A MOBILE FOOD PANTRY TRUCK!

I push Bear aside and look up at him. "Please tell me you didn't drive up here in the church truck that says MOBILE FOOD PANTRY." He did. "Bear, what were you thinking? You've got to get that thing out of here. If Pops sees that in his driveway and thinks our neighbors saw you bring it up here, he will get out his double barrel shotgun and shoot you through the head. Did anybody see you pull that monstrosity up the hill toward our house?"

"I don't think so."

"Get it out of here before Pops comes outside." I know Pops has a lot of pride. If he believes anybody thinks we're needy, he will die.

"Bejesus, I'm bad at backing up, especially down the mountain. I'd planned on using your turnaround in front of the house."

"Why did you drive it here? Did you forget to make your truck payment or something?"

"No," Bear groans at me. "What is the big deal? I borrowed it from the church to get you out of work. I told Don Smiley I needed help from someone at the grocery filling it up for the church and taking it to drop off food."

"Why would you do that?"

"I don't know," Bear says. "It just sounded like a good idea at the time. I figured you wouldn't do it unless there was a reason, like helping somebody. You don't seem to like being with me."

"Give me the keys."

He hands them to me. I give a backward gaze to the house. Thank goodness the air conditioner sounds like a military jet taking off. I don't see Pops.

Driving a truck really isn't that difficult. Mama made me drive one when she got drunk, starting when I was about twelve and could reach the pedals. She didn't want to get a DUI. I don't think it occurred to her she might get in more trouble letting a pre-teen operate a monster pickup truck she 'borrowed' from our neighbor when he was out of town transporting groceries for Pickett's in his eighteen-wheeler. Regardless, there was no option of getting dings, pings, or damaging any part of it. I think at the time, she would sneak it up the hill while Pops was at work and make me back it out and take her to the Crazy Kettle or the Lazy Eight Pub in town.

I back the church truck down the hill until I get to the intersection of Buck Hollow Road. I'm not going that fast, but Bear's turning ten shades of white until I come to a slow stop in the gravel. "There," I tell him. "Can you get it from here?" I'm planning my walk back up the road and not really looking forward to it.

"Is there anything you can't do, Brandy?" He asks me. Then, on a side note, he gave me a half smile. "I mean, other than hold down a job."

"Haha. Too soon. Besides, half of losing my jobs was your fault." I glare at him.

"Will you let me take you somewhere?" he asks me while I'm shoving open the door with my hip. His hand stretches out, covering the expanse between us. "Not in this thing. We'll take my truck. Please. I'll beg." It is hard to say no to those soft brown eyes. I would have declined if I knew it was a well-orchestrated trick to get me face-to-face with Gabe. When we returned the truck to the church, Gabe was out on the front porch of the parsonage, drinking a cup of coffee. Bear waves him over when we hop out of the pantry truck, and then Bear disappears to drop the keys off inside the church.

"You look nice."

I look at Gabe, then drop my eyes to my tank top, shorts, and flip-flops. "Um, no, I don't. I was sitting on the couch eating ice cream and getting ready to go run. I was kidnapped by an idiot who can't drive a truck."

"Beau can't drive a truck?" Gabe asks skeptically. "He takes it up and down the mountains all the time—oh."

"Oh, what?"

"It was probably an excuse to get you inside." Gabe rubs his fingers on his eyes and shakes his head. "Bring you down here." It is funny how out of place he looks in this tiny town in his expensive clothes and fashionable haircut. "He wants me to ask you out so we can double with him and Meghan."

"He's not going to let it drop, is he? Why is he so dead set on this?" I reach out and poke him in the arm. "Oh, unless you really think I'm that *fresh*."

"One beer, and I'm never going to hear the end of it, am I?" Gabe asks. "But I don't know why Beau's fixing us up. I think he wants us to be happy."

"I'm a girl, you know that, right?" I ask him with a peer out of the corners of my eyes. He winces. His eyes reflect the same expression of the little bluebird that hit my windshield yesterday.

"What-do-you-mean?" Gabe studies me, and suddenly, his smile drops. I see a shield going up, some armor. I feel like I almost had a friend, and just as he reached out, I smacked away his hand. I screwed the relationship up even before I got to know him.

"I mean—" I draw the words out. Kenny told me that Gabe liked the boys better than the girls. He heard it whispered down whatever grapevine made it to his mama's ears. She has an inside source, I suspect, at Holy Trinity. His daddy sent him to some school to scare whatever demon out that they thought caused it when he was in high school. I used to wonder if it wasn't his daddy who was the demon because, until this year, I hadn't seen Gabe in town.

"You know what?" I finally muster. "I mean, I dress like a boy." I backpedaled, wanting to see his smile again. I wave my hands before me. "I don't exactly wear girly-girl clothes like Meghan Reynolds. I don't want to embarrass you or anything."

"You won't embarrass me. You're pretty, Brandy. I'll look forward to it if you don't bring your mama to wrestle me down to the ground again."

"Yeah, that's not happening. Mama's in jail."

"Oh, crud, I forgot." Gabe's face turns red. It brings out his freckles; he has two big cherry pies on each cheek.

Bear saves him. I don't know if he could hear the conversation taking an awkward twist, but he is suddenly there even as I reach out and give Gabe a playful push. "It's okay. It's almost worse tippy toeing around it, like Pops did for the first week. I'd rather think it is that far in the past that I can start laughing about it soon."

"Really?" Gabe asks. He has pushed back on a smile and looks sheepishly at Bear, who has sidled beside him.

"No," I say and make my eyes wide. "I just want to be normal and not my crazy mama's daughter. I want to walk into a grocery store, restaurant, or bar and not have someone define me by my mother."

"Don't we all," Bear says. "Don't we all."

Chapter –22
The Trip

"I assumed you were taking me home." I am suspicious when Bear turns left instead of right out of the Holy Trinity parking lot. "You're heading in the opposite direction. Are you kidnapping me?"

"Kind of." Bear's truck is big and nice inside. It has an all-leather interior and a stereo system that I don't have to kick with my foot to stop the CDs from skipping. "I'm taking you where I wanted to take you the other day. Sit back and relax. There's a pillow in the back if you want to sleep."

"You didn't drug me, did you?"

"Damn, Brandy, do you have to be so cynical?" He turns and looks over at me on the passenger side seat. You could put a football field between us; the expanse is so big. "Did I ever question you when you drove us all over?"

"Yes, you did," I told him. "In that ghost town that we found. You whined the entire trip. When I took Bobby Reese back to the retirement village and jumped the hills, you griped."

"Those were all warranted, you understand that, right? We were trespassing. You almost got us killed."

"You're alive, aren't you?" I remind him, and he laughs out loud.

"Only because I kept us alive," he remarks. "You scare the crap out of me sometimes, Bejesus." I am quiet and look out the window. Bear isn't sure how to deal with this. He thinks I'm mad. I can tell because he keeps looking over, trying to read my face. Then he flips on the radio and turns his attention to the road. After a while, he starts singing. He has a voice that is like the singers on the radio. It is deep, and he hits every note, even when being silly, pitching it up high to sing with the girls. He makes me grin when he does this, and I shake my head. "For our first date, I took Megs to a French restaurant. It was Stella's." Bear has a GPS on his truck, and it keeps interrupting him while we get onto the highway. "Have you ever been there?" I see him cringe like he knew I'd never set foot in someplace so nice. "I'm sorry." That wasn't very respectful. I just let it ride. "But it was nice. We had a good time."

"Actually, I have been there," I tell him. I start to push my feet up on the dash. It is automatic. I always do it in Kenny's and Pops' trucks. I stop and sit up a bit. "I went there for a class, and we all ate. I got to meet the chefs and see how they prepared the food."

"Nice."

"I'm not as backward as you would like to believe," I tell Bear.

"I don't know." He looks over. "I've only seen you in your own environment."

"And what would that be?"

"Your dad's house, in your truck, and at a few diners."

"Is that how you see me?" I yawn, and Bear reaches behind the seat until he tugs out a pillow. He doesn't answer me right away and avoids my question while he hands the pillow to me.

"It is going to be a while. Take a nap. And don't ask where we're going. I'm not saying."

"Where else did you go?" I ask him. "Dinner and a movie?"

"Just dinner. She had to get back to train the next morning."

"Too bad. I wanted to hear the sordid details of a lingering kiss."

"That's not happening. Meghan wants to wait for marriage for that."

"Really. Even the kisses? Wow, that sucks. Haha, get it, *it sucks*?" I try not to laugh, thinking about the expression on Bear's face when she told him those words. "Oh, my."

"Oh, my? What does that mean? Brandy, don't laugh." He wags a finger at me, and I can't help but giggle. "Meghan is a nice girl. Her father keeps a close watch."

"It means, oh my. Even nice girls give boys kisses goodnight." I say, settling back against the pillow. "Wake me up when you can tell me a more exciting story."

I didn't wake up for three and a half hours until Bear pulled off the road and nearly jogged me silly. "Brandy, wake up."

I'm half awake, half asleep, and blinking at the highway. "Do you always sleep like you're dead?"

"Not really." I stretch my arms out and blink at the nothingness while trucks and cars barrel past, the wind jostling Bear's truck. I follow his finger pointing upward, and I blink. *Kentucky.*

"Kentucky," I say. Then I'm holy hell freaking out, trying to get out of the truck. "*Kentucky*. That's freaking Kentucky?"

"Yeah, don't get out." Bear's trying to reach for me, but he's laughing at the same time. "Bejesus, we're on a major highway— Brandy, you're going to get yourself killed!"

I toss my phone at him. "Take my picture. I'm going to stand under the sign and do a celebration dance. Oh, my God." I huff and start running along the brim of the highway like an idiot, with my hands flying in the air and semi-trucks blasting horns.

"You can't do that goofy dance on the highway. They will arrest you and take you to jail." He had to drag me back in, and I think he unquestionably thought I was the most home-grown idiot that ever lived while we drove past the sign. I'm practically screaming like a two-year-old who has never been out of her playpen and suddenly realizes she is on the kitchen floor and the backdoor is wide open.

"I know you think I'm an idiot and don't care," I tell Bear. "I am backward." My hand is on my chest while we drive down the highway, and I'm turning my head to look back out the window and see where we've been. "But can you drive back over once more so I can feel the difference?" I pause and see him staring at me with a big smile. "I mean, I know there isn't a real difference on the outside. It is up here, okay?" I point to my head. Bear finds a pull-off and turns around, and he does this two more times until I finally lean back in my seat and sigh, "That was better than sex."

"Well, no, it wasn't," he says. Bear is looking at me all cocky, like he's the one that provided me with this mental orgasm. "But if you sit back and relax for another two hours, we'll do this twice."

"Twice."

It is four o'clock when we get to the bridge that crosses the Ohio River from Covington, Kentucky, into Cincinnati, Ohio. I am still almost high while I make Bear take me from one side to the other two times, no great feat considering some of the exits are closed. Another set of pictures, my goofy celebration dance, and another blast of horns while I almost get run over by rush hour traffic.

"I don't know what to say, Bear." I text the picture of me giving the finger by the Ohio sign to Kenny. "I think I can possibly say this is one of the best days of my life."

He looks at me like he's expecting me to burst out laughing like I've made a joke. I'm not. I know he doesn't understand the situation—that being there with him is a little slice of heaven for me. I mean, I know he's from Mars. I'm from Jupiter. We'll never cross paths other than how we're hanging right now. It doesn't make a difference.

Maybe that's what made me cry right then. I hadn't let the tears fall in a while. I learned when I was little, they didn't get me far. Mama didn't like to see them, which always made her boyfriends mad at me. Pops, he just got nervous and tried to make me happy by feeding me when I cried. It made Josh furious. He always just walked out when I did. I'm trying hard to cover them up, turning my head to the window and scrubbing my wrist beneath my eyes.

"Hey, Brandy, are you alright?"

I know Bear must think my life is so crappy that an event like this, simple to him, was such a big deal for me. I don't think so at all. It is significant for me because somebody other than Pops and Kenny tried to make me happy.

"Yeah, I'm fine."

"Then why are you crying?" Bear's taking an exit, trying to find someplace downtown to pull over. "There's tissues in the glove compartment." I'm overwhelmed again, staring at the buildings towering over us, thinking they could be the mountains, but all shoved up close together. Who remembers to put a box of tissues in the glove box? I'm lucky if I remember to shove the old rag I used to check the oil in my truck under the seat.

"I told you." I'm sobbing now into my hands and feeling awkward and weird and alone even though I'm sitting across the seat from someone. "Because you did something nice for me."

"You do nice stuff for people all the time. Every day."

How do I tell him it is different? That up until this point, he's been a dick about everything with sorries paid off with a credit card. A thousand times, I tried to just be me and stop my mama from drinking and dancing and hanging around crappy men. I tried everything I could to get Josh to find a job closer to home instead of driving his truck, hitting the bars, and being gone all the time. It didn't seem like they believed little me was worth making the change.

"I suppose I'm just overwhelmed," I tell him, taking his offer of the tissues in the glovebox and swiping away the tears.

"Will you let me buy you some stuff without thinking that I'm trying to buy your friendship or get you into bed?" he asks. I turn my head, briefly looking at Bear's eyes before he looks back to the street. It is busy, and people walk everywhere.

"I never thought you were trying to buy sex with your card, Bear," I tell him. He makes me laugh. "Is that what you thought? I'd take your money and tell you no."

"Really now." He has the same look Pops gets when he thinks I've come up with some big lie to cover something stupid I'd done. "I just figured you didn't want to be like your mom." I snap my eyes at him; I almost feel like he punched me in the belly. But it is the picture my mama painted. "I am sorry," Bear blurts. "When I said it, I realized what it sounded like. I'm not calling your mom a—"

"Whore," I finish it for him. "Yes, you did. I would say I deserve that after calling your mom a witch and—stuff."

"Lots of stuff." Bear is trying to smile it off. I know he is embarrassed. I know him well enough. "But I didn't do it because you criticized her way of doing things. You were right about my mother. She is mean. My point was that you —oh, Brandy, I don't know if I can dig myself out of this one."

"It's because you're right. It hurts me, though. Why does it hurt me? I don't know. I'm not her. I could never stop her from being that person."

"I never intended to hurt you."

"I know." I breathe in the deep sigh that comes after a good cry. "Let's just forget about it. I was trying to say that I thought you were buying my friendship. I thought you felt sorry for me because I'm not rich."

"No, I guess I'll be brutally honest." Bear sees a parking lot and veers hard to the right to turn in. "You are with me about losing weight. You're just too pretty to be covering it all up with the crappy clothes you're wearing. I think you're trying to hide behind it."

"Dang, Bear, you're being bold today. Hide what?"

"*You.*" He slides his window down to pay the parking lot attendant, then turns to me. "You keep telling me it is up here."

He pokes his head with his finger, drives through the lot, and finds a space. "You're bailing your entire career because you can't make a speech in three days. It is an excuse to avoid failure, like listening to me and giving up on the Redneck Run. Any girl who can rip the floorboards out of a trailer floor with her bare hands to save her sister can do anything she puts her mind to."

"Kaylee's life depended on it, Bear. It is different."

"I don't know so much about that. I just know you've got so much more going for you than those ditzy girls running the race and those four professional idiots who are demanding all sorts of favors from us like they are extorting us for promotions, free rooms, and cash."

"Ditzy girls?"

"Oh, come on. Megs is—like a plastic doll that her father must put on the shelf at night."

"Then why are you dating her?"

Bear shrugs. "My mom likes her. They are buddies." He holds up two fingers, crossing them. "They go shopping together and go to lunches. It's good for marketing. She's got the right look and the right background. She's small town cute. She's wholesome reading material for the press. Obviously, you don't read the paper much or would have seen the pictures they get of us. What little girl doesn't want to be Megs—athletic and famous?"

"I haven't had the time or the money to buy a newspaper." I shrug it off. "It's like the rich prince in the castle on the hill and the little small-town girl who rides off into the sunset with him."

"That sounds like a bad western." Bear shuts off the engine and reaches for the handle of the door. "Don't get me wrong, Bejesus, she's not so bad. I shouldn't have said that. She's cute. I honestly think I could be content with her for the rest of my life. And she gets along with my mom."

"Yeah, that's important," I tease him. "I suppose that's the difference between us. Meghan is doing it for celebrity status, the cameras, and the money."

"And you just like it. Ah, that sounds like Brandy Alexander Devereauxs, always giving and never taking."

"Is that what you think?" I ask him. "No, dude, I want to run. I want to smoke her bitch ass, leave her choking in my dust."

Chapter −23

Madison

In my dreams, my mom always got rich and came back in her limousine and took me binge shopping."

"This isn't binge shopping," Bear tells me. He just got off his cell phone. He keeps interrupting our conversation to answer it. I think he's gotten twelve calls in the last ten minutes. I don't know what he is talking about. He turns and walks away, going to where there are fewer sounds. "I beg to differ," he goes on. "You haven't seen my mother and sister shop. They have to close the store down for a week to restock. Besides, you don't think I saw all those girly girl dress-up magazine pictures you glued all over your bedroom door? You want this stuff. You know it."

I do. Hell's bells. I admit it, but not aloud. I like the jeans, skirts, and shoes he's buying me at the little shops. I think I'm willing to become his whore to *never* stop doing this forever. No, not really. Oh, yes, really. Oh, listen to me. I think Bear might be Satan himself come to tempt me. What will Pops think when I come home with all these boxes and bags?

"Those are Kenny's pictures," I razz him. I'm looking at dresses. Because Bear has decided he will pick me out something really sexy for the date that he set up for Gabe and me. I thought the last three he bought me were sexy. I'm unsure I can handle anything more than black velvet with straps. What could possibly be sexier? I'm overwhelmed.

"Please quit looking at the price tag." Bear smacks my hand gently. "I'm trying to make you eye candy, and you're working your way down the line going for old lady stuff."

"*Whose* eye candy?" I ask him. He doesn't answer quickly. His face turns a brilliant red. Maybe I just embarrassed him because there are two prim store attendants standing behind us holding things Bear shoves in their arms. I'm sure they can hear me. "The last thing you picked out didn't leave much for the imagination," I tell Bear. "You think I'm going to wear that little dress riding ATVs with Kenny?"

"There is more to life than hanging out with Kenny." Bear shoves a little red dress up against me. "Wow, that looks horrible." He tosses it on top of the rack. Red. Red. Everything he picks out and throws back is red.

"I don't look good in red. Not even flannel shirts."

"That's my favorite color."

"I am so sorry that your dress-up doll looks bad in *your* favorite color. Again, are you buying these clothes for you or me?"

"You. I migrate toward red. And this store doesn't have crap here." I apologize to the attendants, and Bear rolls his eyes. "Don't look at the price tags or apologize to the help."

"No, *you* say please and thank you to them," I scold him. "You treat them like human beings. You know they are human, right?"

"Brandy, stop. It is their job."

"Do you really think for one minute that they got up this morning and wanted to clean up after some jerk who keeps wagging a finger at them and telling them they have poor choices in clothes? No, Bear, they didn't. Make their life bearable. It isn't that difficult." I'm following him because he goes around a rack, sizing up something, and completely ignores me. "If for no other reason, do it for me."

He doesn't seem to listen until he slows along one side, rubs his chin, and looks at me from the tops of his eyes. He rolls his head and looks at the ceiling, then turns around and waves a hand at the nearest attendant. "Can you *please* —" Bear pauses for the drama while his eyes catch mine, "help me find something in red that doesn't make her look like a clown."

"Sir, how about black. It will accentuate her eyes."

"And her soul," Bear leans a little inward to the attendant, who thinks this is funny and laughs. I am glad he is finally bonding with the help, but suddenly, I feel like an outsider.

"Haha. Let's try maroon. It is kind of between."

I left with a black dress with maroon lace and a beanie cap that he told me may look better in the dresses than the ball cap I tend to wear. The dress is too tight and too short, and if Pops sees how much cleavage it shows, he will hit the roof. I'm feeling gorged, ready to go home, while I shove the beanie cap over my head and try to feel at home in it.

I can't help but think Bear's magically trying to replace Josh's hold over me with my beloved baseball hat in exchange for the beanie. Bear, however, isn't done. He takes me to this silly comedy club, makes me eat the worst greasy hamburger I have ever tasted, and listen to two guys who couldn't even get a knock-knock joke right. He takes me down a couple streets, through the pockets of people coming and going from work to home, shopping, or eating. I liked the smells of the city, the scent of shrimp grilling in one restaurant and the tangy taste of lemon chicken in another. He stops and asks me if this makes me nervous, like when I stand in front of a crowd. I think about it. I'm not too fond of the towering buildings and the cars ripping up and down the streets. But the people passing by aren't too bad.

"Then what's the difference? They are still looking at you when you walk by." Bear wheels me to one side so people can pass. "Are you afraid you'll do something stupid? Because everybody does that. You heard those comedians, if you can call them that. They were horrible. Nobody laughed. And they still sat up there telling jokes. I've hit flat notes singing in front of high school kids. You know how that went, right?"

"Yeah, I can imagine. But I don't know, Bear, if it is that I am afraid I'll do something stupid or not." I look up at him. He looks so concerned. "It doesn't matter. I can't do it. I know what you're trying to do. I really appreciate it. But I can't give the speech. I'll black out. Please just lay off. Stop." I am breaking out in a sweat thinking about it.

"I didn't ask because I didn't want to ruin your day," Bear has eased his truck up on the highway. Ohio isn't in the rearview yet, but there are only a couple exits until we're back in Kentucky. "It'll be late, but I can take a different route home, take you past that town in Ohio you wanted to go to."

"Mill Run?" I ask. I know that's what it is. 2049 Mill Street. That's where Madison and Zach Johnson live.

"Yeah, I think that's what you said. It is a good run if you are going straight from Fire Mountain. We can pass it with only a half hour added to the time."

"You checked it ahead of time?"

"Yes. But make the call—yes or no. The exit is coming up to go across the bridge.

"Yes." It wasn't resounding. My voice was pretty quiet, slipping into the air. Bear doesn't want to do this, and frankly, I don't think it is a good idea. I pursue this crazy idea of finding Josh. It probably isn't healthy. I wrestle with it myself.

"Do you still love him?"

"Oh," I shake my head back and forth, then up and down. It is not a discussion I can even have with myself. "I would love the idea that he is alive. There are so many romantic movies with amnesia plot line twists. I've toyed with the idea that he had some concussion, and I know how stupid it sounds, but he doesn't remember me until I show up. I'd love to embrace the fantasy that I discovered it is not him on all those driver's licenses, just his double. Maybe he works for the CIA. Maybe he'll see me and say, damn, I missed her. I quit. I'm going back to Fire Mountain. Happy ending."

"So that is a *yes*."

I watch the trees go by. Ohio and Kentucky aren't so different from West Virginia. "I know in my dreams that Josh never yells at me," I say. "He never walks out the door in the middle of a fight, drinks too much—"

"—hits you?"

I look up and fiddle my fingers on my knee. Bear is simply watching me. Do I lie? Does it make me weak that Josh shoved me to the wall a couple of times and slapped me a few more? I don't even acknowledge his question. I just shrug. "In my dreams, he has not. He isn't turning off some other woman's bedroom light and hopping into bed. I imagine he tells me I'm pretty and worth some epic battle with an evil villain, not staying out too late with his friends, and always hunting. In my dreams, he's not standing there with me until a more beautiful girl walks by, and he grabs her hand and escorts her into the sunset." I look out the window. There are the same gas stations, the same roll from hills to flat, farms to subdivisions. "I know I'm a much better person without him."

"If he isn't dead, would you go with him if he came back?" Bear's voice is loud in the truck.

"That's the big question everybody wants to know, right?" I say it to the window, see my reflection. I see me and know why he never came home. My hair is too dark, fine, and wavy until it looks like one big knot. My face is too silly, with a funny nose and delicate lips. I've got too many freckles, and my eyes look sad.

Bear doesn't answer; he drives on. It is too quiet in the truck, even with him belting out the song on the radio. I think about what I'll do if the Johnson's house is burned down. That will be a whole new ballgame for me. I'm trying to keep an open mind. Is Madison still alive, or is Zach still living? Then he makes me laugh with this crazy seat dance until his phone rings. He glances at it, turns down the radio, and answers it. I snatch my cell phone from my purse, plug in my earphones, and turn up my music so I don't have to listen to his conversation. I'm not quick enough. I can still hear him saying: *Hey, honey, yeah, I'm almost done with the meeting—I won't forget. You know I won't. Yeah, I miss you too.*

It is nine thirty before we get to Mill Run, Ohio. It is mostly made up of subdivisions. Two are old and run-down, with 1960s brick ranch houses and dried grass yards. The third is just one step up. The houses are newer, maybe from the 1980s. It looks like whatever funded the town went bust not too long ago. Most of the houses are for sale; two look abandoned.

It isn't the subdivisions we are heading for, nor the little town we pass through in less time it takes for Bear to take a couple swigs of bottled water he's got stuck in a cup holder by his dashboard. His GPS guides us along the Ohio River until, about eighteen minutes from town, a little flag comes up to mark the spot just as we drive past an old field.

"We must have missed it." Bear stops the truck and cranes his neck to look around. "Sometimes the GPS is off a bit."

It is getting dark, and the last fading edges of summer sky crawl lazily over the horizon in a pretty orange and green. We are between two newer homes, huge log houses with twinkly lights all around a wooden fence and a view of the Ohio River across the street. Bear starts to turn around in the driveway and catches a glimpse of the mailbox while I'm scrutinizing the amount of land between.

"Well, this one's 2049 Mill Street. If he's living here, dead or alive, he's moved up in the world. He's doing just fine right now."

I turn to look at the mailbox where Bear's finger is pointing. JOHNSON. 2049. I'm kind of sick to my stomach. He reads my mind while we sit there. "Do you think maybe he's living up there, or it's another Zach Johnson?" Bear's fingers are playing on the steering wheel, tapping out some tune I don't recognize. "Do you really want to knock on the door and see?"

"No, not really." Because in my mind, Madison Johnson is opening the door. She is everything I'm not—blonde, beautiful, big-boobed and classy.

"Alright." Bear starts to pull out. I throw my hands before me.

"Stop." While he puts on the brakes and eyes me warily, I breathe. "Okay, what if you pull up the drive. I'll get out and knock on the door."

"Bejesus, one of two things is going to happen." Bear shifts in his seat. "Some stranger is going to answer the door, or Josh is going to answer the door. What are you going to do if it isn't a stranger."

"I don't know," I say. "You're right."

"How about stopping at that little restaurant up the street and getting a cup of coffee. You can think about it. If you decide to come back, I'll walk up there with you."

I agree, but the coffee is stale, and the restaurant is only open for another ten minutes. The bill is four bucks, and Bear starts to push back his chair to pay. I stop him. "I have ten bucks in my purse," I jump up before he can stand. "I'm getting this."

Bear nods and waves me away with his hand. I see the waitress flirting with him while I'm paying. She sits in my chair, and they appear to be having a lengthy discussion. I'm sure it's another date to be, so I work my way to the restroom, walk out, and sit on the curb by the truck.

"Where'd you go?"

Bear comes out a good ten minutes later. I roll my eyes. "I didn't want to get in the way. I figured you were flirting up another date. You've got a thing for waitresses."

"Yeah, no, I don't," He waves a finger for me to get up. "Get up. We're going somewhere. I got some information. The waitress went to school with Madison. I know where she is."

We are at Mill Run Old Fundamental Church Cemetery. Bear's got his flashlight out waving it at the stones while he marches through the grass on one side. I'm using my cell phone, letting the light spray on the headstones on another row.

The cemetery isn't really that big. The church is a tiny wooden building with a steeple and a front porch. I don't know why we're even bothering. We know she is dead. The waitress said Madison died of natural causes—she had diabetes and a bad heart murmur. She remembered the family talking about how she never took her medication for it.

Her husband was another story. If he had Josh's red hair, she'd never seen it. It was bleach blonde. The couple would come into the diner on Sundays with Madison's family. The waitress said Zach moved away after a year or so. She remembered asking Madison's mama why he didn't come in on Sundays. He was a big tipper with a cute smile and a chip on his tooth. She said he sold the house, took off, and they hadn't seen him since. She said Madison's dad just rolled his eyes and shook his head like he expected no less.

"Big tipper. Yeah, Josh was like you," I tell Bear when we meet in the middle. He'd waved me over, squatted down, and pushed aside some flowers to see her name. "He liked the cute waitresses and gave them darn good tips."

"Did he have a chip on his tooth?"

"Yeah, Kenny busted his mouth with a fist once when Josh pushed me down the trailer steps. Josh fell backward and hit the stove."

"You know, Bejesus, there are a thousand guys that look like that, give big tips. It could have really been someone else." Bear reaches out and slips his finger along the writing. "Damn, she was only twenty-two. She died two years ago almost to this very week." Bear reaches out, grabs my shoulder, and gently shakes it. "I don't know what else we can do. I feel like we're chasing a ghost."

We are just rising when the cop car comes. Bear scratches his head as he watches the car pull up behind his truck in the little gravel drive that circles the cemetery. The lights are flashing, but there's no siren. "Folks, the cemetery closes at dusk." The police officer comes up in front of us and flashes a light in our faces. We both squint against it. "I'm going to need to see some IDs."

I must go to the truck to get my purse, then fork out my driver's license. Bear's already dug out his wallet and handed over his license. The officer scrutinizes them, looks up at me, and then at Bear. He's younger than the cops around the mountain and looks like he's fresh out of high school. I see a name embroidered on his shirt. It is Tom Hensel. "What brings you out here."

"We were driving from Cincinnati to Boar Mountain down in West Virginia. My friend here thought her ex-husband was buried here. Since we were coming through, we thought we'd stop and pay our respects."

"What's his name?"

"Um, Zach Johnson."

"Zach Johnson," he repeats. I see him hesitate and flash his light on my license again. He's clever, that I'll give him. "Your last name is Devereauxs, and it is on your license. Did you remarry?"

"Well, not quite. I've got to be honest. His last name was Devereauxs when I married him."

"I see." He fiddles with the driver's licenses and looks up at Bear. "Boar Mountain. That's where the big resort is, right? There's a spa there and skiing. Vega. I know that name. My girlfriend is talking about going there. Your family owns that place?"

"Yeah. If you want to come up sometime, give me a call. I'll get you a night on the house." Bear reaches into his wallet and gives the cop a business card. He takes it and nods.

"Nice. But you folks will have to leave. I won't cite you for trespassing this time, but it will be a different story if I ever catch you here again." He's smiling, though. Giving Bear the same kind of flirting gaze the waitress gave him from the diner's window when we left. He probably gave her a hefty tip, too.

"Yes, sir," Bear answers. The officer hands us back our licenses and adjusts the hat on his head while he escorts us to the truck. He stands there waiting for us to enter the doors, but I stop, turn around, and stand in front of the hood in the beam lights of Bear's truck. "You didn't know Zach Johnson, did you?"

"I did. It's a small town, Mill Run. She was my stepsister. He was a good guy. I built my house next to his."

"And you haven't seen him since?"

"He was distraught when Maddy died. I mean, I suppose we all knew it would happen eventually." He waggles his flashlight at me. "If you're looking for him, I got no clue where he could be. I didn't know he was married before. You sure you got the right guy?"

"Maybe not." I turn and walk through the dust shoved up from my shoes and glinting in the beam lights of Bear's truck.

"You didn't ask if Zach had a tattoo," Bear says, scooting into the seat. I close my door. "Do you want to ask him before he leaves?"

"Not really," I say. I didn't need to do it. I know it is Josh.

A little more than a few hours later, we're almost home. Instead of heading north to Fire Mountain, Bear turns a bit east. Twenty minutes later, his truck crawls up the far side of Boar Mountain and then along a black asphalt drive. He stops just short of a log home. It is enormous, a mansion, and ten times the size of Pops' house.

"You wanted to know more about me." He puts his truck in park. "This is where I live." I can't tell if he's trying to rub it in that he has more money than me. Then, I'm not sure because it's almost like he's keeping stuff from me because he thinks I'm so poor, I would be held aback by it. "Do you want to come in and watch some TV?"

"No, I've got to get home before Pops returns from my uncle's. He's playing cards. He'll be back by one o'clock." I shift in my seat. "I don't know if he'll like the idea somebody bought me clothes and stuff. Pops, he would rather see me in cruddy clothes than think some guy's buying me stuff, so I'll sleep with him."

"I'm not doing that, you know that, right?" Bear pats his steering wheel. "It's payment for helping me lose weight and stuff."

"And stuff." I laugh. "Like priming you up for Meghan?"

"What do you mean by that?" His head turns, and he almost looks angry. "If you are implying that I don't know anything about women, you are sorely wrong. I don't need your help with that."

"Isn't that what all this has been about, our relationship?" I ask him. "You are losing weight and tidying up, so she likes you? I'm kind of your trial version of Meghan, the dollar store doll you toss away when you get the pretty doll from the expensive place. Yeah, you've got plenty of money. And there are lots of girls who'd marry just for that. But Meghan, maybe not. She's famous now. I mean, Bear, let's be brutally honest, have you even kissed her yet?"

"That's none of your business."

"Have you ever really kissed a woman at all?"

Okay, it was a mean thing to say. But I know that's what everybody will think: Bear's buying me stuff because I'm sleeping with him. But that part wasn't his fault. I open my mouth to apologize and hold out my hand so he doesn't say anything. Before I can think of the right words to spit out in my defense, Bear crosses half the football field between us, raises his hand, and slides it around my neck. He shoves his hand around my waist and nearly drags me like a floppy baby doll the rest of the distance before he slams his lips on mine in one incredibly long, beard-scratching kiss.

I'm not one to sleep with a lot of guys. But I've kissed more than a few in my lifetime. I always heard you're supposed to see fireworks when the right guy kisses you with the right kiss. I didn't see fireworks. I just went completely blank. And I can't say there was ever a time that any guy has ever kissed me so damn good that I was afraid to take a breath for fear he would stop. Never. And I *do not like beards*. But that's where I was maybe a minute later when Bear let me loose and sat back.

"What the hell, Bear?" I shove him with my hands. He's just giving me this cocky, still-mad scowl.

"Is that what I should do with Meghan?" he asks. "Tell me, Brandy, will that work for her? I'll be happy to try you out on other things if you want. Because that's what everybody expects, right?"

"Stop!" I snap at him. "Please, stop. I'm sorry. I shouldn't have said that. It isn't you. It is my mama again haunting me. No, I don't want it that way. I'm surrounded by men all the time. I don't know why I say that stuff to you."

"I shouldn't have done that. Gosh, what was I thinking?" Bear scrubs his face with his hand and starts patting his leg while he slides back over to the driver's side. "Did I traumatize you?" It is funny, his words. I look up, and he is as serious as anything, and it makes me laugh. My mama's boyfriend tried to kill me. I find out my ex-husband may have more wives than I can count on one hand. And Bear, he's worried a kiss will mar me for life.

"Please don't laugh at me," he says, looking hurt.

"Bear, I've been through hell the last three months. Your kiss—"

I sigh, shake my head, and smile softly at him. "Your kiss was like heaven, no damage done. Just a little shocking. I hate beards." Oh, why did I say that? I'm rattled from the kiss, flustered.

"You hate beards?"

"Yeah, most girls do, I would think."

"Meghan likes it. She's always touching it, telling me it looks nice. She's the one who went to the barbers with me to show him the cut she liked."

"I don't know. It's like kissing a horse—" I bite my lip. A horse? *Stop*, I tell myself. *Just shut up before you say too much.* "It really wasn't that bad. Maybe I'm wrong. Some girls like beards. It caught me off-guard like I was kissing—" I tell him. "Nothing. It was great. The entire day has been great."

"Then why are you making that goofy smile at me?"

"I don't know. —just take me home." I try to wipe it off. I can't. "Let's not screw it up by lingering on it, alright? Bygones."

Chapter −24
The Speech

Pops' mama was a McAllister. I called her Mamaw even though she wasn't really my grandmother. I was born a MacCabe down a hollow different from where the McAllisters grew up. But Pops and his family took me in when I was four. Mamaw's name was Annie, and her family came from Rinndown, Ireland. She used to tell me stories about her own grandmother being called a witch because she used the local herbs to cure people in her village. Her grandmother had taught her mother. Her mother had taught my mamaw, and Mamaw taught me. She lived with us until I was seventeen, and she got pneumonia. She told Pops she had a dream that he took her to the hospital, and an owl burst into white flames through the window of her room, and she died. Pops said she was probably hallucinating from her fever. He put a blanket around her, gently laid her on his truck's passenger seat, and drove her down to Grant Medical.

They admitted Pops' mama, and he came home that January night, driving along in a blinding snow. On his drive back, he was heading up Fire Mountain, and suddenly, the snow stopped. It was eight after two in the morning. He remembers he was looking at his radio clock. Just as the full moon poked out of the clouds, he looked up and saw an owl sitting in the tree staring down at him. He was so mesmerized by the owl that he didn't realize the right tire of his truck had slipped over the edge of the road. There's a hundred-foot cliff on that side. He jammed on his brakes, slid into a tree, and the owl burst into the air in a spray of glittery snowflakes.

Now, Pops isn't superstitious. There are owls all over Fire Mountain because the forest is so thick. He doesn't think he will have bad luck if he walks under a ladder and doesn't blow dandelions and make a wish. He doesn't carry an acorn in his pocket for good luck. Still, the following day, Mamaw was dead, and the reports all said her time of death was eight after two. To this day, whenever somebody's sick, I see him looking up past the giant old oaks on his farm and looking for that omen, that owl.

Even though Mamaw had that dream, it wasn't a sign she was trying to tell my Pops about. She just knew she was going to die.

Mamaw said that stuff that makes up people doesn't come from the outside but from what's inside. It's a bit of magic, superstition, and taking control. It's a bit of looking at someone and seeing on the outside what's making the inside sick. It is taking the ingredients you've got available and using them to feel better.

"That's what I do when I prepare my recipes," I say. "I brought some today for everybody to try out. You better do it soon, though. I have a horrible phobia of standing in front of people, and I faint dead away." There is laughter. The students believe I am kidding. I am standing in front of a class. Eighteen people are staring at me. I find the little piece of tape on my skirt and pick at it. I focus on it and tear my eyes away from those prying into mine. It's one of the things Bear dug up online to help get me through. He also got me a hair tie to wrap around my wrist. I pulled it out a couple times, letting it flip my skin. Ouch. It hurts. I'm focused again.

The professor nods and lets them crowd forward. It isn't so bad right now, almost like the city street and folks walking around Bear and me the other day. Still, my heart is racing, and my forehead is sweating. I hardly even notice that they are tasting my food and telling me it is scrumptious. I excuse myself, rush to the bathroom, and vomit into the toilet. That is something new. However, I've never made it past a minute in front of a crowd.

When I came out, I saw the man who did the talk at the wellness resort getting a drink from the water fountain. He looks up and smiles at me. "I probably just took three years off my life drinking that water. God knows what's in it." He sniffs a chuckle and pokes a finger on the center of his trendy glasses, so they ride a little up the bridge of his nose. "Oh, you are pale. Are you alright? I thought you were joking. You really do have a phobia."

"I'm fine. It is over. I'm Brandy Devereauxs." I stick out my hand. If Pops didn't teach me anything else, he taught me that a firm handshake and letting folks know who you are so they don't have to feel stupid trying to remember your name is a good start to a friendship. He looks pleasantly surprised and shakes it. He's one of those people who follow up by pulling you in, giving you a slight hug, and then gently pushing away. When you're back on both feet, you feel like you've got a new best friend. "After what I had to go through to get it, I better at least get a B."

"I'm Ben Wright. Rough, was it?"

"Oh, you don't know the half of it." I tell him how Bear took me to Cincinnati and made me walk up and down the street, people-watching. And then how he made me sit through the horrible comedians. "And tape." I reach down and pick at the Scotch tape still clinging to my skirt. "He texted me about forty ideas to get me through the speech."

"I'll have to remember that," he says. "But that's not why I'm harassing you in the hallway. I'd like to see you interview for one of the part-time assistant chefs at Little Bend of Salt Springs. It's just a few hours a week, but something to get started on while we work on our budget. Your advisor wanted me to listen to you. He called the other day. We've got about thirty people to interview. We've got a small resort, and it's getting bigger. Dean Popovich recommended you. He said you've got promise and lots of tuition you owe."

I wince. "Yes, I do owe and owe and owe."

"I'm still paying off mine, and I've been out six years," Ben says. "I bet I've got twenty more to go. I think we all struggle with the banking industry's deceptive practices." He's got shaggy hair and reminds me of the clever and stylish side of my cousin, Kenny, that never existed, barring the time my Aunt Jenny got him in a suit to stutter through the scriptures one Sunday morning at church when he was fourteen. He's laid back, easy to like, and comfortable as a new pair of expensive tennis shoes. "I tasted your snacks. They were incredibly delicious. Were they really low calorie?"

"Yes, low salt and low sugar. And I need a job." I nod. "Do you have a card so I can call and schedule an interview?"

"Yes, I do," he digs out his wallet and laughs a little. I think he sees my expression. I'm confused. I don't know why he's laughing to himself. "I'm so sorry. Here, look," Ben tugs out a little card. It is the size of a business card, and on the front, it says: You have to add the words 'Holy Shit' three times into your following conversation with the person in front of you.

"What is—it?"

"My friends have an idiotic sense of humor," he tells me. "It is this game we play. Life's boring. We try to spice it up when we can. Occasionally, we sneak some dare into another person's wallet. It really is stupid now that I'm saying it. Holy shit—"

I burst into laughter. It feels so good to meet somebody with the same stupid sense of humor Kenny does. "You need to do it twice more," I tell him.

"I can't. I'm too embarrassed." He's laughing too.

I'm riding so high that I stop at Boar Mountain on the way home to tell Bear. Big mistake. As I look back on it, even a phone call would have been a bad idea. It is Evan at the security office with a big smile. "Well, if it isn't Brandy Devereauxs." he sticks to his office and eyes the building above us. "I love your name. It's so cool. I'm supposed to call up and let them know you are here." *Them.* I should have taken that as a yellow warning sign like the ones you see right before a big pothole on the highway that's too big to fix with just a shovel full of asphalt from a city truck. He points me off to a visitor parking area. I see him talking on the radio before disappearing into his security building.

It is seven minutes later when I'm poking a text into the phone to Kenny. I look up at the shadow coming by my window. It isn't Bear. I can smell this too-sweet perfume wafting to my window, something like the cheap fruity spray-ons they sell at the stores at the mall. I think the scent is supposed to be pear.

"Brandy, that's your name, right?" I twist my head around and peer upward. I have to assume it is Meghan Reynolds and not Michelle. It is one or the other. It really doesn't matter; the matching of the two is right behind her, with Janie Mills and Carrie Edwards so close together, I swear the two are holding hands.

"Yeah, that's me." I put down my phone and got the same tickling sensation in my belly that I used to feel when Josh's sister and his mom would come to visit. As soon as Josh's back was turned, they would pick on me with a jab about my hair being frizzy, how bad my cooking was, or how I never cleaned the house. Then they would eye me, dark and brutal, like they were warning me that one step in the wrong direction and I'd be in a garbage bag buried six feet under.

"I just want to tell you to stay away from Beau." Meghan's not so scary, though, like a bunny rabbit wiggling its nose at the fox wanting to carry it off. She spits when she talks, and I have to blink against the slobber flying. "You're not to come here. I don't want to have to tell you this again."

I'm caught between laughing at her soft voice and the spittle that I am wiping away with my wrist, and her coached speech. She is nearly foaming at the mouth. "Listen, Goodwill, if she won't say it, I will." Janie sidles up to the side of the truck and puts her arm around Meghan. "Stay away from Beau. Everybody knows what you're up to, slutting around like your trashy mama looking for a sugar daddy. It ain't happening."

"And where is that mama of yours right now?" That would be Michelle wiggling her hips just in my peripheral vision. "Jail, right?" She holds up her fist and lets her forefinger loose to waggle it back and forth. "Oh, one for Meggie's team, none for Goodwill."

"Listen, he can dress you up like a dollar store dolly," Meghan says, her eyes veering into the truck. I am wearing this business-looking suit jacket and skirt he got me. *Dollar store dolly.* I feel my jaws tighten. Where did she hear those words? Did Bear say something to her about the other night in his truck? "But it doesn't change that you'll never be good enough for him. Never." She stresses that point. "He doesn't like you. He likes me now. He's just using you. Accept and go on."

"We should change her name from Goodwill to Dollar Store Dolly." Carrie Edwards has short, sandy hair that falls into her eyes.

"Using me for what?" I ignore Carrie and stab Meghan with my eyes. "I don't know what he's told you, but we're friends. That's all. This whole bully thing isn't even warranted. I'm not having sex with him if that is what you are implying."

"Bullshit," Janie says. She swings her hand up, pushes it back from her face, and rolls her eyes. "That's not what he's been saying."

"I'm just going to tell you this, Dollar Store Dolly," Michelle says. I see her smile smugly at Carrie. She looks above my truck. I don't want to turn my head. She leans in and pushes a finger on my shoulder. "If you come here again, we'll call the cops. Then you can go share a room with your mama in jail."

"Girls. Go on back to what you were doing."

I know that voice anywhere. It is Amelia Vega. That she flew this far from her castle walls surprises me. I see her shooing her dream team away from my truck, shaking her hands like she is drying them off beneath those bathroom fans at the highway rest stops.

"Well, I suppose we need to have a talk," she addresses me. Sitting in my old truck is awkward, staring up at Amelia Vega in her five-hundred-dollar gray suit dress and matching gray pumps. It's that weird, discomfiting feeling when you're sitting still, strapped into the seat of the amusement park roller coaster ride you just finished. You look up to catch the eyes of the next person dangling over and trying to get in, but your seatbelt is still attached because the ride attendant hasn't released it yet.

"I'm not sure the reason," I say honestly. "But I assume it is the same as what Meghan blathered and slobbered on about."

"See, I really don't know you. You don't know me. I don't even think I was amused enough at your interview to warrant looking at your resume." She curls her arms together above her waist and tips her head to one side. She reminds me of the old Bear right then. The one who called me trailer trash in his mind. "Your application ended up in the trash with all the other bargain-bin, sale-priced applicants from New Alliance and Fire Mountain who are better suited cleaning the rooms at the fifty-dollar-a-night New Alliance Motel off the highway or the shabby New Alliance Nursing Home at the bottom of the mountain." She pauses to take a breath. I am holding my tongue, feeling the tickly tummy sensation turn to a burning hate. "But I do know plenty of women like you. I probably don't need to, but I will sum up your existence in just a few sentences, and you can tell me if the description is correct. You come from some little house in the woods, a shack, or a pre-1970s trailer in some mobile home park. Your daddy was a drunk and ended up in jail for hitting somebody over the head in a bar scuffle. Your mama spent most of her time looking for a new husband at some dirty hotel off the highway or concocting methamphetamine in her trailer."

"No, you don't know me," I say. I'm tired of looking up at Missus Vega from the seat of my truck. I push open the door, step out into the hot sunshine, look her eye to eye. "You just described a mama and a daddy for me. You didn't tell me who I am. *Because you don't know*. And I am certainly not defined by my parents. They were not around. So, you are wrong, Missus Vega. Oh, wait a minute. I don't know your mama or daddy, but I do know some things about you. It is still Vega, isn't it?" I give her a questioning glare. She doesn't back down and stands there staring back at me.

"It seems every time somebody blinks," I go on. "you've got a new rich man around to fund your long line of unsuccessful business schemes and bail you out when they fail. I think Bear said he lost track after his fifth daddy which, if I can count correctly would be your fifth commercial flop. Fifth. Five. It is the same number of letters in the word Bitch." I pull up my hand and count out each letter with one finger at a time. "B-I-T-C-H. That word best describes you and is probably also one of the reasons you can't keep a husband around or a business afloat. Does everyone who has invested in the Redneck Run know about your long trail of unprofitable businesses? Do you have another man lined up after they close down the event and resort to bail you out?"

"Are you going to continue? I will call the police."

"Yes. Call the cops. Just because you're rich does not mean I don't get my say." I poke a finger at the phone in her hand. "Because you are a bit difficult to swallow, even to strangers. When you've got a lot of money, you can flash it at some folks who become spellbound. Not everyone is like that, you should know." She turns and walks away, flagging her hand at Evan at the security booth. I follow with my steps hard behind hers. "But someday, you won't have all those credit cards to hide your personality behind. You're going to look into the mirror and realize a witch is staring back at you, and no spell in the world will make you younger. And everybody's going to see you as what you really are. You'll probably end up in some dirty nursing home in New Alliance, surrounded by all those bargain-bin, sale-price employees who you have shunned. And when you're sitting in your own pee thinking, what the hell, why isn't anybody helping me? You'll realize that you, after all, caused this by simply being so despicable all your life."

I am yelling the last part at her while Evan, with wide eyes, comes staggering out of the booth to save his employer. I don't think he knows what to do. He holds his arms out wide and pushes himself between us. I can see Amelia Vega poking 9-1-1 into her phone. I hold up my hands and take a step back. "I'm leaving. Evan, I'm backing up. But only because your boss is too much of a coward to fight a battle on her own, and she must call in someone with a gun to finish off her enemy. That was for your benefit, you know, since the last time I made her cry, you had strep throat."

When I get down to the bottom of the road, I hear the last of my brakes try to grind to a halt at the stop sign. It hits me what I had done. I do that thing that Bear teases me about—I punch the dash, waggle my hands at the ceiling, and kick the floor. I hate myself a little for doing this. It is worse than Kaylee's temper tantrum this morning when I cooked her eggs over-easy instead of scrambling them.

Big Don Reynolds is waiting for me a stone's throw from the intersection of Boar Mountain Road and the main highway in his gray and blue New Alliance Police Station cop car. His lights flip on, and his sirens wail while he hunts me down until I pull over, sweating bullets. Didn't I mention once before that he is Meghan and Michelle's daddy?

"Well, looky here if it isn't one of Ruby MacCabe's kids." He stands outside my truck window, legs splayed and his hands on his side. He isn't tall, probably only five foot and six or seven inches. I think I heard he got the name Big Don as a joke, but he's such an idiot he thought folks were serious when they called him that. The placard on his door even states: "BIG DON" REYNOLDS in bold, black letters. His finger tickles a long, black baton at his belt. He's got a buddy with him, a tall cop with broad shoulders and that cold, state highway patrol gaze that screams, *I got a gun, so my dick's bigger*. He's a younger version of Big Don but probably seven inches taller. Unlike Big Don, whose bulky muscle he once carried has jellied down to fat, he's muscled. "Surprise, surprise. Aren't you the only one left who isn't in jail?"

"We are misunderstood," I retort. I don't know why. My mouth is much faster than my brain today. "But the McAllisters claimed me when I was four."

The younger deputy twitches a smile that Big Don Reynolds swipes from his lips with a little growl. He's afraid of him, I can tell. Big Don's the kind of cop who won't give tickets to other cops if they are speeding. He's the bad guy, the bad cop, the type of cop that sees an old truck with a few bangs and dents and defines the person inside by the vehicle's character. They are either drug users or dealers. Then, he uses his baton to bang the lights out and give them a ticket. The city of New Alliance won't control him. More tickets mean more money coming in.

He's known for abuse of probable cause because, sniff-sniff, he *thinks* he smells weed in the car, then he can arrest the alleged criminal and drag him to the police station. The county judge's job is paid for the next three months through court costs and fees.

"Yeah, it is that mouth of yours that's always gotten you kids in trouble. Thought it'd be wiped off your face by now by some drugged-out boyfriend who got too high. Step out of the truck." I try not to let my eyes get wide. I know it is the leading flaw demonstrating my weakness to my enemies. Still, they are as big as fists while I push open the door.

"Step to the front of the truck." It is the younger cop that beckons me to the front of my truck bumper. I follow, feeling a bit numb. I'm looking around, not seeing any other cars. Hell's bells, they could shoot me in the head right now, swipe up enough blood to make folks think somebody hit a deer on the road, and toss me in their trunk.

Big Don goes to my truck. I see him reaching inside, snatching up my purse. He rifles through it while the younger cop stares at me. "You got drugs in here?"

"No."

"Are you smoking weed?" Big Don yells at me. "I smell weed." He snatches the keys out of my truck, leans over, and investigates inside. I start to lean against the hood. Big Don stands up, tosses my purse back into the car, comes around the front, and snatches up my arm. "You will stand up straight when I speak to you." He shakes my arm and doesn't let go. His fingernails bite into my skin. My heart starts pumping, and my belly is turning flat. I'm not sure what I'll do if he whips out his baton and starts to beat me.

"I'm sorry," I say it. "I didn't mean to do it. Whatever I did."

"Yeah, that's what all you MacCabes say right before you end up either in jail or dead."

He snaps my arm downward, and I'm not expecting it. I keel forward and drop to my knees. I feel his right hand come out, kind of latch onto the back of my head. He's got me held like a man sticking his pup's nose into its pee on the kitchen floor. *Bad pup. Bad pup.* I'm waiting for the newspaper to come out and swat me on the rear.

"I'm going to give you a warning. Once. Stay away from the resort. Don't even think about going up there again. I don't know what you had in mind, robbing the place or just trashing it with paint. But I'm watching your skinny little ass. I'll catch you, gobble you up faster than a wolf gobbles up a little piggy." I'm kneeling in front of him, squatting. I am praying he can't see up my skirt. I know my panties have to be showing. It happened so fast; I was in mid-balance, looking at the ground with my hands out to the sides.

I kneel there. I wonder if my shadow slipping across the toes of Big Don's shiny black shoes is my dignity trying to run away. I know not to move. Pops told me you can't fight the cops no matter what. They got the badge, the gun, and plastic body bags to bury you with. Still, two trickles of sweat are running down my forehead. I would swear they were sucked out of my body from anger. I am shaking, trembling, wondering if this man ever sat at his daughter's bedsides when they were little and read them bedtime stories. If they wrapped their little arms around him and gave him butterfly kisses, not knowing that he would someday be digging his fingernails into the flesh of a woman at the nape of her neck like he was to me right now, thinking about killing her.

"Big Don, sir, I think she gets the point." I can't see his face, but I see the foot of the younger cop stepping forward. His hand comes out and gently pats Big Don's.

"Back off, son, you don't know this family. They are no good, nothing but trash. She could be hiding a weapon."

But the younger cop doesn't back off. He stands right there, an arms-length away.

"I told you to back off, son."

"Sir, you have checked her person, vehicle, and purse. She doesn't have any drugs."

"You're right." Big Don grunts. He starts to stand, and the other cop backs up. Then Big Don snaps downward, leaning hard with his lips two inches from my ear. "You're nothing but a ten-buck whore. But you're cute. If you come to my hunting cabin sometime, I'll buy you for five bucks. I bought your mama one time. It would be nice to have the fresher version." He gave me a shove with his knee as he got up, so I skidded along the ground. "You're not so sassy now, are you? Amelia Vega is already going to press trespassing charges."

"Jesus, Big Don," the younger cop says. His eyes veer from me to Big Don, who is walking toward his car.

"Here, let me—" the younger cop starts to lean over like he's going to help me. I don't know what game they are playing. Is this a good cop/bad cop like I see in the movies? I shake my head and hold my trembling hands up. "No, don't touch me. Can I leave?"

"We're getting the truck impounded," Big Don calls out while he snatches his little radio near his collar. "We're going to tear it apart, make sure there's nothing inside."

"Can I get my purse, call my—dad?"

"You got a direct line to heaven, sweetie?" Big Don is talking on the radio and talking to me simultaneously. "Because last I heard, he was buried behind the prison he died in." He pauses, tips his chin, and smiles wide and extensive, exposing his yellowed teeth. "Naw, you can call him from the station."

"I'll get your purse." The other cop struts away. I stand there, feeling each prickling scratch where I skinned my knees on the asphalt road when he pushed me down.

"Hey, here," The other cop stretches out his hands and offers me my purse. "I got your lipstick, too. It fell out onto the floor.

"Thanks." I look away and down. I don't want to stare above the sun and try to catch the cop's eyes.

"I bet you don't remember me," he says, looking over his shoulder at Big Don, who is laughing on the radio. "I was that little skinny kid that moved into the trailer park next door to your mama's place. Little Pete's cousin. You used to sit by me at lunch all sixth grade so Big Don's son, Alvey, wouldn't beat me up."

I do look up. I catch the glint in blue eyes. "They called you Bubby. Bubby Jamison."

"Well, Big Don's boy called me Retard's Cousin and Butthead and some even worse names than those that I can't say. But yeah, my real name is Calvin." He clears his throat. Big Don must be coming. "If you ride this one out, don't badmouth Big Don. Eventually, he'll get what's coming to him."

I'm that person, right?" I ask him. "Not what Big Don makes me out to be." He doesn't answer. He slips to the left so Big Don can escort me to the police car.

Chapter –25
Taylor and Mandy

I find myself snatching up that stupid lockbox every time something goes wrong. I dig through the envelopes, stare at Josh's face, and read the addresses aloud. I ask myself why I am torturing myself. He obviously didn't like me enough to stick around. If he is alive, I'm probably not even a bad memory in his mind. I have to sit on the side of my bed in my room, let the darkness surround me, suck me in until I feel like exploding.

It isn't just Amelia Vega or Big Don putting me in a funk. While I am sitting in the police station waiting for Pops to pick me up, the lady at the front desk keeps looking at me. Finally, she struts across the room in her too-thick rouge and wire-rimmed glasses. She's chubby and wearing a miniskirt. "You are Brandy Alexander Devereauxs," she asks. "Correct?"

I nod. I know she will not tell me they are giving back my truck. It is in the back lot right now, awaiting someone to pull up the carpets and check it for drugs. One week? Two weeks? They didn't know how long until Big Don got around to it. "I don't know if your father told you. We called the other day and talked to him, a Lee McAllister. It was a couple days after the incident at your mama's place. A police station in Whitcomb, West Virginia, called. They found some remains. It had some things with it they thought you might be able to identify."

I sit and stare at her with my hands folded on my lap. My face feels prickly, numb, and puffy, just like it always does when they call about finding something about Josh. "Sometimes, they fax a copy of the—of the—*stuff*," I struggle through the words, push my hair from my face, and turn to a lady sitting in the waiting room and staring at me. "It's easier, I guess. He was my husband, you know. I mean, it isn't easy looking at anything even if it is on paper, but—"

"Probably because some skin and bones are still showing on the carcass. Some police stations don't like to send these out—they are disgusting, pieces of jawbone and part of a nose here, teeth and—"

"Oh, my goodness! That is enough, Jean!"

I recognize the voice. It is distinguishable and soft-spoken, with words stated in a sing-song tone. It is Gabe's mom, Gabby Murphy. She is just about everywhere in town, volunteering her time. She helps kids with reading at the elementary school, makes cookies for the library, and sets up the church meal drive for families if they have a mama or daddy who is sick. She must bring cookies and snacks here because she had a box of little bags of potato chips in her arms when I came in earlier.

I know my face must be a pasty shade of green. I am wobbling when she shoves a little cone-shaped paper cup into my fingers from the water dispenser by the front desk. "Oh, honey, you'll be okay." She is tiny, smaller than me, with a soft, mousy voice and a sweet tip to her head when she talks to me. Her hand is patting my back. "Oh, you need some Band-Aids for your knees," she tells me. "What happened to you? Did you fall?"

My eyes veer upward and over to the office where Big Don is sitting. He narrows his eyes. "Looks like she tripped over her own two feet, doesn't it, Gabby?"

"I don't need anything," I tell her softly. "Thank you."

That is what I am doing when Pops gets there, his eyes wary and his hand continuously catching on the brim of his hat. He doesn't say a word. I figure it doesn't matter if he's mad at me again. Nothing in the world will change that I'm Mama's daughter and Josh's ex-wife, no matter how hard I try. Even Pops wouldn't believe me if I said Big Don shoved me down for no reason at the bottom of Big Boar Mountain.

I get a text from Bear about twenty minutes later, just as I leave the police station. *Hey, did I pass you coming back down the mountain?* I feel deceived. I wonder what Bear's been telling Meghan about me. How else would they know about the dollar store dolly phrase? I stare at the message and delete it. I'm scared they'll come after Pops next or Aunt Jenny while she runs to the nursing home to check on her aunt. Kenny's big dream is to work for the volunteer fire department. He rides along when he isn't working at the hardware store. They are trying to get a restraining order against me, so I can't go near the resort. If I can't go near the resort, I can't do the Redneck Run. I kick myself for still grasping for that stupid dream.

All that happened and now I'm sitting here with the lockbox in my lap, twirling an envelope in my hand the following day. I am in the town of Whitcomb. It is two hours and twenty minutes away from Fire Mountain. It is raining, and I can hardly see outside the windshield. The rubber is coming off the windshield wiper on the driver's side. It drags a little strip back and forth before me, barely cutting through the driving storm. I'm not sure what is worse, the annoying flap of the rubber slapping when it reaches the far side or the sound of the blade metal screaming bloody murder each time it crosses over. Pops let me borrow his older-than-the-hills truck he keeps in the barn. He was wary and asked me: "Do you know why you got pulled over, baby girl? Because that's got my mind reeling now. I'm trying to imagine why the police would pull you over for no reason and impound your truck."

"Yes, sir, I mouthed off to Missus Vega at the resort," I tell him the truth. "Pops, please don't think I do drugs. I don't. I think we established that fact when we discovered it was Mama's joint in the ashtray on the table."

"Why the hell were you up there?" He cranes his neck to see me and tosses his hands into the air.

"I wanted to tell Bear I passed my classes for the semester. I did the speech I was scared to do." Pops doesn't show any approval of my accomplishment. "It was a big deal for me." I didn't expect it. He never went to college and doesn't understand the importance of it.

"Now, you know I don't like to tell you what to do." He does. "But maybe you better step away from that boy for a while. It sounds like his mama doesn't like you."

What do you think? I told him okay so I could get the truck. I'm trying to figure out why the Whitcomb police station had remains of Josh if he was Todd Winters when he was there. Nonetheless, I don't want to go into the little brick building with the city offices inside. The sky is gray, and so are my spirits right now. Yet, I do.

"We need you to identify some things we have here." The cop is a woman. She wears a polo shirt and blue pants. She is straight-lipped and damning me with her eyes while she tugs on a pair of deep blue rubber gloves. She reminds me of my high school math teacher. He stared at me when we had a test like I was cheating.

I liked math and got good grades. He didn't believe trailer trash like me could add some stupid numbers and know one plus one wasn't three.

With that in mind, I sit on a chair in a meeting room. I know there is a camera in the corner. I can tell it is pinned down on me. I wished I hadn't come here. I feel like I am the one who has broken the law. The officer's name is Sandy Cantrell, and she sits opposite me. There has a cardboard box with WINTERS written on two sides in a permanent black marker. "We can't divulge why we're asking you to look at a few things right now. Another agency is working on an investigation. However, when they are completed, we will call and let you know what we concluded."

I could really help them out. I could plop the lockbox Mama found in her closet on the other side of the table, give them a looky-look, and expose my ex-husband's antics to the cops. Considering the cop's shitty attitude and Big Don's little charade, though, I'm not interested in giving them information. However, I am curious what is in the box. Maybe I can get some info for myself.

She lifts the cardboard lid off the box and sets it to one side. Six plastic baggies are within that she pulls out, one by one. I can see a dirty blue shirt, a gold band, an open wallet with credit cards, a pink teddy bear that looks like it got wet, one white sock that appears to have been worn, and a little blue crystal the size of my pinky finger.

"None of it looks familiar." I shrug and look up. "Why would I be able to identify any of this stuff?"

"I can't disclose that right now." For good reason, I suppose. I'm betting it is Josh's, also known as Todd Winters. I'm betting Taylor, his wife, died within the last three years. I think they are on his trail.

"What's your story?" the cop asks. I look up at the camera, then back at her. "It's pretty boring. I am going to college and working two jobs. That pretty much sums it up. She rises and tugs at her pants like men do when they sit up. "I mean, what is your story with the Todd Winters case. How did you know him?"

"I don't. My husband was Josh Devereauxs. He came up missing three years ago. We all assume he is dead. I assumed this was his. I don't know anybody with the last name of Winters." Officer Cantrell waves her hand to show me to the door. She waits until we get outside the meeting room and stops me in the hallway.

"Thank you for coming out here. I know it was a long drive."

"I hate not knowing. Anything I can do for closure gets me one step closer."

"You're not afraid, are you?" She leans in and says this. "Because if you are, we can probably help you."

"Scared of what?"

"Taylor and Todd were murdered. Didn't you read it in the newspapers? The Winters Case?"

"We don't get any newspapers, and most of the time, my Pops watches baseball games. Again, I don't know Taylor or Todd. I have no ties to them that I'm aware of."

"Okay, if you think of anything, please don't hesitate to tell me. If you are hiding anything, you could be considered an accomplice."

"To killing somebody? My Pops says I've got a mouth on me, but I can't even punch my cousin and yell slug bug when I see a Volkswagen before he does."

She smiles and hands me her card. "Call us if you have any information that will help the Winter's family also have closure."

I drive down the street, park on the side of the road near a gas station. I look up Taylor and Todd Winters on the internet. I thumb down, find an article, and pull it up. It is a website devoted to finding the killers of Taylor and Todd Winters, ages 34 and 36. Todd was an independent contractor and built houses. Taylor designed floral arrangements out of her house. They were found dead in their Wittcomb home three and a half years ago, both bludgeoned with a tire iron while they slept. Then, the house was set on fire, but the local fire department dispatched it within ten minutes, and the blaze was kept to a minimum.

I scrub my forehead with my hands. What could the police possibly have connected Josh to this murder? I mean, I can get a good idea. Maybe the fire. Do they know more than I think? I can't wrap my mind around why Josh would have Todd Winters's driver's license and his picture in it. It can't be that easy to get a fake ID.

I pull into Michigan, West Virginia, at noon. It is a long drive from Whitcomb, over two hours and twenty minutes. I've want to know what happened to Mandy and Mark Walters. I'm so curious.

I looked them up online but couldn't find an answer. The six numbers on a phone look-up corresponding to any Walters in West Virginia were nowhere near Michigan. I'm driving slowly along Ridge Road, looking for a mailbox with 032790. I'm tired and grumpy, and I'm sure I will not find anything that will lead me to Josh. I am sure one minute that he will be killing these women and their husbands. The next, I think maybe he just stole their identities afterward.

Bear keeps texting me on my phone—*where are you? What is wrong? Are you mad?* He calls, I don't answer. Then, I stopped even looking at the calls. 032790. 032790. I'm praying I don't find a burned-up house. Odds are, I will. But I can't even find 032790 Ridge Road.

"Excuse me." I see an elderly lady out watering her garden. I flag her down in her driveway and hop out of the truck. "I was wondering if there is a 032790 Ridge Road."

"032790." She looks at me and shakes her white head of hair. "Well, honey, I don't know any addresses starting with a zero. And we don't have any on this road that goes that high." She waves a hand toward the hill I had come down. "Ridge Road is only a few miles long."

"I'm looking for Mandy and Mark Walters," I tell her. "You don't happen to know them, do you?"

"I can't say that I do." She smiles politely. I smile back. "I've lived here all my life. The only Walters I remember owned the feed store in town. I think some of their kids still run it."

I'm on my way to the feed store in town. I feel like I'm on a wild goose chase, as Pops calls it when he has to chase down one of his workers and can't find him. The boy who was working at the hardware store tells me Amy Walters is at home today with a sick kid. Tim, her husband, went to take a deposit to the bank. I leave my cell phone number and go to the home. Amy left with her little boy, Kyle, to visit the doctor. Her babysitter is there with her little girl. When Tim returns to the feed store, his worker calls me. By the time I get there, a shipment of corn has arrived, and Tim is busy signing the paperwork and loading it from the dock. Finally, twenty-five minutes later, he comes out where I'm sitting on the hood of Pops' truck. He's smiling, and he holds his hand for me to shake.

I've got the name and address written down, and I shift my hands to give him a handshake.

"Del said you wanted to know if I knew of any other Walters who live here."

"Yes," I slide off the truck and stand before him. "I'm trying to find Mandy and Mark Walters. They may not exist because I can't even find the address where they could have lived. I couldn't leave until I find out."

"I don't think there's anyone in the family named Mark. I don't even know an Amanda," he says while I hold the paper. "Oh, but Ridge Road." He pokes at the address. "This might be your problem. Ridge Road got cut off by the highway overpass about five years ago. They just stopped the road about where it goes out of Michigan and toward the town of Texas." He pauses and smiles. "The town of Texas doesn't exist anymore. It was only ten or so houses. They tore all but a few down to build the highway. They lost their post office in the 1960s or 1970s. They would have been considered Michigan since then. You may be able to find the house number out there."

I have a headache as I drive back out of town and take a route Tim Walters gave me to go around where the road is cut off. But it isn't one of those headaches caused by stress. Searching for Josh is taking my mind off Big Don and Mama, and I know I will lose Bear.

I pull onto Ridge Road. Tim is right. The new highway is overhead, and the grind of truck tires rolling along the road makes a shrill sound. To the left, the road ends. To my right, it goes on into the rolling hillsides. Beside me are old house foundations I can make out in the tall grass. Big stones and pieces of fencing pock the property on either side of the road. Nobody drives here anymore; the grass is growing in the cracks of the asphalt.

I drive Ridge Road for about a quarter mile before I see it. It is an old cemetery, the grass overgrown. A wrought iron sign is keeling at the front—HIGH RIDGE CEMETERY. I pull off into the gravel in front of a raggedy iron fence surrounding a small lot with overgrown weeds and small trees. As far as I can see, there isn't a house or a car. If there was once a church there, it is long gone. Only three old steps leading nowhere show any sign of a building that once stood along the roadway. I tromp through the grass. It is knee-high and tickles my skin between my shorts and shoes.

There are probably fifty graves, and I start walking between them, staring at the headstones for names that had not been rubbed off by time and weather. I bear the heat and the sun baking the skin on my shoulders for a half hour. Then, my feet come to a standstill by a high stone in the back. I blink hard. *Bingo!* Amanda Walters. Wife of Mark Walters. Died March 27, 1890. "March 27, 1890." I returned to the truck and grabbed the envelope and a pencil to write down the information. I start to simplify the date: "Oh, March 27, 1890. It is the address, 032790." I whisper to the stifling humid air. On the other side is Mark's name. He died three days after his wife.

"What does this mean?" I groan, tossing back my head. I turn in a circle, trying to find anything to give me a clue as to why Josh would have a driver's license with the names of two dead people from way over a hundred and twenty-five years ago. Yes, this was their address, but for what damn reason?

I take a picture of the grave with my phone. I use my foot to push down the weeds in front to make sure the names are clear in the image. It is almost immediate. I feel something hard beneath the toe of my tennis shoe. I kneel and rub away the grass. Something shines beneath my fingers, and I dip my head, push back my hair, and peer at the tiny shiny object exposed there.

"Holy hell." I reach down and snatch it up. It is a tiny pearl necklace complete with a chain. Oh my, it is mine. It is a necklace. I kept it in a little jewelry box in my dresser. How long ago I remember seeing it there, I don't know. I had not pulled it out in a long time. No, *no I had gotten it out less than six months ago!*

Chapter –26
A date with Gabe

I get back to Pops' house at six-fifteen.

"Blessed Jesus, where have you been?" Aunt Jenny meets me at the garage, wringing her hands and follows me toward the porch. "That boy has been here three times in the last ten minutes."

"What boy?" I ask her. "I've been running errands all day."

"The little red-haired fellow that belongs to the preacher at Holy Trinity." My uncle Lyn pipes up from his fold lawn chair on the porch. He is Pops' closest brother. They are only twelve months apart and could pass for twins when they are wearing their matching camo during hunting season. Now, not so much. Uncle Lyn favors those bright yellow high visibility uniform t-shirts they have him wear down at the city transportation department where he works. He stands out like a torch, sitting there, holding a half-full water bottle he is using to spit his tobacco. It looks like sewage inside and makes me want to gag.

"That's Gabe," I reply. "Why was he here?"

A whole bunch of Pops' family is sitting on his porch enjoying the oncoming evening breeze. It is hot out today but clouding over like it will rain. They are watching me walk up like they've been waiting for me to come home. I hop up the steps and give Uncle Lyn a quick peck on the cheek.

"He said you were supposed to do something tonight." My papaw is sitting next to my uncle and gives me a big old wink. Pops' dad doesn't look like either of his sons. He's got a round face and a big belly, and I was sure he was Santa Claus when I was five. He works up a chuckle from deep down in his belly and scrubs his hand on his white beard. "Baby girl's gots her a dandy boyfriend."

"Not really," I say. "I forgot all about it. I'm hoping Gabe doesn't come back."

"Oh, honey bunch, you can't do that to the boys." That's my Aunt Jillian. I've always wanted to have her name. She has black hair and brown skin and wears these pretty flowered dresses that look like they were made in the olden days. She reminds me of spring.

"She's spendin' too much time running," Aunt Jenny says. "She's turning into a boy."

"I'm going to go get a lemonade," I tell them so I can slip away from the conversation. I decided that's what happens when you get old. You talk about young people and try to make their heads explode. I hear them all discussing me as I leave, as if I can't hear them. I go into my room and fall on the bed, arms splayed and eyes on the ceiling. I lay there for a while, soaking in the darkness. My head still hurts a little, and I'm dead tired.

"Dear God, if Josh is alive, please don't let him do anything else that is stupid, so I have to kill him."

He doesn't answer, so I sit up, tug the little pearl necklace from my jeans pocket, and dangle it in front of my face. The chain is rusted, and the pearl's clasp looks worn out, but it is still as beautiful as it was the day I got it.

Then comes the knock on my bedroom door. I eye it cautiously. "Come—in?" It is more a question than anything. Everybody always barrels through my door like I'm four, and it's okay because back then when I was naked, it didn't matter.

"Hey," Gabe is slipping into my room, the scent of aftershave following him. He is looking around, up and down. "Please do not stand me up tonight. I swear to God, my mom bought a corsage for you. Wear it for two seconds to get at least a picture."

I laugh because I think he is kidding. He isn't. I see him hold out a little plastic container. Inside is a pink orchid.

"You know, this is kind of cool," I say, taking it from him and peering inside. "Josh wasn't big on the dances. I never got any flowers."

"You'll go?"

"Look at me, Gabe." I hold out my arms. I'm wearing shorts and a tank top. He's wearing suit pants, a nice button-up shirt, and even a tie. He's probably got the jacket in his car. "I have been in my Pops' stinky truck all day driving around."

"I'll help you get dressed up." He says it without even laughing. "No, seriously, I have three sisters. My brothers were all grown up by the time I came around. I'll get your clothes. Hell, I'll straighten your hair if you want me to."

"You know how to use a straightener?"

He points at his hair. "My hair is one big frizz. Without a straightener and hair serum, I look like a clown. Please, Brandy, I'm begging you. It is Bear and Meghan, Janie and some guy named Chase and me. It can't just be me. It's got to be *somebody and me*."

"Nobody mentioned that Meghan and the girls on her team ambushed me yesterday?"

"What do you mean?" He looks serious and shakes his head.

"I drove up to the resort to tell Bear something, and Meghan and her team came tearing out of the country club to tell me to stay away from Bear. They were ready to fight."

"I don't think they've said anything. Bear didn't mention it."

"Gabe, his mom came out and ripped me a new butthole." I puff out my cheeks. "She called the cops, and they impounded my truck at the bottom of the hill. Your mom was at the police station. She didn't say anything?"

"Well, now that you mention it, she did," He raises his shoulders. "When she was putting supper on the table, she said *the pretty girl that fainted at church was at the police station today. I wonder if she'll come back to church.*"

"That's it?"

"Yeah, that's it."

I don't know how long everybody in Bear's big truck stared at my family on the porch, staring back at them. Gabe stifles a laugh while he elbows me gently and nods to the two faces peering out of the truck window.

"If you say boo, I bet they'd scream," he whispers while we walk onto the porch.

"Who, my grandpa and my aunts or Janie and Meghan?"

He thinks this is funny and laughs while I have to listen to everybody telling me goodbye, winking, smiling, and telling us how cute we look.

"Make sure she's back by midnight, or you'll find yourself chasing her through the forest past Crazy Willie's with a single glass slipper to reveal her true identity, because she doesn't usually look like this," Pops taunts us, and everybody laughs."

"You owe me big time for this," I tell Gabe when he grabs the latch to the back door of the truck so we can slip inside. I'm wearing a slinky black, ruched dress that barely makes it past my butt and high black heels. He picked it out. Typical man. My hair is straight and pushed to one side, and I have some jingly bracelets on my wrist. I've got enough makeup on my face to pass as a clown. "You do know by the time we get to the end of the driveway, they've got our wedding planned."

"Yeah, you're not the one who brought the corsage."

"I am wearing it, though," I tell him, pointing a finger at my dress. "Proudly. Your mama called me pretty."

"I knew you shouldn't have brought the truck, Beau." Meghan is leaning over and saying when Gabe slips in beside me. She is sidled up next to Bear and examining her shoe. I think I sloughed off part of my heel. Oh, my gosh, you have got to buy a car for when we do this." She stops and turns because everyone is silent and staring at me. "What?" I ask them, tossing my hands upward.

"I thought we were getting Brandy." Bear is looking at me through the rearview mirror. I narrow my eyes. He looks different. He's shaved his beard. The only thing left is a bit of scruff on his cheeks, chin, and upper lip. He is smiling at me, giving me a nod. Maybe he looks a little too good because I can't seem to force eye contact. Still, it almost makes me mad. I know he shaved because I told him girls don't like beards. The guy next to Janie chuckles agreeably. His hair is short and handsome like the models on the magazine cover, almost girl-pretty. He smiles, I smile back, then turn away.

"We didn't. We got Goodwill." Meghan giggles.

"Megs, it isn't Goodwill anymore. It is Dollar Store Dolly." Janie laughs into her cupped hand, and they both burst into giggles.

"Oh, my gosh, that's right. We changed it. I forgot." Meghan turns around in the seat and pokes a finger at me. "Ha ha, we're just kidding. Not." I feel myself sinking in the seat. I want to punch her. I want to get out of the truck while my eyes work slowly over to Gabe to tell him I am going to rip his ears off for guilting me into this. He is staring at Meghan, his expression something short of unbelieving.

I don't think he has ever been around when those two have laid into me. His jaws are churning. "God, girls are mean," Gabe replies. Just as quickly as his eyes set on Meghan, he turns and pushes his arm around me.

"Not all girls," I mutter.

"True," Gabe agrees. "Since Brandy's not going to say it, because she is not a mean girl, I will say it: she's definitely hotter than anything I'm looking at." My expression changes. I lean into Gabe and let my head fall on his shoulder. It is the least we can do. I'm getting the feeling he hates this as much as I do.

The drive to the restaurant is nearly unbearable. There is incredibly awkward small talk that keeps leading over to Janie and Meghan chit-chatting about nothing but the Redneck Run and how it is affecting their lives. Meghan keeps sliding up next to Bear, tickling his new scruff and whispering stuff in his ear. Janie's date had yawned eight times before arriving at The Fiddle, an Irish restaurant near Salt Springs. For twenty minutes, he plays a riotous game of rock, scissors, and paper with Gabe and me.

I've been to this specific restaurant more than a few times. Of course, it wasn't to eat. I couldn't afford The Fiddle. It was behind the scenes. I knew the owner because I had interned there during my first year of college, helping in the kitchen. The chef was an arrogant jerk, and he had a difficult time keeping any kitchen staff. He yelled at everyone right in front of the customers from the table cleaners to the workers who cut up the potatoes. I pretended he was Pops on a bad day and did what he said. The owner still calls me once in a while to come and help. I try, but working at Beverly's and Smiley's, I couldn't take the time off to get over here often.

We're seated right away even though the line is out the door and into the parking lot. Meghan shakes her shoulders haughtily to everyone in the line. She shoves her little arm into Bear's and struts past them. Cash Register Girl has a new, exasperating attitude.

"I hope you don't mind if I'm clingy tonight," I say to Gabe while I take his hand. He doesn't seem to care at all. "I'm afraid Janie is going to suck my brains out at some point." I think he knows that Janie's date has warmed up better to me than her. He keeps migrating toward Gabe and me, following me like a lost pup. With Gabe, I feel like I'm holding my cousin Kenny's hand, though.

Traditional Irish foods are on the menu. Everybody's looking at it like they are staring at words in French. "What do you like to eat, Gabe," I ask him.

"What's Boxty?"

"Potato pancakes. They make them here with squash and garlic."

"What's Colcannon?"

"Mashed potatoes and cabbage."

He sighs and lets the menu fall. "Do they have anything normal, Brandy?"

"Go with the Irish Stew. Lots of meat, lots of potatoes. It's safe and good, and I know the chef who created the dish from an old family recipe." It was me. The one that the chef used when I worked here tasted like cardboard. I showed the chef how to kick it up a notch from one of my Irish Mamaw's old recipes passed down in the family.

Gabe starts a long conversation on some TV sitcom with Bear to his right. I am sitting next to Janie's male model, Chase, realizing that although he's nice, he's dumber than a rock and completely ignoring her. Chase keeps nudging me and trying to show off by telling me about his wannabe acting career. He works for a commission at one of the stores at the mall. He keeps smiling at me while I help him find something on the menu, and then he stares at my boobs. I keep looking for a shut-off switch on his shoulder, thinking he couldn't be human and that dumb. Then, it occurs to me that the laughter I hear across the room sounds familiar.

I turn just in time to see Ben Wright from Little Bend of Salt Springs sitting three tables over. He's with a huge group of people who all look like him. The girls are all wearing LL Bean clothes, and the guys are all wearing American Eagle beanies and glasses. They are drinking wine and having some heated discussion as if they are passing around jokes.

"Hey, I'll be right back," I tell Gabe. I walk over to Ben's table, lean over, and push my hand on his shoulder. "My cow got out today. We found it at the church. It got in the doors, crapped all over the floor." They are all looking at me with confused faces. The table is silent. Then, as if he is suddenly getting punched in the gut, Ben turns his head, and his mouth breaks into a smile.

"Oh! Holy shit all over the church."

"Yes, it was."

"Holy shit, Brandy Devereauxs, that's you."

"It is. Holy shit."

"Holy shit."

The man sitting across from him, leaned back with a hand on his forehead and groaned with a grin. "Ben got the *holy shit* card," he says aloud, and they all kind of take in that breath of realization and start to laugh loudly. "Dude, that was a hard one too! Did you pay her?"

"I didn't." Ben gets up, does his hugging thing, and then introduces me to his friends. He has his arm over my shoulder, dragging me in, and I suddenly sit down at the table with them, talking and chattering. It is much more fun at this table than the one with Janie and Meghan and the creepy boy candy.

"You're here with—?" he asks just as the server comes up with their appetizers. I realize a good twenty minutes have passed, and I wave a hand over to Gabe.

"Friends." Okay, it is a lie. But what am I going to say? *Yes, I'm here with my mortal enemies.* Instead, I turn and point to the table just across the room. I can see all of them staring at me as the conversation had long ago turned to the traitor who changed tables. Gabe gives a little wave of his hand. "I am. I let somebody fix me up on a date. The guy who's waving is really nice. But ug. Everyone else, I don't know, and it's awkward. So—just wanted to say hey."

"Well, hey, then," Ben tells me. "You can come sit with us if it gets any worse. We can share a plate."

"Yeah, come on over," one of them says, and I hold up a hand.

"I'm already in over my head. Ask Ben here what happens when I'm around a crowd. You'll be sorry."

"She faints."

"Yeah," I joke, "so I'm throwing my weakness out there for anybody who might be my archenemy undercover. It makes for a better battle at the end. You can bring in a dozen or more people, watch me black out, and use a butter knife to kill me dead."

"I can't imagine you have enemies." One of the girls is chuckling at me. "You're just downright entertaining."

"Oh, no, you don't understand. It's a bloodbath over at the other table." I lean in and nod toward Janie and Meghan. "See those two girls?" She nods. Everybody is almost silent, trying to hear me over the restaurant sounds. "You probably recognize them. They're doing the Redneck Run."

"I do," she says. "That's one of the twins— Michelle or Meghan."

"Yep, that's Meghan. They got wind I was going to do the Run, and they've been trying to stick a sword in my back all night." I drop my voice, and everybody leans in. "I think they are scared to death that they'd be up against a genuine redneck, and beneath their two-hundred-dollar haircuts and their tailored workout suits, they're nothing but those mean cheerleaders in high school that can't even work up a cartwheel."

"It wouldn't surprise me. Those women are cocky on the TV shows."

"A *real* redneck. You really don't look like one."

"You didn't pull into my driveway tonight and see my family sitting on the front porch with the flags waving and the ATVs parked in the drive." I laugh, and they laugh along. "Yeah, it is all tucked up inside this dress, just dying to get out," I tell them, patting my chest. "It would've shown, but my date won't let me punch any girls at the table. He tells me I must wait until we're in the parking lot." They are quiet, trying to read me. "I'm just kidding about the punching."

"You're doing the Redneck Run?" Ben asks me. "I didn't know that. What's your skill?"

"I like to run. I do about twenty miles daily up and down our mountain," I tell him. "Chased by our neighbor's dogs, shot at, screamed at, and jumping over creeks." I'm feeling a little itchy at all the attention. I hold out my hand. "But I'm not doing it now. I thought I could do all the events by myself. They changed the rules when they learned I was entering the event alone, so you must have a team now."

"Can they do that?" someone asks.

"*They* can always do whatever they want if they've got enough money and political ties," Ben grumbles. "That's Beau Vega over there. I met his mother once at some tourism event. She has her sword drawn before she even walks into a room. I heard he's worse."

"Yeah, right!" I bob my head up and down. "But Beau, he's not so bad."

"He lost a lot of weight since I saw him in the newspaper last year. That's not the guy you mentioned you worked with to lose weight, was it?"

I nod and wave my hand away.

"You should find some people for your team," one of the girls says. I look up, and she's smiling and pushing her hair behind her ears. "You've got a month and a half. You should do it to get back at them for pulling the plug on you."

"It wasn't just the lack of a team," I start to rise. The servers come with little fold-out chrome stands to hold the food trays they bring out. I turn and pat Ben's hand while I start to rise. "I couldn't find a sponsor willing to bank the thirteen hundred dollars and the t-shirts on me. I'd do it, but I'm a starving college student. It looks like it's time to eat. Thanks for getting me off the battlefield for a little bit." I leave on that note with a hug from Ben, sit back in my quiet seat, and wait for the girls to draw their swords again.

"I thought you bailed on me." Gabe pokes me in the arm. "I really thought you bailed." He keeps looking over at the table. "Next time, be a hero. Drag me with you away from here. Janie's date is an idiot, and Beau's back to being a shit again."

We both regret letting Bear drive. We're stuck, and we know it. Our food finally comes, and everyone picks at their plates except Gabe and me, who dig in like we haven't eaten in weeks. I am having a good time with him. He's not critical of me stuffing the bread in my mouth and laughs when I keep dropping forks on the floor. I look up to see Bear looking at me with his fork poking into his meat, dividing it up, then leaving it. He gives me the strangest smile, forced and maybe trapped. I'm figuring, after watching him let his girlfriend dig her nails into me and letting her do it, he deserves it.

As soon as we're done eating, I want to show Gabe the waterfalls they have just outside the restaurant. Most people don't know they are there, but a little stream runs past the side doors, and there is a walkway where you can access it. If you go to the very end, you can stand above the waterfall and see tiny lights floating in the water. It is beautiful, and I think he will like it.

"Come outside," I tell him, leaning over his seat while I get up.

Everybody is still chit-chatting while I snatch his hand and sneak out. He follows me down the back steps, through the doors, and into the tiny patio. It is starting to get dark, especially beneath the canopy of trees above us. "They've got big goldfish." I show him. "Coy." I slip off my heels and look right and left to make sure nobody is around. Then, I take a step into the cool pool of water. "Okay, wearing heels sucks. This water's nice."

"What are you doing, Brandy?"

"Nobody can see me, Gabe," I say. "You got a penny?" I point to where they've built a tiny water fountain. "I want to make a wish."

"Sure." He wiggles his hand into his pocket and pulls out a handful of change. "Take two. Make a wish for me, too." I take the pennies and start to shuffle across the slippery pool.

"Alright, wait up." Gabe makes this huge sigh while I come to a halt and turn. "No girl has to swim an ocean to make a wish for me. I can do it myself." He's peeling off his shoes and socks, tugging up his pants legs, and walking in the water.

"It's hardly an ocean." I can't believe he is wading right in with me, no questions asked.

"That's not the point. Damn, this is cold." I'm not sure what the point is, but Gabe comes up behind me and puts a hand on my arm. "You do know if I go down," he says. "I'm dragging you with me."

He never should have said it. I see him get this funny, surprised look on his face. His eyes get wide, and he lurches forward. "Aw, no," he whispers. I keel to the right, my toes hitting a slippery moss-covered rock. One second, I'm standing there with my mouth open, trying to come up with a witty remark to end this banter, and the next, I'm sitting in the pool of water, Gabe tumbling in right behind.

"Aw, shit," Gabe moans, grabbing my arm and towing me up with him. "Where did you come up with this brilliant idea?" He lets his voice rise, a sad mimic of his rendition of my words while the water dribbles off. "*C'mon, Gabe, let's put a penny in the waterfall.*"

"That is not exactly how this played out," I refuse to take the blame on this one. "You didn't want a girl outdoing you, making it to the waterfall and maybe wishing —" He is cursing low on his breath, holding his arms out and watching the water pour off both of us. I think he is going to scream at me. I'm waiting. He doesn't.

"Wishing what, Brandy?" he asks. "Finish."

"I don't know." I start to turn toward the restaurant, but he points a finger at the fountain. "I don't know what a guy like you, who has everything, would wish for."

"I don't have everything. And I'm not turning back now. We're going to make a wish even if I have to drag you across the water by your hair." He takes my arm while we both slip and slide toward the fountain. I look up, and he is looking down at me, laughing softly under his breath. "You looked pretty funny going down."

We are still dripping. It is warm, wet, and uncomfortable. "Why did you follow me? Do you not know anything about me, Gabe?" I return. "I can't take one step without trouble following." I stop at the fountain and stare at the murky water inside.

"Beau calls them adventures."

A dead fish is floating on top, and we look at it, lock eyes, and laugh. "I suppose that's the last guy who came out here on a date from hell whose girlfriend wished he wasn't around and turned him into a fish," I mumble. "I think I'll wish you won't be so stupid to follow me next time."

"Don't wish that. I'm having fun. It isn't a date from hell." Gabe pokes a thumb behind us. "Beau's date is a date from hell. I think my head will explode with Meghan's shrilly baby whine."

"Okay, I wish I could be in the Redneck Run." I don't know why I made that wish. I suppose deep down, it is really what my heart is set on. I have a million other wishes I could have asked for like a new truck, a job, Big Don to get a flushy in the police bathrooms like his son used to do to Kenny, Calvin the cop, and Little Pete. I didn't. Gabe is looking at me. "You really want to do that, don't you?"

"Yeah. What's your wish?" I watch him toss the penny into the fountain. The dampness is creeping up my hips while he tosses his in, too. A dribble of water slips past my left knee.

"I wished you'd be in the Redneck Run."

"Oh, you're kind of being sweet," I say. "We know it can't come true." But I'm turning to look at him, and he's looking at me.

"You never know."

"I do know. Big Don said Amelia Vega is filing trespassing charges against me for stopping up there the other day at the resort.

There's a judge that will get a restraining order, so I can't go close to her."

"Brandy, I know you'll figure something out." My hand is still clinging to his shirt. His hand is on my arm. I'm misty-eyed because it was an adorable thing to do. Those things, lately, seem to come in smaller quantities. I'm thinking we're about to have a moment, about to kiss. It's almost like we both are really trying to work on it; maybe it isn't coming, isn't the right time, isn't the right person, but, oh-what-the-hell, we'll give it a shot because we're both standing here. We do. It's a kiss, warm and soggy and kind of uncomfortable like the damp clothes I am wearing—

"Hey, lovebirds, we're getting ready to take off."

I don't know why I can feel the red slip down my cheeks. It's Bear. It shouldn't bother me. He caught Billy putting his hand up my shirt. I know he can't see us too well. It is dim in here. I'm glad.

"Come on," Gabe gives me a little nudge with his hand, and I step out. I should have been more attentive, but my mind was on Bear watching us.

"You've got to be kidding me—!" This time, I managed to land in Gabe's lap, belly first and right on top of him. I'm splashing after he says that, flapping my arms, trying to get up from this awkward position. He's got his hand on my slippery wrist and trying to peel me off, and I can't do anything more than sit back and feel the water seeping into my dress again. And belly laughing loudly.

I hate my laugh. When it is heart-felt, full-bellied, I-can't-control-it burst of laughter, it is loud and sounds like a witch cackle ending in an owl's hoot. That's what I'm doing right now. I can't control this one. I can feel my sides aching while I look at Gabe squirming from a full sit-down position. It is the expression on his face like he bit down on a pickle after sucking on a sweet lollipop.

Gabe is mumbling something to himself when he looks up at me, his eyes questioning before he starts laughing like an idiot too. We can't even hardly get up. By the time we get to the other side, Bear has some staff people holding towels. I slip to the bathroom to see if I can dry off in one of the air dryers. The moment I go in, I feel like I am in high school again. I'm face to face with Janie and Meghan, grooming their hair in the mirror. I stop dead, slip on my heels, and approach the dryers. They are staring darts into my back.

"That was classy, Goodwill," Janie finally says. I knew it was coming. It was only a matter of how long it would take. "If I could be any more embarrassed by what you just did, I would die."

"It's Dollar Store Dolly," Meghan corrects. "We keep forgetting her new name. I told Beau we shouldn't have picked you up."

"Did you not think we would see your *kin* sitting on the porch a'spittin' in their jars and drinkin' the 'shine?" Janie tells me. Would she really start a fight in the bathroom? "I wouldn't want anybody to know those were my family."

"Your daddy works down at the sewage plant," I remind her. "That's a pretty shitty job."

"*Works* is the keyword, though," Janie says. "He has a job that is better than any of your poor white trash hillbilly family."

"Enough, Janie," I say. "I don't want to fight you. I'm proud of my family. You can call them anything you want. I don't care because I see the mouth it is coming from and you're like this big as far as I'm concerned." I hold up my forefinger and thumb, just barely pushing them together. Then I look at Meghan. "And I don't want to fight with you. It isn't because I couldn't beat the crap out of all four of you. I could. You're a bunch of weakling scaredy-cats."

"You can't do squat."

"I can't when you have your daddy pulling me over in his cop car and impounding my truck, threatening to arrest me, and offering money to get me in bed. No, I can't."

"What! How dare you!"

"Yeah, that's what I said to your daddy." I swat the towel around my neck. I want to dry off more but know I've got to get out of here.

"I'm telling on you. I'm going to get an attorney and sue you for being a redneck and saying that. I can afford it now. I'm famous and I'll tell everybody on T.V. how redneck you and your family are."

"I don't think you can sue anybody for being redneck, princess. But I could sue you for defamation for ruining my reputation if you announced something bad and untrue in the press about me. Then I'd be the rich one." I toss the towel by the sink. "But sue me if you want. You are mean. I don't know why you even bother picking on me. I'm not hanging around Bear anymore like you told me not to do. I don't even answer his texts and calls." I turn to leave.

"We'll get you back, you know that, right?" Meghan says, coming up around me, poking a finger in my mid-back. "You just wait. Sometimes, when Bear isn't around, I will get you good. Better watch your back. If you say anything about my daddy ever again, I will have him shoot you while you are running some night! Yeah, I've seen you running after dark and in the morning. I know your route. I'll tell him and he'll kill you dead."

It is quiet. I hear a toilet flush. Meghan snaps her attention back at the stall. The door opens and I see one of the girls from Ben's table coming out.

"Hey, you alright?" she asks me, scooting between me and Meghan. "Are these to women you are riding with? How about I give you a ride back to your place?"

Chapter −27

Loving Bear the Only Way I Know how

I woke up the following day in Ben's guest bedroom. Gabe and I never made it back home last night. I accepted the ride. Gabe did, too. Janie and Meghan were whining to get home. They had early training days tomorrow. Janie's date was begging to come with us. I told Chase we'd be out too late. It was a couples' thing. It gave us an excuse to bow out of riding with Bear. We stopped at a couple apartments and hung out. I had fun even in damp clothes. We finally ended up at Ben's house at about two-thirty in the morning. He's got this new log cabin overlooking a lake. It's got a framed back porch and sits at the bottom of a mountain. I follow the low sound of voices from my room and see Gabe and Ben sitting on a couple of rockers, sipping on big mugs of coffee.

"I guess we are officially at morning," Ben says.

"Don't tell me you two stayed up all night." They were sitting there when I strolled back to the bedroom last night. I could hear their soft voices trickling through the hallway until the sounds lulled me to sleep.

"Wow, we kind of lost track of time." Gabe looks at his watch, then looks at Ben.

"I'm hungry." Ben leans over and rises. Fifteen minutes later, we are all three in the kitchen cooking up a storm. Before we eat, Ben pulls me aside and hands me a check.

"What's this?" I ask him.

"You said you needed a sponsor. There's fifteen hundred there." I'm staring at the check, at Ben, then at the check again. "I can't accept this." I try to hand it back to him. "I'll never win. I've got no team, and I haven't all the stuff the big teams have." He stops me.

"Everybody loves the underdog even when they don't win," he says. "After seeing those two girls in person that you would be racing against, you'll dust them."

"I'm going to design your t-shirts," Gabe says. "We already talked this out last night. My degree is in graphic design. It's the fun part of my job that I like and usually can't do because the jobs are few and far between."

"Don't worry about anything but getting your team together," Ben adds. "Between four-thirty and five, we had everything else worked out. If you still want to do it, I'll call the resort Monday morning and get the ball rolling."

"Wishes do come true," Gabe laughs. "They do." However I see him looking at Ben, and I think he didn't wish for me to be in the Redneck Run at all. I think he wished for something a little more.

Pops is giving me an angry stare when I get home. He does this thing with his eyes, narrows them to fine slits, and tips his chin down. I think when he does this, he can read my mind. It is Sunday morning, and I usually cook lunch for everybody after church. They are all sitting around waiting when Gabe drops me off at half past one in the afternoon.

"Have fun last night, Brandy Candy?" Kenny comes in and grabs me around the neck and gives me noogies with his knuckles on top of my head when I go out of my bedroom, redressed in camo pants and a crop top. "Get you some something-something?"

"God, leave me alone!" I growl at him, shoving him away. My Aunt Jenny yells at him, saying he shouldn't do that to a girl even if I am his cousin. I'm tired and grumpy, caught between walking on a high because I have a sponsor for the Redneck Run. Then I realized maybe I was using the lack of having a sponsor as an excuse to not run at all.

"You better get to making something," Pops says. "It's almost two in the afternoon." I know he must have thought Gabe and I got a hotel room or something last night. He says nothing about that, probably because Gabe's the preacher's son. He hints, though, and the whole time I'm cooking lunch, he keeps coming in and standing in the kitchen with his arms folded across his chest like he wants to say something, but he doesn't. This time, he leans back against the sink, and I turn. "I think you don't want me to finish college because you won't have a slave in the kitchen to cook for you all the time," I tell Pops while I finish in the kitchen.

"You told her that?" My papaw uses his cane to walk into the kitchen. He has his glass in his hand and walks around Pops to the sink to fill it up. He leans his hand solidly on the counter and stares hard at Pops. "Why would you tell her that? She's the only grandkid I got that's gonna have a degree."

"I never told her I didn't want her to finish school, Dad. I think she needs to make sure this is what she wants. It's a lot of money she owes. She's not got a dime to pay it back. No job—"

"No, you were pretty clear," I tell him. "You told me that I should find a good man, get married and—"

"No, Brandy, I did not."

I throw my hands into the air and groan loudly. "Yeah, you did."

We lock eyes for at least seven seconds. I finally break and look away. I can never win in a staring contest with Pops.

"Bear's out there." Pops is still watching me. "He's been sitting on that couch with your papaw since he finished church at eleven. Said he was worried about you. You and the preacher's boy left with a different crowd they didn't know. He felt responsible. He tried a bunch to call you. You didn't call him back."

"Because I blocked his calls, Pops, on my cell phone. So Big Don will eventually give me back my truck."

"Is that what this is all about?"

"What is this?" I ask him. "I'm not sure what you mean. I don't want Bear here. He can't come around here anymore. They are making my life miserable if that's what you want to know. His mom, his girlfriend, her friends. Big Don. They ganged up on me at the resort just like they used to do in high school. I really thought high school was over. But now I'm reliving that hell every day, and I don't have Josh around to stick up for me. I can't even punch those dumbass girls in the face because they'll have me arrested."

"You don't have to put up with it, baby girl."

"What would you suggest I do?"

He didn't have an answer; he simply looked at my papaw. "I'm taking the ATV out for a ride." I snatched up a hair tie and ponytail my hair behind my head.

"Are you freaking stalking me?" I confront Bear while opening the barn doors where Pops keeps his ATVs.

"In your dreams." He looks at me and starts to laugh like I'm joking with him, then realizes I'm dead serious. "No, your Pops told me you were out here."

It is muddy, and it looks like it is going to rain again. I just want to get out of here and be by myself.

"What's going on, Brandy? Why are you mad at me?"

"Because you are here. When you are here, your girlfriend gets mad. And I am mad because she called me Dollar Store Dolly. Where did she hear that? What did you say to her about us sitting in your truck the other night? When your girlfriend gets mad, she calls in the National Guard. Did they not tell you what happened?"

"What happened?"

I fold my arms across my chest. "You know what? Nothing, nothing at all."

"Did something happen last night?"

He really doesn't know. "You should ask your girlfriend."

"You mind if I ride one?"

"If you don't mind looking at my ass and a bunch of mud flying at your face."

I've been riding ATVs since I was four. Pops used to stick me on his lap when he went hunting, and not long after, he got me a miniature version that I could ride around the yard. He lets Kenny and I use his two oldest ones whenever we want as long as we're careful with them. Kenny always leans over when Pops tells us this and whispers, "Define careful?" Because we have this thing about racing them and getting a little goofy. Kenny likes to ride the puddles sideways. I like to do cartwheels and jump over them while they are running. I can even catch up sometimes with Kenny when he goes out alone and is slip-sliding up a steep hill. I come up behind, walk up the side of the ATV, and ride it like a ballerina standing straight up. Then I pivot, lunge off the front on my hands and feet, and beat him up the hill. He hates this. "I'm a puma," I tell him with a silly grin.

"I'm gonna shoot me a puma one of these days," he tells me in return.

We can't touch the one Pops calls Old Yeller. He and Uncle Craig modified it from scraps and engine parts they found online and at a junkyard. "Don't touch the one under the tarp," I tell Bear. "It's sacred." He shies away from the tarp like there is a monster underneath. He should. It gets up to ninety miles an hour now. I'm unsure if Bear has ever been on an ATV. I've got to assume he has tried one out before because I don't necessarily leave him in the dust. However, I do have some tricks that me and Kenny always do to each other. The one I like the best right now is getting close enough ahead of him to spray mud all over him every chance I get.

Bear finally seems to tire of my game when I cut along the creek and send a spray of water in his face. It's misty on the mountain, and he slows down and disappears. I start feeling sorry for him. It makes me mad because I blame him for not sticking up for me.

"I'm stuck." When I go back to see where he disappeared, Bear is standing by the ATV, knee-deep in water and milky mud, and trying to push it out. He looks like a four-year-old who just got caught crossing the street by himself.

"Yes, you are." I shut off the engine, lean back in the seat, and wipe sweat from my forehead. "How'd you get mud in your face?"

"Funny. Haha. Can you help me push this stupid thing out?" He's using the bottom of his t-shirt to wipe away the mud on his face. "I'm going back to the house."

"You're almost to the top."

"Yeah, I think you just want to be alone. I'm in the way." Bear looks down the hillside, then back at me. I can see his eyes falling on my cropped shirt and then below to where my bare tummy is. My pants are low-rise, and there's a good gap between my shirt and the waist, my belly button about halfway between. His gaze, then, snaps away. I'm surprised. He's never given any indication he was looking at me this way. I think of how many ways to next Tuesday this would tick his girlfriend off if she knew I was walking over to him right now, stopping just short of the right tire and getting just close enough that we're almost touching. "Why'd you leave last night, Brandy?" Bear's looking down at me. I'm close, but he doesn't take a step back. "Was it that Mark guy? The one Janie was going out with. I know he wasn't leaving you alone." Bear leans up against the front of the ATV and shoves a hand through his hair.

"His name was Chase, Bear," I tell him. "He wasn't bad. He was cute showing off. I didn't think I could stand the long ride home with Janie and Meghan. It made me mad when she called me Dollar Store Dolly. I wasn't as much mad at her as I was with you."

"Okay, I'm sorry. It won't happen again."

"It didn't matter. I ran into somebody I knew. We decided to hang out with them. They were going out, and I know the girls wanted to go home and go to bed."

"You seemed to know just about everybody. I think that's what made Megs mad. She's backward."

Backward? Last night, there wasn't any part of Meghan Reynolds that showed she was timid. She had a pretty good hold on getting in my face, calling me everything but crap. "Shy, she is not, Bear."

"No, I mean she just isn't very cultured, like classy."

"I'm hillbilly. What do you say about me when I'm not around?"

"You're not—" He looks down and seems to chew on this again. "Yeah, you're hillbilly. Please don't get mad at me saying it because I'm not being mean. There isn't anything wrong with being that. It's just how you handle it, how you handle everybody else. You've got class when you want to." And there he goes, trying not to stare at my belly again, scrubbing his arm across his face like he's trying to hide it. "Did you sleep with him?"

"If you mean Gabe, it is none of your business."

"You're right."

"I'm standing here wondering, Bear," I say, leaning back on the ATV. "Why would you even ask that question? Don't you think it's strange you'd ask that of a friend?"

"Yeah, you're right about that too, I suppose."

"Do *you* want to sleep with me?"

I can see the anger in his eyes. But my own, I'm just blinking up at him as innocent as a newborn fawn. And there's a tiny part of me that I wouldn't admit aloud that kind of likes that wild-angry glint to his eyes, the way he's working his jaw. I'm thinking about the mud all over him, the way he's standing there with his long legs stuffed in those jeans that fit designer right around his butt. My mind's already peeling off that skin-tight T-shirt, rolling my fingers along his chest, belly, and wondering what's in the package below.

But what's the sexiest part of standing right there? I know that he doesn't know he's hotter than hot. He still thinks he's this fat guy with a lot of money to throw around and enough confidence to ask a girl out if he's holding a hundred bucks in his hand.

"I see you looking," I say, leaning in. We're almost touching. I can smell Bear, catch a whiff of sweat, cologne, and everything, man. "You want to touch it?" I reach out, take his hand, and let it rest just above the material of my pants on the bare skin of my belly. He lets his palm settle there and gets this scared rabbit look in his eyes like he wasn't expecting me to do this at all, but he doesn't want to pull away.

"Brandy, don't do this."

"Don't do what?" He does start to pull away, and I feel his fingers tickle along the skin just above my belly button. I reach out and gently pull it back. "Isn't this why you come around?"

"You don't want to do this." He doesn't deny it and lets the words fade until I can't hear them above the water trickling in the creek. I can see his chest rising, falling like he's breathing heavily.

"I don't want to do this?" I ask him softly, leaning in. "Or you don't want to do this?"

He looks away, down to the creek. I figure, okay, maybe he doesn't. Maybe I read him wrong. Perhaps he sticks around because he likes hanging with me, Pops, and my family. I back up and let his hand fall away. "Alright. Enough said. Let's get this ATV out."

Bear doesn't even say anything. He nods, and he has this miserable set to his lips. He goes to one side, grabs the handlebars, and starts to push. I know it isn't going to move much. But I back up to the rear and begin to give it a good shove. Then I realize I'm the only one doing any of the work. I look over and see Bear standing two steps from my right shoulder. "I don't know how to do this, alright?" I'm leaning hard still into the back of the ATV.

"I don't know what you mean," I say.

"I think you do." He looks me straight in the eyes, serious as I've ever seen him. He seems different then; he's scared, but not scared and timid like a mouse standing up to a cat. It's more like the wary gaze of a kid who knows he must take a test and knows he won't pass.

"This." He waves a hand between us. "I've been staring at your ass all the way up the hill, your perfect, perfect ass. Your perfect belly is flat. Every time you stand up to go over a big rock, I can see right up your shirt to the little lacy bra. I'm trying not to think about it. Let it go. I'm trying not to wonder what it would be like to touch that lace, touch your skin underneath. You made those little circles around me, that's sexy as hell. I let it ride. I think of other things."

"Okay, well, let it ride," I say with a smart twist of lips and a waggle of my head. "Think of other things."

"You know, you've got a mouth on you that just won't quit." The next thing I know, Bear's right up in my face. He's got his arm around my shoulder, his hand sliding up along my neck and in my hair. He's kissing me hard. I can't catch my breath, and my heart's pounding like a line of drummers in a band at a high school football game. He startled me at first. I wasn't expecting him to do it. I jumped like a rabbit flinches at the sight of a coyote. I think he liked it. He was the one with the sly smile then. The kiss is fast, like one of my short runs, that I take off a little faster to get a better workout.

He switches us around so he's partly sitting on the back of the ATV, all relaxed. He grabs me up around the waist with his free hand, lifts me, and I automatically wrap my legs around his middle. Now he's got a free hand sliding under my shirt, under my bra, while he presses harder into me. My head is spinning because it isn't what I expected. It's a little more feral, a little more like the woods around us grabbed up the city boy I thought I knew and made him into a man, something rough and definitely not tame.

I can feel him working his pants, I know what he's doing, so I shimmy down to help him out. My hands are on his arms like I imagined, feeling the muscles tense every time he shifts. He freezes for a moment, I look up, and he's looking at me. Deadset, his eyes are on me. We have a moment I can't quite describe. It's like our two worlds cross right then. It doesn't matter what planet we're from. We're like one. Then, I see something cross through his eyes. It makes me feel like what we're doing is wrong. I don't know why.

"Tell me this is what you want," Bear's voice is almost a whisper, deep and controlled. I nod, forcing my eyes to stay on his own. Then that bond passes, and he's pressing me hard to him, making those little huffing whispers that mingle with mine.

Chapter –28

Weird Martha

I didn't think it was going to play out like that. Those are the very words Bear tells me before he leaves in his truck. I don't know what it means. I don't ask him. He hadn't said more than three words to me, even after we got the ATV out of the creek. Then he mumbled those words to me while he stood at his truck. Surely, by now, he knows nothing ever plays out as it should with me.

Two days later, I haven't heard from him. It's not what I want. Sometimes, you've just got to live with other people's choices. He had to live with mine when I pushed his hand back on my belly. It was what I wanted, wasn't it? To get back at Meghan the only way I know how. Like my mama would have done.

Accordingly, out comes the apparently cursed lockbox. I stare at it and open it up. I've got notes written on the tops of the envelopes: ***Taylor and Todd Winter/Dead/knife/Fire. Hannah and Tyler Heaton/fire/Dead. Madison Johnson/fire/Dead. Mark and Mandy Walters/Cemetery/necklace. Ashley Mills: Alive/white truck.*** I jiggle the envelopes, listen to the license slip up and down the paper, and hear the key slide until it stops. The keys. I tug one out of Heaton's envelope. It is small. I turn it around in my hand, lay it flat on my palm, stuff it in my pocket, and take it down to Grant Rehabilitation and Nursing Center.

"You know what this key goes to, Bobby?" I ask him while he sits in a tan vinyl chair where the T.V. sits in the lobby. He's got the warmest brown eyes I've ever seen on anyone. He used to be the janitor at the New Alliance Middle School. That's where I met him. He smiled big-toothed at all the kids while he walked down the hall with his mop bucket and mop. Some smiled back, some did not. I did. He used to point at me and say, *You're gonna be somethin' big someday, girl, yes you are.*

"Why, it's a key." He takes it from my fingers and pokes it with a gnarled forefinger.

"I figured that out." I roll my eyes. "Since we agree that it is a key, do you know what it might unlock?"

"Um, no, I don't think so." He shrugs and hands it back. "You came down here on a Tuesday to ask me that?"

"I came to see if you'll do the Redneck Run with me."

He laughs loudly and claps his hand on his thigh. "You hear that?" he tells everyone in the room. "This little girl, she wants me to run in a race. How about that." He elbows the catatonic man next to him, then pushes himself to his feet. Bobby Reese pretends to run in a circle, then sits down again across from me. He's out of breath.

"Are you done?" I ask him blandly.

"Listen to me, I'm wheezing. Baby girl, I can't race anymore. My legs, they ain't what they used to be."

"And neither is your brain," I tell him, poking his knee. "I can run. I'm just not so good at hitting the target with a bow. You saw me. I need somebody to shoot a bow and do the archery division."

"I thought that's what we've been doing all along, teaching you how to use that bow."

"Okay, let's say this." I lean into Bobby. "You're not allowed to eat anything this winter but stuff I shoot with a bow during hunting season. How does that work for you?"

"I'll starve to death."

"*Bingo.* I'll take you out hunting this winter. I'll put up my pops' best blind with a space heater and sit in it with you while you hunt if you do it."

"Yeah, baby girl, I'll do it for you. It sounds better than sitting here and watching the old girls do their Jazzercise dancing." He bends his arms akimbo and dances with his elbows flapping like a furious rooster. "Except Lydia. She's got giant bazoombas, and boy when they turn on the Hot Rock of the 1970s, and she starts jumping to the beat, they do wiggle and shake—"

"Oh, Bobby!" I cringe, turn my head, and cover my ears with my hands. "Stop! You're going to make me deaf. You're going to damage me worse than my mama did in the four years she had me."

Martha Hershberger is a different story. I figure she's the only person I know who can swim above a doggy paddle or that flappy stroke most folks do across the water. Kenny drives me to Owl Hollow, and I stand on her porch with my cousin.

"No, I'm not that good," she tells me while her twelve sisters take turns curiously peering out between the thick blanket curtains in the pretty two-story house windows. "When we go to the creek, I spend more time diving after my sisters to keep them from drowning than swimming. Besides, I've got to watch the kids on Saturdays." There's a horse and buggy in the driveway tied to a post. Beside it is a big, new church bus with **God's Holy Temple – Prayer works!** written on one side beneath a rainbow and a pair of Jesus' hands in prayer.

Her mother brought us some chocolate chip cookies and milk. She doesn't look anything like Martha. She's pudgy and has rosy cheeks. Kenny, Martha, and I sit in a couple chairs and dip the cookies in the milk. "I don't know why you don't. Can't you get somebody else to watch them for just a day or two?"

"I don't think my family would approve. It is vain to compete. We spurn vanity."

I see Kenny tip his head to one side and size Martha up. Her hair is still pitch black, but she has lime green highlights this time. I'm scared he might say something stupid like, *They approve of the crap you're wearing on your hair?*

He dips his cookie and pulls it out. "And volleyball isn't a competition?" he asks, and I nod in approval of his cleverness. "Because there is a volleyball net in every one of the Amish yards we passed coming in here."

"Maybe we should pray about it." Martha reaches out a hand to me and one to Kenny. Kenny stares at her hand like it is a dead rat, then Martha's face, then he turns to me.

"I'm not praying with her."

"She's not trying to exorcise you. Just do it," I tell him. I'm willing to do anything to get Martha to join the team, even if she is trying to banish whatever demon is inside my cousin.

"No."

"Just do it!"

"No."

"Kenny, you will sit here and pray with her or I swear to God—" I growl before Martha's wide eyes stop me cold.

"Brandy, you can't swear to God. It is blasphemy."

242

"Okay." I bob my head up and down. "You either pray with her, or I will. I will—*you just will!*" I reach out, snatch Kenny's hand, and hold it tight with my fingernails, ready to dig in like brakes if he tries to pull out. Martha reaches out and snaps up his other hand frantically like he is drowning, and his head just went under.

"Let us pray," she starts. I see Kenny's eyes dead set on me, narrow and enraged. "Please help my friend, Brandy, understand that I must obey my parents. I must not be vain. Please guide her in her endeavors and, perhaps, show her the way to our church and Godly ways."

"Okay, it's my turn," I say before Kenny can wiggle his fingers out of mine. I speed my prayer up a bit and tip my head for effect. "Dear God, please scratch what Martha said. She knows not what she does. Instead, make Martha see the light. I beg you to guide her in joining our team and swimming for us. I'll go to church with her two times, one for each of her churches if she does, and I will get saved at least twice with her if I must do it."

"Dear God, please get me out of this place." That was Kenny, and he got his wish ten minutes later, even if Martha was about ready to grab up her broom and hit him with it.

"God, she is so weird," Kenny tells me when we hop into his truck. "Who wears hair like that?" His vehicle is new and still smells good inside. He has a little air freshener clipped to the air-conditioner. "Who goes to church every day?"

"You're close-minded," I tell him. "Your mama goes to church on Saturday, Sunday and Wednesday. Then she goes between to choir and picnics. I'm sure Martha's family thinks we are weird."

"What's weird about us?" Kenny makes that stupid duck call, puffing out his cheeks when he does it. I shake my head.

"Nothing, Kenny," I grunt soberly, pushing the hair back from my face. "Nothing at all."

About fifteen minutes out on the road home, I got a call from Martha. "I'll do it if your cousin goes to a party with me at one of my neighbors. Kenny's hot."

"Kenny isn't hot. But, of course, he will," I tell her. "So, I can count you in?"

"Yes."

When I turn the phone off, I look up at Kenny. "Hey, you're going out with Martha. You're taking her to an Amish party."

"Oh, no," he tells me, turning his head away from the road long enough to shake it hard back and forth. "No way. I'm not going out with Weird Martha. And I'm not going to some creepy Amish party with her."

"Yes, you are," I tell him. "I covered for you when I thought you'd smoked the dope at Pops. I took the blame for it. Oh, yes, you are."

"But I didn't even smoke the dope. It was your mama."

"It doesn't matter. I took the fall. It still counts, and you owe me."

"I freakin' do *not* owe you."

"Oh, yes, you do."

Kenny makes the duck call. Then he completely changes the subject and starts talking about new camo coveralls he bought for gun season.

"Can you drive me someplace?" I ask him.

"I just drove you to Weird Martha's."

"Have you ever heard of Sunshine Forks, Tennessee?"

"You're kidding me."

"I'm not. I've got an address, which is only a few hours away."

"Brandy Peppermint Candy, I've got a thousand things to do, and that ain't one of them. Why don't you get Bear to take you? He likes doing that crap with you."

"He's got a girlfriend now." I shift in my seat, sigh, and look out the window. I've got to admit, Bear was right. There is more to life than hanging out with Kenny.

Chapter −29
Finding Josh

Yesterday, I ran so hard up the mountain that I thought my lungs would burst. Mama's lawyer called. He said if I didn't press charges and she could get out of jail, she would go through another drug rehab, and she'd give full custody of Kaylee to Pops. That was the deal. I love my mama—I do. But I know the rehab isn't going to help, and jail is the only safe place for her. I also know that at any minute now, without her signing custody papers, she can say Pops did something to Kaylee and have her taken away to some foster home. I go into my room to my little table and pull up the pearl necklace. I stare at it long, trying to remember how I got it.

It was the summer, and I was about three or four years old. Mama was gone. Nobody knew where she'd taken off that time. I was in a foster home. I don't know where, but the lady who took me told me to call her Mama Jean. Nobody was mean to me, but Mama Jean took in lots of kids to make money and not necessarily to love them. I wanted to be with Pops. It was all I could think about, so I kept running away and trying to find his house. The sixth time I walked out down the sidewalk and knocked on a front door, the lady from the foster care services sat me down and told me I'd never be able to go live with Pops if I was a bad little girl and ran away.

I started crying, and I think she realized how much I loved him then. She took the chain she was wearing from around her neck and put it around mine. I remember she pointed to the little pearl at the end. "I am going to make sure you go live with your Pops. I'm giving you this necklace so that you trust me. Will you trust me enough you won't run away if I give it to you?"

To me, the pearl necklace became my first lesson in trust. It was everything that my mama wasn't—leaving me alone in the house, smoking a joint on the couch while I watched cartoons in her lap— a hundred other things that toddler shouldn't have to live with or know. But at what cost would it be on me if she was out of jail again, begging for money, calling me up at all hours of the night to pick her up from somewhere? I can no longer pay her rent or Kaylee's food and daycare to keep my sister safe at least part of the day.

That's why I run. It is always because I'm trying to get as far away from Mama and my problems as possible. I let the necklace dangle in my fingers, knowing what I'd have to do, and then I lay it down and take off down the road at a dead run. The only problem with this outlet is that I always have to go back. It doesn't solve anything. If Mama isn't on the other end of the phone call line, she's always in my head.

"I think you're doing the right thing," Pops says when I get out of the shower. He is lying on the floor, playing a board game with Kaylee. I'm wearing one of my new outfits, leaning over and rubbing a towel against my head to dry my hair. I see Pops note the clothes with a curious expression that drops to him biting his lower lip. "Did Bear buy you those?"

"Yes. I would not take his money, so he paid me in clothes for helping him lose weight."

"Uh-huh." His knowing gaze says he thinks I'm up to something, and it isn't good, but he'll sit back and let me make the mistake. "Protecting your little sister is a good thing to do."

I know it is the best thing for Kaylee, too. She'll have a chance. If not, she is only one tiny footstep away from one of Mama's drugged-up boyfriends doing something awful to her.

"Who is going to protect Brandy?"

I jumped, startled. I don't even hear Bear step in the door. This is new. He used to knock. Now, he's family? Pops looks up from where he is leaning against one elbow.

"Brandy will be fine," Pops says. My eyes go from him to Bear. "She's a big girl. Kaylee's not." Bear won't look at my eyes.

"Yeah, we saw that last month when she almost got killed, Lee. You say that but look what happened before. How will you know if her mom starts all that up again? It's like you're trading in one daughter for the other." Oh, no, Bear called Pops by his real name.

"Excuse me?" Pops utters. "Don't you say anything like that, son." I feel like this is something he's doing, man to man. I'm not comfortable with this. I'm not thirteen and need two grown men making decisions and fighting over me. It's too late. Pops' eyes cloud over with a storm. I'm not used to somebody sticking up for me. I mean, Kenny sometimes does it in his own half-assed way.

He used to tell Pops I was at his house when I was really hanging out with Josh. My family backs me up. But when it comes to important family decisions about me, nobody defies Pops and gets away with it. It's just how it is while I live under his roof.

"Brandy won't let it happen. She knows better now."

"She knows better?" Bear lets the door close behind him. I feel like a little kid while my parents fight over my head. "I don't think you have to worry about her decisions. It is her mama's choices that are bad."

"Son, you have no right to come into my home and tell me if I'm right or wrong. Buying my daughter clothes does not make her yours to decide for." Oh, shit. I see where Pops is going.

"I'm not making a decision for her. That doesn't make sense. If you are wrong, you need to be called out for that wrong. Her mama almost killed her. Big Don said she laid into Brandy just as hard as that idiot John John. They'll let him go too if she doesn't press charges on her mom. Without her complaints, they've got nothing. Do you *not* think that her mother might recant giving you custody once she's out, and John John might go after Kaylee again too?"

I look at Bear, my eyes sliding over to Pops. He didn't know Mama swung the first few punches when I knocked over her table full of drugs. I didn't think he needed to know. I didn't want him to know Mama tried to hurt me like that. But Bear is right. My mama is bad enough that she might change her mind about the adoption so she could have something over me and Pops forever, extorting us for money to fund her habits with our desire to keep Kaylee safe. I had not wanted to come face to face with that reality.

"Stop it!" I yell. "Both of you! I am old enough to make decisions for myself!"

That said, I'm in Sunshine Forks, Tennessee, where Josh's Katy-did lived when he was William Hill Junior. The lockbox sitting next to me in Pops' truck is closed tight. I grabbed it up, took Pops' keys off the table, and took off. I know Pops will be furious when I return for taking his truck. I don't want to go back. I'm six and a half hours and a time zone away from him. I am also way too dressed up to be standing on a truck loading dock for Elkton Logistics. It is hot, dusty, and dirty. I'm wearing a skirt and a lacy top while I walk up the ramp in the back in high heels.

The guys give me a strange gaze, like I'm a doe during hunting season, and they have a really bad hankering to shoot me. "I'm looking for William Hill Junior," I say to the first man I encounter. He's sweaty and work-dirty, carrying a box. This was the second stop I made. The first was a restaurant I visited in town to get coffee. The waitress knew where William Hill Junior worked. It was with her ex-boyfriend right at this dock. My heart pounds walking up the ramp. I'm thinking that Josh is going to come walking out at any time. Josh, that is, as William Hill Junior from his driver's license.

"That's me."

I turn. Another guy is rolling out boxes on a cart along a ramp and into a semi-truck. He's halfway up and stops, so he lets the cart rest. He's tall and thin with short red hair, but not Josh. "You're William Hill Junior?"

"Yeah, who's asking?"

"Um, me," I say. I'm flustered. I hadn't reasonably thought ahead that this might happen. "You're not the William I'm looking for. I was expecting somebody else. My ex-husband changed his name—I thought it was the same as yours."

"Oh, no, she's hunting some poor dude down for alimony," the sweaty guy says behind me.

I twist and shake my head, then turn back to William. "Do you have a wife named Katy?"

"Katy was my sister. Why do you want to know?"

"*Was*? Is she still—around?"

"She died six months ago." He wiggles his foot on the cart and leans forward. "You're not really looking for your husband, are you. Are you a reporter or something?"

"No, I'm not."

"I don't believe you. It is the same thing that's been in the papers, and the same on the police reports. I can't tell you anything new if that's what you want. Somebody broke into Katy's house. Probably thought she was at work. The cops think whoever it was got surprised by her being there." He shakes his head, takes both hands, and rubs his eyes. "They hit her over the head with a brick they found out front that they kept over the garbage can lid to keep the raccoons out. Then, whoever did it tried to burn the place down.

They must have been in a hurry. Only the bed she was on caught fire. Whoever did it still hasn't been caught. Johnny found her when he got off work. That's it. That's all."

"Johnny?"

"Johnny Mills. That was her husband."

Johnny Mills. My heart skips a beat. *Johnny Mills.* Holy crap. The image of frizzy red hair and freckles comes to my head. It was the girl from Brink Hollow with the kids. Ashley. Johnny Mills was her husband, too.

"Is Johnny still around?"

"You know what? Yeah, go bother him. He's pissed me off just taking off like he did. I think he's staying somewhere in Bluffton Hollow, at one of those live-in hotels off the highway."

"It is Pine Estates," another guy loading hollers out.

"Yeah, something like that." William has the worn look of someone sick and tired of trying not to think about something terrible that happened to him. "But I will tell you this—there isn't anything new. It would be best if you left us alone. Quit sneaking up the driveway and peering in the windows to get your stupid stories. It nearly killed my mom and dad. We need closure. We need to put this all behind us. Go away. Don't put it in your paper."

I'm car-sick by the time I get to Bluffton Hollow. Pops' gas tank is almost empty, and I can't find a gas station. I'm crap out of luck today, I'm thinking. I think there is only twenty-four dollars left on my debit card anyway. I will be running home on fumes if I go any farther. However, it is only a few miles to Pine Estates. I've had to stop to get directions twice, but when I slow down across the street from this brick building, I see the sign out front. **Pine Estates Motel. Nightly Rentals.**

It is a shabby old off-highway motel, the long ones with ten or so rooms all on one floor and little red doors. There's nothing but pine forest around it and an abandoned gas station with sideways pumps. It's the kind that used to be off just about every exit ramp, big enough to hold a family for one night while they made their way to Florida or South Carolina. There's only one parking spot per room on the buckled asphalt. I stay settled where I am, sit in the shade, and try to decide which direction that I am going with this.

I'm not knocking on the doors, asking if anybody knows where Johnny Mills lives. I'm a little nervous about some creep grabbing me and lugging me inside. One room has a big white truck in front of it. I pull up the lockbox and dig out Ashley's envelope. I've got this written on the front. **Ashley Mills: Alive/white truck**. I sit, thinking I could do this for days, and he doesn't show. But there's the white truck, and everything else seems to fall into place.

I'm assuming someone at Elkton Logistics told Johnny Mills that some reporter, undercover cop, or crazy girlfriend is coming after him because Johnny has decided to bail. I see a head peering out when the door opens to Room Number Six. White-blonde hair. Tall. My eyes narrow while I stare through the bug-pocked windshield. I can't see the face. I'm not sure. My heart rides upward like a rollercoaster rolling up the first hill, waiting to crest, and fly down the other side. Back and forth, the head looks, and then out comes a man, head tucked low and moving fast to the car parked in front of the room.

He's the right height, the right build. He wears the same kind of distressed jeans and pale T-shirts. The tattoo. I see a bit of orange bird tail slipping out from the sleeve of his T-shirt. It is a phoenix. It is him. I bumble for my cell phone and juggle it with trembling fingers to get a picture. I hold it up just as the man approaches the driver's side door of a big, four-door truck. He wiggles his keys and looks at me, and I see something flash in his eyes. Josh's eyes. Josh's freckled face and cocky tip to his chin. *Click*. I got the picture. I think I am going to throw up. It is Josh. It is him.

I duck. He takes off out of the parking lot in a spray of gravel. I fire up Pops' truck and follow him. I'm unsure if he knows I'm behind him, but he keeps going faster and faster. Odds are, he knows it is me tailing him. I keep looking at my gas gauge when he hops onto the highway. It's less than a quarter tank. The little red light is screaming EMPTY! I'm almost to him, swerving around cars and a semi-truck in the fast lane, and then he veers a quick right and goes off the next exit. I follow. I see Josh looking through the rearview mirror when he drives right through the stop sign and makes a right down one county road and then another. The streets are going from buckled gray asphalt to brown dirt and gravel, and dust is fully consuming his truck.

I'm right on his butt when I see his brake lights go on. He skids to a halt, and my right foot jams hard on the brakes. Not quickly enough. Pops' truck tires are sliding like a stick of butter slips down the edges of a hot baking pan. I swing to the right, but the truck bucks and grumbles. Then, the front bumper slams hard into the back truck bumper in front of me. It isn't as much a crash as it is a crunch. The sound of metal bending and then scraping screams in my ears. I've got my seatbelt on. The airbag doesn't release. Still, the truck goes sideways onto a gravel pullover and almost into a tree. I feel another bump while Josh backs into me, pushing me sideways about forty feet

Then, nothing but a foggy layer of powdery dust envelops the truck. I stop and watch Josh kick his vehicle into gear and take off again. I sit there three seconds before I push the gas pedal and start forward again. "Pops is going to kill me," is all I can say over and over. I don't get six feet when the truck comes to a dead halt. I'm out of gas.

It didn't occur to me that Josh might come back. I was more worried about Pops killing me for the massive dent in his front bumper and the scratch on the driver's side panel where Josh's truck banged it sideways. I stand there, staring out in the direction he went, watching the dirt settle and the air clear. A four-way intersection is only about ten feet away. A crossroads.

I kick the dirt, return to the truck, and pull out my phone. I'm not sure who I'd call, maybe Kenny. But there's no cell phone service here. I've got no choice but to walk. I grab the lockbox, stick it in a little plastic dollar store grocery sack, and carry it. It is twenty minutes later before somebody passes me, and I flag them down to take me to the closest gas station.

"Honey, you're not going anywhere soon." I'm in the car with Natasha Taylor. She lives about three miles from here. She has a gas can at her house and takes me to town to fill it up. But she is right. As I slide out of her car and stare at Pops' truck, I see four dead flat tires. Every one of them is slit deep. I called Pops, and he called a place with a tow truck. I'm shaken and can't get rid of the feeling. It latches on to me like a moldy, damp cloth clings hard and fast to the side of a bucket after it dries. Josh is alive. My stomach lurches like the roller coaster climbing the hill, has gone down the other side.

The coaster is getting ready for another twist, veer, or careening downhill ride. What if he wants to kill me now, too? *No, he loved me.* I suppose that's what all the other girls he burnt to a crisp or bludgeoned thought, too.

The tow truck driver stopped at a rest stop. I took out the business card the cop gave me in Whitcomb. *Officer Sandy Cantrell—Investigator* is written beneath a badge logo. I called her up and told her I had seen Josh in Tennessee. "Okay," she answered lifelessly. "I'll let them know."

"You're going to check it out, right? I think he might be killing girls all the way up and down the highway. He ran me off the road."

"This is Josh Devereauxs with the same last name as you?"

"Yes."

"I think we are talking about two different people. I know sometimes we want to have closure so badly that we dig for anything to solve the case of a missing family member."

"*We?*" I ask. "Have you had a missing person in your family?"

"No, I have dealt with this in other cases. There isn't any connection with your Josh in Whitcomb. You should go through your local police station from now on. We talked to Officer Reynolds after you left, and he said that you deal with mental issues."

"You're kidding me, right?"

"Missus Devereauxs, let the police handle this. Get some help. The two cases don't match. I've got hotlines that can help you out."

"I'm not crazy."

"He says you sit in a bar and buy your dead husband a beer. Reynolds stated that he has stopped you from committing suicide several times at a local railroad track. You recently broke into your mothers' house." She sighs. "*Brandy*, can I call you that? Everyone deals with personal issues. You can get through this. The loss of your husband has made you a little irrational."

Nobody's going to listen to me. "He's not dead. You can call me anything you want, but crazy, I'm not. Drugged out, I am not. I am not my mama, are you? Because I bet you try to be as different from her as you can be even if she goes to church every Sunday," I say and hang up the phone. "I'm not," I yell at the windshield. "I am not crazy."

Chapter –30
Getting in Trouble with Pops

It is almost dark, and the crickets are chirping when we pull into Pops' driveway and get out of the truck. A few trucks are in the driveway, including Aunt Jenny's car. Crap, why is Bear here too? I hear the front screen door slam and look up. It is Pops first, then Kenny and Uncle Craig.

"We've been worried sick about you." Pops passes me and doesn't look up. The tow costs three hundred and fifty dollars. He pays it with cash. I can see him counting it out into the guy's hand. Then he stares at the front of his truck after it is unloaded. I see him running his hand down the bumper, tugging at his chin while he looks at the tires.

"Holy shit, girl, you are in one big ball of trouble." Kenny has come down the steps and is standing behind me. I'm tired and miserable. "Uncle Lee has been looking for you all day, called everybody he could think of."

I wish this day would go away. I know it isn't done yet. "Pops," I mumble. "I'm sorry." He says nothing at all. He stands there staring at his truck with his arms crossed. Uncle Craig comes out and rolls his hands over the tires.

"I hope you've got a good explanation for this," Pops finally says to the ground.

"I just ran off the road."

"Don't lie to me. You don't get four dead tires from running off the road."

"I saw Josh, Pops." Holy cow, that was the wrong thing to say.

"You can't see that boy because he is dead, dammit! Dead! Can you not get that into your head!" He reaches out, grabs my lockbox, and throws it at my feet. Pops blows up right then, one colossal spiel about chasing ghosts and being crazy. "He's not coming back! He's never coming back! You've got to get your crap together, girl, or you're going to end up in jail! My God, look at my truck. What the hell were you thinking?"

He is waving his hands, screaming at me while I stand there holding my breath, my eyes as wide as my fists. "And do you know who showed up at my door today?" he goes on. "One of Big Don's boys. He said that they were done searching your truck. Kenny and I go down to pick it up, and it is in nothing but pieces all over the compound."

"My truck's in pieces?"

"Baby, they tore everything down to the carpet and the steering wheel. This is stopping now. Now! You are not to tell anybody about this, you got it? Brandy, folks already think you are a loopy for always sitting at the bar and running down that stupid mountain. I honestly have my doubts about you now, too. Normal people don't get into this much—trouble."

"Okay. I'm sorry, I'm sorry, I'm sorry—" I keep saying repeatedly. It just seems to go on and on. But I think it will be better than the next three days when he won't talk to me. "Please don't be mad at me, Pops. Please. I'll drop the charges for Mama so you can take care of Kaylee. Heck, I will say I lied and go to jail for her."

Finally, Uncle Craig comes out and lugs Pops toward his truck with an arm around his shoulder. "Kenny, boy, come on!" he shouts. "Let's take Lee for a ride and get a beer."

I sit on the front porch steps, watching them all trickle toward their cars. They all file past Pop's truck and shake heads like funeralgoers filing past a casket. Now, it is quiet, and the fog is creeping up the mountain, little tendrils slipping from the creeks below.

"Here." Bear's leaving, too. He jingles his keys in his pockets, which means he's heading toward his truck. His steps halt at the porch deck, and he gently bangs my shoulder with a large manila envelope. I look up. He's keeping his cheeks scruffy. He looks nice.

"What's this?" I take it and turn it around in my hands.

"It's your registration for the Redneck Run and all the pamphlets and rules and your competitor bibs and numbers. It got approved."

"It has to be approved?"

"Yes, by a committee. Closed doors and all. I am on it."

"They didn't want us, did they?"

"No, not really. It doesn't matter. You're in."

"Did you carry a sword in with you to battle?" I ask him. I lift my arms and pretend to swing a sword in the air.

"I did. And a shield. My mother was there. She was quite concerned about Bobby Reese's health and age. The attorneys were called in. We came up with a happy medium. I went down and asked Bobby to sign a second waiver. All fixed."

"Thanks." I look up. "I hope your mother isn't mad at you."

"Oh, she's always mad at me. It just comes in different degrees and intensities. I'm starting to realize it doesn't bother me so much." He steps down so he is on the same level as I am. "I guess it bothers me still. However, I know we're not going to agree on things. She must give a little if she wants me to stick around. And she doesn't want me to leave."

I tug my purse onto my lap, pull out my phone, and find the picture I took at Pine Estates. "Take a looky-look."

"I see a guy—" he starts to say, then leans over and takes the top of the phone in his fingers so he turns it a little. "Holy crap."

"That's Josh."

Bear sits down next to me and stares at the image. "Where'd you take this?"

"I was about six and a half hours away in Pine Estates in Bluffton, about ten miles away from Sunshine Forks, Tennessee," I tell him.

"Is that where you were?" he asks, and I nod. "You should have taken me with you."

"I was ticked that you and Pops were fighting like divorced parents over their kid. I just—I had to get out."

He blows me off and turns back to the phone. "I honestly couldn't go either way on knowing if he was dead or alive," Bear says. "Still, I'm blown away that he's still flesh and blood. What is that on his arm?" Bear is looking closer. You can see the orange coming out of the sleeve. "Is that just the light?"

"No, it's the phoenix he had tattooed on his arm before disappearing. He was into the mythology stuff. It is a creature that has the head of a dog and a body like a bird. It explodes into a fire when it dies, and a new phoenix is born from its ashes."

"Josh, you sneaky, creepy, crazy bastard," Bear says. "Does he freaking think he is one of these, you think?"

"I don't know, Bear. He used to tell me they could turn into people."

"Who was he in Bluffton?"

"Well, he was from Sunshine Forks, but after his wife died, he went to Bluffton. Up until about seven hours ago, he was still Johnny Mills. You know, the same Johnny that married Ashley with all the kids. His driver's license in the lockbox belonged to his last wife's brother—William Hill Junior. His sister, Katy, was found dead. Somebody hit her over the head with a brick, then laid her in the bed and torched it. However, the house didn't burn down.

"Why'd he have the brother's license?"

"I would assume he was going to kill him too. It just didn't happen. And the big question is this, Bear," I say. "How did Mama get all these licenses because Katy's only been dead six months."

"Six months. Your mama doesn't seem like the killing type." Bear's jaws are working hard, and he looks like he got stung by a wasp. "I would assume he hid it there thinking your mom wouldn't find it. Why? Who knows. Bejesus, the bigger question is: are you safe?" he asks me. "What if Josh came back six months ago, and what if he comes back again?"

"I don't know, Bear." I swallow hard. I can hear my tummy growling. I haven't eaten all day. "Three days after he disappeared, my trailer burned down. Three days. The trailer park manager figured it was a contractor's mistake. I knew better. Little Pete told me Josh was trying to fix something under the trailer while I was at work, and before he went to the bar the day he vanished. I figured, up until a few months ago, that he was working on the furnace because it had broken. That's why I didn't say anything to anybody. I didn't want to have to pay for the trailer if Josh had screwed the furnace up to make it catch on fire. I just let it ride. Bear, I think the damn furnace was fine. I think he tried to burn me up in it. I don't think he drove past the trailer park that night to see if I was home; I think he was using it as an alibi, along with screwing Lisa Perkins in his truck. The trailer just never burned up."

Bear's eyes work back and forth between my own. I remember when he didn't look people right in the eyes. Now he does. It's cool.

But it is also unsettling. I think he can see into my soul. "You need to call the police, tell them what is happening. Get some protection."

I try not to laugh. He is so naïve sometimes. As if someone is going to come watch over me. "Well, Bear, the National Guard has more important things to do than babysit a girl everyone thinks is delusional," I tell him. "I did call the cops as soon as I lost sight of Josh. They said they would look into it, but they aren't. Big Don told them I was a risk, you see, a druggy and a person with a mental health condition. They acted like I was crazy."

Bear lets this soak in. I can see he wants to deny it by the cock of his chin, the way he leans back. I'm ready for him to tell me he'll call Big Don and fix everything.

"You know what? He's the one that's a crazy-extreme." Bear rubs his forehead. "I thought it was just me that he didn't want the twins around. Maybe Big Don thought I was creepy or something. He won't let me within a five-foot radius of his daughters unless somebody else is around. Do you know that? It doesn't matter if it is a date or just eating at my mom's; he's always got somebody tagging along with us like it's the eighteenth century or something. He treats his girls like frigging ten-year-olds." He reaches out and puts a hand on my shoulder. Another something new. "I'm just really unsettled. Because now you're not only on Josh's radar, but Big Don's too."

Chapter −31
Hanging out with Bear

"Hey, what are you doing —back?"

I am lying on my bed with my feet hanging over, still in my dress and heels, tossing a football in the air, catching it, and tossing it again. I have my radio on low and soft, and it eases into the air, only muffled by the bottom of the door slipping over it. Bear is standing at my bedroom door, staring down at me. I watched him leave. He said he was having dinner with Meghan's family at seven. He only has fifteen minutes to get there. I come in, fall on my bed, and stare at the ceiling. "It was only a meal," he tells me. "I wanted to check on you. For most people, dinner is about an hour long. It isn't a five-star restaurant, a five-course feast that takes an afternoon like it is with your cooking here. It was just my mother and me, Meghan and her parents. We had bland pot roast and store-bought bread. Have you moved since I left?"

"No."

"Are you okay?"

"I'm trying to come to terms with what happened today." I watch him sit down in my little chair across the room. "You don't need to be here."

"I want to be here. I want to hear all about your speech and your grade. I didn't get to the other day."

"No, you *can't* be here," I rephrase. "I'm going to be upfront with you, Bear. Josh and Big Don are just the icing on the cake."

"What do you mean?"

"I stopped at the resort the other day after my speech to tell you about it. I was confronted by your girlfriend, her little coven, *and* your mom, who called Big Don to impound my truck. I can't lie. I said a few things I shouldn't have. That's why Gabe and I bugged out of the dinner early the next night. Big Don threatened me, pushed me down and stuff."

"Big Don—pushed you down?"

"Yes, they don't do that in your rich, protected world. But in mine, they do." I sit up and put the football down on my pillow.

"I think you should rethink coming here anymore."

"You don't want me to come here."

"There's an ATV out in the garage." I smile a little. "If it could talk, it would tell you she's lying if she says she wants you to go. *She* is *me*."

"I don't want to be like my father, Brandy."

"What does that mean?"

"I don't know." Bear leans back in the seat. He pats his finger on his knee to the beat of the song on the radio. "If I say it, you'll take it wrong."

"I get it. You have the pretty girlfriend you take home to mama, who you show off in the crowds. Then you have one that does the fun, dirty stuff on the kitchen table and everywhere else, hidden and dark."

"Well, it's a bit harsh. But yes."

"Why can't I be the pretty one you show off, Bear?" I say a little snottily. "You bought me the clothes."

"Don't say that, Brandy." He sits up and rests his elbows on his knees. "It isn't all that. We're just from two different worlds. You've said so yourself. I like hanging out with you. It is incredibly— exhilarating."

"Yes, it was exhilarating today, too, going a hundred and ten miles an hour in a high-speed chase and then realizing the idiot in front of me is jamming on his breaks. I call that terrifying," I say. "You missed it. You also missed walking in the sweltering heat to flag down somebody to help get gas. That was nerve-racking. And it was hardly thrilling getting yelled at by a man still grieving his sister and thinking I'm just another newspaper reporter trying to exploit him for tonight's interesting commentary on the eleven o'clock news. Wow," I mumble flatly while I roll my eyes. "That was white-knuckle fun."

"Finding a little treasure box with a marble in it exactly like my dad used to get me and that matches your eyes was damn near the coolest thing I've ever experienced. Holding you over that basement was scary as hell, but after it was all said and done, I felt— elated. Sitting with you in a diner and joking about what happened was better than the stupid roller coasters at the amusement parks."

Bear points at the football and holds up his hands for me to toss it to him. I turn, snatch it up from the pillow, and give it a throw. "Bending over laughing so hard at you when you do something goofy like get your hair caught in the weight machine or try to close your eyes driving the ATV and running into a tree, it is—I don't know, better than eating cherry popsicles. Going out to dinner with you, watching you having fun with Gabe, and hanging out with a bunch of people I don't know was hell."

"You really like hanging out with me?"

"When you're not being a bitch."

"Likewise," I say. "So how do we make those two worlds collide so we can still hang?" I hold my hands over me and make fists, bringing them together hard. "Boom," I say softly. Then I open my hands wide and wiggle my fingers downward, so they look like lady-finger fireworks falling from the sky. Then I hold them up so Bear can toss me the football.

"I don't know, Bejesus, I don't know if it can be done or not." He yawns into his fist and sits up. "Just because we've established the fact between us that we like hanging out doesn't mean everybody around us is going to think we should. Your Pops, for one. He thinks I'm the key to the lock that opened the box of your troubles."

"And your mommy likes me," I say sarcastically. I catch the ball he tosses back, stand up, and stretch my arms over my head. Bear's eyes are working upward, doing that thing again, watching me and trying to be cool about it. The way he looks at me when he does that, you'd think he'd never seen a girl before. I suppose it's only natural that if you put a guy and a girl in a dim bedroom together, you're going to get some sexy thoughts.

But he stops and stares up at me from the chair, elbows on knees and feet tapping to the beat of the radio. He looks like he's going to say something but doesn't. He cracks his knuckles and stares down at his feet.

"What are you thinking about?" I ask him.

"I'm trying not to think of you on that ATV. The scent of your skin reminds me of something sweet, wild, and free. I'm trying not to think bad stuff while you wear that dress and stand before me."

I laugh a little. Then I lean over and push my hand on his chin.

He automatically looks up. I lean in and kiss him softly on the lips. He kisses me back but doesn't reach an arm up and slip his fingers around my neck. Instead, he takes his hand and gently pushes me away.

"Brandy, don't. I thought we weren't going to do that."

"I don't remember having that conversation," I say. I'm not hurt. It's almost amusing. I don't truly understand him. Of course, I married a guy who would sleep with anything.

"We did. Kind of. Now you really look nice in that dress, and so my mind went to the other day on the trail. I'm trying to say that it doesn't mean we have to do anything. I was saying. It's not that you're not pretty or—"

"Don't justify it. That's fine."

"Then why are you doing that?"

I shake my head. I'm not sure what he's accusing me of doing. I only know that he is really, really sexy when he's trying to be cool and not look like I am doing something that he thinks is a turn-on. There's something in his defensive stance, the way he keeps tugging on that little fuzz on his chin where his beard used to be, and the way his eyes are trying to meet mine, but he's shying away.

"I don't know. Just being—you."

"Okay, I'll stop being me."

He stands up, then. Bear stops, takes in my eyes, and reaches out a hand. He lays it on my shoulder and lets it ease down. The lower he goes, the hotter I feel below my belly. He gets to my elbow and stops, leans down, and slowly eases his other hand behind my neck.

"If you don't want to do anything, Bear, you need to stop," I tell him, "You don't know what—your touch does to me."

"Yeah, I think I do." He has this smug smile, cocky and self-assured. Now, I know he is going to kiss me. I'm learning it, waiting and waiting. But he stops right there and bows back. I'm wavering, wanting to lean in and get the kiss, begging him with my mind to do it. Yet, he doesn't give it at all.

"Now, you know how I feel. Sometimes, I think you are evil, just doing what you do to make me crazy. You tease. Then, I think, maybe it is just me thinking you are teasing. You're just being you, not knowing you even do it."

I reach out, tug at his T-shirt, and quickly draw it up.

"Don't." He snatches at my finger. "I'm still not comfortable with my shirt off. I still feel—fat. I know you don't get it, but it's there. In my head."

"I don't care." I tug a little more. He pushes me back quickly with one hand.

"Stop. Please don't do this, Brandy. I really don't want to hurt Meghan, alright? Can you—be my friend like you were before?"

I step back until his hand is released from me. I think about what he said, and my feelings are hurt. "No, I can't, Bear," I tell him. "I'm just not looking for friends now, so I don't need you around. And what man does not want to have sex, Bear? Tell me that."

"One that has a girlfriend already. Can you not just be friends with a guy. Do you have to have sex with every man you meet?"

"Ouch," I huff. "That was mean. But, okay, I'm not going there with you. I get it. You don't like me in that way. Fine. Then don't look at me like you do. Don't stare at me at the table like you did the other night at the restaurant, prying off my dress with your eyes, pissing your girlfriend off. Hence, she does everything but knifes me in the girl's bathroom. But just so you know, I've only had sex with Josh and then you. That's it. And I don't know this for a fact, but Meghan Reynolds was pretty hot and heavy in high school with a few guys on the football, soccer, and basketball teams."

"Stop it, Brandy."

"No, you need to hear this. I'm tired of your mean girlfriend slamming me, and I just smile like an idiot while she does it. And you watch, don't defend me. I know people lie, but the boys were pretty open about what she did for them, to them, and all of them."

"I said, stop it, Brandy."

"No, I think Big Don has bigger plans for you two." I stop, lean in, and poke my finger at his chest. "I have a right to defend myself. Until you, Josh was the only man I'd been with. All those guys you've got lined up in your head because you see my mama in me, they *aren't*. I'm not some dirty whore. I don't need you to pay for things, to give me a roof over my head, or give me money to buy drugs. I can take you or leave you. I do quite fine on my own, Bear.

I'm not the slut you've made me out to be, so don't pretend you're using me like your daddy used women. You need me more than I need you. Period. I thought you were different because you didn't think I was slutty at all. Obviously, I read it wrong. You know, I've said enough. It's time for you to leave now."

He exasperates me. I sit down on the side of my bed, trying to understand our fight. I know his mother sways his view of me, just like Pops has his doubts about Bear. Bear was right when he said Pops thinks he is the key to my problems.

"Aw, why didn't I think of that?" I huff a breath and stare at the key.

"What?" Bear has his keys wiggling in his hand.

"The keys." I drop to my knees and dig up the lockbox from the floor. I sift through the envelopes and tug out the one with Crystal's name on the front. I take it and wiggle it until the key comes out. Then I hold it aloft. "Mailbox keys. You made me think of it when you said Pops thinks you are the root of my problems. I thought of what Josh and I used to fight about. Bills. I would go to the mailbox in town and have to get them out and think they were the root of our fights the entire time." I hold up a key. "Ten bucks says this is a mailbox key."

Chapter –32
David and Goliath

The only guys that ever seem to beg me for anything are the ones I know don't like me for more than a friend. Gabe is one of them. He called me on the phone to come to church with him on Sunday morning. I think he has no friends except for his new association with Ben. I go because he was so nice at dinner the other night.

It isn't that at all. Gabe's got a crush on Ben. I could even see it for the few hours I spent with the two the other morning. And the day after and yesterday when we went to work on T-shirts and marketing stuff for the Redneck Run. At twelve-thirty in the morning, Gabe texts me on my phone. I'm in bed, but I hear the buzz. I think Bear is having a food crisis.

Gabe: *Hey, I need some advice. Did you see a connection between Ben and me? Am I just reading into it?*

Me: *Really, are you asking me this at midnight?*

Gabe: *Yes. It was love at first sight.*

Me: *Does Ben know this? I mean, you do understand you can't just make people gay, right? It's a two-way street. Oh, then again, you're good-looking. I'm sure there are lots of folks that would cross over for that.*

Gabe: *Haha. No, but he just got out of a long-term relationship. And it was a guy.*

Me: *Honestly, Gabe, until a few weeks ago, I was still waiting around for my ex-husband to rise from the dead. Do you really want advice from me?*

Gabe: *I can't talk to anybody else. I know, you know. You had that funny smile on your face when we were talking today. You get that goofy smile on when Bear's around. You don't realize it.*

Me: *See? You shouldn't ask me for advice.*

The conversation ended not long after. But by then, Ben was calling me at one in the morning to see if Gabe and I were serious.

Me: *You realize it is one in the morning. I'm not yelling at you because I need an internship with you.*

Ben: *Yeah, sorry, I can't sleep.*

Me: *So you call me and ask me if Gabe is dating me.*

Ben: *Okay, I'll be honest. I can't stop thinking about him.*

Me: *I will tell you what I told him. You shouldn't ask me for advice.* I wait about ten minutes because I know Ben is nail-biting on the other end: *The feeling is mutual.* I wonder why everybody thinks it is okay to call me at night with their problems. I think I am going into the wrong field. I should be a therapist.

That was nine hours ago. "We really need to see Ben about the shirts," Gabe whispers in the church pew. Ben. Ben. Ben. Good God, I'm beginning to hate that name.

Yes, I am in the back row at Holy Trinity on Sunday with all the other big-time sinners. I can't hear his dad preaching because Gabe has not stopped whispering to me the entire time. Preacher Murphy is talking about David and Goliath. The story is getting good, playing out like the old suspense movies Pops likes to watch. I am nearly giddy with anticipation at the end. The big bully, Goliath, had already challenged the Israelites. This little guy, David, just brought food for his big brothers. Goliath's an absolute crap, one of those tyrant's that keep coming up to the little guys to beat them up just a little bit, then rubbing it in that he's going to finish them off next time. The preacher was getting to about the tenth 'next time', and the plot was thickening; tempers were about to explode.

"Why don't you just call him?" I barely lean toward Gabe. I'm trying to hear the ending. My tummy is tickling in anticipation.

"I don't know."

"Are you using me as a buffer between you two?" I ask him. David has just grabbed his sling and five little stones from a creek. I missed something. Was David the good guy, or was Goliath? I can't remember.

"No."

"Does he win?" I can't stand the suspense.

"Who? Ben?"

"No, idiot, David. Does he kill the giant? Or does the giant kill him? You keep talking, and I can't hear."

A few people turn when I whisper that a little too loud. One lady narrows her eyes, shoves a forefinger to her lips, and shushes me.

"Yeah." Gabe nods. "Everybody knows this story. David hits Goliath in the forehead with one stone, then cuts off his head."

"Oh, so cool. Blood and gore in the Bible. I'm going to have to open that book and check it out. He's a good guy, right? Or am I cheering for the wrong team?"

"Yeah, David fought on God's side," Gabe tells me. "That would be the good side." I look over, and Gabe smiles and shakes his head. "I'm never going to the movies with you. I'd probably have to tell you the plot step by step. By the way, how's everybody doing in your training?"

I stifle a laugh and get another round of shushing. "Well," I whisper. "Martha made it all the way across Fire Mountain Creek without drowning. She's quite fast when she doesn't start doggy paddling. The only problem is she closes her eyes and goes a little off-path. We might be fine if the river is running hard. She's used to fighting the Ohio River current."

"Oh, boy."

"Kenny is fine on the ATV. He might hit fewer trees if he would stick to the course Uncle Craig laid out for him and quit trying to show off. Pops went to the eye doctor to get Bobby fit for a new pair of glasses. He kept missing the target and breaking the windows of the garage. Pops figured buying a new set of glasses for the old guy was cheaper than getting new windows."

"And you?"

And me. Kenny and I rode to a shoe store in a big mall in Ohio where Noah Hartley signed autographs and marketed his new line of trail running shoes. You could either buy a pair of Noah Hartley Official Running Shoes of the Redneck Run or pay ten bucks for an autograph. I couldn't afford the shoes that were allegedly extra special and made for running trails, jumping over roots, and so on. They just looked like regular tennis shoes to me anyway. Still, I thought of my old sneakers and gluing the bottoms on every time I ran. I think it would be nice to have something new.

Kenny loaned me ten dollars, and I waited in line with his fans for an hour to get an autograph and ask him what his best time was so far. It would have been far cheaper to simply walk up and ask him, except he had two big gorillas who wouldn't let anybody get within a ten-foot radius.

I finally get to the front of the line and hold out my hand with Kenny's ten dollars. Noah Hartley looks up past me and to the line behind me. "I'm sick of doing this. What do you want me to write? Make it short."

"I really don't need anything signed. I'm just racing you next week in the Redneck Run. I wanted to meet you and find out your time."

"Seriously?" He looks up and flashes me a grin. But it isn't a nice one. There is something strangely cruel in the quiver of his lip. "You've got to be kidding me. Is this a joke?" He looks around like he's waiting for everybody to jump up and say surprise, you've been pranked! Nobody does. They stand there, probably not hearing him because his voice is low.

"I'm running against *you*? A local yokel? I'm sick of doing these stupid runs with inept people running them. Redneck Run. Who names a professional competition something like that? It's a joke. But it's the only way my manager says I can sell my shoes." He leans in and snaps the ten dollars from my fingers. "Here, instead of an autograph, let me give you some advice. Don't get in my way and screw up my time because you're plodding along with the rest of the idiots on two left feet. Have fun because I'm complaining to the board for letting locals in on the challenge. There won't be a next year for simpletons like you."

I don't tell Gabe that, though. I tap on my knee. "Your daddy's a good preacher," I say. "I should have started listening to him long ago instead of texting on my phone during the service." The lady who shushed me a minute ago shushes me again. I waggle my head at her and roll my eyes.

The choir gets up to sing before the last hymn. Bear is up there directing. He starts with a solo, and his voice is as perfect as I've ever heard anyone sing. People lean in as if his voice pulls them in with his song. My eyes slip over to where Meghan and Michelle hold their hymnals in the choir stands. If I didn't know them, I'd say they looked like two angels with their mouths in O's, providing a soft backup with the rest of the choir for Bear's solo. When Bear's solo is done, he turns his back to us and starts directing again. I see Meghan tip her head to the right, a loving gesture while she mouths something to Bear.

It sends goose pimples up my arms, and a shiver makes me shake slightly.

"Uh oh, I don't think I've ever seen anybody get goosebumps of jealousy." Gabe rolls his forefinger up my bare arm, then pokes me with it.

"You've got to be kidding me," I grouch back. I realize, then, how much Gabe and I are alike. I like hanging around with him. He gets me even when I don't want him to know what's happening inside my head.

"You know, he's obsessed with you."

"You could have fooled me, Gabe. I'm not somebody's side dish. Bear can screw off."

"Um, that guy, Chase, that was with Janie, remember him? He keeps calling you his future wife. *Hey, where's my future wife?* That's what he says every time he sees me like he's got the next fifty years set aside with you. Every time he asks for your number, Bear won't give it to him."

"You can give it to him. I liked him," I say, thinking it would be a nice jab at Janie.

"You sure?"

"Yeah."

Gabe doesn't say anything. He grabs the hymnal and rises with everybody else for the last song. A smile plays on his lips, and I'm not sure why. I mouth the words along with him and yawn into the cup of my hand. I'm running three times a day now. It tires me out.

Half the mountain comes to eat Sunday lunches at Pops' house. Even Preacher Murphy, his wife, and their kids have come today. They brought some potato salad, which I can tell is store-bought from Mister Smiley's. I don't say anything, but I know I must have gotten into the preacher's head about bringing anything but a box of food, and it makes me feel good that he listened. "We're going to Salt Springs later, right?" Gabe has asked me this every fifteen minutes since we left church. He is sitting with me on the front porch after eating, nestled between my papaw and Aunt Jenny. I assure him we are. He knows we are. He has Ben's cell phone number. He texted him twice this morning. This is the third time this week that we've gone there. They chat. I hike. I run. I run more.

"Hey, come here. Let's go for a walk." He grabs my hand, and I'm giving him a wary gaze. But I'm going with it. I think he's got something up his sleeve. We leave the old trail behind the garage and stop just where everybody can see us.

"Okay, give it maybe five minutes."

"For what?"

"You'll see." He's got a sly smile on his face. He drags me over by a tree, puts both his hands on my shoulders, and positions me right in front of him. Then he leans in, lets an armrest just over my shoulder, and takes my fingers in his hand. He is only inches from my face. And it would be a damn sexy posture for him if I knew he had any interest in girls. But he doesn't. I'm confused while he kisses my forehead really gently. "Look up and smile at me."

"This is weird."

"Just do it. You'll know why in about four minutes."

I do, and I can't help but grin because he's crossing his eyes before he kisses me on one cheek and then the other. It makes me giggle because it tickles. "You see," he whispers. "Bear is over there, and he is about to lose it. How do I know? I can see him talking to Kenny and looking over Kenny's shoulder. Every time he does it, I give you a kiss, and his face is getting redder and redder, angrier and angrier. As much as this grosses me out, I like seeing Bear get jealous."

"Gabe, he doesn't really like me," I say. "I appreciate what you're doing, but he told me yesterday he just wants to be friends."

"He's lying. Or he is just being a jerk again. Don't you see I'm his insurance? If you're hanging with me, you're not dating anybody else. And we're not doing anything, right? In his case, what better guy to fix the girl you like up with than a guy who likes guys?"

I reach up and push the hair out of Gabe's face. "Why are you doing this?"

"Because I like you. I like Beau. You both are idiots, and you need to be idiots together."

"Thanks for the compliment, butthead. Bear doesn't know you like guys?"

"I don't know. I think he does. It doesn't matter right now. I could be a tree limb touching you, and he'd be turning green."

Gabe nods toward the woods, pulls me out from the tree, and tosses an arm around my shoulders. "Let's walk for about ten or fifteen minutes, then head to Salt Springs. About that David and Goliath story today. I think my dad did it for you, going up against all those dream teams you're up against. I thought you'd want to know."

I suppose this is when my instincts kick in, the teeny-weeny finger of doubt poking me right in the gut, telling me there's something more profound and a little more sinister going on in a seemingly innocent situation. I look up at Gabe. I know it is a fine line he walks with his parents. I understand I'm somewhat of a shield for those things he knows they know, but nobody wants to discuss. It is a small town.

"Okay, what's going on, Gabe?" I push him back with my palm. "Why are your parents being nice to me?"

"I don't know. Mom and Dad like you. You do nice things. And they are here because you told Beau how New Alliance got its name. He's been telling everybody about it. My dad said he needed to do a little more work getting out into the community and bringing everybody together again like that minister, Piper, did. He figures he could get more people coming to the church. He means well. But my parents, their intentions were good from the start."

"*Their* intentions, but somebody else's intentions were not good? And from what—start?"

"Oh, boy," he sighs, leans back and scratches his head. "You know what? I'm going to tell you the truth. They can arrest me. I don't care."

I'm just standing there, my eyes working back and forth between Gabe's eyes. "Why would they arrest you?"

Then he gets interrupted. Kaylee pushes her way between us, patting me hard on the leg. "Crazy Willie wants to see you," she tells me. "Pops told me to tell you."

"Crazy Willie?" I snap my eyes from Gabe to Kaylee. She is wiggling her fingers at me, so I'll hold her hand so she can drag me with her. I reach out and take it into my own. For the moment, my conversation with Gabe is forgotten. The only one I have never seen eat at Pops' house is Crazy Willie. Something must be wrong. I've been consistently dropping food off at his house about every other day, he shouldn't be mad about me cutting through his property.

But something out of the norm happens. He shows back where Bobby shoots at the targets while my cousins watch.

"He backs up whenever we start to go over," Pops says low in his breath. "He said he wanted to see you. He doesn't have a gun."

"That's nice to know." That's Bear standing next to Pops. "He could break her in half with just his hands."

"I think he's okay," Pops answers. But he's not taking his eyes off the man.

"Can somebody go get him a plate of food?" I ask Pops before I go. "Geez and make everybody move back. They're acting like he's a gorilla or something that's escaped from the zoo."

Pops waves at Kenny, who shuffles off toward the house. Kenny keeps looking back, almost walking backward, staring at the scene. I think he is a bit upset he's missing out on me getting dragged off into the woods by Crazy Willie. They are all staring at Crazy Willie. He's standing alone, staring back at everybody and holding a brown paper bag in one hand. I let Kaylee's hand go and walk through last autumn's leaves. I weave through the little trees, feeling like everyone's staring at my back, and wait for Crazy Willie to pull out some weapon and murder me.

"Here. You need these."

He throws his arm out as if he is handing me the bag. I take it. The top is crumpled over and over to make a handle. Slowly, I open the sack and peer inside, praying it isn't some missing girl's head. It isn't. It is a pair of high-top tennis shoes close to my size. Probably boys. They are a bit dirty and definitely used and were perhaps made in 1985. "The shoes you wear, they fallin' apart. I found these in that big Goodwill bin behind the grocery store. Been lookin' and pokin' around there for a long time. I heard you gonna be in the Redneck Run. I figure I got stock in you cause you run my land. I was a pretty big redneck in my time."

"Thank you," I say it and smile. "I will wear the sneakers. Will you come to watch me run?" I think about that stupid Noah Hartley and his ugly line of shoes. They aren't anything compared to the sneakers inside this bag. I think how Crazy Willie probably got up in the middle of the night to trudge down that hill in the dark to find them. He'd probably been sifting through the Goodwill for three months before he hit the jackpot.

"No, crowds just ain't my thing."

"They aren't mine either," I declare, feeling a bond. "People scare me if there's more than ten or so. I get a little dizzy."

Crazy Willie is looking over my shoulder. I hear the sound of feet on leaves. He looks like he's going to buck. "That's my cousin, Kenny," I divulge. "He's bringing you some Sunday food. I can sit with you while you eat. Just me and you if you want."

I sit with my legs crossed in the leaves across from Crazy Willie, squatting with the plate on his knee while he eats. I babbled about Pops and told him who was in my family. I talk about the Redneck Run while he sips on a lemonade Aunt Jenny brings out because she can't stand not seeing the legendary Crazy Willie up close. Now she's got bragging rights in her bible study club. She'll be the only one of them who has been within an arms-length of the old man, whom most still think is a phantom. Then, all of a sudden, as quick as he came, he shoved the plastic plate and fork at me, rose, and left. He fades into the woods while I pick up my new, used shoes.

I'm sitting on the bed in my room, trying on the sneakers. Bear knocks on the door and comes in, looking down while I finish tying them. They fit really well and are nice and worn in.

"Crazy Willie got them for me to wear at the Redneck Run," I tell him while he sits down in my chair. I stand up and jump up and down in them. "Oh, they are fine, just fine."

"It's okay for Crazy Willie to get you a pair of shoes?" Bear growls at me. "But it is different when I pull out my credit card to buy you something? What gives?"

"We know your history, Bear. You try to buy your friends. It isn't because you're doing it for that warm feeling you get in your heart." I use my toes to slip both shoes off and hug my arms over my chest. "That's assuming you have one."

"Ha ha."

"I'm poorer than dirt, but Pops says I don't have to get a job until after the Redneck Run, so I've got one less worry. Then, I've got to pay him for the truck repair." I shrug, lean over, pick the sneakers up, and put them by the registration folder. "So, what's up. I'm getting ready to head out with Gabe. I need to put something else on besides a Sunday dress, you know?"

"Can I tag along?"

Oh, no. I don't think Gabe wants Bear to come on this trip when he's dying to see Ben. "Not this time. We're—it's like a date. Just the two of us."

"Another date?"

"Oh, yeah. We're a couple now. Sometimes. Not all the time. You know. Lots of dates. Lots and lots of them. And sex. Lots of sex."

"You know he likes men, right?" Bear has a funny, knowing grin on his face, and he is trying to rub it off.

Holy shit. I stand there weaving my shoulders back and forth, trying to think of something to backtrack, make up for my lies, and still cover for Gabe because he isn't sure Bear knows. Bear shrugs. "I guess some people swing both ways. You're beautiful. He's nice looking."

"I know, right? That's what I said."

Bear furrows his brow and tips his head. "You said what?"

"I—that it is great he swings both ways." I hold up my hands, feel proud I'd covered my tracks.

"Bejesus, he doesn't swing both ways." Bear groans, reaching out and giving me a little shove with his hand. "I've known him since kindergarten. He knew which direction he was headed even back then."

I'm mildly embarrassed. If it was anybody other than Bear, I'd probably feel like I wanted to hide under the covers. "Well, regardless of the relationship status, we have a date." I reach out and give Bear a little shove, too. "I need to find something to wear that isn't—a churchy dress." I pass him on the right of the chair, open my closet door, and look inside.

"You know, if I had a choice, I'd be with you, not Meghan."

"Why are you telling me this?" I ask him. I stared at a skirt, thinking it would be cool and cute. "It would take much more than that to get me in bed with you. I don't—want to know this. You're a full-grown man. You can make choices. I don't even believe you."

"I don't know how to prove it."

"That's pretty simple. *Don't be* with her."

"You don't understand the political complications that will happen if I do. She's a big tie with the community, the church."

"Oh, my gosh, are we living in the Middle Ages?" I ask him. "You said you wanted to be friends, and that's all good and well. Okay, we're friends. Stop this crazy *I want to be with you* bullshit. You're with me now. We're having the time of our lives," I tell him flatly.

"Well, I'm not. It is ripping my gut out."

I wonder how many men told Mama that. A hundred, maybe more. I know she slept with all of those liars. Bear's right behind me when I turn and almost trip over him. I'm holding the skirt, and he's catching my arm so I don't fall.

"Brandy," he says it like he will say more. He doesn't. Instead, he looks down, slips his hand around my shoulder, and gives me a long kiss on the lips.

I push away. "Please stop. One minute, you're all up in my face, *let's be friends*. The next, you're staring at my boobs. If I wanted another guy like Josh, whose eyes never stopped looking for something better at the next trailer park, they are a dime a dozen. I could pick three up at the Crazy Kettle. Four, if I wear this skirt."

"Cripes, I'm not like that. And you'd get more than four if you wear that skirt."

"Thanks," I say to what I construe as a compliment. "However, you slept with a waitress because you could see down her shirt."

"I didn't sleep with her. I just told you that. I was drunk."

I'm sure Mama heard that a lot, too. I can't count the number of times I remembered her screaming out that it was *she* who was using the guy. *She* wasn't a whore.

Okay, here's where it gets a little shady about how I end up in bed with Bear, me sitting on top and riding him like a cowgirl, complete with a little pink cowboy hat. One minute, he's all up in my face, trying to kiss me. I tell him no. He stops. When he backed off, I guess it hurt my feelings. I don't cry much. But for some reason, I did. Then Bear kisses me on my cheeks and lips and works his way to my neck and shoulders. I vaguely remember shutting the door and turning the lock. Oh, yeah, that's where the hat came in. It is one I wore at the fair one year. I have it sitting on my dresser with the little third-place trophy I won for showing a cow. I pull my dress over my head, so I am standing there in nothing but my pink bra and black panties with little pink bows and say something like:

"Okay, cowboy, you want to play?" and I put the hat on my head. Bear stutters: "H-holy shit." And it makes me feel like I'm the most beautiful woman in the world. Two seconds later, we don't even bother getting undressed. However, I remember feeling quite self-satisfied for ripping off Bear's shirt without leaving a tear.

And that's what it takes to get me in bed. I realize Bear could have thrown my words back in my face while we lay there cuddling after. Cuddling. It isn't something I'm familiar with. Josh just did his thing and jumped out of bed. I like cuddling. I like how he tickles me with his fingers along my arm and keeps telling me how great I am in bed. I like how he holds me, plays with my now-frizzy hair, and tells me it looks great. I know better. I like the pillow talk and the opening up a little because we do. We talk about stuff we'd never say outside of holding each other now. Then I think that Bear is getting ready for round two because he puts my hat back on my head and starts kissing me again. And there's a knock on the door.

Another round of holy shit, and we're dancing into our clothes. It's funny, and we laugh. It's Pops, and I tell him to go away, please, I will be out in a minute.

"Here's some cash. Please buy yourself a new pair of shoes," Bear whispers to me after he's dressed. "You don't have to give Meghan more hay to chew on, wearing the ones from the dumpster. Noah Hartley has a new line out. He's displayed them at the resort, and we're selling them. He's got a women's line of shoes—"

"You're kidding me." I am just about to unlock the door. My hand is on the knob. I turn. Bear is laying a whole wad of bills on my little table by my bed.

"What? Bejesus, you need shoes. He's right. But you need to look nice while you run, too. You need to be comfortable."

"What?" I have my hands out, flabbergasted. "You are putting money on my end table after we had sex. You do know what that implies, right?"

"Oh."

"Put it back in your wallet or leave it there. Whatever choice you make will define our relationship for future—intimate—um, meetings."

He snatches it up almost desperately, and inside, I feel elated.

Chapter –33
The Key

Pops is under the truck in the driveway, assessing the damage. I can see his feet sticking out. I push down an old bath towel on the gravel and scoot beside him. He's peering into the black above, and I follow his gaze.

"I don't even know where to start," he mutters. He doesn't look at me except for one second when he seems to note the beanie hat on my head instead of the ball cap. "I can fix about anything, but this here is extensive damage."

"I'm going to talk to Mama," I say softly. "Get her to sign the papers."

He nods. "It's the right thing to do. I don't think your Bear agrees with me."

"Yes, sir, I know."

"You like that boy?"

"Yeah, Pops," I say, and then there is an uncomfortable silence between us while Pops tinkers around. I tug a little on the beanie hat. He sees this and smiles, reaches out a hand, and taps the hat. Then I sigh. "I like him a lot."

"We're talking love?"

"Yeah," I feel my face getting red.

"He seems to think a lot of you."

"Well, he's got a girlfriend in town. She's Big Don's daughter, Meghan."

"Well, that's a can of worms I wouldn't want to open." Pops turns around, but he smiles at me. "Likin' somebody so bad your heart feels raw, it's hard sometimes."

"I don't know what to do."

"You're asking me for advice?"

"Yeah, Pops," I tell him. The other day, Pops sent me to fix a cow fence at my papaw's house. Pops also said that Bear should ride along and use some of his huge muscles to help repair the fence.

I told Bear that if he was going, he had to respect my papaw, and it was all *yes sirs* and *no sirs* to him. He nearly knocked himself out to be respectful to him and to help. He even remembered not to offer to buy a brand-new fence. Papaw shook his hand, and I'd never seen him do that to any of my friends. He winked at me and brought his hands out, tossing them like he had a fishing pole. He was reeling in a big one, which was embarrassing because I knew he was implying that Bear was a catch. I can't stop thinking about Bear trying so hard. I want to take the next step, but I'm scared to take it.

"Have you let on that you like him?" Pops asks.

"Yeah. No. I mean, kind of."

"Have you told him he needs to choose you or her?"

"No. I'm at that point. I'm there. But Pops, he's not the kind of guy that likes quitters. I'm quitting school. I thought maybe he—"

"So maybe you shouldn't quit school."

I turn and look at Pops. Did he really tell me I should finish school? He did. I don't say anything.

"Well," he says, "you're not usually afraid to jump right into life. I suggest you follow your gut. Do what you usually do. Jump and look how deep the hole is while you fall." He stops, gives me a sly smile, and rolls his eyes, "Baby girl, that never gets you in trouble."

"Pops, please," I groan. "My gut tells me I should run like hell."

"No, I don't think so. I think your head's thinking that." He pokes at the beanie. "But you're making a choice somewhere inside, don't you see? If you love the guy, you must let him know. You know I'll be there with my hand outstretched if you need me." He sighs deeply. "Brandy, can I make a suggestion?" I nod. "You ever thought of praying to God about it?"

I grit my teeth and shrug. "I pray. He doesn't seem to listen. I mean, I prayed for Bear to be a better person—"

"Is he?"

"I suppose."

"Maybe God's busy answering other prayers, and he has to make room to fit yours into the schedule he's already laid out for you." Pops pokes at the dark air under the car. "You know, you are the answer to a lot of people's prayers, don't you? That's what Preacher Murphy told me the other day."

"He did?"

"Yeah, nobody in a hundred-mile radius of that little shine you give off gets left out. Nobody goes hungry like all those folks you buy food for and make food for on Sunday. Nobody has to do stuff alone like that old lady you take to the cemetery or Kaylee. Keep on praying. God'll fit you in somewhere."

I nod. "Thanks—daddy." I turn and smile at him before I wiggle out.

He snickers. "Aw, bugger off. It's always daddy when you need something."

"No," I bend down, peering at his elbow under the truck. "It's daddy all the time. I just call you Pops."

I sit with Mama at the county jail. They have a little patio area with metal tables and chairs. Two policemen stand guard at the corners. "I am not pressing charges against you if you sign the papers the attorney is bringing over today for Kaylee."

She looks worn and tired. There are bags under her eyes and dark circles beneath. Her cheeks, however, have color. It is something I can't remember seeing on her, probably because I have never seen her off drugs or booze.

"Yeah, okay. I want out of here."

"I'm sure you do," I say. I raise my hand and hold it out flat. In my palm, I expose the tiny key I found in the envelope with CRYSTAL D. "Do you know what this is?"

Mama stares at it. She blinks and starts to shrug. "Just tell me the truth. I'm so up to here with Josh stuff." I hold my hand up over my head. "I know he's alive. I saw him in Tennessee. You're not hiding anything from me. It doesn't matter. Nobody believes me. But I need to know what the key is."

"It is time for me to go," she says and gets up. I rise with her and put out a hand to stop her. The cop in the corner threatens me with a *hey*. I back off, step back.

"Did it cross your mind to stop John John from killing me?" I ask her. I doubted it. She hasn't even bothered to ask me how Kaylee is doing or how my own wounds are healing. "When you stopped hitting me and he started in, did it occur to you to stop him?"

I see an angry cloud cross over her face. Mama's jaws are rubbing up and down, teeth grinding.

"Baby, you was flipping out at me. I was high. You know what? I'm the only thing that's kept you alive so far," she spats at me. "Don't make me out as a monster."

"You kept me alive?" I laugh sarcastically and shake my head back and forth. "You've done nothing for me. Nothing."

"Nothing." She cackles a snarky laugh, eyes the cops, then turns around and points to my fist, holding the key. "Me and those keys is the only thing between you and that dumbass husband of yours," she growls low. "It's a mailbox key like all the others in the box. I get the mail for him and the checks. I put them in different envelopes and sent them out to him. They's insurance checks and the likes, baby. His payment to me? He gave me a couple hundred bucks in each envelope to do it. Well, and one other thing. He said three years ago he'd kill you if I didn't do it. It's kind of your own insurance. I'm kinda what's kept your little ass alive. And I'm not doing a good job of it here, am I?" She pokes a finger at me. "I would suggest you figure out a way to get me out of here or start going to the boxes and sending the checks yourself."

Chapter –34
Emma

Red sky at night, sailors' delight.
Red sky in the morning, sailors take warning.

The morning started with a red, raw sky peeling back from the horizon like a fresh scab reopened. I suppose I should have paid attention to my Mamaw's old saying. I should have looked out the window and not ignored the warning. There was a hell of a storm coming. But who would have thought? Until last night, it seemed everything was going alright for once.

If it had, however, I wouldn't be standing in Bryant, West Virginia, with that stupid lockbox clasped in my arms, waiting for the cops to come, watching the black clouds pile up on the horizon. There's a warrant for my arrest. Big Don's on his way right now. I know this because Bear just told me that. One minute, I'm standing on the edge of a quarry, looking at a burnt-out building. The next, Bear is walking the same little trail I took, stalking me like Pops tracks a deer during hunting season.

It wasn't a part of my plan. Just a matter of time. As soon as I left the jail, Mama got her attorney. She signed over the papers for Kaylee. Then Big Don came in to question her about her contact with me. He started threatening her, and she started talking louder than the blue jays Pops feeds off his back porch, telling him about the box, and about Josh. Now, I think I had better catch up with Josh before he catches up with me, right?

Oh, we're at the last place Emma Weber was seen before—SURPRISE!—her mobile home exploded into a million pieces. She lived on Mix Road. Number 12. It was an ancient mobile home and the old office for Rampart's Stone Quarry. When I found the Bryant Journal newspaper article on the explosion, Dave, with the Bryant Volunteer Fire Department, told the reporter that the blast was so great that they found pieces of her couch embedded in a stone conveyor six hundred feet away.

There's a cliff here, about a hundred feet high. I am standing on the grassy ledge overlooking the quarry below; the wall is dug out.

It hasn't been used in a long time. Trees are growing along the ledge. Pieces of Emma were found down there. It took divers three days to scour the water. However, the water is over a hundred feet deep. For the safety of the divers, the search eventually ceased.

Her husband, Nick, however, set up a memorial fund to help pay for funeral expenses. Blonde-haired, baby-blue-eyed Nick disappeared with the donation money and a one-hundred-thousand-dollar insurance payoff. Another no-shocker for me. I imagine Josh in Cancun, Mexico, on a sandy beach, sitting on a white, plastic chair with his toes in the ocean water, sipping on a can of Bud Light Beer. The color of the water probably matches his eyes, baby blue.

I'm also looking at baby blue water while standing on the tippy top of a cliff wall. The quarry is a long way down, though. I won't be dipping my toes in it from here. Bear has the fingers of his left hand wrapped around my wrist. He's using the other hand to talk on the phone. There was only the sound of little birds above me just a few breaths ago. I was alone. Then, I hear a dog barking far away. I listened to the toes of his shoes snap a twig behind me. I turn, I'm startled. Bear shouldn't have known where I was. Two steps, and I'm only inches from the edge of the quarry wall, looking a hundred feet down to the cold stare of water below. And he catches my wrist with his fingers, nails biting into the skin below my palm.

"What-are-you-doing-here?" I ask. But I know. It is like the last three years of my life were little pieces of a puzzle I hadn't put together yet because some of them were missing. No big deal. I'll put the puzzle aside. Then, I find those little pieces strewn across the floor. I pick them up, analyze them, and, like an idiot, try to put the puzzle together.

"Please don't do this, Bejesus. Please. Just be nice to the cops. You can't run, or it will never stop. You're going to be just like Josh."

"Just like Josh?" I snap at him. "Do not compare me to a murderer. How would you know what he is like? I'm nothing like him. I didn't do anything wrong!" My eyes are set on the water. The rock wall is jagged. Still, I'm willing to take the jump. I'm not going back to jail. Back to jail. Yes, last night. I was in a dead sleep, and Big Don banged on Pop's door. He was about to bust it down. Pops got up half-asleep, and Big Don knocked him hard to the floor.

The cop's shotgun was drawn at my God-loving, law-abiding Pops who never broke the law other than going five miles over the speed limit once in a while when just the right song comes on the radio.

Pops was on the floor, and Kaylee was screaming, and they burst into my room and told me I've got to go to the police station for questioning in a murder. Did they realize they were screaming at the girl who uses a glass and a piece of paper to catch the little spiders that can't climb out of the slippery stainless steel kitchen sink so she can set them free? No, they don't take that into consideration. I got dragged down to the little dark New Alliance building and shoved into a room with a locked door. All the way down the hallway, Big Don poked and pushed me, banged my back, and tried to trip me.

Big Don was all cocky and gave me little taunting pokes on my arm. Poke. Poke. "You thought you could get away with it," he disclosed, then looked up at the camera in the room's far corner. "Where is that boy, Josh? Your mama told me everything. You saw him. Where were you meeting him? I talked to your mama in jail. She said you had a box with Josh's things."

"She is the one who gave it to me."

"That's not what she says."

"Am I under arrest?"

Big Don didn't say anything. He left and returned four hours later, saying he was going to get a warrant and would be back for me. Uncle Craig and Pops came to get me. I got home, packed a bag, and left. Pops stopped me. "You're not taking my truck."

"Pops, I've got to get out of here. I've got to—figure out where Josh is or something. They think I am a part of this—this murder thing."

"You can't run, baby. They will find you. It will make you look like you did something wrong. If Josh is still alive, he isn't going to be happy about being found. Sit down. We'll get you a lawyer."

"With what? We don't have a dime to our name." I was smart mouthing then, pretending to pick up a phone. "Hi, my name is Brandy. My ex-husband is on a murdering spree, and the cops think I helped him because I'm quicker than they are figuring out he did it because I know every place he went, every person that he's killed.

I've got a lockbox with all his fake IDs. Oh, and my wonderful mama, who my Pops begged me to get out of jail, told them I did." I worked my eyes upward and put down my fake phone. Then I walked to the window and looked outside. The sky was bloodshot red over the trees, enflamed like a wound with swirls of blues and greens. Ruby red, flushed with big black clouds rolling in.

"Pops, I've been to the police," I divulge. "They won't help me. And Big Don, when the cameras aren't on him, he hurts me." I raised my arm and showed Pops a skinned elbow and a bruise on my wrist. Then I just stared at the colors of the sky, didn't really see them. I remembered Mamaw looking out the window one morning before a tornado ripped through our valley and wiped out a swatch of trees. "Red in the morning," she said, only a few hours before the storm came. "Sailors take warning."

"I know where this all started. I knew that boy was trouble all along." Uncle Craig was pacing in the living room. Pops kept getting out a pack of cigarettes he hid in the bookshelf and slapping it on his leg. He hasn't smoked in five years.

"What boy?" I asked, shoving the curtains back.

"Your friend who comes over. Bear. He's the the root of all this."

"What do you mean?" Pops asked.

"He's the judge's boy, the judge that took our land. Just as soon as he showed up around here, things started up. I saw it—you remember his father? They found him dead in some cheap hotel. I remember them talking about it on TV like they were trying to link Josh and the judge's death together somehow."

"Why would Josh murder a judge?" I asked.

"Hells Bells." Pops grunted. "Why would he murder anyone?"

"I didn't know Bear's dad was—murdered." I rubbed my forehead. I felt a bead of sweat gathering there. "I figured he had a heart attack or something because he was overweight." I stopped and touched my face, tingling with realization. I wavered there, my hand on my face. "Oh my, do you think Bear knew this? Oh, Pops, do you think he's been hanging around me just to see if I knew where Josh was, maybe thinking I helped kill his daddy?"

"How would he know this?" Pops looked at me hard. "That's crazy, right?"

"I don't know." I felt the tears come, and I felt my tummy ache with a sudden panic. That's why Bear didn't want to sleep with me, get close to me. That's why he told me: *I didn't think it would play out like that.* The cops told me they were investigating something. I didn't even think about it. I didn't—have a clue. "Oh, Pops, why do I migrate to these idiots? Why didn't I see the clues?"

"Because you want to believe everybody is as good inside as you are good inside." Pops dangled the keys to his truck in his fingers. "Because you liked the boy. I thought he liked you, too. He had us all fooled." He looked at me, looked at the door. I know Pops understands. He's always getting fooled by Mama.

"Never again," I hissed. I felt dizzy with anger.

"No." Uncle Craig wiggled his keys from his pocket and tossed them to me. "Brandy, stop it. Don't jump to conclusions. He may not have known. And you can't change because other people are bad. Don't let the dark in others make you dark too. You've always been that little bit of light. That's why your Pops couldn't stand to leave you with Ruby. Here, take them. They are going to be looking for your Pops' truck first. Take mine." He brought out his wallet and dug out every bill he had inside. "I think there's forty dollars here, sweetie. Take my truck. Get out of here. Don't call us. We'll figure out something. We'll get an attorney somehow." Pops was staring at Uncle Craig before tugging out his wallet. He had another thirty bucks.

"Where you gonna go, sweetie?" he asked me. "Sixty or seventy dollars, it's not gonna get you far."

"I don't know. Maybe I'll head to the city. I'll go to Charleston. There are cheap hotels off the highway. Pops, I'm so sorry I'm so much trouble." Charleston. They both knew better.

It is probably a mistake, but I didn't go there. I emptied the lockbox and shoved the envelopes under my mattress. But before I did, I grabbed the last envelope and ripped out the fake driver's license for Emma and Nick Weber. Then I paused because I saw the envelope with Ashley's name and phone number splashed in Josh's handwriting along the right edge. I ripped it off and shoved it in my pocket. Then, beneath the red sky, I drove down Fire Mountain, and instead of turning left to go to Kenny's, I headed toward the highway. I tried to call Ashley six times. Maybe Josh has called her.

There's no answer.

That's where I ended up in Bryant, West Virginia. I'm standing in my eighty-dollar jean shorts, and a sixty-dollar baby blue T-shirt Bear bought me in Cincinnati. The leather boots have heels and are challenging to stand on in the grass. I'm wavering. I suppose it seems silly, this little note of my clothing. But when I hear the twig snap and see Bear standing only a step away, I think: *Oh, my God, why didn't I see this coming? Why the hell would a guy like Bear even look in my direction? And I am wearing clothes that this dumbass traitor bought me—*

"I've got her here, Don." That's Bear. The traitor. The turncoat. "She isn't going anywhere." Laughter. I hear thunder in the distance and feel the pressure of the storm as the hair is standing up on my arms. Lightning. It peels across the sky. Bear looks up absently. "She's not getting past me, that's for sure. You've got them coming down Mix Road, right? Well, there's no other way out but the quarry behind us. She can't swim. Sinks like a rock."

I am here, though, not to verify Emma and Nick's existence or their death. It isn't to stand in awe that Josh murdered someone else, and why did I live? Bear and Big Don were waiting for me to lead them here. They figured last night that if they took me to jail, roughed me up a bit, and set me free, I would run back to my ex-husband. It is the only place I know Josh won't be.

Right now, though, Bear is pushing the little button on his phone, turning it off. He stuffs it in his pocket while I wiggle my wrist free from his fingers. My cell phone is in Uncle Craig's truck. I parked it in the gas station lot about a quarter mile away, hoping nobody would recognize his vehicle or follow. I was wrong. Bear knew exactly what vehicle I'd taken and where I'd go.

"Please just hear me out. It is going to storm. We are going to get hit by lightning." What the hell? He turned on me like a rabid puppy when I told him I knew his secret. He turned defector, called the cops, and now he's doing his best to hold on to me, so I don't get away.

"At what point were you going to tell me the big secret?" I ask Bear. He is standing right in front of me. I am trying to peel away his fingers by wriggling my wrist. I'm not letting go of the empty lockbox. I don't have a gun to his head, but you would think I did.

"Big secret. Bejesus, I don't know what you mean. Will you stop this? Hear me out. Go with the cops. Just put your hands in the air and do what they say. I'll get you the best attorney in the U.S. We'll have you out before you go to sleep tonight. You can tell your story."

"My story? Do you mean the boring one where it starts out with me working at Mister Smileys and Beverly's? I work. I go home. Then I do it again the next day. I meet some guy, try to be his friend, and he shits on me. In case you didn't pick it up, that friend is *you*." I feel my lip twitch. I know Bear sees this. He doesn't know what that means because he's never truly seen me angry. "How about, Bear, that we start with your story? The one Gabe was scared to tell."

"Stop pulling, Brandy."

I can see him looking toward the cliff, which is not three steps away. He shifts and lugs me over the best he can away from it. However, I lean back and put the brakes on with my feet. Oh, the black clouds are working their way toward us. The crackle of thunder eases across a valley, followed by a louder bang.

"Okay, if you're going to be a bitch about it, I'll hash it out for you," I hiss. "But, you know, I never saw it coming. I think they call it being—blindsided. You know, when somebody you know is directing your attention somewhere else, and so, you look. You know, because you trust them. They wouldn't do anything to hurt you. They've got your back. Then, you get hit out of nowhere, on the other side, just outside your peripheral vision. Boom! Wipe out. Right on that vulnerable side, the side you leave open just a bit to let people in, even if you've gotten hurt again and again and again. You know that side, don't you? Because you've been standing back all this time, watching it, assessing it, testing it out. Poke, poke. That's where it hurts, Brandy. Poke, poke. I better lose weight, or she'll know that I'm here to find out about my father. Poke. Oh, this is even better. I think I'll screw her and get a little something-something out of it while I'm at it. Poke. Watch her squirm. Aw, cool, there's that scared look in her eyes."

"Please don't do that. It isn't true. I wouldn't hurt you."

"You're hurting me now," I declare, looking at his fingers biting into my wrist. He tried to grab me around the waist and drag me a minute ago. I kicked and swung my arms, so he settled on latching on to my arm, waiting for the police here. "You set me up, Beau—

I'm sorry. It really isn't Beau—Vega. You changed it back to your mom's name after your dad died. It was Beau Patterson. That's what you've been doing for the last six months. You've been following me around, trying to see where I meet up with Josh like I'm helping him on his murder spree, taking in a little cash. Was it like some superhero movie for you? Are you avenging your father's death?"

"It wasn't like that." He is gaping at me—the mouth-dropping, wide-eyed, what-the-hell look people get when something goes incredibly wrong and it freaks them out. "I had no clue who you were when I met you. How'd you find out who I was?"

"I looked you up on the internet, idiot! I should have done it months ago. But it never occurred to me to do a background check on the choir director at a church and a guy I thought was my friend. Does it matter? I kick myself, thinking I should have recognized you, the big old fat bully. You were Judge Patterson's boy, who used to make fun of Little Pete on the bus. That's why he kept telling me at the hospital, 'I don't like him. He's mean to me.' But it just didn't click. I thought he meant John John. I wouldn't have known you. You went to live with your dad when he got into politics and tried to get into the Senate. I don't know if, outside of stopping you beating up all us trailer trash, I'd had any encounters with you." And that is why he's looking at me like a pup that just got caught peeing on the floor.

"That's not the point," I hiss at him. "Your dad was the judge that said a dam would be built along Fire Mountain Creek. The one who moved everybody out, and took all their homes from the bottom to the top. Bobby Reese and Janie Murphy, I can name twenty-five other families whose spirits died the day he did it. Then, your snake father said it was too expensive to pay for the dam. He sold the mountain to your mom. You come back to make friends with me, blindside me, and get me put in jail. Why? What is in it for you? Why would you go out of your way to hunt me down like some jerk-off bounty hunter?" I push out my hand. "You don't have to say. I figured it out. When they found your dad dead, you figured Josh might have killed him too, right? Because all this started with our little trailer tucked up on Fire Mountain and having the land taken away by some conniving bastard judge."

"How'd you know he was my dad?"

"Uncle Craig told me. God, why didn't you tell me yourself? Why did you let this go on? You know I didn't do anything."

"I assumed you would eventually find out. I'd deal with it then. I assumed I'd lose you as a friend, so I held out. I thought you'd get to know me, know I wasn't like him, and maybe you'd stick around. Bejesus, there are lots of people who wanted my dad dead. He was mean. Josh is just one person who could have killed him. As soon as we started hanging out, I knew you didn't do it, Brandy. I swear I tried to tell Big Don that a hundred times. He kept telling me to keep hanging around you. And Preacher Murphy kept saying, yeah, it's okay. Do what the cops say. But you kept talking about the damn Redneck Run and getting right in his face and mom's face. You kept putting yourself out there, and the more you did, the more pissed off they got. I tried to get you to stop."

"I shouldn't have to stop."

"It wouldn't have made a difference. The cops just wanted what was in the box, for you to lead them to Josh."

"So Big Don can be a hero and solve the big case of his life. And while all the media is focusing on the Redneck Run, the reporters are all there and ready to take his story."

"Brandy, they are coming. Please don't pull away. Just give me the box. That's all they want."

I stare at him. They didn't want the box. They want what is in it, which is sitting in my Pops' house under the mattress of my bed. If I open the lockbox right now and spill out the contents, which isn't anything but air, they are going to Pops' home and tear it apart and think Pops was a part of this.

"Let me go, Bear, or I swear to God I will wail into you right now worse than when I wailed on your chubby, cowardly ass on the school bus that day."

"Where are you going to go, Brandy?" he asks like he's consoling a two-year-old. "Come on. Where?"

Another boom, another resounding crash of thunder. I feel the sprinkle of raindrops on my arms. Oh, my God. I hear them coming up the trail. I listen to them talking. I see Bear's eyes work upward, so I turn my head and catch a glimpse of clothing along the gravel road where a gate shuts it off from the highway.

"The only place I got to go, Vega, is down."

I don't know if fear makes me stupid or if I am just plain stupid with it. I am true to my word, though. I take a step toward Bear, drop the box, rear back my fist, and let it fly right into his face. He doesn't expect it. I don't know why. It hooks him right between the eyes.

Maybe he's the stupid one. He knows me. I'm not going to go down without a fight. I think he harbors this foolish idea that all girls deep inside are like his loyal dog, meek Meghan, sitting around waiting for a guy to make the decision to protect them. It doesn't work that way on Fire Mountain. He should have known better. Because his first experience with a redneck girl left him with a black eye and a bloody nose on Missy Smythe's Bus 7. And she hasn't changed since.

I wrench my hand away when he steps back oh-so-close to the cliff's edge. I snatch up the box. I can't go back. I listen to my gut just like Pops says I always do. I make the jump before I look. I go forward, right past Bear and into the blue water.

Chapter −35

Sinking

Jump. Just like Pops said, I jump first and think later. I listen to my gut and take off without thinking. I can't swim worth crap. I don't know why I sink when I get into water. I used to sit in the old clawfoot bathtub in Pops' bathroom, fill it to the rim, and hold my breath to practice floating. I tried to glide there on the surface. Even in there, my skinny body would drop until my butt would bump right off the bottom.

I asked Mamaw once, and she told me it was because I was skinny and had more muscle than fat. It was a good thing. Fat people float like marshmallows on the surface of hot chocolate, she told me. I was more like a chocolate drop added for an extra treat. They fall to the bottom, and you can dig them out with a spoon.

After I shatter the quarry water's surface like a bird hitting a windshield, I lounge there a second, thinking about marshmallows and wishing I'd float like one. I feel the box falling from my arms. I don't care. Maybe it will hit the bottom next to pieces of Emma and lay there forever unfound. I know I'm going to die here as I go down, down, down. I feel my sinuses ache. My head feels like it is going to explode. Light goes to the darkness above me. Kenny is right when he describes my ability to swim. I float just as well as a Bud Light can filled with rocks. It is getting darker and darker, and hell's bells, I hear a splash above me. It is like a muffled *ploof-splosh* sound. Then, something is latching onto my arm, tugging me upward. I think it is upward because it is so black where I am.

"Bud light." It is what I am choking and coughing when I break the surface. The raindrops splatter on my face. I don't know who has me. I am assuming it is a cop. Or Bear. It's Bear because I hear him curse. He's got me by the neck, but I can still hammer him in the gut with my elbow. "Dammit, stop it!" His voice is low. "Just shut up!" He's looking up, and I'm making a sloppy flounder of my arms and feet. I'm finally realizing my head is going underwater. It freaks me out. Bear says, "Why the hell do you do these things you do?" He is trying to paddle backward toward the wall. "God almighty, I've never seen someone sink like that."

"Mamaw said I'm like a chocolate drop." I choke and gasp.

"Ouch, dammit, stop! What the hell are you talking about? No, you are like a sour jellybean. I am trying to get us up under this ridge so they can't see us, so we don't get hit by lightning. If you hit me one more time, I'm going to dunk your head under and hold you there!" It is a steep edge, nothing but a tiny crest of rock roof before it's a straight climb up the wrinkled surface of the stone wall. He must see my eyes get wide as apples. "Okay, I won't really do that. Just trust me. I will not let you go."

Does he not realize trust is an issue with me? I gave him enough demonstrations.

"Brandy, you definitely have trust issues." It's like a revelation for him while he backs onto the wall. I know his feet aren't touching anything. I see his hand patting the little stones sticking out. They keep crumbling and falling. He's got this kind of scared look in his eyes.

"Well, I started to trust you, and look where I am now."

"Yeah, not down at the bottom of the quarry dead. What did you think was going to happen when you jumped? You'd magically float and swim away?"

"The other option sucked, Bear."

He presses a finger to his lips. "If they find us, I will turn you in. I'm going to say you jumped. I didn't want you to die."

"Imagine that." I am still choking quietly, still trying not to wallow with my arms flailing and my legs paddling aimlessly. "I wonder why I have trust issues with you."

"No, so I am not an accomplice. If I am, I'll go to jail, too, and I can't help you. I don't think they saw us. Quit moving. Just be—still. They'll know we're down here if they see the water moving."

"So, what you're doing, then, is kind of like our relationship." I let myself relax then. I feel Bear's arm turn me, and I shift and shove my hand around his neck. We are belly to belly. I am tired of fighting him. "You want to be with me but don't want anybody to know."

"You're going to discuss this—now?"

I swipe my face with my hand and set my forehead on his chest for lack of a better resting place. "You know of a better time?" I look up. He gives me a hard, dark stare.

I hear somebody yelling, "Hey, anybody out there?" I see his eyes work upward. A male and a female voice are calling almost in unison. Then, it is quiet. We wait. We watch. Nobody walks around the rim. It is silent.

"Where did they go? What did you tell them?" I whisper. I'm watching Bear's hand clasping the rock. His fingers keep slipping, and we dunk down a little.

"I told the New Alliance police we were heading here. I said we would be waiting for them. Big Don said he would contact the Bryant police because they had jurisdiction. I parked my truck pretty far away. He probably thought I lied to him to get him off track. It's raining hard. They won't stay."

"Why would he think you lied, Bear? I think you're like his lapdog now," I say. I am looking out across the water. I can't even see where the shoreline ends. I'm terrified he's going to yell and catch their attention.

"You're mean. I don't know, but I can't hold on here forever," he tells me. "And as far as you are pointing the finger at me for disrespecting this relationship, I'm not the one that initiated the relationship. I already had a girlfriend. I wasn't making passes at you, flirting, or whatever you want to call it. I was perfectly happy with what we had without the sex."

"And that would be you acting like you are my friend so you can find out if I was with Josh when he killed your dad," I mutter. "That's some relationship, asshole." My heart falls right then. I'd seen this happen with Mama a hundred times. One incident, though, sticks like hot glue in my mind. In sixth grade, Pops let me go to Mama's house overnight while he went hunting. He told me later it was against his better judgment. Still, Mama had asked, and she told him she'd been sober for at least six weeks. She wanted to bake me a birthday cake and give me a little ring she'd gotten me.

The guy she was dating came over. He was mad at Mama because he didn't want some stupid kid around. Now, I know he didn't want anybody around. He didn't want anybody to tell his wife he was fooling around, getting some bar waitress tail on the side. It was one of the local cops, a big, burly man. I sat on the couch while he yelled at her, and then Mama came out and told me to go for a walk and come back in a few hours.

I remember telling her it was only ten degrees outside. She wouldn't take no for an answer. But before I put on my coat, I remember what she said: "I don't have those kinds of men hanging around, baby girl. Some men want to be with me like I want to be with them, get a little something-something. They don't want nobody to know. I don't care if they got a girlfriend or a wife. They pay my rent, buy my food, and take me to the bars. The guy on Saturday bought your mama that ring you're wearing right now—"

I still have that ring. It was cheap and left a little green circle around my finger. I take it out occasionally and remember the story and the hundred other times I heard about my mama and her men. I guess I didn't understand until now, that some of them she must have really liked, maybe loved like I did Bear. Mama probably got the tickle in her tummy if she knew he was coming. She probably felt her heart beating fast and dreamed of having a wedding band on her hand. But she never got it, just a little something-something on the side and rent and groceries. And a fake ring.

I thought Bear was different. He's not. It is a defining moment for me, I suppose, baptized in that frigid water of the quarry and clinging to the man who likes me enough to hang around, get that something-something, but has another he flaunts on his arm for everybody to see. She's the one he likes, the one he'll end with at the end of my story. The future trophy wife—Meghan Reynolds. But that ring, it's the reason I made Josh marry me. It is why I waited around in the Crazy Kettle for three years for him. I didn't want to be my mama. Mama might have loved those men like I love Bear. They didn't love her. And he doesn't love me.

I must have stared at him for a long time. When I blink past the comprehension, Bear has a strange expression. I'm expecting him to say something profound, he says: "It's like this. I can't do this much longer. I'm running out of steam. Regardless if they are out there, we can't hide here forever." We bump along the wall until we find a rocky ledge. The rain is getting harder, banging off my head. There's something of a beach, a place locals must come to swim because a rope hangs out over the water from a tree. It is swinging in the wind. Nobody is around. It is quiet except for the pelt of rain and the clap of thunder. We walk through the raggedy grass and back along the gravel road to the gas station.

As we break through to the highway, Bear stops me with his hand. "Maybe they saw my truck. Maybe they are watching it." I am shivering.

"What are you saying?"

"You need to stay here."

"Bear, I've got my uncle's truck. I'm not sticking around with you. I'm not standing out here in the pouring rain. Right now, I don't want to be anywhere near you." But I realized right then that while I pat my back pocket where I stuck them, I didn't have the keys. "Son of a bitch!" I kick the dirt and waggle my arms into the air. My eyes veer behind us. However, I knew the keys were in my pocket right before I jumped.

"Nice dance, Brandy." Bear rubs his forehead. "Just chill out. I know you don't understand this. Your family's entire reputation isn't at stake here. But mine is. If the police think I am aiding someone who committed a crime, the reporters will be here in ten minutes. We're the big story now with the Redneck Run. They are looking for any drama they can get." He takes in a breath; he must see the irritation in my eyes. Surely, he knows he insulted me by making it appear my family doesn't even have a good enough reputation to lose. "If they get ahold of this—my mom can be ruined." Bear reaches out and touches my shoulder with a knuckle. "I'll go find a hotel, someplace we can think this out, call Pops and a lawyer. Then I'll come back for you when I make sure nobody's around—two or three hours, tops."

"How do I know you're not calling the cops again?"

"How do I know you're not going to take off, that you don't have your keys tucked in your shirt or something?" Bear retorts.

"You want to feel me up, look for the keys?" I spat at him, waving my hands at my chest. Bear grimaces.

"No, I don't. You don't have the keys. I'm not going to call the cops. I guess we're just going to have to trust each other. You think I'm any better at this than you?"

A big ball of tears settles in my throat. "Why did you do it?"

"Do what?"

"Everything," I say. "Why didn't you tell me about your dad and Josh? Why'd you be my friend? Why'd you turn me in?"

"Because when I saw you, I just saw the outside. You're beautiful, knock-out gorgeous. I thought you'd be easy to collect hanging out at a bar, wearing—"

"—skanky clothes."

"I didn't say that." Bear shakes his head almost sadly. "It used to be easier hanging around people who don't expect anything from me and don't care about me, who would just as soon screw me like I'd screw them." He wiggles a finger near his head. "I just don't always have the tools to figure stuff out, Brandy. I'm new to this. Just stay. I promise I won't mess up again."

I've got no choice. Bear is right. Even if he does call the cops and brings them right to me, I've got no place to go. My phone and purse are in his truck. I nod. He sees the distrust in my eyes. As he walks away, I call out to him. He turns. "Promise me you'll come back. Promise me you won't call the cops. Promise me—" *You won't just use me like Mama's men did. You won't kiss Meghan. You won't leave me. You won't—*He's tipping his head to the side, waiting for me to finish. I don't and shrug instead.

"What, Brandy? Is there something else?"

"No," I lie. "Nothing." Not that I can say aloud.

"I promise. I'll come back. If it is up to me, I will be alone. But I really, really believe Big Don is trying to help you. He is weird, but not a bad person like you all make him out to be. You've got to trust somebody. Big Don's a cop. They are always the good guys, right?" He looks at me and points a finger. He is sopping wet, still dripping from the quarry. "You promise you'll stay?"

It is ten-thirty at night before Bear returns. I have nothing to do but think. It is dark. Nothing but the crickets are chirping. The rain is still coming down. The storm has eased. I see blacker than black against the dark sky again. He looks surprised when he sees me and says he can't believe I didn't buck. "I promised," I tell him. He has a blanket in his hands that he tosses at me.

"I borrowed a coat hanger and unlocked the door to your Uncle's truck. I used your phone, called your Pops," he tells me while I wrap the blanket around me. "He says Officer Calvin Jamison called his house at seven tonight. He looked for you like he had no clue there was a warrant or anything for your arrest."

I stand up and swipe the leaves from my rear. The moon is full. I can see the roadway, a trail of gravel leading toward the sky glow from the gas station on the highway exit. My clothes aren't damp anymore; they are clammy and stick to my skin. "What does that mean?" I ask. "Why would Calvin call me?"

"Pops didn't know. He didn't ask," Bear tells me. "Officer Jamison was going to do some research. He was waiting for a callback. Your pops was really wary of me. I don't know what was said. Brandy, Don said he was trying to help you. He's not a bad guy, you know?"

I'm learning not to try to convince people of things they don't believe. If I look in the mirror and don't like the person looking back at me, how can I expect anyone else to respect me? I look at my hands twiddling together.

"It'd only been twenty minutes or so when I left," Bear says. "I didn't want to leave you out here any longer. Pops agreed. I got us a place to stay about twenty minutes from home tonight. It's far enough from New Alliance that nobody will notice my truck. He doesn't want you to take off. He said Officer Jamison thought we should stay where he can contact us."

Less than an hour and forty minutes later, we are at a hotel off the highway. It is much nicer than the one Josh lived in; it is newer and has a pool. Not that I want to swim. Instead, I'm watching T.V., sitting on the end of one king-size bed, and chewing on a stale candy bar from the vending machine in the hallway. Bear is leaning with his back to the wall. I think he's using my phone to text somebody and tell them he's alright. His is gone. He says it might have slipped out of his hand halfway down the quarry wall.

"Here." Bear reaches out. He hands me my cell phone. "Take a look." I look up at Bear. He's not looking at me. I take the phone from his fingers and focus on the front. He's pulled up a social network page with an image. It is the chubby Bear with a full beard, business suit, and tie. It's just the upper half of him, the old Bear from six months ago with a glum, apathetic look on his face and eyes.

"What is it?" I ask.

"You told me you know nothing about me. This is me in Chicago before I moved back to New Alliance to help run the resort."

"Okay," I say, handing him the phone back. "Cool." It isn't the Bear I know staring back at me. I suppose I don't really care anymore. It's not like I need to know because—that's what people who hang out with each other are—close, and might have a future together. (God, what was I thinking? Was some guy like Bear with looks and money going to marry me? I've got way too much of Mama in me.) I've decided that's not going to happen anymore.

"Cool? That's all?" He smiles at me, but his eyes are questioning. "I thought you wanted to know more about me." He taps the phone. "I worked for Strategic MG, Inc. I like to say we go in and help dying businesses cut costs. That usually isn't the case. We go in, find the weaknesses, and clean house, if you know what I mean. Lots of firing of people. Lots of—pressure to build the business back up." He laughs. "But it's hard to meet people when everybody runs when they see you coming. Everybody hates you because you're the guy who comes in and exposes weaknesses. Of course, it has its perks. Lots of money. I suppose that's good. It's a multi-million-dollar firm, and I had all the answers. There is a sense of power involved in being the one who makes the decisions."

"Why don't you go back?" I ask.

"I liked it until about six months ago. Then, my perspective started to change once I got back home. I got bitch-slapped by reality. I looked in the mirror one day and saw my dad looking back at me—an old fat guy one step away from a heart attack and dying in a bed-bug-infested motel all alone. Then I met you, and you led me down a road I'd never taken. I realized I liked the direction I was heading. Besides, my mother needs me at the resort, and I get to do what I always wanted to do, work with music even if it is only a tiny church in the middle of nowhere."

I pretend I'm not looking, but it is right there in front of me. Bear has folders with pictures of Meghan and her team on his page just below his picture. There are probably ten more with Bear in newspaper shots and linking arms with local celebrities and radio station hosts. It's almost like he's taunting me with it, showing off he was popular, had a great job, and had a beautiful girlfriend.

And me, I've got a warrant for my arrest, and I've lost my jobs, just to mention a few reasons why I am a loser without a dime to my name. An excellent way to rub it in, Bear.

"Cool, Bear." I nod and push the button on the phone so the page disappears. I go to my texts and flip through them. Chase has texted me twenty times a day. Ben texted me to come tomorrow. Gabe has phoned me twice. A couple of Ben's friends we met want me to do stuff with them. And Kenny left a text about picking up ice cream. *Ash. Ash?* I see the name and push the little line so the message comes up. The text says: *This is Ashley. Got your message. Call me. Now.* My eyes are glued to the message. It was from three hours ago. My heart seems to stop, then start pounding.

"Why do you keep saying that? Cool." Bear snaps back and interrupts my stare. "What does that mean?"

"It means what it means," I answer. I start to rise. "I'm going to take a shower. "

"Then you'll lie down with me and watch a movie or something? You're still shivering."

Or something. Really? He's going to show me pictures of his girlfriend and then want sex?

"I'm tired. I'm not—interested."

"Oh, so that's how it is now." Bear waves a hand at me and plops down on a reclining chair next to the bed. "When you want to do something, we do it. When I do, it's like: Bear, I'm all tired." He makes his voice higher for the last part. I was insulted, so I snatched up my phone so he wouldn't use it.

"I'm not sleeping with you tonight. I'm not sleeping with you ever again. I think—I think you have a girlfriend like you said."

"You are just mad."

I roll my eyes and go into the bathroom. Lock the door.

I turn on the shower and the bathroom fan. I stuff a towel at the bottom of the door and dial the number from where Ashley called.

"Hey," I whisper. "This is Brandy. You called me?"

"Oh, God, oh God." I hear her like she's walking from one room to the next. "He's here. He's here. Brandy, he says if you don't come, he's going to kill my kids. It's Johnny."

"What?"

"He saw you at some town. You were hunting him down. He said—" Ashley is crying, sobbing, and I swear I hear breathing beside her.

"Call the cops," I hiss. "Can you call the cops?"

Thwack! Ashley makes a funny whimpering sound. "He's—he can hear you. Brandy. He's standing right here."

"Hey, baby," I hear. It is a little muffled. Still, I'd know Josh's voice anywhere. My heart races and my toes feel numb. "I seen you in Pine Estates. I saw you at your Pops' house not too long ago, too. Watched you through the window. Have you been talkin' to your mama? Because she called me, and I know the cops were listening."

"What do you want, Josh?"

"I want to see you, baby," he says. "You tell anybody, call the cops, I'm killing her. And I'm killing the brats."

"No, Josh."

"Yeah, Brandy," he says. "Who do you think you are, huh? Why didn't you leave it alone."

"You tried to kill me, burn the trailer down."

"Well, you're sleeping with my brother. Now we're even."

"What?" My eyes go to the bathroom door. It is metal and tan. But on the other side is Beau Vega. "You don't have a brother."

"You figured out how to find me but are too stupid to know the guy you've been hanging out with is Judge Patterson's son?"

"I—I knew that. How does that make him your brother?"

"Half-brother, idiot. We have the same mom. He knows it. Didn't he tell you? His daddy spent a lot of time at the Crazy Kettle before we were born. My mama used to hang out there a lot—"

He hangs up. I'm shaking. I stand there feeling like I have run twelve miles. I'm out of breath. I shower, play it out like I'm getting ready for bed, and let the hot water run down my head and body. I wish I could wash off Josh just like the dirt from the day from my body. All I have are my jean shorts and T-shirt, so it isn't like Bear's going to know I'm taking off as soon as he falls asleep.

He's sitting on the recliner when I get out. He ignores me and leans back like he's getting ready for a long night of watching shows. I eye his keys on the table where the T.V. is standing. I can't think of any excuse I can make to snatch up the keys and sneak out to the truck. I'm going to have to steal his vehicle, I know. He's one step closer to calling Big Don again if he hasn't already phoned him from the hotel office or some payphone at a gas station.

"I'm going to bed," I tell him, hoping he'll turn off the T.V. He doesn't. Bear doesn't even ask me if it bothers me. I could only look at him, see his eyes, and know I was right the first time I saw him. I saw Josh in Bear the first time he visited Pops' house. It was the twinkle in his eyes. After he lost weight, it was the swagger.

"Suit yourself. I'm going to be up a while." He actually looks at me, then looks at the door. It is secured shut and zipped tight with a chain lock and padlock. "I'm assuming you're a flight risk tonight. Pops was worried. I told him I'd do everything to keep you safe."

"If I was a flight risk, wouldn't I have taken off already?"

"I don't know. I've heard coyotes will chew their paws off if they are stuck in a leg hold trap." He scoots up in his chair and tugs on his lip. I hate myself for thinking this, but he's picture-perfect sitting in his skin-tight jeans and muscles sticking out of his t-shirt, better than Chase any old day. "There's two windows and a door in here. I think if you don't want to go to jail, you would claw your way through the floor like you did at your mama's trailer. Or jump out a window like you jumped off the cliff at the quarry."

"Don't go there," I say. I wish I could tell Bear I knew the truth: Josh was his brother. I can't. He'd know someone told me. He'd guess it was Josh.

"I'm sorry."

"That would imply you thought you were wrong," I toss back at him. I walk up and tug the covers back.

"Will you please talk to me? We really need to talk."

"No, Bear, I won't. Shut up. I said, we are done. Let me sleep."

"Please don't be mad."

"Mad? Because you compare *this* to me trying to save my little sister? Or—or jumping off a cliff so I didn't get shot? You know what? I guess what really pissed me off was that jumping into the quarry was not the jump I was planning on taking, *Beau*. Just so you know. Pops thinks that might be what you were waiting on. Me, I wasn't so sure. I was ready to take a step and trust a little bit. You're gutting me because I think my pops is always right."

I leave my shoes, purse, and phone by the side of the bed. I don't look at the keys or draw attention to how easily they would be for me to obtain. Then, I lay down and waited for Bear to go to sleep.

Chapter −36

Sneaking out of a hotel room

There's nothing on the radio but advertisements about the Redneck Run coming up in three days. It is two in the morning. The storm is blasting shards of golden lightning before me. The crash of thunder hides the sound of music when it explodes above me. I'm in Bear's truck, barreling down the highway toward Brink Hollow. The GPS takes me southwest along the four-lane route, almost to New Alliance, before I turn off at a smaller highway.

It was one o'clock before Bear fell asleep on the recliner, snoring away with his head lolling back. I'd snuck out of Pops' house more than a few times in high school to meet Josh. Pops once told me if he ever caught me sneaking out at night to meet a boy, he'd shoot the boy and ask questions later.

I assume he was exaggerating. However, there was a slight chance he could be telling the truth, so I got good at unlatching the locks by practicing during the day when I had just gotten home from school, and he was still at work. The key, I learned, was working each latch and each lock in slow motion.

It is precisely the skill I use to snatch up Bear's keys and slip out the hotel door with my boots in my hand and my purse over my shoulder. Rain. It is pelting down hard. I steal fifty bucks from his wallet. It wouldn't have been a simple feat, but Bear was reckless. He left it sitting on the bathroom sink. Idiot. Of course, I was the one going out of the hotel door like a twenty-buck whore with half the money stolen from her john's billfold.

I don't think I really thought out any plan for meeting Josh. Sitting in the truck right now and watching the lights from the safe little houses nearly hidden in the hills and valleys on either side of the highway gives me a feeling of doubt and doom in the pit of my stomach. Why can't I be tucked into a bed with some balding and pudgy but gentle husband holding me to sleep? Maybe a kid or two is lying in a bed with a kitten wrapped in chubby arms in the other room. The halls are lit by gently glowing lamps, warm and safe. Outside, the front porch light twinkles and reminds those passing that there is something everybody wants, I want, inside.

But I'm not. Instead, I am doing ninety-five miles per hour in a stolen truck and heading straight into the storm and toward hell, where Satan, himself, is waiting to drag me down with him. My course is only slowed by the local cop who pulls me over when I pass his car in the left lane.

"Yes, sir." I am sitting in the truck, staring at the highway patrolman who pulled me over. He's looking at my license and flips open the little book I dig out of Bear's glovebox with his registration and insurance. He seems uncomfortable with the rain cascading off the plastic wrapper over his hat. His eyes blink against the drizzle, slapping his face. I'm thinking that it's all over now. I will have to take off and have a high-speed chase.

"I was speeding. It's my boyfriend's truck. I was with him tonight and didn't have my car with me. I —I am in a hurry to see my friend who is sick. I'm—I'm going to take her to the hospital."

"What town are you heading to?" He is tolerant, if nothing else.

"Brink Hollow."

"Slow down."

That was it. I almost burst into tears. The one cop that's ever been nice to me and trusted me, I've deceived. I'm an emotional basket case. I take off slowly, forcing myself to stick to the speed limit if for no other reason than to respect that one cop who had an actual soul. It occurred to me that he ran my driver's license. Surely, he would know if there was a warrant for my arrest, right? Are they all just playing tricks on me?

Two and a half hours later, I'm sweating bullets, pulling along the curb of Ashley's house. The rain won't go away. The storm is settling right above me. I sit there in the truck. It is silent except for the drops of water pelting the roof. I don't think I realize until that moment, when I am turning my head to the fifteen steps along the brown-grass lawn strewn with a broken plastic slide, a ball, and a blue plastic swimming pool, that I will die. Knowing Josh, it will be slow and agonizing. He always liked to draw things out.

Fifteen steps, and I know Josh has some horrible end waiting for me. He'd tried it twice. Once, when he attempted to burn the trailer down and the second, making me nearly roll over in Pops' truck. What will it be inside? A knife, an axe, a gun?

I must take those fifteen steps and slowly reach the front door. It opens even before I knock. Ashley is standing there. Her mascara is dripping black tar down her face. Her cheeks are red and bruised, and her bottom lip is busted. I look on the floor. Two little boys are sitting on a tattered blue blanket. They are silent, unmoving, not watching the TV. Their skinny little arms are wrapped around their knees. Their eyes are wild-scared like Kaylee's the night John John nearly killed her. Guess who sits on the couch with a beer in his fist and a cigarette in the other?

"Hey, baby, I saw you the other day."

I slip in the door. Ashley shoves a piece of crumpled toilet paper to her eyes, blotting the tears away.

"When did you start beating up on girls, Josh?" I ask him. "Or is that your name at all?"

"You've still got that mouth on you, girl."

Holy Cow. He jumps up off that couch in one leap. He approaches me, and I don't have the cunning to open the door and run outside screaming. I stand there unbelieving. The Josh I knew was a crappy guy, but not a killer, not a guy that beats the shit out of girls. I've never seen a man fight like this before, but he lifts up both his arms and starts flailing me with the outside of his fists until I sink to the floor.

"Stop, Josh! Please—!" Stop. Do I fight back? No. I would suppose Ashley is the same. I would suppose his Hannah, Katy-did, Maddy, Taylor, and Emma didn't either. We're all dead broke like old hard-run horses, not fighters. The only thing I can do to stop him is bring up my arms in defense. One of the little boys screams. Josh lifts me by my hair, and I know he will slam me up against the front door. Then, it is like I feel this thump on my head when he does use his elbow to punch me into the door. It doesn't hurt as much as I am consumed in browns and grays while my brain sloshes around inside. The world is swimming while I fall on my elbows.

It only takes Josh four minutes to drag me into the kitchen, shove me into a chair, and tell Ashley to start tying me up with a green electric cord he rips from behind the couch. She is shaking so severely doing it that her entire body is jiggling. "I'm sorry. I'm sorry. I'm sorry," she keeps choking this out over and over. Her eyes go to the living room, where the two boys are quietly huffing sobs.

"I'm just wondering what went south in your head to make you do this?" I'm saying to Josh's back. Eight gas cans of different sizes and colors are lined up along the wall. "What the hell happened? Didn't your daddy give you enough attention? Maybe your mama gave you too much." No. That isn't it at all. I can tell by the skin and bones body, the sallow cheeks, and the red gashes on his nose and cheeks that he's deep down in hell with heroin, coke, or meth.

He is lifting one gas can. I know his intention. Josh was never much for conversation. He turns and gives me one of his winning smiles but doesn't say a thing.

"Please don't piss Johnny off," Ashley is saying. "Please, I've got babies in the other room. I don't want them to get hurt."

I had a good idea they were going to die. Maybe Ashley did, too. She tries to console Josh and tell him she can make everything alright. They can leave and go somewhere far away, and nobody will ever know. "Oh, please let the boys go, please, Johnny," she mewls. "I'll do anything you say."

He turns and laughs, grabs another old, dirty kitchen chair, and pushes it back-to-back with mine. My hands are tied behind me, and the chair pinches them intensely.

"Sit down, my lovely lady." He then mumbles something to himself and smacks himself on the head. "Oh, I'm bad. No, I'm mad. Bad, mad, BAD!" He swivels around. He looks at me and points a finger. "I'm not crazy, you bitch."

Ashley is down to sobbing. Her eyes are ogling him. Josh pivots around again, stares at the wall, and then, all of a sudden, lunges at it, smacking it with his head. He follows it down until he can't get past the sink. My ex-husband lunges downward, and jerks open the doors under the sink. He slams one once, twice, three times. I hear Ashley screech each time they slap together.

"Oh, my God, he's having an episode," Ashley hisses. She doesn't seem to care that Josh can hear her. Apparently, he doesn't. He has no interest in her now at all. "There's a gun down there. There's a gun—*oh, a gun*. He can't have the gun."

An episode? It is more like an attack of the crazies. She tries to buck and get to the living room. I'm trying to remember how many kids she has. Is there one missing? Did Josh already hurt them? She nearly collapses on the boys, screaming for them to run.

The boys sit there sobbing, saying they won't leave her. I think they are Kaylee's age; one might be smaller. Suddenly, Josh is in front of me, a flash of gun barrel coming at my face. "Bang." He hits my forehead hard. I'm blinking blood away. Josh drags Ashley back. I start yelling, screaming for somebody to help, and he says he'll kick the kids if I don't shut up.

"Take the boys. Take Jared Michael," Ashley is saying while he slaps her down in the chair and uses the cords that he ripped from behind the refrigerator to tie her hands and her feet. "Oh, my God, please don't burn them up with us. Please!"

"If you had just left me alone, you'd be sleeping soundly in your Pops' house right now. You know that, right?" Josh leans down with his hands on his knees. "You'd read in the paper tomorrow morning that a woman and her kids died in a fire. They are strangers to you so you would forget by that afternoon and go on with your life." Josh has a rifle in his hand. He holds it to my head and says: "Boom." Then he giggles. His freckled, boyish face contradicts the wicked I see in those blue eyes. *Wicked. Josh.* I'm hitting the wall right now, thinking how stupid I was. No, nobody would have seen this coming. Nobody. *Oh, Pops and Bear did.*

"What the hell were you thinking, babe?" The eyes match the quarry water I jumped into yesterday with Bear. It wasn't that long ago I swam in those eyes staring at me, almost drowned in them too. Josh reaches out a hand and slides it along my jawline. "The perfect woman. The perfect face. What a waste in a trailer park. You know, I screwed your mama more than once while I was in ninth grade. She needed some weed. Of course, it was way back before she looked like the hell she looks like now."

"Just let the boys go, Josh," I say. His lip is twitching. I look at his eyes. Nothing is in there. It is like his mind just went POP! "They are yours. How can you hurt them?"

He doesn't seem to care. He steps back, folds his arms across his chest, and nods. "Wow, if I shoot you two, someone might hear. I'll just shoot one of you. Haha, that was a joke. Who will it be? Who wants to go first?" He holds the gun up again and puts it to his face like he is aiming at each of us. "Boom! She's dead." He says while he touches the tip of the barrel on Ashley's nose. He turns to me. "Boom! She's dead." I wince, startled.

Josh stops and lets it drop to my chest. "Don't want to mar that beautiful angel face. Got to see it in heaven. Or, maybe I'm going to hell. Yeah, I'll take you to hell with me. Eternity in Hell with Brandy. Ah, sweet Jesus."

Ashley and I are tied to a chair, our backs to each other. I'm scared to try to wiggle out of the electric cords. They seem slippery enough to do so. I think I will wait it out, wait until Josh turns his back. He looks back and forth between us, seemingly satisfied we're not moving. Josh pours rivers of gas around the house, walking from room to room until each gas can is empty. It is overwhelming. He removes his lighter, flicks it in my face, and then snaps to Ashley. I'm too numb to cry. Ashley, maybe she was numb before I got here. She is just sniffing now and trying to drag herself from the chair in little springs upward. Josh leaves the kitchen. I can hear a baby crying in another room. I think I hear someone knocking at the door. Josh snaps to attention. "What's going on out there?" he asks the two little boys. They shake their heads, little mouths wide open in terror.

"Jared Michael is awake. He's going to climb out of his crib. I can't die because Johnny will hurt him." She is talking to herself. Not to me. Josh is taking the lighter into the hallway, leaning down, and flicking it. "I'm not going to die," she says softly. "I'm not going to leave my babies. I'm going to kill that bastard."

It's a funny thing, maternal instincts. I suppose while some women, like my mama, lack in protecting their children, it is ten-fold in others. Once Josh figures out that he can catch the envelopes of their electric and water bills on fire and lay them down on the carpet for more fuel, Ashley is a ten-fold mama. He first goes to the two bedrooms on the right, and smoke starts filtering into the kitchen. Fire. Heat. It spurs her on. Jared Michael is crying while he runs down the hallway in a diaper. His little feet are soaked in gasoline. You can see the footprints on the kitchen linoleum. "Mama!"

"Oh, my God, if he gets near the fire—" Ashley wiggles her hands. I am wiggling my hands. Nothing is happening. The cords aren't slipping.

"Okay, okay," I say. Because I don't want to die, and I realize I AM REALLY GOING TO DIE. But I've made it out of worse things.

I escaped my mama and John John. I jumped off a cliff today. "I thought Josh picked us because we weren't fighters like the others. But we're alive," I tell Ashley. "Still. He was wrong. We're fighters. We can—break the chair. We can break the chair." I lean into her and see Crazy Josh slip into the baby's room, which Jared Michael just ran out of. "We can jump in the air and come down on the legs. It will break the wood. We can slip out of the cords."

Obviously, Ashley doesn't know that I'm just winging being clever. Because she says: "Okay, count to three. Jump. Then we'll push up and jump toward the oven."

"Well, that was a brilliant idea," Ashley hisses while we lay on our sides. The chair's are completely intact. We did count. We did jump. But we never made it to the oven. Both of us just keeled to the right and fell over. And oh, my shoulder is killing me. I think I have a splinter from the wooden seat on my butt.

"Do you have a better idea?" I'm asking her. But she's already coaxing Jared Michael over, whispering sweet nothings and telling him to go outside. "Run!" Her eyes veer toward the back door, her head bobbing in the direction. "Go, baby, go, go, go!" She comprehends what I'm finally grasping. We're almost dead. The house is one big burning ball of hell. The smoke is pouring into the kitchen, and the scent of burning wood and plaster makes my nostrils ache. Then, we can hear crashes in the living room. BOOM! BOOM!

"I'm out!" Ashley lifts a hand into the air, then another. It seems like an eternity; she is tugging on the cords on my wrists, pulling. I can feel them come free with the prickles that come with wrists, hands, and fingers caught in a death grip. That's when the gunshot blows in the living room. That's when Josh comes barreling through the room, across the linoleum, and stands where Ashley is snatching up Jared Michael. I don't know what he shot at or who. I am just rising from a squatting position, watching his wide-eyed frantic retreat and watching him bring up the gun again.

Everybody always tells me I've got a mouth on me. I'll admit I do. I can't say that I throw a punch often. One time, on a school bus when I knew two boys were going to beat up Little Pete, I did. But it is like my reputation began preceding me after that. I just had to use my sassy mouth, swagger a bit. Still inside, I cowered.

When Josh lugged up his gun to shoot into the kitchen, it was one of those rare times I got my punch on. I know he knew we were heading out the door. The cops must have been in front. He was trapped. I think he was ready for a standoff. I wouldn't let him get to that point because I'd had it. I had enough of getting the crap beat out of me by jerks. But he's not a little guy. I knew I wasn't a match for him unless I did what Pops told me *never* to do to a boy again after I did it to Kenny when we were wrestling in the backyard when we were ten. Kenny cried for a half hour when I drew my leg back, aimed it between his legs, and let the pointy toe of my cowboy boot fly. Such I did to Josh. The man keeled over with a wispy trail of breath slipping through his pursed lips. I knew I only had so much time for him to catch his breath, think past the aching balls. I lunged on top of him and started whaling on him with my fists just like I did Bear so many years ago.

I think I was still on my knees on Josh's back, still pummeling him, when I felt the fireman's arms wrapping around me, dragging me out the back door. Josh didn't make it. Just as we crested this little wooden back porch, the furnace in Ashley's house exploded. They said you could hear the explosion a mile away. Right before the blast pushed the fireman forward, I saw Ashley with Jared Michael. I saw Josh, his face being peeled back by the flames. Then, the fireman and I were buried in a blanket of smoke, ash, and bricks.

Chapter –37
Hospital Drama

"I've seen better decisions made by Kenny's pigs when they bust between his legs to get away from getting slaughtered," Pops grumbles at me.

"HAHA," I fake a laugh. It is a little loud. I can tell because Pops leans back and winces. "SORRY, THE EXPLOSION HURT MY EARS." I see him looking around. People stare at me with these little pursed lips like I just burped out loud. I slide down in my chair. My nose is still bleeding a little. I have a black eye again. I have two fat lips and a massive bump on my head, and the doctor told me I don't have a concussion, but I need to be watched for twenty-four hours. And I still can't get the smell of gasoline out of my nose.

"It hurt all our ears," Pops says.

"HUH?" I ask.

"IT HURT ALL OUR EARS."

I nod. My ears are ringing. We are sitting in the waiting room at Brink Hollow Community Hospital. I, Pops, Uncle Craig, and Kenny are on one side. Pops has his arm around my shoulders so hard I can't breathe. Kenny is holding my hand, something he has never done except when I dug my claws in and made him pray with Martha. It's creepy and comforting both at once.

Amelia Vega's entourage of family and friends, Preacher Murphy and his wife, Meghan Reynolds, and her mother, are on the other side. Amelia has been down in the recovery room with Bear. I am getting dirty stares from everyone but the Murphys. No surprise. But I'm not the one who told Bear to try to knock on Ashley's door. Unfortunately, he didn't have all the weight to shove into it anymore. Josh let out a shot from his rifle that went straight through the door and caught Bear on the shoulder. He just got done with surgery.

"You know, if it hadn't been for that police officer pulling us over, we wouldn't have headed to that woman's house," Pops says. Bear heard me start his truck. It is loud. It's got that guttural growl of a diesel truck. When he heard it, he ran to the office and called Pops.

Pops picked him up, and they were heading back home, having no clue where I'd gone when Pops got pulled over for speeding. "I told him we were in a hurry. We had a sick friend we were taking to the hospital. He said to me, 'That's funny. Where are you all from? I had a girl pass through here about an hour ago, doing about ninety-five miles an hour and heading to Brink Hollow.' Bear knew exactly where you were heading."

"It was a good excuse," I say, poking Pops in the shoulder. "Some old man I know told me to say that if it's an emergency."

"Baby, what you did was a dumbass thing to do." I have never seen Pops cry. When he saw me crawling out of the bricks with the fireman, he had tears running down his cheeks. I can't get his face out of my mind. It freaks me out. I keep looking at him, trying to read him. He keeps smiling a flat-line smile in return.

"Yes, I know."

Kenny is slumped in his chair. He nods toward the hallway. I follow his gaze and see Amelia Vega coming down the hallway. "Brandy Andy Pandy, if you're going to talk to her. Now's the time to do it." He releases my hand and gives my elbow a pat forward.

I don't want to talk to Amelia Vega. I know I *must* do it. There's no chance that we're going to do the Redneck Run if I don't. I still have no clue if she is pressing charges. For the first time in a long time, my cousin Kenny is pumped to do something other than hunting or watching wrestling on T.V. I've never seen him excited. He really wants to kick Lynn Houck's butt in the ATV racing. It seems he looked the guy up online. He used to race cars about ten years ago, some little foreign things. Then he went into selling cars. He's not even a hunter or an outdoorsman. He lives in some little swanky town in California, far away from what Kenny would define as being anything close to redneck.

He made a remark in American Pro Hunter magazine about having some hillbilly blood two generations back. That's why he'll win the race. There was a picture of him on the front cover wearing a camo suitcoat with a can of chewing tobacco in one hand and a rifle in the other. A Confederate flag waved behind him. Kenny was livid. It was insulting. He went off about stereotyping, then went out and shot at the magazine for an hour. *Passion*. It was nice to see this in my cousin.

I catch Amelia Vega before she makes it to the waiting room, where we all sit. "I was wondering," I am trying not to yell at her. I just want to talk to Beau a minute before we go. The doctor said you aren't letting anybody see him. There might be some sort of restraining order." I have to stop her just as she comes out into the hallway. I stand up against the wall, my hands behind my back, trying hard to look as meek as possible. It just doesn't come naturally. I know I'm as rigid as a two-by-four. She nearly walks past me. "Beau is busy with his fiancé now."

"Fiancé?"

"Yes, that is what I read in the newspaper last week," she says unemotionally. "But we haven't crossed paths much lately." She is ready to walk away. I see her looking over my shoulder vying for an escape. I shift toward her, trying not to lose her attention.

"I'm sorry."

She stops and turns her attention to me. "For what? For dragging my son into this mess? A thousand sorries will not get you out of the trouble you've caused him, the terror you have put me through tonight. This is going to be a disaster for our reputation." Amelia Vega doesn't have an expression. Her eyes are just plain cool, staring at me. She is looking impatiently from left to right. I feel like an ant that she is readying to squash beneath her little black flats.

"And letting a serial killer go is much better for your reputation? He helped save three little kids and their mama." I growl, then snap my jaws shut as if it will help me control my temper. "My mamaw used to tell me we are no better than the company we keep. If I were you, I'd be more worried about your bodyguard, Big Don." Stop! I force my anger down with a hard swallow. "There are rumors you are going to press charges against me and get a restraining order at the last minute so that I can't do the Redneck Run. My team has worked hard at it. Our community is rooting for us. They *need* it. I need it. We need it."

"Really? You are going to bring this up now?" She laughs sarcastically and starts to walk. "You're ludicrous. And you should be happy I'm the bad guy stopping you from letting them down."

"I have been banned from your resort and country club. I can't talk to you anywhere else. So *yes*, right here. I am asking you to let us do this. My sponsor invested a lot of money so we can compete.

I—guess what I'd like to do is make a deal with you. I don't want to let anybody down. I was wondering if there is anything I can do to stop you from pressing charges and getting a restraining order."

She rolls her eyes, looking over my shoulder. "Sometimes I forget where you came from until you say something ignorant like that," she says. "No, I won't make a deal with you. I make too much money to make deals with people like you. I can get a thousand of you knocking at my door for eight bucks an hour, willing to do anything for a job. They are willing to sacrifice everything—their families and pride." She gets this little stiff smile on her lips. "What will you sacrifice? What if I said you'd have to stay away from Beau?"

I knew this might be something she would throw out there. I didn't really have a set plan if she did. But I recognize the fact that as much as Bear doesn't want to believe he's the one who initiated the relationship, he is the one who has been pursuing me. "I'm not the one who is knocking at his door all the time, Missus Vega," I reply, probably a little too smugly because I can see the glint in her eyes that she knows this already. "You know, you're going to lose him eventually," I declare. Her face is expressionless for a couple breaths. Then she sniffs a haughty laugh.

"*We're* going to lose him eventually," she returns. She smiles, and her eyes veer to the waiting room where Meghan's mother is sitting. "And just so you know, I'm not so worried about me. If you mean Meghan, she'll keep him around. You, I'm not so sure. Megs probably doesn't want a girl that's prettier than her hanging around with her husband." I start to say something; she holds a hand and shakes her head to halt my words. "No, you listen to me this time." I know she waits a moment to see me sweat, just to draw out the fact she knows she's got me under her thumb. "Just so you know," Amelia hisses. "I'm not cutting a deal with you because of what you came from or because you're argumentative. It isn't bad to have the confidence to speak your mind," she tells me. "The reason I'm not cutting a deal with you is because I see you made it out in one piece from whatever ill-bred pigsty you came from. I see my son as a different man; I see what you did for him—everything I couldn't do, couldn't understand. I'm not cutting a deal with you because I think if you put your mind to it, just like you did with my son, just like you do with everything else, I have no doubt you'll win that race."

I know I must have had the same expression someone would have if Preacher Murphy came strolling down the hallway without any clothes on, doing a jig, and singing a bawdy song. My mouth is slightly parted, my head tipped to one side, and my brow furrowed. Did I hear her wrong?

"So maybe you're thinking nobody else believes in you. You are wrong. And you're wrong about my son. I don't think he even let his gaze sweep past those two dullard in-bred twins. He made a beeline toward you from the very start. But I've been married enough that I know it isn't you, and it isn't me who makes the choices. It is the man. They marry one for the money or the show, and the other they keep around because they love them, they desire the outside appeal, or they love to wear the bling around their neck. He'll choose; if he listens to me, it will be the money or the show. Girls like Meghan are easier to get along with, easier to hide the defects, and easier to mold. You'll be the necklace like you are now, sweetie."

"I'm not somebody's whore if that is what you are implying."

"Well, yes, you are. I know he bought a ring. It was actually in the newspapers before he said anything to anybody. You don't have it on your finger and are sleeping with him right now."

"You don't know that."

"I was married five times. I knew each time when my husband was running around. I think there's something in the swagger, something in the smile."

"Oh, just go to hell. I don't need you defining me based on you and your twisted relationships."

"And that's how you always end your battles. You make a big show, blow up, and walk out."

"It's kept me alive this long," I spit, and then I feel my shoulders fall. I'm just too tired to fight. "I don't know what else to do. I could call a few newspapers and let them know the real hometown team is getting barred because you don't like the way we look, the way we act, and the idea we might win."

"Haha, that's pathetic. Do you think after this, they'll believe it?" Amelia mutters. "I'll make it easy on you. Stay away from my son, and you can run. Easy-peasy." She pushes a finger into her hair and tucks it behind one ear. Then she holds up one manicured finger.

"Before you answer, just so you know. He's been asking for you. What choice will you make?"

"Was Bear really Josh's half-brother?" I spit it out, flinging it at Amelia Vega like a snowball packed with shards of ice. She flinches, freezes, and wavers.

"Who told you that?"

"Josh did. On the phone last night."

"Did—did you tell Beau?" She reaches out, latches on to my arm, and draws me close. "Does he know?"

"I didn't tell him anything. I just assumed he did. I thought it was the reason he set me up and turned me in to the cops," I tell her. "Before I go in and start yelling at him for not letting me know, I just thought I'd get a heads up."

She snatches my arm tighter and pulls, eyes wavering over my shoulder. "Don't. Please don't. He has enough issues worrying about turning out like his father. I don't want him —knowing his mother is Elizabeth Devereauxs and that he will go crazy like Josh."

"Josh wasn't crazy until his mom built a meth lab in their back garage, Missus Vega. He was just as normal as you and me until he started dabbling in the drugs."

She is looking back and forth between my eyes. It doesn't matter to her. I see it. "I'm horrible with secrets," I say. "You need to tell Beau."

"No."

Chapter –38
Dandelion Seeds

It is seven in the morning. Pops doesn't ask why I stay at the hospital. He sits there with me, snoring with a blanket tucked under his head. Kenny is playing some games on his phone. Bear has texted me ten times from the work phone his mom brought him. I haven't answered until he writes this. *I'm starving. They keep wanting me to eat this fattening, unhealthy hospital garbage.*

I laugh to myself. It is like a thousand times he called me in the middle of the night, sitting there with a fork stuck in a gigantic slice of coffee cake and knowing I'll talk him down. I push up from my chair. Kenny looks up and gives me a smile. "You going to see him?"

"Yeah, I suppose." He heard the conversation between me and Amelia Vega. He knows the consequences. He doesn't judge me. That's why I like my cousin so much.

"And it's like phone sex to you, talking to me about food at two in the morning," I tell Bear when I walk around the corner of his room. "Hey, baby, I'm really craving whipped cream and cherry. I'm begging you, let me have the cherry."

"Well, I'm not thinking about food anymore."

Bear looks pale, lying in the bed. They've got him sitting up, and the TV is on. He's watching some 1970s sitcom, and the canned laughter bounces off the walls. That's when I tell him, "I hate your mother." He laughs a little. I sit down on the tan vinyl chair in the corner. "She said you wanted to talk to me. She didn't tell me you got all dressed up for the occasion." I point to the bit of hospital gown sticking out of the sheets at his shoulders. "That said, I'm still wearing the same clothes I wore two days ago."

"Nice, huh?" he jokes back. "I just wanted to see you, and make sure you were alright." He keeps looking at my face. I know he wants to say something about bumps, bruises, and scratches. He doesn't. Instead, he gets this puppy-eyed gaze like Pops does when I skin a knee, and he yearns to wish the pain over to himself so that I don't suffer.

"I know. Me, too." I yawn into my hand. My back hurts, my legs are sore, and my face looks like I was tackled by a professional football player.

"No, not as much physically as mentally, Bejesus," He says softly. "Your ex-husband is dead. The man you've been sitting in a bar waiting to return for the last three years, chasing around West Virginia, Tennessee, and Ohio."

"I know. But that's one phoenix that isn't going to come flying out of the ashes." I do know. He didn't have a chance. My last sight of Josh was him rolling just enough to get up. Then there was the explosion. When the coroner came in a few hours ago, he told me there were no remains except for a piece of his wallet and a wedding band. "Hmmm, wonder which wife it was from?" I answered. Everybody wouldn't stop staring at me after that. Most people hadn't heard the whole story yet. I don't know what they expect. I just stood there and nodded. I refused to talk to the reporters that poured in the doors. Pops got the security to make them leave.

"And you're alright?"

"Would you be? I don't know. I'm numb and feel a little sad. I guess—I guess I've spent so long already thinking he was dead. Knowing he is dead now isn't so bad. It is just—it hurts. But everybody else made it out alive. Oh, and I hear you're quite the hero." I can't get comfortable in the chair, so I slide up. Bear blinks at my change of subject matter. He goes with it, though. "Pops said you came through the front door after you got shot and grabbed up Ashley's two older boys while she was scrambling to get out with her littlest one."

"You would have done the same thing."

"Yeah, I wish I could, but I was tied up. Haha," I say dully. Bear chuckles. I hold up my wrists. They have bruises from the cords. "I've never been tied up by a guy before. I don't like it."

"Wrong guy. Wrong situation."

"We need to stop this," I say flat out. I start to get up. Bear drops the smile. I know he knows I'm not talking about the insinuations. "We have to stop *this*."

"I knew this was coming." He pushes himself up.

"What did you expect, Bear?" I ask him. "You proposed to her.

You know me. You know I don't want to be my mama. I don't want to be somebody's second choice. I want a guy that looks at me and says I'm the only one. Period."

"Like Chase? He says you're his future wife."

"I know, and yeah, I think so."

It is quiet. "I didn't propose to anybody," Bear says quietly. "And I wasn't the one who started it." There's a shadow slipping across the door. I snap my eyes upward, waiting for a person to enter. The warning of a clearing of a throat lets me know it is Gabe who rounds the door and leans on the frame.

"Hey, sorry to interrupt. We have to head out and get some sleep." Gabe is strangely solemn. Maybe he heard what I said. Perhaps he's just being like everybody else, staying out of my way. Nobody seems to know how to talk to me suddenly. It is like I've got an incurable disease, and they are afraid they'll catch it. "I, um, just wanted to stop in. I think they will release you soon anyway. Did they tell you that?"

"Yeah, late this afternoon." Bear still has his eyes on me. So does Gabe. He looks like he wants to say something. He doesn't. I'm easing toward the door. Bear gives Gabe a wave. "Thanks for sticking around."

"I'm coming with you," I say to Gabe. "Hang on."

"Brandy, wait a minute." Bear is scooting down the bed like he's trying to get up. "Don't leave. I wanted to talk to you. I just thought I'd wait until after the Redneck Run to deal with everything —"

I stop and throw my head back. I'm at the door. I take a breath and watch Gabe stop a step away. "What, Bear? Make the decision of whether you're sticking with Meghan and keeping me on the side? Or keeping me after all the press is off your back because I'm not good enough for you? I'm not an idiot. I've heard men tell my mama that about every weekend since the day I was old enough to understand the meaning," I tell him softly. "Okay, so maybe I started it. It was for the wrong reason. She pissed me off, you get it?" It was a belly punch without a fist. I saw it in his face. I should never have said it. It was true. And then again, it wasn't.

"Okay, if you want to play that game, Brandy, I used you too. You are just like your mama, flirting it up and then following through.

Do you have no morals? You knew I was dating her. You knew I didn't want to hurt her. I didn't want to spoil her ability to run that race. You've got a stone's chance in hell of winning, Brandy. Come on, be realistic. They've been training daily on the best equipment available in the world, and you? You've been running around in the woods."

"Ow." I hear Gabe say. I see him putting on the brakes, his eyes closed like he doesn't want to say anything. Oh, but he will. "Okay." Gabe comes around me and steps back into the room. Bear has to turn to see him. He's pale and has dark circles beneath his eyes. "I'm going to say something. I'm not doing this anymore. Dude, you realize what you are saying, right?" Gabe pivots on his feet and holds a hand out at me because my mouth is open to finish what I'm saying. "Because what I'm hearing and what everybody else on the floor of this hospital is hearing is that *it is more important to you that Meghan's feelings aren't hurt*. It is more important that you don't ruin Meghan's team's ability to win. I assume the resort has dropped an incredible amount of money into the local coffers to use them in their promotions. You forget, bud, that's what I do. Art and marketing. I get that. But when it starts hurting other people, you've got to step away. Right now, the almighty dollar is making the decisions for you. To hell with Brandy. To hell with all your friends who have supported you for the last six months and an entire town that supports her. Why would you say something so utterly stupid, so insensitive, so incredibly cruel? If you said that to me, I'd be out the door, too."

"He's probably worried he'll go to hell because he promised your daddy he'd fix me," I say. I start around Gabe. I am tired, and I want to cry. "Isn't that right, Bear? Preacher Murphy gave you a job when you came back. Save that poor hillbilly from turning out like her mama. And I'm still broke. Oh, wait, I forgot. This entire charade started with Big Don using *you* to try to get me to squeal that I knew who killed your father. But you couldn't get me to do it because I did not even know anything about your dad. Well, and I'm broke."

"I have no clue what you are talking about." Bear scrubs a hand over his head. "Damn, guys, I don't get what's going on. Brandy, please don't go. It's just the medicine making me loopy. I didn't mean it."

Gabe has a puzzled furrow of his brow, eyes narrowed. But it isn't at Bear. It is at me. "What are you talking about?" Gabe asks.

"I'm not an idiot, Gabe. I know what everybody thinks of me."

"Maybe you don't. Because I think Brandy, it was the other way around. My family didn't have a clue about Bear's father; he wasn't even in the picture. My dad brought Beau's conduct up at the supper table one night after he fired two busboys because they were *local*. Dad said if anyone could make that boy see the light, be a better person that it would be that little girl who lives up on Fire Mountain, Lee McAllister's daughter. She's got heart. I took him to the bar that Friday night to meet you. *He's* the broke one, not you."

I grin at Gabe. I know he must see a world of deliverance in my face because he tips his head and for just a moment, we get this friend-bond when I let him in. I feel almost as if this great burden is released. Then, I turn to Bear. "Well, it's a good thing I didn't die in that house last night. I certainly wouldn't be going to heaven, would I?" I utter. "Because I've failed orders from higher up." I narrow my eyes and focus back on Gabe. "A heads up, please, next time, so I can put more effort into it? He's still a shit." He gives me a thumbs-up.

Gabe is walking beside me in the hallway. I told him about the deal Amelia Vega made with me. "I just ruined it, didn't I?" I say. "I shouldn't have gone to see him. My team's out of the competition. Big Don's got it out for me. She knows it."

"That's bull. Big Don is out of the picture. He is on administrative leave. My mom heard it yesterday when she went to drop off cookies at the station. It's internal. They won't say what it is."

We stop when I get to Pops. I knock his knees with my own. "Come on, old man, wake up."

"I'm awake." He wasn't. I could hear him snoring down the hall.

"Come on. I'm done with Bear. I want to go home."

"You're not sticking around until he's released?" Pop yawns.

"No, his fiancé is here. His mom is here. He doesn't need me—"

"Brandy, the man busted a door, got shot, and walked through fire for you. What more do you want him to do to show he cares about you? I don't know many who would do that for a woman."

"I wanted to make sure it was really me he was looking for on the other side of the fire, not somebody like Mama. I think I know now."

We're halfway through the parking lot when Pops suddenly stops. "Kenny, go get in the truck. I want to talk to Brandy." He tosses the keys, and Kenny takes them. Pops turns around. He grabs my arm and forces me to look up at him. "Brandy, look me in the eyes." I did, and I saw him working his gaze back and forth between mine. "You worry so much about being your mama. You don't see the forest for the trees. I will tell you something, and I know it will hurt. But you, right now, are your mama when she was your age."

"What?" I try to pull my arm away, but Pops holds on. "It isn't that she —" he leans forward, gets close to my ear. "slept with every man she saw. There are a lot of people who don't find it necessary to wait three dates or get to know somebody before they hop into bed with them. It isn't even that she used them for the money they gave her for it. It was the only way she could put food in your mouth. It was how she did it. She went for the bad ones. And she went for the good ones. But she *pushed away all of them* when they got too close. Every one of them. She pushed me away. I would have loved her for what she was back when you were little and before the drugs. She blew me away. But she just ran."

I am smirking at him when I finally jerk my arm away. "Stop it, Pops." I start to turn and walk. "I know what I'm doing."

"Do you? Because you're walking away. And walking away is what you do best. Because it is exactly what your mama did and what you are doing now, dammit! I do not like talking to your back!"

I stop. Right there in my tracks, throw back my head. I sigh and pivot on my feet. I am almost face-to-face with Pops when he shoves on his brakes.

"Now what?" he asks in defeat.

"You think I should stay." I say, don't ask. I look into Pops' bluer-than-blue eyes, and he looks back at me.

"Yeah, Brandy, I do. Don't do to Bear what your mama did to me. Baby, I still love her. It hurts."

"Okay, I'm scared."

"You just crawled out of a burning building, for heaven's sake, girl. How can anything be more terrifying than that?" Pops groans.

He shakes his head, and then sighs. "If the boy doesn't know you like him, he will always be floundering around wondering. Then, one day, he's gonna be gone. You're a fighter, Brandy. Put up those little dukes and fight for him."

"That doesn't help make the scary go away. What if he leaves?"

"I stuck around, didn't I. I ain't leaving you, Brandy, never. You're tough to live with. You're tougher to live without."

"Okay, daddy." I bob my head up and down. I trust those eyes looking at me, especially when I call him daddy, and they twinkle.

I'm scared. I'm nervous. I expect Meghan to be in Bear's room when I get there. She's not. He's alone.

"Hey," I say. Bear is on his phone texting someone. He looks up, startled, maybe when I waver at the door.

"I thought you left."

"You're still a shit. I'm like that, you know. You're my work of art. I want to finish things I start." I stop. "Scratch that." I sigh. "Pops says I always walk away. I'm trying something different. I'm sticking around." Standing there while he stares at me, I feel stupid, so I thrust my hand out. "But—everybody else brought you flowers. I didn't. I found you one." I raise my hand, holding out a little dandelion with white flower seeds still sticking on top that I picked in the grass next to the parking lot. "I couldn't find you a fresh orange one. But maybe you need the wishes, huh?"

He puts down his phone, and I walk across the room, handing him the flower.

"Are you staying a while?" he asks.

"Do you want me to?"

"Sit."

"You know, we were kind of like—boom!" I wiggle my fingers in the air in front of me, tiny explosions, while I sit in the vinyl chair and tug it up next to his bed. "Pops says people are like those little dandelion seeds that catch in the wind. I used to pick one, blow those little seeds into the air, and try to make wishes on each of them. Sometimes, they'd collide, catch on each other, and I'd try to peel them apart." Bear is looking intently at the little orange seed petals of the dandelion, poking the teeny top with his huge finger.

"I mean, I was scared they had different directions to go because they had different wishes I'd attached to them. If they went the wrong way, the wishes wouldn't come true. Pops told me not to. Just let them be. They'll figure out if they'll stick together, which way to fly, or if they will grow together. Sometimes, we're in situations we can't get out of when we collide. It isn't easy. It's messy. I don't know if you want to be my friend or what. Regardless, it is wrong of me not to say anything and think you'll figure it out. It is time to make a choice."

"That was deep."

"I can be quite profound if I want to."

"So —are you asking *me* to make a choice?"

"I wish I was," I tell him. "But we're not the two seeds clinging together. I'm not the dandelion, not the seeds. You and Meghan are the ones floating there. You two are alike, from the same world. Yeah, maybe you'd like bumping around with me a while. You'd like the messy, the adventure of it. But then, you'd get tired of all that." I look at the floor and stare at my bony knees. "So, I suppose I'm saying that I'm the one holding the dandelion still in my fingers, puffing out all these wishes, hopes, and dreams around me. I could reach out and pull you two apart. I can't. You'd hate me for it."

"I'm the one holding the dandelion, Bejesus." He pushes his fingers in the air, holding the flower aloft. "I suppose I'm the one in control of the situation, right?"

"Yeah, maybe you're right." I shove my feet up on the side of his bed.

"Each of these little seed thingies is a wish, right? And I can have all the wishes on here?"

"Yeah, sure." I nod.

"Okay."

Bear is still staring at me. He's not smiling or frowning, just looking at me hard. "The gunshot in my shoulder didn't hurt as bad as thinking I lost you."

"Yeah, I'm sorry I stole your truck." I poke him with the toe of my boot and work up a little smile.

"Yeah, that was wrong. I get three free car washes and a hand wax for that one. You didn't ding it like you did Pops' truck, right?"

"No. I treated her like a baby barring the paint peeling off one side in the explosion. But that wasn't my fault."

Just then, he looks up. I crane my neck around and see Amelia Vega just inside the doorframe. Meghan and her mother are standing with her. "Oh, we didn't know you stayed around," Amelia Vega says. She looks wary before the expression passes. Almost immediately, Amelia is smug, as I figure Satan would be after she closes a deal. Yes, I suppose she won this one. I see Meghan trying to catch Bear's eyes. She doesn't seem to know if she should come into the room or turn around. Her eyes veer to Amelia as if she expects her to make the decision.

"Beau," Meghan says, slipping inside after a nudge from her mother. She walks right in front of me and places herself shrewdly between me and Bear. My foot falls off the bed, and I sit up. "Mother and I are prepared to stay with you this afternoon. I am skipping the interviews with the journalists from Canada. Michelle and Janie can handle them." She pauses, leans over, places her hand on Bear's arm, and kisses him on the forehead. "I want to stay with you. Your mother approved my absence. I thought we could—hang out and watch T.V." She turns to her mother first and gets approval, then spins around to look down at me. "Just you and me, nobody else."

I am finishing a text to Bear. It goes like this: *What do you want me to do? Leave. Stay. Girl fight.*

"Brandy," Meghan clasps her hands at her waist. It is a defensive posture. "I'm sure you are ready to leave, go home, and get some bed rest. You've had a long night."

I can hear Bear's phone ring with my message. Since I can't see around Meghan, I don't know if he even looks at it.

"I kind of planned on staying." I am sure she can read my posture, too. I feel like I'm surrounded by her wolf pack. "My Pops and Kenny left to get my uncle's truck and take it home."

"I can catch the Murphys," Meghan says. "You can ride with them."

"Excellent then," Amelia Vega waves her hand at me like she is shooing me toward the door. "That means we're all set. Brandy, I can walk you out if you like."

I get a text, look down: *Girl fight. Oh, please. Ringside seats.*

I lean to the right and gaze at Bear around Meghan's side. "Are you sure?" I start to rise. Meghan snaps her eyes to Bear, then to me. "Is he sure about what?"

"Nothing, Megs," Bear's eyes are wide. I know he thinks I'm serious. "I already talked to Brandy about staying. Maybe you can come back later." He can't see the smile playing on my lips. He's caught between being alarmed that I might grab Meghan and flop her to the floor before his mom and being a bit turned on about the entire concept.

"Beau, I think it would be best if Meghan stayed with you, sweetheart." Amelia primps her hair with her finger. She leans forward and tugs on my shirt. "Come on, Brandy, I'll walk—"

"No, mom, Brandy's staying." Bear is sitting up in bed. "We've been through a lot today. I need to talk to her. She needs to talk to me. You all go back. You've got work, and the girls have interviews. Don't make it complicated. Brandy can sit with me."

"I won't!" Meghan is clenching her fists at her waist and stomping her right foot. "I won't leave, I won't. I won't." I think she is kidding at first; she acts like Kaylee when she misses her eight o'clock bedtime by five or ten minutes. "It isn't fair. I don't like her. I don't want her to be around Beau! Mommy, go get Daddy so he'll make her go home! It is his fault! He told me he was going to put her in jail until she rots for saying mean things to me, and he didn't! He promised! All's he did was tear up her truck!"

I have no clue how to deal with an adult two-year-old, and she is staring at me with a stink eye, her lips pursed. I watch her bring back both her hands like she is going to shove me. I hold up my own to keep her at bay. "You don't want to do that," I say flatly. I am leaning back a bit on the chair, planning a way of escaping to the door. She would have gone through with it if Amelia Vega hadn't stepped between us and grabbed her hand.

"Meghan, maybe you are sleepy. I think you need a—nap."

"She is," her mother coos at her, giving me a dirty look. "She's been through a lot today. I'm going to take her home. Let my little boo-boo get some rest."

I don't say anything after the three leave through the door. Bear is eyeing me cautiously. I sit down, scoot the chair, and shove my foot on his bed. "Okay, where were we?" I say. "I was apologizing for stealing your truck."

"Can we skip forward to the girl fight?" He works up a smile.

"It wouldn't have been much of a fight on any level," I mutter. "I'm not judging you for wanting to be with her. She is cute. But dude, she's like a seven-year-old."

"Yeah, a bit spoiled."

"A bit—*something*." I look at him.

"Listen, I'm lying here thinking about the dandelion, about choices and wishes. Before I immortalize it in gold, I need you to know something. Some stuff I can hide from my mom. I can't hide it from you."

Oh no. This is where Bear tells me he's really in love with Gabe, or good God; what could he possibly tell me that would be worse than what he has seen me go through over the last six months? "Break it to me gently," I kid him. My stomach jumps.

"You know, I told you I was adopted, right?"

"Yeah."

"Josh was my half-brother. That lady at the bar that wanted to fight you, Lizzy Devereauxs, she's my birth mother. It wasn't my dad that I wanted to end up like. It was her." Bear is pale. "Now it is him—Josh. I'm scared you'll find out and think I will go crazy like Josh."

"Bear, Josh already told me that last night. I'm here." I move my chair closer, lean, and rest my hand on his arm. Then he slides his hand over. He's got my fingers twining in his. "Yeah, it was a shock. I just never even thought about it. Unless you're a meth addict, you will *never* be him. I guarantee it. I can tell you the exact moment Josh changed from nice to his evil counterpart and transformed from good Dr. Jekyll to bad Mister Hyde. It was the day he went to his mom's house, and she turned him on to meth. It was like the Josh I knew died that day. That was when he started getting mad at me constantly and going out. I just didn't want to believe it. I didn't understand." I look up. He's gazing at me. "You are just so lucky your dad wanted you, that *your mom*—Amelia wanted you."

"You know, speaking of moms. It was always my dream to sing. That's why I minored in music. Mom told me it was a pipedream. I should have just bucked and changed my major from management to music. I didn't. I always feel like I'm putting everybody else's priorities first."

"I did notice you were not good at prioritizing because of the way you overlooked me and followed what your mother wanted you to do," I tease him. "Seriously, though, if it is your dream, you must go for it, Bear."

"Naw, it isn't so much now. I like directing the choir at Holy Trinity and singing for the church. It keeps me centered."

"Like me running. I can't do it for a living. Wish I could."

"Well, right now, I'm thinking about dandelions and not living up to somebody else's dreams right now."

"It's your dandelion now." I shrug. "Your decision."

"So—you're not going to freak out, do this?" he waggles one arm in the air and winces. I roll my eyes. "You're not going to run to my mother and tell her I have different dreams. That I know about my birth mother. Because I think she would wig out."

"You're an idiot, you know that, right?"

"You keep telling me that. I don't see it."

He makes me laugh. I suppose that's why I put up with all his shit.

Chapter –39
Breaking Bobby Out

The town is filled to the brim with people and crowds everywhere. It is like some bizarre county fair. Every street is jam-packed with booths, games, and people running around in straw hats and bandanas. Instead of a rodeo, there's a mud bog race. The horse shows are replaced with the ugliest pickup contest. There are wheelbarrow races, live bands, and a huge pig roast. I think I just saw a man lugging around a toilet as part of a float for the parade. There are three hours and ten minutes to the starting time.

I'm with Gabe and Ben at a little booth in front of Mister Smiley's. It is a large tent with a big, nice banner advertising, LITTLE BEND OF SALT SPRINGS–SPONSORS OF THE *GENUINE* FIRE MOUNTAIN REDNECKS. It matches our shirts, except on the back of the shirt, it says: Kiss my Bad Ass. The 'ad' is crossed off, so it looks like it says 'Kiss my B Ass.' A smallmouth bass is embroidered at the top, and a girl in jean shorts and a t-shirt is leaning over, kissing the bass. That was Gabe's idea. There is a stuffed bass my Aunt Jenny sewed together hanging from the front of the tent. It has a little sign that says: Kiss me for good luck! People have actually come by and kissed it.

Our tent is one of eighty-two, each representing the teams in the competition. Inside, there are brochures and a big picture of our team. I've worn the same camo jean shorts as in the image. They are way too small. Pops about crapped when I left this morning. And I'm wearing a black teeny-weeny tank top squeezing me so tight, I can't breathe. It keeps crawling up my tummy and almost to my boobs. And I am donning cherry red lipstick Gabe picked out that sticks better than the permanent marker trail of circles Kaylee left along the living room wall this morning. Oh, and I'm wearing my beanie cap like the binky Kenny used to suck on and hide under his pillow until he was four. Between luck and heavy foundation, I don't appear to have a single bruise. I'm like a dress-up dolly for Gabe— the same kind of half-naked girls in the Backwoods Babe soft porn magazine Kenny keeps tucked between his mattress and bedsprings that slip out occasionally.

I'm glad for this. It is keeping my mind from running back to the image of Josh's face before the explosion over and over again. However, I am not comforted by Gabe's presence, nor Kenny's and Martha's. They keep noting how many more people are here than last year. I'm feeling ill to my tummy waiting and watching for Bobby Reese. Ben's friends keep stopping in to wish us well. I think he knows everybody in West Virginia, half of Ohio, and Tennessee. I know some of them from going to his place. They honestly seem to like me and Gabe and have welcomed us into their pack like one of their own and like we've always been among them.

We're handing out homemade beef jerky to people walking past. It just stopped raining. Everything is puddles, mud, and humidity, making me sweat. And mosquitos. I can't stop scratching my arms with all the little bumps on my flesh. Right now, I'm lying back in the claw foot tub that is holding all the jerky, and I'm texting Pops. He's picking up Bobby Reese and bringing him down. People keep stopping and taking pictures of us. I don't know if it is just because they've never seen real rednecks before, or they think we're just plain weird. I feel like I'm in a freak show.

"God, you are beautiful. Can I take your picture?"

That deep voice is Junior Riley. He's nineteen and drives a jacked-up truck parked in the lot at Smiley's a few minutes ago. His pickup has this guttural growl like Bear's truck. It is big and hurts my ears each time he drives by and tries to show off by hitting the gas. He has plump cheeks that remind me of a beaver, and he hangs out in Smiley's parking lot with other boys after closing. He keeps standing over me and taking pictures of me with his cell phone. This is the third time he's stopped today. He brought four friends with him this time.

"No," I say. "Go away, Junior." He has gotten to the point where I think he is stalking me. The other boys stand there and gawk at me with big stupid grins, taking pictures.

"Yes, you can," Gabe says. "Have at it!" I turn my head and glare at him. "It's good for marketing." He tells me. He fiddles with his phone for a minute while the boys smile stupidly at me. "See? Remember those three men from Huntington who came over a little bit ago? They gave me their info. They've already got pics of you on their websites."

I scoot up and look at the image he is showing me. Pops is going to hit the roof. It is mostly me posing with each as I've done with what feels like a thousand people today. Gabe set up a few bales of hay for a backdrop. But one of those idiots got me leaning over the cooler, tugging out a bottled water. You can see down my shirt and up my shorts all the way to my black panties with red lace, both at once.

"Nice," Ben says with a low whistle. "It has our Salt Springs name all over it." They both analyze it like it was actually my intention to look like a porn star for promotional purposes on every social network and hunting website from here to Alabama. "If she turns just a little bit so her knees are to the left, we can add our logo to the bottom and make a poster."

Gabe thinks this justifies him taking the boys' phones and me standing with each to take a picture. I groan and listen to the little clicks as the boys in front of me take pictures. If that isn't bad enough, a small crowd of onlookers thinks I'm some kind of celebrity and starts taking their own shots.

I groan and text Pops again.

"These people are in so much better shape than we are." That's Martha Hershberger talking. She is chewing on the last remnants of turkey leg she bought at a food booth. She has taken off her bonnet and laid it back. Her hair is beautiful, and she says when it lays down, it goes almost to her butt. Kenny seems to find this curiously fascinating. He keeps reaching out and petting it like it's his mother's toothless, ugly poodle. Kenny is looking at Martha in a whole new light.

The turkey leg was almost as big as her arm. It is now nothing but bone, and the grease riding down her forearms. "I looked up the famous guy I am swimming against. His name is Neal Whitley." Martha rubs her elbows to get rid of the grease. "When he was a kid, he was in the Junior Olympics. I don't know if he's ever swam in anything but a pool. He shaves everything, even his legs." She pulls up her dress to expose the hairiest, whitest legs I've ever seen on a man or woman. "Maybe I should have shaved. I wonder if it really helps make you go faster."

"Have you ever shaved?" Kenny is looking down. His face is all scrunched up like he's looking at a pig's butt. "That's disgusting."

"No, we don't shave." Martha doesn't seem to be bothered that Kenny speaks his own mind. "Do you?" she asks him.

Kenny thinks this is funny and pulls up the hem of his camo pants near his ankles. "Nope. We match. "

Unfortunately, they do, and three or four people passing give us a puzzling gaze. "Real rednecks," I tell them, pointing a finger at Kenny and Martha. "You can pet them if you want. They don't bite." They tuck their heads and walk on while Kenny snorts a laugh.

"You are embarrassing to be around," Gabe tells me. "Oh, you want to compare?" I crane my neck and look up at him. Ben and Gabe are wearing matching outfits—a flannel shirt, tight blue jeans, and cowboy boots. "Dudes, you look like cowboys. There's nothing farther from a redneck than two gay cowboys."

"Brokeback Mountain," Ben says.

I let it go. "You don't have some wiseass reply?" Gabe asks. "Because *we* are the coolest, most fabulous guys here." He grins and bobs his head up and down with a cocky tip of his chin.

I shrug. Using coolest, most fabulous, and guys in the same sentence pertaining to wearing costume cowboy outfits should speak for itself. Dorks. I don't. I'm just lounging in my own pity today. Three hours until the starting time. Everybody's standing on eggshells like they know I will wig out. I'm starting to get nervous, and I think this was a ridiculous idea. I shouldn't have dragged all my friends into something that will humiliate all of us.

Then it happens. I get a call from Pops. "Bobby Reese isn't coming. I'm so sorry. The nurses had no idea he was involved in this, and they won't let him leave."

I had him on speaker. Everyone in the entire tent is silent. "Pops, can't you talk them into it?"

"I tried. Uncle Craig tried. They won't budge."

"Can we sneak him out like we usually do?"

"They've got everybody outside watching the festivities."

I lay there in my bed of jerky. I can hear them announce the beginning of the day's activities. I'm not surprised to hear Bear singing the National Anthem. Ben comes up and sits next to me, pats my back, and tells me it is still cool we're here anyway. Maybe next year we can do this again.

An hour goes by. I pass out jerky and force a smile so folks can take pictures. I check my texts. There's one from Bear. It says: *Did u hear me sing?*

I write back: *Yes, like Angel.* And put an emoji of a smiley face.

Bear: *You okay? Your booth looked crowded.*

Me: *Fine. Little scary, not much. Got tape on my leg to help.* Bear's little list of freak-out helpers.

Bear: *Ready to run?*

Me: *No running. Bobby not coming.*

Bear: *Huh?*

Me: *Nurse won't let him. Kenny mad. Martha cry. Brandy pissed.*

Bear: *I'm sorry.*

Me: *I miss u, Bear. Sorry. I b like Mama 4 u.*

I send it. I wait for the regret, but I don't feel it. He didn't text back. I let it rest and feel stupid. I tell everybody I am going for a walk. Junior is in my face again. I am tired of smiling and afraid I will punch him. It is only one hour and ten minutes before the start time. I hear them begin the announcements over the speakers mounted along the streets. It is just making me feel melancholy and left out. I know I'm walking toward the nursing home. I'm trying to think how I can get Bobby out. I know I can't.

I hear Junior's truck behind me. He is revving the engine. I'm waiting for him to hit his gas, fishtailing around me, showing off. He honks his horn. I jump and flip him the middle finger. "Go away, you idiot!" I yell at him with hands in fists, turning to make sure he sees my face all screwed up in anger. It isn't Junior. It is Bear.

He pulls up and looks hurt. His perfect lips are in a pout, and his eyes look like a pup that just got butt-spanked with a newspaper for chewing up a shoe. "Obviously, you're mad at me. I'm not sure what I did this time. Is it too much to ask for a hint?"

"No, not really. I thought you were—somebody else." I say instead. "I really did." I'm still upset, but seeing Bear makes me feel better, and I recognize that with a surrendering sigh. "What are you doing? I thought you were in charge of announcements and stuff."

"I thought maybe we could break Bobby Reese out of the nursing home."

"You remember the drill. You pull in the back, and I climb into a window. Bobby comes out the back door and jumps in." I recount to Bear when we pull into the parking lot. The only problem is that they are having a picnic on the lawn in front of Bobby's room, where I usually crawl in if the staff is doing their rounds. They all know me. One look at me, and they'll know I'm here to get him. We could pull around back and load him in if I just let him know I was here. The problem is, I need someone less conspicuous to find him.

"Martha." I tug out my phone and text Kenny, asking him to bring Martha over. Kenny is sliding beside us in the parking lot in less than eight minutes. Gabe is on the passenger side, and Martha is in the middle.

"I have a mission for you," I say to them. "We're going to have to break Bobby Reese out if we still want to do the Redneck Run. It isn't going to be easy. But are you all in?"

There isn't a booming whoop and cheer. Martha bobs her head up and down cautiously, and Kenny yawns in the cup of his hand. I think they are just as happy that we aren't going to be in the Run. Kenny's wearing his ball cap, removes it, slaps it on his leg, and puts it back on. "Sure, can somebody grab me a can of pop up there on the picnic table while we're at it? I need some caffeine."

"I take it that's a resounding 'yes.'" I mutter, feeling a bit slighted by their lack of enthusiasm. "Okay, here's my plan—"

Nothing ever goes as planned for me, not even remotely. I get a strategy in my head, and it always seems to play out differently than it does in my mind. I am thankful Bear doesn't remind anybody of this while Gabe slides out of the truck, sneaks around one side of the lot, and lumbers toward one of the nurse aides. He asks her a couple questions. I can see her pointing him toward the inside of the building. His job is to ask her to take him to his fake uncle Rudy, one of Bobby's buddies, who has the room next to him. Gabe can tell Rudy to tell Bobby we are driving to the back of the building where he can sneak out.

However, nobody arrives when we get to the back door and wait. Five minutes pass, then ten.

"Crap. This isn't going to happen, is it?" I ask Bear.

"Okay, you single-handedly chased down a serial killer and caught him. You saved your little sister from John John. And you almost have your college degree," he reminds me. "You've convinced a hard-assed, hard-headed man that he was on the losing side, so I'm here. Surely, you still have enough of that spunk left to bust an old man out of a nursing home for a couple of hours."

"Maybe God's trying to tell me it isn't going to happen." I stop and realize what he is saying. "You're on my side now?"

"Yeah, Bejesus." He looks at me strangely, like I knew this all the time. "I've been here the whole time. I've just been going about it the wrong way; at least, that's what my mother says."

"Your mother?"

"Um," he lets that slide. I don't have time to ask before he goes on. "You see, this little girl, she was about to die in a trailer, and she prays for me instead of herself."

"You prayed for me when I fell through the floor at Brink Hollow."

"I wasn't the one that was going to die, Brandy. You were. You could have prayed for just yourself. Instead, you thought of me and decided some stupid jerk's life was more important. It was pure, steadfast, and selfless. What kind of person does that kind of thing? I don't know. That kind of stuff flips a guy out a bit." He pauses. His face is lacking expression.

"This is different, Bear. My life isn't on the line. I don't see how this is going to work."

"Yeah, and God just handed David those stones to hit Goliath while sitting on his back porch sipping coffee. You heard at least a bit of Preacher Murphy's sermon between your texts and your conversation with Gabe, right?" I stare at him. Is he talking about the race or our friendship? "I don't think so. He had to find the stones. David was on a battlefield in the middle of a losing battle against a giant. Sometimes it's messy. You get mud in your face or have to drop a hundred feet into the nothingness below to kill whatever giant is after you. Hell, girl, I didn't do anything but work in a cubicle and go home before I met you. I'm having the time of my life. Please take me to a new level. Get the old guy out, and let's win this race."

Oh, yes, it was messy. I am walking around the back of the building, finding windows that might be open. I finally feel a wiggle in a frame and creep over the edge. I slide inside to the screams of a little old lady while all the plants on her sill crash to the floor. I swear, I hear Bear laughing while I pop my head up, and sure enough, he's banging the steering wheel with his fists. I decide if I make it out of here without getting arrested, I'm going to whale him again like I did on that school bus.

I'm trying to pick up the little pieces of ceramic planter and plop the plants back in them. I hear a nurse's voice calling over the loudspeaker in the room. "Missus Reed, do you need something?" I'm doing praying hands and begging the old lady not to tell her in mouthed words, but I think she is sure I am going to murder her. I back out of the room while the lady picks up her lunch tray and tosses it at my head.

I swoop from room to room, but almost everybody is outside at the picnic. I finally came across the old man with long hair who smoked the weed in the truck with Bobby when I picked them up for practice. "Randall, you remember me—Brandy? I need to get Bobby and get him to the competition."

"Yeah, I remember you. I'll help if I can come too." *Great.* While I'm unaware that outside, Bobby has already gotten the message that we're trying to break him out, and he talks Edna Hill into pretending a heat faint in her chair to grab attention, Randall goes to the far side of the building and pulls the fire alarm. It is not something I expected. It suddenly sounds like a prison breakout, with people running everywhere and sirens and fire alarms already blaring through town.

"You wanted messy?" I am asking Bear this while he is looking through his rearview mirror, watching twelve old people from the nursing home clambering up into the bed of his truck. "Here is messy." Oh, no, there are thirteen.

"What happened?" he's scratching his head. "I thought it was just Bobby?" I eye three little old ladies donning cheerleader outfits climbing in, and I groan.

"And twelve of his friends that will blackmail me if I don't take them too."

The fire trucks are pulling in, and Bear is nearly peeling out of the parking lot to get to the roadway before they block us. Bear's driving along, trying to blend in with the traffic. He is sticking out like a sore thumb. Bobby keeps holding up his bow while the others cheer him. People walking the sidewalk applaud him, asking him when he will compete. He's a distinguished warrior god going into battle and he has worshippers everywhere. Kenny, driving behind us, isn't helping. He keeps honking his ahooga horn while Martha leans out the window with her fist as if praising Bobby from below.

I laugh nervously and peer over at Bear. He must have been looking at me because he quickly turns his head back to the windshield. I lay my elbow on the window. The sun is hot, but I'm glad the storm has gone. I'm worried about Martha swimming the creek with all the surplus water flowing over the edge. She's not worried at all. "I passed a couple of logs one day on the Ohio River when it hit peak during a flood," she told me earlier with a shrug. I didn't know if she was kidding or not.

"What?" I invite Bear to explain his funny gaze at me.

"I don't know. You look—"

"Yeah, I know. Please don't say it," I respond, smacking my cherry-red lips together. "Like a soft porn star in a Camo Babes magazine. Just give me an ATV and a flag, and I'll stand on a toilet seat planter in somebody's front yard and sell—heck, I don't know, hunter orange boxer shorts or something. Gabe has this demented idea of what a redneck runner should look like."

"I like camo." That's all he says. "I like red lipstick." I'm unsure if he is evoking the memory of our ATV ride up the hill or just being matter of fact. "I suppose I like it a lot."

"It's like you enjoy being a part of this freak show."

"Oh, you don't know how much," he laughs. Then he taps his thumbs on the steering wheel. "I'm going to have to get back. I can drop Bobby off at his starting point first. Listen. I've got to tell you something." Bear stops at a light and scrubs a hand over his face.

"Okay." I laugh a little because he's so serious.

"No, Bejesus, please." He is solemn, unsmiling. "You need to know this."

"Okay."

"Noah Hartley's got two security guards that ride behind him while he runs. They ride on either side of him on the road. You can pass anywhere while they are on asphalt as long as you don't touch Noah. They cannot impede a runner's path or a runner in any way. The tricky part is when he's on the trail. That's when they ride behind him. The tires will take up ninety percent of the path, and you can't go off the trail. If you get caught behind them, you're stuck. They'll be tossing mud in your face like you did that day we went out riding —"

"Why are you telling me this? How do you know?"

"Because they've been practicing on the trail for three weeks."

"I thought that was against the rules, practicing ahead of time on the competition trails."

"Well, they have been doing it," Bear tells me. "I was there watching them. Here's the thing. That means you *must* get around him before the last leg of the trail. Because only four or five miles on the other side is the finish line. If you are close at any point on or before that trail, those security guards will do everything in their power to slow down so you can't catch up to him. What I'm telling you is this—when you are on the last five miles before Boar Mountain, you've got to pass him, or that's it. You're done."

"That's not fair. The packet says the track is kept safeguarded before the event. Hence, everyone has the same degree of experience on the trail. And how can his bodyguards get away with blocking another runner? That is cheating."

"I don't make the rules. They don't follow a standard. That's what gives them the edge, Brandy. The bigwigs at the resort and the visitor center don't want anybody else to win. There's a lot of money sunk into endorsements."

"You still don't think we're going to win."

"The odds are so stacked against your team; I don't know how you can. Martha's up against an Olympic swimmer. Bobby's slow and can't see the targets anymore."

"Pops bought him new glasses. He's gotten much better."

"That's good," Bear clears his throat. Then his smile drops. "Then there's Kenny's race. They got rid of the rules stating all ATVs must be factory-built and pass a third-party, non-biased inspection."

"When did they change this? Kenny had to get his inspected."

"When Lynn Houck, who is riding against Kenny, got an endorsement from an ATV company. His ATV now has a special engine that is incredibly fast and also has special parts developed to take the specific turns made on the course. They have also been using the course to finetune the steering, suspension, and axles," Bear says. "It is a hybrid model one of the companies is designing and putting on the market. They want it to win and use the race for commercial purposes. Houck wants it to win because they've given him half the money upfront. He was drunk the other night and admitted he had already spent that half. He'll do anything to win."

"Gabe is right. This is one big endorsement for products. I wish they were still just mud bog racing out behind the Crazy Kettle."

"Well, they aren't. I want you to win. Does that count for something?" He reaches into his glovebox and pulls out a brown paper sack. "Here. This is for you. No rules against plugging in a cell phone and listening to music while you run, huh? Think about the music, not about the crowds. Mom knows your weakness. She's got a frigging fan club for the Fire Mountain Shadows lined up at every turn on your run. In revenge, I got you a cell phone when I got my new one. I put on a whole bunch of music you can focus on."

I look at him, trying not to seem wary when I take the bag. "What other rules can be bent to make it fair?" I ask him.

"There's really not that many. I think they try to keep it simple."

"If there are outside things like dogs that get on the course, it is just part of the run?"

"Yeah, I suppose."

"And the rules are pretty general about modifying an ATV?"

"You have an hour and ten minutes before the race. I don't think you have enough time to modify an ATV, Bejesus."

"You are underestimating me again, Bear Vega," I reply. He is looking at me. I cross my eyes, but he still doesn't turn away. "Why are you staring at me?" He looks like Kenny's old pig he ended up saving at the end of 4-H week because the kids sell all of them for slaughter to make money. Kenny loves that pig. And that pig loves Kenny, giving him coy sidelong glances when he walks into his barn.

"I don't know. I can't stop."

Chapter −40
Redneck Run

"Pops, we need to use Old Yeller for the race."

It was more than an hour and a half ago, I was standing on the side of the road talking to Pops on the phone, fifty feet from the starting line for the race. I'm watching the runners standing on the sidelines waiting for their ATV rider counterparts to hand them the baton to finish the run. I'm in the dark about my team. Nobody knows anything about their starting or ending times. If we're going to have a chance, Kenny was going to have to kick butt with his ATV.

"Oh, there ain't no way in hell." Pops made a chuckle-laugh, deep and low on the other end. It's the same laugh and line he formerly used when I wanted to stay out later than eleven on a Saturday night in high school.

"Please. I'll clean my room if you let me."

"You need to clean your room anyway. But there ain't no way that boy can ride her. Old Yeller, she's modified, baby girl. She ain't a toy. He's never ridden anything like her before."

"Well, actually, he has. We used to skip school and take it out."

"See, therein lies the problem. You don't respect her or her sire. She's not an 'it'. I'm assuming that's where the dime-size dent on her front end came from six years, four months and three days ago from last Tuesday."

I didn't know if I was helping my situation or not. "Please, Pops. You know what this means to us."

"*Us.*" he seemed to taste this like his first, beloved cup of coffee in the morning. "It isn't just *Brandy* anymore, huh?"

"Huh?"

"You know what?" he said. "What am I hiding that old girl in the garage for anyway. I'll get her down there for Kenny."

"Pops, one other thing. I need a bag of jerky from the booth, opened and in a brown paper sack. Can you take a drive up Crazy Willie's road and ask him to bring his dogs about halfway down the last hill on the run? There's a little gravel pull-off right above Owl Hollow, where Uncle Craig used to park his old truck to coon hunt.

He always said he could hear his dogs baying up that hollow, knew where they were when they got away from him."

"Willie won't shoot me?"

"Just tell him I need him. He'll come. He ate with us. I figure he knows he's family now."

"Baby girl, I hope you know what you're doing."

"Yeah, Pops," I told him softly. "I'm adding a little bit of redneck into this silly, watered-down version of the Redneck Run. It's running like one of those new lemon-flavored light beers now. We need to make it more like Uncle Craig's moonshine. I'm adding some hillbilly juice, if you know what I mean, making the odds a little more in our favor."

There was silence on the other end. I figured Pops would hang up or give me a lecture. Not so. "Well, girl, I suppose a man couldn't be prouder than to raise a girl that knows the difference between the real things and the not-real things in life," he told me. "Win or not, I'm going to die knowing I raised at least one hellion right."

I laughed and felt a little of the woozy leave my tummy. "Oh, before I hang up," I told him. "Tell Crazy Willie when he hears Hartley's ATVs coming up Owl Hollow to let loose the hellhounds. He'll know what that means." I ended the call and shoved my phone into the back pocket of my shorts. Now I'm sitting on a curb waiting.

"Friggin' backwoods hillbilly. Who wears shirts with something like that written on the back? Kiss my Bass. It's just ignorant. And if it isn't ignorant, it's prejudiced."

I barely hear him. I wish I hadn't. Noah Hartley is standing next to me doing these goofy-ass stretches and jumps. He's super skinny and not the pretty kind of slim. His head is shaved, his face is sallow, and he is bony like somebody sucked the juice out of him. He reminds me of those life-size cardboard skeletons Pops glue-sticks on the front porch door on Halloween.

"It's kiss my bad—ass." I stand up bobbing my head up and down to his feminine little jumps. "You know, Kiss my ass. My ass being what you'll see when I pass you."

"You're kidding me in those shoes and those scraggly legs. You realize you'll have to use them to run, right? You'll be lucky if you place."

"She got them at Goodwill," Meghan calls out behind me. "The shoes, I mean." She does that stupid giggle into her palm and looks around at the people lined up along the sides of the asphalt road to make sure she has their attention. "That's the girl I talked about at the banquet last night: *Goodwill.*"

Everybody there can hear her yell it. I don't know if she doesn't realize most of the crowd assembling on the sidelines waiting for the next step in the race has come from the hills and mountains and places between. Some might be from the resort, folks who have seen her on T.V. But I see folks just like me standing there. Not everyone is decked out in the holier-than-thou state of mind like she is. I can see it in the suddenly pinched expression on their faces while they look at Noah, then at me before their eyes fall on Meghan Reynolds. I think she just lost some fans. I see one woman tucking her WE LOVE MEGHAN FIRE MOUNTAIN SHADOWS sign down to her knees.

"I happen to like Goodwill," I shrug while Noah jogs away. "Regardless," I yell after him. "I'll be sure to point that out again when you're staring at my butt after I pass you. Let's say you can kiss my bass. We've got it hanging in front of our tent if you lose. How about that?"

A few people cheer. Noah turns suddenly and gives me a big, fake smile. He caters to the crowd, holding his hands high, marching with skeletal knees popping up high, and clapping. "How about that! I'll do it. I'll kiss the redneck's bass at her booth if she wins. *And she can kiss my ass if she loses!*"

There are more than a few people who find the idea of me kissing Noah's butt appealing, I suppose. There is a lot of laughter that sends my belly into spasms. I let out air from my lips and push in my earplugs to listen to the music Bear put on the phone. 1980s. I'm cool with it.

I'm staring at the phone, wishing I could be anywhere, but here, when I look up just enough, I see a police car stopping ten feet away. Aw, crap. This is it. Amelia Vega is actually pressing charges—

"I have received a complaint of kidnapping from the Grant Rehabilitation and Nursing Center." Calvin the Cop is stepping out of the New Alliance city police car. He slams the door behind him and walks out to me.

"Oh?" is all I say. My eyes are on the volunteers. They are on the sidelines waiting for instructions. As soon as the ATV riders finish, they are informed and run across to tell the team members so they can get prepared. In my case, I will stand at the start line, Kenny will park his ATV at the log at the bottom of his run, sprint over to me, and hand me the small baton with our numbers coded on it. I'm suddenly more focused on watching three runners taking off, keeping my eyes peeled for Kenny. Strangely, Noah's teammate, Lynn Houck, has yet to arrive.

I force myself to look at Calvin the Cop. I hope the crowds watching us will keep him from bullying me like Big Don did. I know what's coming, though. It's the excuse he'll use to drag me into his car, arrest me, and take me to prison.

"I just didn't want him to do it to anybody else," I blurt out. I'm talking about the city prosecuting attorney calling me last night and asking me to make a statement about Don Reynolds abusing his authority by bullying me and impounding my truck. I guess there are cameras everywhere in the station that picked him up hurting me. And there is a bit of a controversy over his inability to solve a crime and a little redneck girl on the mountain figuring it out for him. "Big Don, I mean. I didn't want him to pull any other girls off the road and hurt them."

"Yes, I understand that." Calvin takes a step back. "I'm not here for that." His voice is low, he is bent toward me as if he doesn't want anyone else to hear. "Regardless, I thought you knew I filed the complaint charges on Big Don. I was the one who needed the statements and evidence. That was the reason I pulled you to the front of the car. We have a camera there. I got Don Reynolds harassing you on the camera. I got him misusing his authority to drag you down and question you like he did."

He loses that cop stance and then smiles. "I was hoping you knew I wouldn't let him hurt you. He's been doing this crap for a long time. Four years ago, he arrested one of my uncles and broke his glasses and his nose. It had to stop, and I figured that becoming a cop was the only way I could get close enough to Big Don to bring him down. I didn't realize it was so incredibly out of control. And now—" Calvin smiles. "He's down, and more than a few folks have come out of the woodwork and are pressing charges against him.

It's taken me three years of getting to the point I could smack it back to him, but it's done."

"Are you arresting me for kidnapping still?"

"Naw, I don't see Bobby anywhere around. He's an adult. He has the right to leave the home. I was kidding." Calvin looks right to the left. "If whoever got him out gets him back safe, no harm done."

"Okay. How'd he do?"

"Strangely well," Calvin says. "Although he was like fifteenth getting done, he hit the bullseye on the target dead on. Nobody else got all the bullseyes. I mean, the guy hit the target perfectly. The judges were out there taking pictures. He's probably going to be on the news."

"What does that mean even if he placed fifteenth on the time?" I am halfway focused on him. I hear the ATVs starting to roll in. Twenty to thirty runners along the sidelines are getting sent in. I see Meghan clapping her hands and dancing to the starting line.

"I don't know. I know that when he was finished, he was mobbed by about a hundred old ladies asking for his autograph."

"Great," I grunt, but with a smile. I find it strange that I'm not let down. I think it is just because I'm nervous about the run. "And Martha swimming?"

"I don't know. They had an ambulance call down there. I think it was someone in the crowd. Without Big Don, we're down in numbers and winging it as far as patrol. I've been from one side of the mountain to the other a hundred times today." His radio blares, and he looks down. "I'm sure that's for me. I came to give you this. Sorry, it took me so long. Your Pops was busy unloading the ATV and asked me to bring it to you."

He hands me a small paper bag. I look at it, open it up, and peer inside. "It's what you asked your pops for?" Calvin, the Cop, asks me. "It smells like beef jerky."

"Yeah, something for the race."

"You going to have time to eat?"

"Probably not." He holds up a finger to put our conversation on hold, tips his chin, and says something on the radio. "Alright, the first of the ATVs are coming in. I've got to get down here and make sure people stay out of the parking lot so they don't get hit."

Calvin starts to turn, then partway. He tips his head to one side and looks at me very seriously. "Hey, just so you know. I probably would have turned out differently if it wasn't for you beating the crap out of those boys on the bus," he tells me. "I figured if this tiny little girl wasn't afraid to take on some giant kids to protect Little Pete, I could do it, too. And running down your ex-husband because you figured out that he was killing women takes guts. Good luck with the race."

I stare at his car while it is leaving and tuck the bag into my shorts. Then I hear cheering along the roadway. More of the ATV racers are starting to come into the lot. People were pouring down the hillside where the ATV race was ending. Most, I assume, were there to watch Lynn Houck compete. It is like a herd of buffalo stampeding along the roadway. Someone bumps into my shoulder. It is one of the runners excited about getting out of our boxed area. A man slips past me and excuses himself. Then I feel the bang on my shoulder again.

She must have been waiting for the volunteers' attention to be focused on the event once things got busy with the ATV riders coming in. She must have been counting the seconds with bated breath, anticipating the moment Calvin the Cop would leave. Lizzy Devereauxs must have been biding her time patiently awaiting that first punch to my right cheek because when she hauled off and hit me, it was like she'd been holding on to that energy until it grew to epic, superhuman proportions. Her fist hit my cheek so hard that I whipped around, and I completely lost my balance, landing on my belly with a short, hard slap. "You kilt my son, you kilt my son! I heard it on the news today! It was you who kilt my son!"

I rolled. It is a defense mechanism. I am like a little mouse that's seeing the paw of a tomcat come down on her when Lizzy's foot starts doing a chopping block aimed at my chest. She is screaming at me, and I can hear a lady yowling over her. Suddenly, somebody's towing Lizzy back, and I see one of Josh's uncles with big, burly arms trying to take her place. "Holy hell! Somebody help!" I scream. Tim Devereauxs is a barrel-chested, massive beast of a man. One swipe from his fist, and I knew I'd be as beat up as the gross pulp at the bottom of Uncle Craig's moonshine glass. I shouldn't have screeched because people are spontaneously pouring onto the road.

Fists are flying everywhere. Just as Tim raises his arm, somebody grabs it and jerks him backward. I don't know if anybody knows who is hurting or hitting who. I can only see Lizzy pulling back her fist for the second round.

"I didn't kill him, Lizzy!" I yell over the riot that seems to be stemming from my scream. "He killed himself. You know that! Don't listen to the reports. He tried to kill me. He tried to kill his kids. I had no choice but to leave him!"

She hits me, doesn't care, both fists baring down on me while I do my usual arms in the air protecting myself. Then her angry punches stopped. I see Crystal grabbing her by the waist, lugging her mama back.

"Mama, stop!" Crystal grabs her arm hard when her mama kicks her to be released. She shoves her mama back. I see one of the runners come between us while Crystal grabs my shirt collar in her fist. "Tell me you tried to pull him out."

"Crystal, nobody could have saved Josh. He wasn't Josh anymore. He wasn't Tyler Heaton, Johnny Mills, or any other aliases he had for himself. He's been addicted to meth for three years at least, murdered people to feed his habit. There wasn't anything left in his eyes. Crystal, if you know me at all, you know I would have gone in there and grabbed him out. I sat at that bar waiting for him to return to me for three years. Nobody does that who hates a guy and wants him dead. But—he wasn't the boy you grew up with, the boy I—loved."

"He didn't feel any pain, right?"

"No," I lie. "It was fast. The house blew up. Boom. He was gone in a second." I don't know how long I stand there and stare at Crystal. She finally releases my hand, then nods to the man holding her mama back. "Let her go," she says, pointing to her mama. "We're leaving."

I'm sitting on a little curb, taking out my earphones plugged into my ears. The cops came and broke up the fight an hour ago. It was crazy; people were hitting each other. There must have been fifty of them not knowing who to hit because there weren't any sides. I guess that's what you get when you invite a bunch of hot-headed rednecks. I nursed my wounds with a cup of water to my cheek and slip out of the chaos with the help of one of the volunteers.

"Hey, Kenny will be here in about five minutes."

I felt his hand on my back and looked up to see Pops. About twenty-five minutes have passed since Noah Hartley left. Every now and then, a runner comes past. I'm not sure if I feel let down or not. I only know it is lonely sitting here by myself.

I smile at him. He's got that old concerned look on his face like he's going to tell me a story of something that happened to him when he was my age. He doesn't. Pops sits down next to me.

"Wow, sweetie, did you fall?" He touches my cheek with his knuckle where Lizzy hit me.

"You didn't hear? There was a freaking riot here. Josh's mom showed up after seeing the news about Josh. She started punching, and then one guy hit another, and boom!"

"You're alright?" He is really looking at me intensely. "You didn't get hurt? It was so crazy at the river. I don't think we even heard anything."

"I'm fine, Pops.

"Crappy way to end the day, huh?"

I'm not interested in me. I'm trying to get him to tell me what happened with Martha. "What happened?"

"Well, your little friend Martha was late getting in the water. They blocked it on both ends, so the current wasn't so bad. She started across. About ten or so people were going across, fighting a little bit of current." Pops clears his throat. "There was a woman, and suddenly, she just stopped and disappeared. People on the shore were jumping up and down and screaming. It was horrifying. Martha saw her. Neal Whitley, the professional swimmer, saw her. There were a few more, but everyone except Neal and Martha kept swimming. They dove down a couple times, and Martha dragged the lady back up about ten feet away. Neal pulled her to the shore."

"Wow, is the lady okay?"

"She's fine. Got the fire scared out of her. They didn't have to do CPR or anything. But Martha got slowed down behind everybody else. She stuck with the lady about twenty minutes more to ensure she was alright."

"That's Martha," I giggle. "Now she'll be telling everyone that God sent me to have her in the Run just to save that lady's life."

"Maybe he did." Pops shoves me with his shoulder. "You'd do the same, wouldn't you?"

I know he knows I'm disappointed. "Well, I'm more concerned about losing to Noah Hartley."

"I understand."

"No, you don't." I bite down on my bottom lip. "I bet him if I won, he'd kiss that bass Aunt Jenny sewed. The one sitting at our tent."

"That's funny."

"But this isn't." I get ready to hear him groan. "He bet me in return, if I lost to him racing, I would kiss his butt."

"Cripes almighty, how do you get yourself into this stuff, girl?"

"I've been hanging with you for too long."

Only six people are waiting for their teammates when Kenny comes strolling up. He's barely recognizable underneath the mud on his face and body. He's got the baton in his hand and gives it a little toss in the air. "I held them off as long as I could for you," Kenny mutters, swiping the mud from his eyes with his wrist. "I figured I could gain some time." I wasn't quick enough and watch the baton fall to the ground. I'm not in a hurry, so I sweep it up with my fingers.

"Yeah, that was the funniest mud bog race that poor Houck guy ever saw." Pops sniffs. "Nothing but spray in his face all the way down the hill. Kenny just stayed right in front of him, fishtailed and caroused around. It took an hour to come down that hill and should have been fifteen minutes. He didn't get around him until the other side."

"Did you hear him yelling at me? His face was purple."

"Yeah, you were really rough on him." Pops reaches up and slaps Kenny's arm with his hand. "You made your daddy proud. But there better not be a dent in Old Yeller."

"No, sir. Just a little muddy."

"Well, Brandy, we'll meet you on the other side of the mountain." Pops gets up and pats my back. "Bear said he'd be there too."

"Really?"

"Told me to tell you he'd be there until the cows come home if he needed to wait that long. But he also said he didn't think he'd have to."

"I haven't heard that saying since Mamaw was alive," I laugh. "I wonder where he heard that?"

"He probably found it online," Kenny rolls his eyes. "That guy spends more time trying to impress you than anyone I know. And you just stare at him like he's an idiot."

"I do not." I reach out and punch Kenny. He takes my wrist and twists it.

"Ow, Pops, make him stop!"

Chapter –41
Riddles along the Trail

It is too hot for September. Maybe I should not scoop up this particular month and toss it in with all the rest of Autumn, bulking them into the season that's supposed to be setting the course for winter and the cold winds that blow with it. As I think about it, it seems tolerable to be warm in the beginning and cooler at the end. Still, I'm not expecting the temperature to be ninety-one. I overhear somebody saying we might have gotten a record today. It's usually in the seventies, well into the middle of the month.

Two miles. It is when I start seeing the white paperboard signs taped onto random trees. They seem to happen in the pockets where most spectators are collected.

WHAT COMES DOWN BUT NEVER GOES UP? I'm wondering what the heck it means, this riddle. But it's in Bear's writing. I run about a quarter mile more and see the answer: *RAIN*.

Four miles: *HOW CAN A POCKET BE EMPTY AND STILL HAVE SOMETHING IN IT?* Four and a half miles: IT HAS A HOLE. Not long after the second riddle, the runners start dropping like flies. The first six miles are straight up and along the side of Fire Mountain before there's just a tiny expanse of hillside flat toward the top. It's the back side, which is federal land. Then, suddenly, the trail starts dropping down along a rocky ledge. You have to jump and climb up a few and then get through the deep ruts of mud that the ATVs for Noah Hartley have left behind in their wake.

"You okay?" I ask everybody I pass. The fourteen people so far are pretty good about moving to the side when they can. I think it is just the polite thing to do. I'm not used to the marathon attitude. One of the men I catch up to on a rock tells me Noah Hartley spit his bottled water on him when he passed. He pokes his finger at his shirt. He's almost out of breath.

"Lots of bleach will work on that," I tell him, then proceed. "Lots and lots." He laughs and tells me he's throwing the shirt away. It probably has snake venom on it. "Hey, do me a favor. When you catch up to him, spit back at him for me."

I've yet to get winded. I look for the signs. They help pass the time. I've been running so long that my lungs are better adapted to it than the runners I overtake. I know it doesn't mean much. We're not even going to place. Still, I'd like to see if I can catch up to Noah. Maybe spit on him when I go by. I break out in a sweat when I sprint down the mountain on the other side.

"You alright?" A woman is limping. I figure she's got blisters. A volunteer is helping along the path. "She was running right behind Hartley, and one of his ATVs ran over her foot."

"I swear, he did it on purpose," the runner says. There are bystanders packed in there, and I feel my stomach getting jumpy, like panicky mode has set in. I see the sign and find myself focusing on it: *THE MORE YOU HAVE OF IT, THE LESS YOU SEE. WHAT IS IT?* A few hundred feet later, when the observers are at their peak, I see the answer: *DARKNESS.*

I'm thinking that I've got about five miles on the road between the two mountains before the race goes back up again and ends another six miles at the top of Boar Mountain along Boar Mountain Road and the resort's parking lot. I'm still not tired or even winded.

I PAID OFF THE LOANS YOU OWED FOR YOUR TUITION. YEAH, BE MAD. I DON'T CARE. YOU NEED TO STAY IN SCHOOL. I stop and stare at this one. I almost cried. I didn't. I started to run again.

"You alright?" I see Meghan Reynolds two miles along the road. She isn't going fast, probably pacing herself the last eight miles.

"How—how did you get here so fast?"

"I ran—haha." She doesn't laugh, so I turn and run backward in pace to her forwards. "That was a joke."

"It's not funny."

"It's funny. Come on."

She can hardly catch her breath. I can't tell if she knows Bear did the signs for me. If she does, she doesn't say. She has an angry pucker on her lips. Her face is beet red, and her usually pretty hair is sweaty. "Okay, maybe you'll like this one." I must keep turning my head to ensure I don't trip on anything. "What do you call a can opener that doesn't work?" There are volunteers along the road handing out water bottles. We run right past them.

"I don't know." She rolls her eyes and looks around me like she will pass, so I turn and pace myself with her.

"A *can't* opener. Haha. You had to like that one." I swipe my hand through my hair and try to reach out for a bottled water. I'm not too good at it and knock it clean out of the lady's hand. "Oh, crap." I stop long enough to pick it up and return it to her. "I'm sorry." Then, I have to run faster to catch up with Meghan.

"Hey, how do you catch a bra?" I ask her.

"I don't know."

"A booby trap." I reach out and point a finger. "Now that was a good one."

She laughs, takes a swig of her drink, and then hands it to me. "You want to share spit?" she asks. I reach out, and she pulls it away just before my fingers reach it. "I'm just kidding."

"Are you or not?"

"I am. Here." She does it again, and I cross my eyes at her.

"What do you do," I ask, "when a blonde throws a pin at you?"

"I don't know." She hands me the bottle this time, and I pour it on my face.

"You run. She's got a grenade in her hand."

"That was just bad."

"It was, but it passed the time," I say. "I'll see you at the finish line, yeah?" Then I feel a little bit of my redneck slipping out. I bite my lip, then slide this in. "I suppose it was good that you girls stole that name, Fire Mountain Shadows. Because that's what you are right now, *in my shadow*. But not for long. I'm out of here." I don't look back; I take off in a mad dash. I can't help but wonder from her attitude if Bear made his choice. She wasn't ripping my eyes out.

Occasionally, I can hear the helicopter passing over from the TV stations. When I see the clusters of crowds, I'm more interested in the damn riddles. Bear's writing calms me like he's here with me. But it isn't easy to read. He has a tendency to get messy at the end of a sentence. Small pockets of crowds are getting thinner as those runners that they have waited on have already passed. Whenever I see a gathering coming up, I pop on the earphones, turn on the music, and watch for the riddles.

Most of the spectators have headed up to the resort for the finish. Then, about three miles later, I hear the hoarse growl of ATV. My stomach jumps in fifteen directions, a bag full of bouncy balls rebounding in my belly. Noah Hartley. I am on the last little bit of road before it goes up the mountain again. I realize I've got maybe a quarter mile when I see Hartley's sweaty back to pass him. I remember what Bear said—that it would be impossible to get around the ATVs on the trail on Boar Mountain.

Once I was off the road, I saw the two security ATVs side by side behind Hartley. I know there have to be runners ahead of him. He got started later because his teammate was part of the water rescue. I don't care. My aim is to get past him. I ease up until I'm almost to the ATVs. I know they are about an arms-length away from me on either side. I'm going to slide between them. As I up my pace, the one on the right slips inward.

"Hey, runner behind you!" I yell. They can hear me, I'm sure. Kenny and I constantly scream back and forth on the ATVs, no problem. There's a small crowd and cars parked on the roadway, or I would go to the right. I can't.

Again, I try to slide between them. This time, I hear muffled laughter, and the ATV on the left slips to the right. There's no way I can pass them. The gravel from their tires is pelting me. I snatch Bear's phone from my waist and poke in Pop's number. "Pops, is Crazy Willie up on Owl Hollow?"

"Are you calling me while you're running?"

"I am," I say in puffy breaths. "There are two guards on ATVS riding by Hartley, and they won't let me pass."

"You've caught up with Hartley?"

"Yeah. I'd pass the idiot if I could—ouch." A big rock hits me on the side of the shoulder. I slip forward and skid on my belly. Pops is no longer on the other end, so I stuff my phone back into my pocket.

We do this dance all the way to the mountain trail. Maybe I'm kind of glad for it. There are hundreds of faces on the sidelines dancing in my eyes. Upward. I can feel my body getting pulled as my legs pump hard, but not as hard as I like, behind one ATV. The other is getting a reasonable distance ahead. I know I've got to bide my timing just right. I know when I jump the first little creek, I'm in Owl Hollow.

The trail is a muddy mess. The tires are sending muck and mud into my face. I'm flecked brown and black. I see Owl Hollow. I push my pace a little faster and slip up to the right. I know the ATV in front of me is going to do the same. He's a chubby guy driving it, the kind that's borderline buff and overeats. He turns and waves at me with a big smile like it's okay that he is blocking me and preventing me from passing.

"Let me through," I huff at him. He won't, so I bide my time, wait for the bay of Crazy Willie's hellhounds. Four minutes later, I hear them.

"Hey!" I yell at the driver in front of me. "Let me around!" I know those old hound dogs know my voice. They've chased me down Crazy Willie's hill for three years and probably chased Kenny and me down the mountain on our ATVs for ten years. When that pack of dogs come barreling down the hillside, I hold up the bag of jerky in my hand. They know I'm trying to bribe them. I toss the bag on the front of the ATV on the driver's lap. The idiot driving doesn't see it. He's looking at the dogs. The next thing I know, five hounds are making a devil's leap onto the ATV while the guy starts screaming holy hell and runs into a tree. I watch him roll. He gets up and starts running down the side of the hill. The hound dogs are too interested ripping apart the bag of jerky.

Okay, I'm starting to get a little winded. The mountain is steep for the next quarter mile; unfortunately, I know this. The mud on my face makes my skin tight, and my eyes burn from the gravel spit into it. I'm starting to feel it when I am about four steps from the back of the remaining ATV. If I don't get around it, I'm not passing Hartley. But the driver is veering right, veering left, so I can't get around him. I can't do it. This is it. There's no way. What was I thinking? I'm too tired. I realize I'm seeing Mama's face. She pops up in my head, stands there with her arms crossed and the pickle-lips staring at me: *Baby girl, why the hell are you always thinking you're building castles in Spain? You ain't never going to be more than what you got right now. Get down from your high horse. You ain't better than nobody else 'round here.*

Around here. Like at Mister Smiley's Grocery. He would never sponsor me because he wanted to be surrounded by four beautiful women who were too good to clean up the bathrooms like I did.

Or at Beverly's because a girl from Fire Mountain wouldn't amount to anything. Nothing. Because I'm nobody. Like Josh used to tell me. *Can't you do something with that hair of yours? I won't be back until tomorrow morning. Don't wait up on me.* And Big Don. *You're nothing but a ten-buck whore.*

And my mama. I conjure up a memory. It was the elementary school spring concert directed by the music teacher, Missus Moffatt. Pops bought me a little blue dress and white leggings because I had a solo, just a tiny part, not more than a few simple verses. I don't know how Mama heard about the program. She did. I don't understand why Mama came to this one out of the hundreds of others she failed to attend. She did. She jumped up from her seat as soon as I stepped up to the microphone to sing my part. She must have been drunk or high because she leaned on the empty seat in front of her, and she and the chair came crashing down. It was like an explosion, and people jumped. Then she wouldn't let anybody help her up. She kept yelling that all she wanted to do was get a picture of her daughter. Bam! Everything went black that horrible day. I hit the stage floor—

I stop then. I try to text Pops. I'm done. I'm finished. The ATVs won't let me pass. There isn't any cell phone service, but I think the text got sent. I sigh, blink, and right in the middle of nowhere is another sign. *THEY ARE NOT REAL. STILL, THEY CAN BE ACHIEVED IF THEY ARE JUST BELIEVED. WHAT ARE THEY?*

"Dreams." I knew it even before I saw the answer written in red on the sign lying on the ground. The wind flipped it off its perch, but I saw it standing over it. I pick it up and stare at it. But it doesn't just say one simple word. While I look down on it, I can see more writing. *DREAMS. BEJESUS, I BELIEVE IN YOU. WHEN YOU MAKE IT TO THE END, REMEMBER I WILL BE THERE FOR YOU EVEN IF THERE ARE A MILLION PEOPLE AHEAD OF YOU. YOU'VE MADE IT THIS FAR. YOU CAN MAKE IT THROUGH WHATEVER YOU SET YOUR HEART TO.*

I realize there's more to Bear than I wanted to believe right then. I let my teeth sink into the cardboard encouragements, remembering his words once when we got into a big fight. He was right. He said I always hit the hill running but stop and turn around when it gets challenging, too difficult to go any farther in my mind.

I let other people define me and worry too much about their thoughts. I'm sitting here thinking that's why I'm not finishing college, standing here staring at a mountain, too afraid I'll fail. Honestly, I've got nothing to lose.

I snatch up the cardboard and fold it as small as I can. I tuck it into my shorts. And I start to run again. I am staring at the back of the man on the ATV. He's not much bigger than Kenny, and I think I've chased my skinny cousin up the hills and along the hollows on Pops' ATV plenty of times. I don't try to go around him. I jump on the back and clamber over him. Which is precisely what I do when we crest a hillock. I jump as high as I can, let my feet walk along the side and to the front, and then jump off in front of him.

He slows long enough for me to get about twenty steps ahead. The driver is forcing my pace now, another tactic I wouldn't have expected. It is an easy fix. The first narrow turn we take, I grab a mid-size sapling, pull it back in a powerful arc, and release it, letting it whip back at the driver's head.

It was enough to slap him in the face, not necessarily stop him cold in his tracks. However, it stings, and he reaches up both hands to swipe away the burn. He keels to the right. The ATV, on the other hand, keeps going left. It makes a solid crash into a hedge, then slip-slides down the hillside before resting on a rocky ledge.

There is a moment when I think Noah Hartley has probably bested me. I don't see him for maybe a mile, and I know there are probably only five or six to go. I'm sore and tired, but it doesn't stop me. I figure my little heart will have to blow before I stop now.

Like a bat out of hell, I am coming through those woods and up the mountain. I see Hartley's back, and then it gets closer and closer. His shirt is sopping wet with sweat, his face is pink, and his skinny legs are trying to pump hard. Yet, this isn't an asphalt racetrack. It isn't an all-weather running track inside an air-conditioned building with staff running out to give him water bottles. It's the real thing with rocks and dirt and mud and roots. It's redneck, hillbilly country, and not his pampered track runner kingdom. He's used to competing against his buddies with the same background. He's not used to people like me. He's having a difficult time. I realize this when he turns, and his buggy eyes open wide at me.

"Hey, buttwipe, I bet you thought you'd never see me—that friggin' backwoods hillbilly from the starting line. Yeah, I'm the one that you said would be lucky to finish." I huff with thick breaths. "You know, I'm not even winded. By the way, you might remember me. I'm the one who stopped in while you were promoting your Noah Hartley Official Running Shoe of the Redneck Run." I come up beside him and look at the side of his bare head. "You told me I was simple and inept. You called me a hillbilly and a redneck. How's it making you feel right now that I'm going to pass you, dust your city boy ass, huh?"

He keeps looking behind him. I know he's watching for his ATVs. "Just so you know, I was really looking forward to you seeing my ass in your face for the rest of this run. But that's not going to happen. You're not going to see me at all in five minutes."

I run. I run like I've never run before. I lift my hand just as I get ten steps away from him and point to my back. "Yeah, buttwipe, kiss my badass!" Then I flip him the bird, and I'm sure it is less than five minutes, I am gone from his sight.

It was strangely subdued when I hit the asphalt roadway off the trail. One mile. I've got one mile left. I can see people lined up along the roadway from right to left and two deep. People are milling around, sitting in their cars, and it is as if they all just kind of stop, startle to attention, and look at me when I round the turn. "Runners coming!" I hear somebody yell.

My heart is pounding. I try not to watch folks slide off their cars like they are surprised to see anyone. A lady holding a cell phone at jerks it up and starts taking pictures. I feel like I'd walked in the wrong house's front door and sat down at a stranger's table. Panic mode. I wait for it to hit. I stop and snatch up Bear's phone and plug the earphones in. Music. I take a deep breath and pretend nobody's there but me, the trees, and maybe a crow or two. Then, I take a little skip and began to run again.

I'm sprinting up the road. I find it easier to push my head to the wind and try not to look up, but I know some faces and wave as I pass. The people I snuck out of the nursing home and Millie Piper. My aunts, uncles, and cousins are there. I see Ben's usual entourage and maybe his mom and dad stuffed there.

Preacher Murphy and his kids are holding up a sign with my name. And there's the people I worked with at Smiley's waving as I pass. There are even some homemade signs with GO! GENUINE FIRE MOUNTAIN' NECKS written on them in bold red permanent marker. There are lots of homemade signs with my name on them.

Suddenly, the finish line is in front of me. Everybody is sitting down and lounging. I cross it with little more fanfare than my own sigh. "Holy shit, I actually finished," I say when I get there. I'm elated. I know it is probably loud because I've got the earphones on. I'm looking for Pops, for Bear, for Kenny. I feel my stomach jerk and jump because everybody's staring at me. I see the TV people look around from their little white vans, strangely subdued. I find the table where they're taking in the times and lean my butt against it and try to text Pops.

Pops. I'm here. I'm up here. Yay. Where r u? I'm ready to go home. People staring. Ug.

"Sweetheart?" I feel a tap on my shoulder. I turn and pop out those earphones. A lady in a race smock is trying to get my attention. "I need to see your number." She is wiggling her finger in a circle, so I turn. She has to swipe the mud off, even on the back. She scans the tag. "She's 222. Brandy Devereauxs." I look at the table. They are smiling. "Congratulations, you've finished the race."

"Thanks," I start to say, and then suddenly, a bunch of strangers are jostling my shoulder and congratulating me. Reporters are in my face, wagging microphones. When I finally get a break, my heart is racing worse than when I was running up Fire Mountain.

"Hey, where is everybody? Where's Martha? I want to see her. I worried about her all the way up the hill."

But Pops is just standing there, feet planted and his eyes going back and forth between my own. "Baby, you're the first one in. Did you run the right route?"

"Is there a wrong way?" I joke. He's not laughing. "Well, yeah." I laugh. "There's only one."

"Where's Hartley and the rest of the runners?"

"I left him about six miles back. Didn't you get the text about the ATVs? They wouldn't let me pass." I'm a big ball of mud splatter. Still, I reach down to the waist of my shorts and tug out my phone.

I pull up the text. "See? One of them bumped me." I hold up my arm and expose a tiny welt on my elbow. "I had to jump over it. Like a puma," I add.

"Yeah, the last text I got said you quit because you couldn't get past them. Hey, look." Pops points over my shoulder. "I texted Bear that, so he didn't hurry. He was talking to reporters at the ATV run." I see a set of stands with a podium. On either side, they have two giant screens that are running videos of the Redneck Run—swimmers, runners, and ATV drivers. I see a picture of Bobby pop up. He's getting ready to shoot a target. However, my attention is turned to a flash of camera in my face. Reporters are converging on me, taking pictures and asking questions. I force smiles and bob my head, hoping I don't throw up on them. My wild eyes turn to Pops. I know he sees the spooked pony in my gaze.

"Pops, I need to go someplace for a minute."

"Oh, yeah, you look like a doe in the headlights. How about you go talk to Martha. She's at Kenny's truck with the rest of your team. They parked in the back. She's feels bad placing so far back."

"Is Bear there?"

"I haven't seen him."

I figure he's probably waiting for Meghan.

"What'd you do, sprout wings and fly?" Bobby Reese is doing his little old man dance, kicking up his heels when Pops and I get to the truck. "I'm just kidding." I can see Martha. She's sitting on the hood of Kenny's truck in the shade and on one of Aunt Jenny's old blankets Kenny keeps in the truck to sit on when he goes fishing.

"I did." He squishes me hard in a hug.

"Hey, good job. Better luck next year, huh?" Gabe's right there, poking me in the shoulder.

"Nice try. We still got a lot of advertising until you got covered in mud." Ben laughs. Does nobody believe I finished the run? Then I walk over and climb up on the hood of Kenny's truck beside Martha. Pops hands me a raggedy towel with bottled water poured over top so I can wipe the mud from my face and arms.

"I'm sorry." She tells me while I scrub. "I feel like I ruined all this for you. You've been talking about the Redneck Run for two years. And I screwed it up. Maybe I should have prayed harder."

"Screwed it up by going back and saving somebody from drowning?" I ask her. "If you were that person who didn't go back, I wouldn't have been your friend in the first place."

"I think you must have prayed enough," Kenny adds. "What would have happened if you weren't there? You're like a superhero."

"Anybody would have done it." Martha shrugs us both off. I think she wanted to win this as much as I did.

"Did they?" Kenny is sitting in the truck driver's seat. The door is open wide, and the window is down. His foot is propped up on the mirror. He looks at Martha over a pair of dark sunglasses and his ball cap. "No, they didn't. I keep telling you that. They kept on swimming. What the hell? *Who* does that? I'm going to call you *Super* Born Again Amish Woman. We're all getting T-shirts."

"We could have Gabe design them," I add, then shove my shoulder into Martha's. "I think it is cooler than winning."

"As soon as the crowds clear, we will go back to Uncle Lee's and eat that pig we stuck in the ground to cook this morning." Kenny does a little drum roll on his steering wheel.

"It's not your 4-H pig from high school, is it?" I ask him aghast.

"Oh, hell no," Kenny grunts and laughs. "That one is tough as rock, and still too mean to catch."

Chapter –42
Party Time

"Hey, I got here as soon as I could." Bear is dressed in a white shirt and tie now. He seems to take note of the beanie hat he got me in Cincinnati. I shoved it on my head for comfort. I see a slight and smug smile, that I've exchanged it for Josh's ball cap. His sleeves are rolled up and he has to be sweltering in the heat when he hops out of his truck. Martha and I are looking at photos of the Redneck Run somebody posted online. Gabe and Ben are on either side, peering over our legs at the phone I'm holding. There are three images of her breaking the surface of the water with Jean Ogle, the swimmer who almost drowned. Her arm is high in the air. They are awe-inspiring.

"Well, what's he doing here?" Gabe asks, elbowing me.

I lower my voice deeply and mimic an evil villain: "I brought him to the dark side."

"Hey, didn't I just see you?" Bear says. He points a finger at Martha and gives her a big grin. "You were amazing."

"See, I told you," I said, bumping her shoulder.

He holds his hands to his sides, showing us his dressy side. "Yeah, I know. I look like an office geek. Go ahead, you two, laugh if you want."

I stare at him. No, he doesn't look like a geek at all. My heart's pounding double-time in my chest. His arms are tan and muscled, sticking out past the sleeves rolled up to his elbows. His hair is freshly cut, his eyes are warm brown, and he is smiling. I feel like I've got marbles in my mouth. I can't talk. He doesn't seem to notice and keeps talking while standing in front of us. He looks out of place. We're all in our T-shirts and shorts, even Gabe and Ben. Bear doesn't seem to care. I think he wants to be like us.

"It is one hundred and ten degrees today, and my mother informed me we have an emergency conference and are meeting with reporters right in the middle of the event. I don't even get through the doors after the emergency at the swimming event, and they call me to come up here. There's always drama, you know?

Now, I've got to get over to do the announcements for each runner when they start coming in." He looks at his watch and winces. His arm still aches from the gunshot. "They said I've got about twenty more minutes."

"Thanks for being there for *me*," I waggle my shoulders, reach out with the toes of my shoes, and poke him. "Yeah, no big deal. I'm just Goodwill and Dollar Store Dolly. I don't count for anything."

"I'm here now." He looks at me right in the eyes. "And you are neither of those names. All the while, my mother thinks I am resting at the resort, recuperating from being Brandy'd again." It's like nobody else is there when our eyes connect. I'm suddenly sweating bullets and realizing I probably look like I've been through the mud bog even though Pops gave me bottled water to rinse off my arms and legs. "And you do count. What do you want?"

Still, as soon as he says that he whips over and gives Kenny's foot a knuckle bump. "Good run, dude. It brought a lot of laughs." He's like everybody else. They are walking on eggshells around me.

"Okay, stop it." I hold up my hands and look at everybody in the eyes one by one.

"Stop what?" Bear asks.

"Acting like —I don't know. Like somebody died." Silence. I throw my hand out and bob my head up and down. "I mean, I guess somebody did die. But I don't mean that." Stares. I'm getting the blinky-eyed, oh-crap-she's-gonna-blow gazes. Honestly, Josh is the farthest thing from my mind. "Stop it!" Damn, can't a girl quietly celebrate on her own? I don't want to take away Martha's sunshine.

"You're going to wig out, aren't you?" Kenny says. "This is where you wig out."

"Wig out. I never wig out. Screw you all." I grump. Okay, they all laugh awkwardly at this.

"Just saying." Kenny nods his head and goes back to texting somebody on his phone. It is quiet with all of us. Maybe it is just the heat or being so tired. I am just about to poke my finger on the phone to bring more pictures to the screen when Bear turns and seems absorbed in something toward the parking lot. It's a police cruiser. I cringe. It stops short of Kenny's truck, and Bear walks out and leans into the window.

"Eye candy?" Martha asks me. I know my eyes are warily set on the cop car.

"Eye candy?" I ask.

"Bear." She bumps my shoulders. "Oh, come on. He's hot. I'd go out with him if he was Amish or Born Again. You're looking at him like he's a chocolate bar on the first day of your period."

"No, he's got a girlfriend," I mumble. Then I realize Bear is turning and wiggling his finger at me.

"Uh oh, Brandy Cop Candy, what'd you do this time?" Kenny's voice echoes from his truck. I see him peering warily through the door window.

"Nothing barring a small riot that I know of," I muttered, sliding off the hood and handing my phone to Martha. They all look at me as if this must be a news flash; they did not know about the fight. "Which technically wasn't my fault. It was Lizzy Devereauxs' fault."

I can see Bear is cautious. Maybe he knows how I feel about cops. I don't know. When I walk up to the cruiser, I only see that he steps back and quietly stands by Kenny's truck away from us.

"Is this you?"

I stare at Calvin until he raises his cell phone, hits a little arrow, and a video plays before me. I watch and wince. Someone managed to catch the ATVs blocking my ability to pass them. Mud is just streaming out from beneath the tires. I can see myself running, pausing, and then the back of the ATV smacking into my right side.

"Yeah, they wouldn't let me pass on the road or up the first leg of the mountain."

"And this?" There's another set. This is up the hillside.

"Yeah."

"Why didn't you report this?"

"To whom, Calvin?" I ask him bluntly. "And what good would it do me? My last run-in with the cops ended with me kneeling on the asphalt, wondering if I was going to end up in the trunk of your cruiser dead. You guys don't protect *us*. You protect *them*."

"Big Don protected them. I protect anybody who needs protection. That includes you and your dad and everybody else, understand?" I nod my head slowly.

"Whether you say yes or no, do you want to go out sometime?"

"You're kidding me, right?" I ask him.

"No."

Calvin came from the same place I did. He's a nice guy. I'm just not the kind of person that would ever date a cop. They are just too arrogant with a gun hanging on their hip. It's like they put on their badge, and everyone must respect them no matter how stupid and misguided they are. I recognize that.

Still, I clown about it to Bear when Calvin drives off. "Well, hot damn, I just got asked out by Calvin the Cop," I tell him. He is sitting on the curb under the tree where there is just an inkling of shade left in the late afternoon heat.

"Brandy, listen to me. What the hell is up with you?" Bear doesn't cuss much. I'm surprised.

"What do you mean?"

"Those ATVs could have killed you." Bear is angry. I don't know if it is aimed at me. "Why wouldn't you say anything?"

"Because nobody would listen to me even if I did. Don't look at me like that. I can't tell if you're mad." I don't like him mad at me.

"I'm not mad at you. And I would listen." He's staring at me. His hand comes out, touches my shoulder, and sits there. I'm unsure. He's never touched me like this before, especially when anybody is around. "Brandy, I would listen."

"They didn't hurt me." I'm thinking, I am going to wig out now.

"Calvin is going to investigate it," Bear goes on. "That was the meeting you missed, I guess. You're okay?"

"I'm fine."

"What'd you say?" He asks.

"I just told him they wouldn't let me pass. They hit me a couple times on the road and up the hill."

"No, when the cop asked you out."

"Oh." I blink and feel his hand slide away. I wish it would stay. "I asked him if he really thought I needed one more guy in my life leaving the toilet seat up in the middle of the night so I can fall in it." I shrug. "And he said you can never have enough toilet seats."

"What the heck does that mean? You're going out with him? Just like that?" Bear groans. I'm not expecting him to go off on me.

"What's the difference, Devereauxs?" he responds. "I don't get it. I've known you for six months. Do I have to buy a uniform to get a date? Why have you never gone out with me?"

I'm taken slightly aback and show it, holding my hands out and waggling my head. "Because you've never asked me out, Vega."

It is like it just never occurred to him. "Oh, I guess you're right. I just figured you wouldn't."

"You've known me this long and haven't asked me out because you *didn't think I would go*?" I tip my chin. Certainly, he is kidding me. "You're joking, right?"

"I don't know, maybe. I don't have much experience in asking girls out, Brandy. Good God, you know that. With my old job, women either ran like hell because they thought I was going to fire them, or they wanted to sleep with me because I'd fire them if they didn't. It's not my character to go to bed with somebody because they're scared of me." He untangles his tie a little with his fingers. "I guess there's always something in the way. Maybe you wouldn't anyway. Maybe I'd freak you out because that's not how we've been hanging out, and you wouldn't want to be around me anymore."

"I would have probably gone out with you since we started working out together. Just saying."

"Why didn't you ask me out, then?"

"Really, Bear?" I toss my hands out. "The entire reason you were losing weight and working out was to impress Meghan and get the girl. I've never seen anybody work so hard for something. I didn't even think about asking you out. Your head was dead set on her. Who wants to be the girl you feel you must ask out because you're hanging with her? Who wants to be the one you settle for?"

"Settle for?"

"Yeah, come on, I was cleaning out restrooms at Mister Smiley's. Meghan's a cashier. There is a certain pecking order in the grocery industry, you know."

"You were working your way through college. Meghan's never going to be anything more than a cashier."

"Okay, that's fair. And I didn't tell Calvin I'd go out with him. I told him I wouldn't. I don't particularly like cops. You should know that."

I was going to tell him I had a weakness for chubby guys with a bad attitude. I didn't get to. Bear's cell phone rings. I see his shoulders drop. "I'm sure it is my mom again. Hold that thought—please." He stands up and walks to the other side of Kenny's truck. I see him pacing back and forth, then his eyes veer toward me.

"Did you finish the race?" he asks me, stopping just an inch from my feet. "Bejesus, did you *run the entire race*?"

"Yeah, of course. Why?"

"I just assumed you didn't. Your pops said you decided not to finish. Holy crap. How long have you been done? How long have you been sitting here? Why didn't you say something? What are you doing here?" He's holding the phone to the side, his face lost of expression. "How'd you get done so—quickly?"

"Oh, my God," I groan. "Bear, what the hell? Could you stop asking me questions? I ran. That's how I got done so quickly. I've been here forty minutes. That's the point, isn't it—running fast, winning the race?" I stop and point a finger gun at him. "I was a bit slowed down by all your riddles because your writing was so crappy, I had to stop and decipher them." I tug out the last sign he had posted from my shorts and wave it in my hand. "But I passed Hartley a long time ago. I finished."

"But Hartley is just now getting to the finish line."

"Which would confirm what I have been telling everyone all along—I could beat him. He's a city-boy idiot, and he managed to piss off a redneck girl. What's your point?"

Twenty minutes later, Bear is called up to announce the runners. Two armed security guards whisk Kenny, Bobby, Martha, and me to the resort's conference room. "Listen," Kenny mutters to me. We are seated on vinyl chairs at a table in a big, stuffy room. The guards are standing outside the doors. We keep peering at their shadows. Kenny is freaking out. He's waving his hands, and Bobby keeps pushing on his shoulder to get him to calm down.

"I didn't do anything. It wasn't me. If we get arrested, I didn't do anything that any guy wouldn't do to that asshole Lynn Houck. He kept idling his engine high so nobody could hear their starts. He deserved mud in the face all the way along the run."

"That's not a crime, is it?" Martha asks me.

"How would I know? Why is everybody looking at me when you ask a question a criminal would know?" I give her stink-eye and hold out my hands. "I've got one parking ticket. One stinking parking ticket doesn't mean I'm a felon." Then, I realized what Bear must have been suggesting in the parking lot. He didn't believe me. He thinks I didn't run the race. "Oh, no, it's probably me. I think they believe I cheated. But I know I stopped and checked in at every table they had along the route. I came to a complete halt even when they told me I didn't have to sign in or anything. I didn't trust them, you know? I even took the bottles of water they gave me even though I didn't want them. Hell bells, was that a trick?"

"Maybe you drank too much water. It's probably from the resort. Maybe it isn't complimentary," Martha offers. "Hotels do that all the time, leave bottles of water in your room and charge you for them. Maybe they want to charge you."

"Oh, I've got ten bucks in my pants pocket if you need it, Brandy," Bobby digs into his pocket and pulls out a crumpled ten-dollar bill.

"They are usually about four bucks a piece. How many did you drink?" Martha asks me.

"About fifteen or so, I think. I don't know. That's a lot of money."

"Or maybe they are coming to arrest us for breaking Bobby out?" Kenny offers, poking his forefinger toward me. He is across the table from me, but I'm willing to crawl across it and drag him down if he's going to play turncoat. "If so, I'm bailing. You and your dumbass ideas, Brandy. You're getting us arrested this time. I always said it was going to happen. You're the leader of this stupid gang. It was your idea. I'm out."

"We are not a *gang*, we are a team. And my idea? You all were pumped and ready to go when I asked you. Kenny. You are not bailing. We are all in this together." I push myself up, so I am leaning all the way across the table, elbow-walking until I can stretch my arm out and snatch up a bit of skin on his shoulder. He winces, desperately slapping my fingers away.

"If you bail," I growl, unmoving. "I'm telling Pops you almost burned his barn down with that bonfire last October."

"Stop it!" Kenny shoves my hand away and nearly pushes me off the table. "You're so friggin' crazy."

There is low chatter at the doorway. All eyes snap to attention, and I slide back to my seat. Crap. Amelia Vega is standing there with a bunch of suit-coated men. I can see she is eyeing us with the same expression my fifth-grade teacher dread-eyed me when she realized she got stuck with one of the MacCabe kids in her classroom.

She's an easy book for me to read, Missus Vega. Before she walks into the room by herself, she sighs, closes her eyes, and rubs a hand over her forehead. All four of us are quiet. We stare at her with the same wary gaze she is staring at us.

"You probably already know this. The internet, it seems, is faster than our team of arbitrators and workers. The unofficial count has been broadcasting for over thirty minutes, and two of the last runners are still not in."

Well, no, we didn't know anything. Bobby is looking at me, looking at Kenny, who I figure, is the weakest link. Amelia Vega nods and then holds out a sheet of paper in front of her. "There was some question about the stats being incorrect. The judges quickly calculated this three times. Volunteers along the routes verified procedures were properly followed. The controversy with Noah Hartley began long before three groups of bystanders took videos of his ATV security guards trying to ram Missus Devereauxs with their all-terrain vehicles. The runner whose foot was crushed by one ATV filed a police report at the hospital. Her injury was also caught on video. Noah Hartley's team was disqualified for several of these types of mishaps. Even so, there was a fair margin that wouldn't even have meant the difference."

"So, we're not in trouble for something?" Kenny pipes up. "What are you telling us?"

"You have won the Redneck Run by quite a large margin."

"We won," Martha is the first one to speak. "Everything."

"I thought there were a bunch of runners ahead of me," I mutter.

"No, you passed them all—significantly," Amelia says in a forced tone. "Yes, your team won."

There is just a moment of complete silence. I think we are waiting for a punchline because we lean forward, our heads tipped to the side, our eyes blinking wide. Her words sink in on Bobby first, and he makes this loud whooping sound. We all jump in our seats.

Then Kenny is high fiving everybody, and Martha is crying again. Bobby starts dancing his little jig and makes me get up and do my goofy dance. This lasts five minutes while the crowd outside watches us with the same amused gaze visitors to a zoo look on at baboons swinging around inside their cages. Then, as quickly as Amelia Vega swept into the room, she said she needed to talk to me privately and shooed the others out to prepare them for reporters.

I am still sitting. I know from experience with teachers that I am in the submissive role. Amelia Vega is screaming dominance, standing above me and two feet away, where she stops short and folds her arms across her chest. "Brandy, I know we have not agreed on—many points," she says as the doors to the room are closed behind us. "I have said some things to you that were—"

"Callous, unkind, cruel?" I answer. "And, maybe, tactless?"

"I'm sure you have said bad things about me to my son."

"That's fair. But it was before I knew you two were related. After and on occasion, I've had to bite my tongue pretty hard," I tell Missus Vega. My eyes are dead set on hers while I rise. "You should know that. He's still hanging around me. I don't think he would give me a second chance if I said something bad about you, and he knew I knew your identity."

"It goes both ways," she says. I think I see a small smile play on her lips. Still, I can't tell if her voice is wary. "Brandy, we don't have much time before we talk to the reporters, and you and your team stand for the award. I am going to ask you a big favor. You will be speaking to reporters. Please do not allow your opinion of me to tarnish your view of the event, the country club, or the resort. One of the reasons we rely on Hartley's team to win is that they are familiar with protocol and proprieties."

"Rely on? I think the verb you are looking for is *bank on*. You allowed them to break the rules. You allowed them to cheat. You bent the rules and changed regulations at every step so there was no way those who sponsored and invested in your resort could lose, so you won, and so all of you profited considerably at everyone else's expense."

"This is common practice."

"It is not common practice where I come from." I narrow my eyes. "How, Missus Vega, is this playing out for you now?"

She sighs. "Even the slightest negative remark can destroy our reputation, business, and travel industry here." She takes a deep breath, closes her eyes for a moment, and opens them again. Then Amelia Vega sighs deeply. "I am begging you. I suppose this is where you ask what is in it for you."

I understand what she is implying. I'm sure she has a relatively large sum of cash within reach and hidden from my sight. I stand there, though, more shaken by the idea I will have to stand in front of a crowd.

"I've already tried to get Bear to date other women. He said he would not —and it pains me to quote his words, *whore himself out for me with Janie or Carrie* or any of the other girls that I suggested were suitable women to drag around public places with him."

"That's not true, Missus Vega," I say. "He has Meghan."

She says nothing at first, just shifts. "I know my son had to toss money at you. I also know from the credit card receipts that you didn't take enough to dent a poor man's wallet. I'm assuming money is not a way to charm you. Such, I'm at a loss."

"You know you are insulting me. Do you think I am so stupid I don't recognize that?"

"I'm trying to persuade you to do something to help us not lose millions of dollars. We need to take the focus off the negatives—Hartley's team, our support of him, and his poor sportsmanship. We're a resort country club, for heaven's sake. It would kill us." She holds her hands up and closes her eyes. "This is what I'm asking. We need to plug it now as our Fire Mountain hometown team won, the underdogs, and you've got to appear like we're a part of that win because we're a part of the Fire Mountains, just like my son said we once were. Use that story you told him. Bring us all together. Your marketing team director Gabe Murphy thinks we can pull it off. It's a win-win. We have less damaging effects—"

"What benefit is it for us other than losing our own pride because of all the crap you've done to me, Missus Vega? That's a hard pill for anyone to swallow."

"Do you know how much commercial advertising we are losing by having Hartley's team disqualified? I will give you a job here if you want. I'll send you to the Bahamas. Name it. You've got it. I'll buy you a unicorn if I can find one."

"A unicorn," I repeat. Then, I gaze at her, narrow my eyes, and draw it out for as long as I think she can handle it. "Okay. I've got two things." I finally spit out. "When I was eight, my mom came to one of my choir concerts drunk. She made an idiot of herself and knocked over some chairs. She wouldn't leave and started chanting my name like I was the star football player during the winning game. I can't go in front of people. I just can't. I faint dead away."

"You must. Your team has to accept the award. You need to make a speech."

"I'd rather not win than pass out in front of a million people, Missus Vega."

"I can stand up there with you."

"Alright. And catch me if I fall."

"And what is the second thing?"

I didn't get to tell her right then. The doors open wide and I hear this: "Oh, please tell me you didn't stick my mother and Brandy in the same room—alone." I can hear Bear's voice mewling outside the closed door. "Sticking two wild tomcats into a cardboard box and closing the lid would be just as disastrous. Oh—"

Chapter –43
Friday Nights at the Crazy Kettle Revisited

It is Friday night. I am sitting on a bar stool at the Crazy Kettle Bar. I'm nursing my third drink. It's a ginger ale. I'm wearing a little black dress with maroon lace. It is too tight and too short, and where it stops at the thigh, I can feel the tear of the vinyl on the bar stool against my flesh. I'm wearing stiletto heels. I'm walking on sunshine. I'm going back to school next fall. Bear did pay my tuition and convinced Pops it will keep me too busy to get into more trouble. Ben is hiring me part-time. They got the commercial contract because we won the race. His resort is already booked solid for the next six months.

The last drunk guy who sat down in the empty seat next to me promised to buy me a new car if I went to the hotel with him next door. I didn't decline. I didn't have to. He was gone in less than five seconds. I made a buck toward my college book fund from Billy the Bartender. I told the guy I knew his wife from Holy Trinity Church.

"Oh, shit." That's Billy the Bartender. He's patting his palm on the bar counter in front of me, vying for my attention. "Hey, hey, hey." I see him reaching down to where he keeps the baseball bats. My eyes follow his, and I turn slightly toward the front door. It is Crystal Devereauxs and her mama. They've just stepped across the threshold and into the bar.

Billy has his bat out. I shake my head and give a little push to the bat. "Not yet. I told them to meet me here." I push myself from my stool and walk through the tables. I can feel the stares on my back. Everyone who knows the Devereauxs knows there's going to be a fight.

"Hey," I greet them. I'm two steps away. That's close enough to talk to them, far enough away not to get whaled on by a punch.

"What'd you want, Brandy?" Crystal's eyes are like a feral cat, wary. Her arms are out as if she is getting ready to hold her mama back.

"Here." I have one of Kaylee's little sandal shoeboxes in my hand.

I thrust it toward them. Both step back, eyeing it like I'm handing them a hand grenade with the pin pulled out ready to explode.

"It's okay, take it."

Crystal reaches out, takes the box, and opens it slowly. She narrows her eyes and slips her hand into the box.

"It's all the stuff I've got left of Josh. I figured you'd want it." There's a little box in there; Crystal takes it out and opens it wide.

"It's Gramma's wedding band, Mama," she says.

"There's an envelope in there, too. It's got a couple hundred dollars in it that Josh left for you. There's an old baseball, a coffee mug, and the ball cap Josh got me in Cincinnati."

"What made you decide to give it to us now?"

"I just never thought about it," I tell Crystal. I rub my face and look at Crystal right in the eyes. "Okay, I'll be honest. Here's the truth. I loved him. He hurt me. I've got to move on. The police took everything else I had as evidence—the envelopes with the driver's licenses and the keys. Before they did, I hid this stuff. I thought maybe he didn't hurt you so bad, maybe you never want to move on because you are blood and all. I didn't think the cops needed to know about this stuff."

"Keys?"

"Mailbox keys," I say. "He'd been getting insurance checks for all the girls he killed."

Crystal closes the lid to the box. She gives her mama a shoulder bump. "Let's go." Lizzy looks like a deflated balloon, old and sad. "Mama, we need to move on." And they do. Crystal and Lizzy leave.

I return to my seat and stare at the clock on the wall. Not much has changed in my actions from the last three years I have sat here on Friday nights. Of course, Mama isn't dancing around the pool tables. She's in a rehab center in Texas. I doubt she's going to get out of jail. She finally confessed to picking up the checks from the mailboxes for Josh. I'm not going to be taking her home, stopping at the trailer park, then standing on the railroad tracks and waiting for the train to come. I know Josh is dead.

I've got a few extra bucks. The company that made the tennis shoes Crazy Willie pulled from the dumpster is bringing back the line, promoting them as the winner's shoe of the Redneck Run.

With my endorsement, that is. And I'm wearing the beanie hat Bear got me in Cincinnati instead of the ball cap Josh gave me, tugging it down a bit over my eyes occasionally before I nudge it back up. The only thing that is the same is the beer bottle sitting on the bar counter beside my ginger ale. It is the same beer Josh used to drink. Guy number seven sits down in Josh's seat.

"Hey, can I buy you a drink?"

I look at Billy. He's getting a beer from the tap, but he turns. This is a fifty-dollar bet, which I slid across the counter four minutes ago when I saw him walk in. "Fifty bucks says I can get rid of this guy in less than twenty seconds," I had said. Billy's trying to buy new tires for his truck, so he's all in.

"Your Pops said you were here." It is Bear, and he's wearing that nice shirt and tie again. I can't hardly stand it. He's beautiful. I don't want him to leave. I know he will. "What's up? I thought we were doing something tonight?"

So here goes my spiel. I'm already ten seconds into the conversation. It's only three words. I'm sure it will send this one packing out the door in less than five. "I love you," I tell him. There's this long hesitation. I'm sitting there looking at Bear in his chocolate brown eyes with my odd yellow-pink ones. I know Billy's gaze hasn't left the two of us because the beer he is pouring is spilling on his arm and down to the floor. And Bear hasn't stopped looking at me, unblinking. I can hear the jukebox and people chattering. Bear shifts in his seat. Is he getting up? I know he's waiting for some punchline that isn't coming from my lips.

"Yeah, okay, I love you too," Bear says.

"Really?"

"Yes, going on six months now," he says so casually it is like I did nothing more than ask him to pass me the salt. "It has evolved since then. It isn't just puppy love." My heart makes this giant lurch in my chest. It bangs and bounces, waking up something jumpy in my belly. It isn't working the way I planned. Fifteen seconds. I figured that would scare him off. I've only got five seconds left.

"I liked being married. Someday, I want kids. Pops wants twelve grandkids; I'll settle for six. I don't want to leave Fire Mountain. I don't want to be far from my Pops, Kenny, Aunt Jenny, and Uncle Craig. Your mom hates me. I can't change. We'll always battle it out.

I'm scared you'll leave me, scared you'll side with her. I'm going to finish school and work over at Salt Springs because I got the job —"

"It's a bet, isn't it." Bear doesn't look really happy now. He's rolling his hand in his hair.

"Yeah, I just lost." Twenty seconds. Billy reaches out to my arm, extended and bent at the elbow, and swipes up the fifty-dollar bill. My eyes follow until Bear taps me on the arm with his fingers. "After I said I love you," I say. "I figured you'd be out the door."

"How much of what you said is true?"

"All of it." I push down my dress with my fingers. It is crawling up. It dawns on Bear right then that it was the one he picked out because red was his favorite color. "You can run. I can't get my fifty bucks back, but I'm giving you a chance to get out alive."

He leans back, cranes his neck so he's looking at the door and then back to me and upward like he's looking at the beanie hat and realizing I exchanged it for the ball cap, made my choice. Then Bear rubs his chin with his hand. "Six kids, that's a lot of kids. And marriage, that's a lot for a man to swallow on the first date."

"Run," Billy says softly from behind the bar.

Bear chuckles. "So how is this bet played?"

"I had twenty seconds to scare you away," I tell him. I watch Bear reach into his back pocket and pull out his wallet. He tugs out a crumpled bill and lays it down on the counter. Then, he uses his fingers to push it toward Billy. "I'll get in on it. I'm not as experienced as Brandy. Give me like sixty seconds to see if I scare her away."

Billy shrugs. "Sure. I'm in." He's got a beer in his hand, but he's too interested in the conversation to give it to the man who ordered.

Bear turns his chair toward mine. He leans back and puts an elbow on the counter. Then he looks up at Billy and waits for him to nod. "Okay, well, here goes. I never liked Meghan Reynolds. It was you. Gabe knew it, and Reverend Murphy knew it. I think everybody knew I liked you since I almost hit you while you were running down the highway in front of the Quick Stop."

"You almost hit me?"

"You jumped on the hood of my car."

"That was you?"

"Uh-huh. I'm the stupid, dumbass."

"Stupid, *pretty boy,* dumbass," I correct him.

"Yeah, that's what you called me. I thought I hit a deer. That's how you ended up in the church choir. Reverend Murphy was trying to fix us up. I went with the stupid story of having a crush on Megs because I could hardly move my lips when I was around you. You were sitting there, and I was shaking, trying to put Band-Aids on your knees where you fainted, and I was thinking, you see it, you know I'm scared to death of you. You're probably laughing at me inside, thinking how fat I am and how ignorant I look. You remember me as the mean boy to little kids and that you beat up on the bus. I knew you already thought I was a complete idiot because I was the fat guy at Mister Smiley's who knocked over the entire pyramid of weight loss meals in the freezer section.

"The cleanup in Aisle 12," I recall. "The man who knocked over the display of Real Meals for Real Men Weight Loss Meals."

"Yes. I was desperate. Meghan was the one helping me work up the courage to go to your Pops to meet you. It was right about when Big Don started asking me what you were telling me. I thought Megs was just being nice, trying to fix us up. It should have occurred to me her and her dad had ulterior motives. It didn't."

I stare at him and nod my head. "Okay, what else do you have?"

"Somewhere along the way, she started liking me, Brandy." Bear shifts uncomfortably in his chair. I'm looking straight into his eyes. He's having a hard time sticking with mine. I'm feeling it again. I see Josh leaving out the door and never coming back. "I started losing weight and gaining confidence. I liked that Meghan liked me. I figured after a month or so, you wouldn't go out with me, you know? I started kind of liking her too. And were were both pushed by my mom and her dad. She was there; the only one there for a fat guy. You were obsessed with your ex-husband, this ghost that's just out of reach since the day I met you. I figured I couldn't compete with that—with him."

"Okay, so you like her." I tap my finger on the counter. "Why are you here?"

"Because it was *never* her. It is *you* I obsess about. *Like* is one thing. *Love* is another. I told her those words the day I left the hospital and how I felt."

"Just give me the damn fifty dollars," Billy starts to slide the money toward himself. "She's not leaving her chair. You only have five seconds left.

"No, you better hold on to it the last five seconds," Bear says, stopping the crawl across the counter with two fingers. "I didn't think of putting the signs up on the trail. My mom did. Surprised? We stayed up and worked on it the night before like we didn't have a thousand other things to do. She just dropped everything she was working on and came into my office and asked me if doing this Redneck Run was really worth all this effort. She'd had it with Hartley and the tourism agency. I told her the only reason I was even putting an effort into it was for you, so I could show you that I believed in you as much as you had believed in me. I just kept screwing it up. I told her the story of Boar Mountain and Fire Mountain, once called The Fire Mountains." Bear leans in. I feel him taking my fingers in his. His fingers are trembling. Maybe mine are, too. We're knee to knee, and he looks down at the floor and back up again. "She even went with me up the hill to staple gun the signs to the trees at three in the morning." Bear takes a breath. "My mother is not an outdoor person. You should have seen her smacking away the mosquitoes with her arms flailing and walking the trail in her pumps." He chuckles. "I like Meghan. I don't love her. I love you and will marry you tomorrow morning if you want me to."

He reaches into his shirt pocket and pulls out a small box, which he opens, exposing a massive diamond ring with little hearts. "I bought this for you about two months into our walks. Falling through floors, chasing that ghost of your ex-husband, jumping off quarry walls—that was like a love potion for me. Marry me, Brandy, please. You scare the absolute crap out of me, but I don't want to be without you. I asked your Pops, and he said if I could catch you, I could have you. I'm not planning on moving away. I'll build a house next to your Pops if you want. I'll have five kids and a dog if you go to church with me on Sundays. How's that? What do you say?"

I am speechless. I stare at the ring and look up at Bear. I've never seen him look so scared. I know he thinks I'm two seconds from bolting. I hardly turn my head. My eyes are still stuck on Bear's.

"Take the fifty," I say to Billy. "I'm shaking when I reach over and latch on to Bear's arm, drag him in for a kiss. "Okay. I'll marry you."

My cell phone rings. I pick it up and see a text.

Okay. I'm here. Will you come out and get me? It is Amelia Vega.

I turn to Billy again. My hand reaches out and one finger pokes at the dribbles of sweat on the bottle of Josh's beer. "Take the beer and dump it. Get Bear the same thing I'm drinking. No, make one a beer."

"You're having a beer?" Bear asks.

I shake my head. "No, it's for your mama. We made a deal. If I say nice things about the resort and the Redneck Run, she said she'd come out and get a real taste of what redneck is all about. Tonight, it is a beer. She's coming to Pops' house Sunday after church for lunch."

"You know what you're getting into, right?"

"No, I don't," I tell him, tugging on the beanie hat. "But I do have some love potion in my purse that will make it easier to swallow."

"Love potion?"

I opened my purse, and inside, there were three newspaper clippings that I lay down in front of him. "There's this murder case that's never been solved. I thought maybe we could check it out."

He smiles, lifts the ring box, and tugs my hand. "I'm in."

www.ingramcontent.com/pod-product-compliance
Lightning Source LLC
Chambersburg PA
CBHW051525250626
47156CB00001B/226